BOOK 4

Brandon Mull

ALADDIN

NEW YORK LONDON TORONTO SYDNEY NEW DELHI

ALADDIN

An imprint of Simon & Schuster Children's Publishing Division
1230 Avenue of the Americas, New York, NY 10020
First Aladdin hardcover edition March 2016
Text copyright © 2016 by Brandon Mull
Jacket illustration copyright © 2016 by Owen Richardson
All rights reserved, including the right of reproduction in whole or in part in any form.
ALADDIN is a trademark of Simon & Schuster, Inc., and related logo is a registered trademark of Simon & Schuster, Inc.
For information about special discounts for bulk purchases, please contact Simon & Schuster Special Sales at 1-866-506-1949 or business@simonandschuster.com.
The Simon & Schuster Speakers Bureau can bring authors to your live event. For more information or to book an event contact the Simon & Schuster Speakers Bureau at 1-866-248-3049 or visit our website at www.simonspeakers.com.
Jacket designed by Jessica Handelman
Interior designed by Mike Rosamilia
The text of this book was set in Perpetua.
Manufactured in the United States of America 0316 FFG
2 4 6 8 10 9 7 5 3
This book has been cataloged with the Library of Congress.
ISBN 978-1-4424-9709-2 (hc)
ISBN 978-1-4424-9711-5 (eBook)

To old friends like Darren, Joel, Larry, and Nick.
And to new friends like Jason and Adam.

CHAPTER
1

SHRINE

"Are there really ghosts here?" Cole asked.

"They're called echoes," Hunter replied. "But, yeah. Pretty much."

Cole, Hunter, Dalton, and Jace strolled along a flat, stone-lined path in the garden surrounding the Seven-Cornered Shrine. The bright afternoon sun, the sculpted hedges, the diverse flowers, the trellised vines, the shade trees, the trickling streams, the splashing fountains—nothing in view suggested the presence of restless spirits.

They had arrived in Necronum from Zeropolis by monorail a little before midday. The station straddled the border between the kingdoms, with the track ending scant feet from Necronum. It had felt strange to transfer from the comforts of a sleek monorail to the clattering confines of a horse-drawn coach, and served as a strong reminder how different the kingdoms could be from one another. The coach had brought them directly to the shrine, along with Mira and Joe, who had gone their own way just after the group reached the sprawling grounds.

Watching Hunter, Cole could still hardly believe he had joined forces with his lost brother. Cole lacked memories of living with Hunter as his sibling back home in Arizona, but that made sense because Hunter had been taken to the Outskirts before him. When people went to the Outskirts, those left behind forgot them, just as Cole's parents and sister could no longer remember him. Hunter had shown Cole lots of photographic evidence that they had grown up together and had offered even more proof with the risks he took back in Zeropolis.

Cole sometimes wondered how many people had been brought to the Outskirts over the years. If all who came here were forgotten, how could anyone ever make an accurate count? Dozens of kids were simultaneously abducted by slave traders when Cole came to the Outskirts. And Hunter had been captured on a separate occasion. How many other times had it happened? How many total people had been taken? Hundreds? Thousands? More?

"You've actually seen a ghost?" Dalton asked.

"I've seen plenty," Hunter said. "The shaping in Necronum is built around interacting with the dead."

"Think we'll see some today?" Jace asked, not quite keeping the uneasiness out of his voice.

Hunter clapped his hands and rubbed his palms. "Not if we stay together. Echoes don't usually like groups. At least not at a shrine."

"Then let's split up," Jace said. "I want to hear Dalton scream."

"How will you hear me if you're running all the way back to Sambria?" Dalton scoffed.

Jace huffed. "There's nothing to be afraid of." He glanced at Hunter. "Is there?"

Hunter shrugged. "Not if you don't mind being haunted."

"Haunted?" Jace asked, looking a shade or two paler.

"Sometimes an echo will take an interest in you," Hunter said. "Follow you around. Work mischief. Watch you sleep."

Jace was trying to nod, as if the information were expected, but he didn't look very comfortable. Cole didn't feel at ease either, but he still managed to enjoy the sight of Jace getting rattled.

"They can't touch us or anything," Jace said, as if confirming common knowledge.

"It depends," Hunter said. "Not usually. There are plenty of exceptions."

"Now you're just messing with us," Dalton said hopefully.

Pausing on the path, Hunter closed his eyes, stretched out his arms, and took a deep breath. "I smell dead people."

"Whatever," Cole said, glancing around just in case. On one side of the path, a row of fruit trees rustled in the soft breeze. Were they moving a little too much? In the other direction, a couple sat on a stone bench staring at a pond. "You don't mean those two?"

Hunter opened his eyes and regarded the pair on the bench. "Normal people. But you're smart not to make assumptions here. At a shrine, the differences between a living person and an echo can be subtle."

"They look like normal people?" Dalton asked.

"Most of the time we can't see echoes," Hunter clarified. "Sometimes you might feel them. Not so much with your fingers. Your spine might tingle, or you might have the suspicion you're being watched. Pay attention to those feelings in Necronum."

"Are you good at the shaping here, Aaron?" Jace asked, using the alias they had agreed to adopt for Hunter. They had decided Mira needed a codename as well. Today she was Sally.

"They call it weaving," Hunter said. "Short for death weaving, or echo weaving. I'm not bad at it. The really talented weavers can summon echoes. They can see and talk to them when others can't. Some weavers can even travel to the realm of the dead. They call it the echolands."

"How good of a death weaver are you?" Dalton asked.

Hunter shrugged. "I'm no expert, but I know some decent tricks."

"Call an echo," Jace challenged.

"No need here," Hunter explained. "In fact, it would bother them. At a shrine, echoes can appear to anyone. They might be a little transparent. Or they might look as solid as we do." He started walking again.

"What exactly should we do if we find an echo?" Cole asked. "We never really covered that."

"Get info," Hunter said. "We need to find Honor and Destiny."

"We have the stars," Jace reminded him. Mira's mother, Queen Harmony, could place stars in the sky to mark the location of her five daughters. She only did so in emergencies. Currently, Destiny and Honor both had stars in the sky, practically on top of each other.

4

"Sure, but we want details," Hunter said. "We know which direction to go, but we don't know how far. And it would help if we could learn exactly what happened."

"The echoes will just tell us?" Cole asked. "Isn't it risky if we let the wrong echo know who we're after?"

Hunter rolled his eyes. "Be smart about it. Don't start by asking exactly what you want to know. Haven't you been to confidence lounges? Feel it out. The echoes who come here do it voluntarily. They want to interact with the living. They may want you to do favors for them. See if you can make a deal." His voice became hard. "But no binding oaths."

"What does that mean?" Dalton asked.

"It's like making a formal contract," Hunter said. "Echoes only have real influence over the living if you give them power. The easiest way to get yourself in trouble is by breaking a promise you made to them. Especially a formal one. They call it a bound oath."

"But we can bargain?" Cole checked.

"If you keep it casual," Hunter said. "Don't make any official vows. And take care how much you say. Echoes use information as currency. Most would happily trade what they learn from you with others."

Hunter stopped walking as they reached the intersection of two paths. "Four directions," he said.

"One of us will have to backtrack," Cole observed.

"Not it," Dalton said.

"Not it," Cole added reflexively.

Hunter stared at Jace. "I don't care either way. Do you want to go back?"

"I'll go forward," Jace said.

"We have a few hours," Hunter said. "They'll make us clear out after sundown. My understanding is that most of the action at this shrine happens out here on the grounds, so just roam and see what you find. Try to relax, and use good judgment."

"Try not to cry," Jace told Dalton.

"Have fun," Dalton replied with a smile. "I bet this will be your lucky day."

Cole winced. As a Sky Raider, Jace had adopted negative superstitions about any wishes involving good luck. "He means die bravely," Cole interjected.

"I know what he means," Jace said coldly. "I make a joke and he tries to jinx me."

Hunter rubbed his forehead, as if he had a headache coming on. "Jinxes? That's a crime now? Come on, guys, get it together." He turned and started back the way they had come.

After a final glare at Dalton, Jace proceeded along the path.

Folding his arms, Cole watched Jace walk away. Dalton lingered. "Why do you always bug him?" Cole murmured.

"Jace started it," Dalton said. "Go ask him why he bugs me."

Cole sighed. "He's had a hard life. He grew up here as a slave."

"And my life has been so easy," Dalton replied, some heat in his tone. "I got taken here as a slave. Ripped from my home. Just like you. Every second we stay with Sally, we risk our lives just like Jace does."

Cole thought about that. After venturing into a stranger's basement on Halloween, Dalton, Jenna, and a bunch of his friends had been taken here against their will. Cole had followed, trying to help, but got captured as well. He had met Jace and Mira after he was sold as a slave to the Sky Raiders. When the three of them escaped with Twitch, he found out that Mira was a princess and got involved helping her find her four exiled sisters.

Nothing since coming to the Outskirts had made Cole happier than finding Dalton. It had been such a relief to reunite not just with a face from home, but with his best friend. In a strange, dangerous world, Cole now had somebody he could talk to and really trust. But ever since finding Dalton, Cole had felt torn about whether his top priority should be helping Mira or finding the other kids who were taken. So far he had compromised by trying to accomplish both goals at the same time.

"I don't mean our lives are easier," Cole said.

"That's what it sounded like," Dalton said.

"Jace is kind of a jerk," Cole said. "I don't see that changing in the near future. He was always a slave. He never learned how to be normal. I know you're better than that."

"So we should let him walk all over us?" Dalton challenged. "How many times do I have to say this? If you let somebody take advantage of you, it gets worse, not better."

Cole shrugged. "Maybe you're right."

Dalton glanced down the path to the left. "I guess I'll go this way."

"Take care," Cole said.

Dalton hesitated. "You haven't forgotten about Jenna?"

Cole froze, trying not to let his irritation show. How could he forget Jenna, his secret crush since second grade who had finally started to become his friend before they were parted by slavers?

"We know she's here in Necronum at the Temple of the Still Water," Cole said. "It's not nearby. But we'll get there."

Dalton looked around to make sure they were alone. "Right. *We know where she is.* We don't have to wander. We could go straight there. We're in Necronum. If we find Jenna, we could search for the Grand Shaper of Creon and maybe figure out a way to get home and stay there."

Cole put his hands on his hips. By all reports, even if they managed to get home, nobody would remember them, and they would get drawn back into the Outskirts within hours. But Trillian the torivor had suggested it might be possible to change how that worked, and Cole refused to give up hope he might be right. After all, isn't that what shapers did? Mess with reality? And shapecrafters could tinker with the shaping power itself. Somebody had to know a way they could get home to stay. "Are you saying we should ditch Sally?"

Dalton raised both hands innocently. "Two of her sisters are already in trouble here. This is where Nazeem lives, the freaky guy who invented shapecrafting and who almost caught you in Junction. Things could get really ugly. I'm sure Joe can help Sally meet up with lots of allies here. They'll be all right. Queen Harmony already told you where to find Jenna. I don't get the holdup. Why make Jenna wait? And after we find her, do we keep her in danger, or do we go look for a way home?"

"The Grand Shapers are in hiding," Cole said. "How would we find the Grand Shaper of Creon without Sally? Staying with her gives us access to all the members of the resistance."

"It also leads us into danger and turns us into targets," Dalton said. "It's complicated. I don't have all the answers. But sometimes I wonder if getting home still matters to you."

Cole frowned. Since embarking for Necronum, he had been especially focused on trying to find Mira's sisters Honor and Destiny. Mira's mother had warned him they were in serious danger. And then last night in Zeropolis, Mira reported that Honor's and Destiny's stars had appeared in the sky.

"Of course getting home matters," Cole said. "But finding Honor and Destiny is really urgent right now. We know they're in trouble."

"I get helping at this shrine," Dalton said. "We just made it to Necronum. But what if Destiny and Honor turn out to be far from the Temple of the Still Water?"

Cole paused before answering. He felt torn. Would he walk away from Mira if she still needed him? It would be so good to finally see Jenna again. But if Jenna was relatively safe, and Mira was in big trouble, shouldn't he help Mira first? Dalton was waiting for a reply.

"With Nazeem around, and the High King still after us, this might not be the safest time to get Jenna. If we can help Sally defeat Nazeem and Stafford, everyone will be safer, including us. Plus, we'll have major resources to help find the other kids from our neighborhood who got taken, and extra help figuring out a way home. Do you think Jenna will want to go home without Sarah and Lacie? How many of the kids who were brought here can we leave behind? It would take years to find them all on our own."

Dalton nodded pensively. "Maybe we can't take on the job of finding everybody. Maybe that's too much. Maybe me, you, and Aaron find Jenna and try to get home. We'd be lucky to pull off that much. Do we really have to fight a revolution and find all those other kids too?"

"I don't know," Cole said. "Leaving the others feels wrong to me. So does abandoning Sally. But I hear you. If we figure out a way home, I guess we could leave behind info on how to follow us. We could hope the other kids find their own way back."

No longer looking him in the eye, Dalton stared over Cole's shoulder. "We have company," he said.

Cole turned to find a teenage girl standing behind him, not much taller than him and rather thin. Her long brown hair hung mostly straight and was parted in the middle. She wore a lacy white top, a gray skirt, and sandals with wooden soles. Cole thought she looked about fifteen.

"There are no private conversations here, you know," the teen said.

"Apparently not," Cole replied.

"She just appeared," Dalton muttered.

The girl giggled.

"Appeared?" Cole asked, suddenly unsettled. "You're dead?" She looked perfectly tangible.

"I'm not dead," she said. "I still have my lifespark. But, yeah, my physical body died. I live on as an echo."

Mustering his courage, Cole tried his best to act casual. "You look normal. How can we tell you're really an echo?"

"She *appeared*," Dalton reminded him.

"I didn't see it," Cole said.

The teen reached out a hand. "Touch my fingers," she offered.

Cole extended his hand, hesitated, then passed his fingers through hers. The contact created only the faintest whisper of sensation.

The girl's eyes widened, and she giggled. "Did you feel that?"

"A little," Cole said.

"That's unusual," she said. "By the way, it's poor manners to touch an echo unless we offer, so don't make it a habit. The others will be mad at me for warning you that you were being overheard, but I started to feel bad for you."

Cole glanced at Dalton. He couldn't believe they were talking to an actual ghost!

"How many echoes were listening to us?" Dalton asked.

"About ten," the girl said. "There were more when the four of you were together. Some of the others followed your friends."

"Echoes have listened to everything we said?" Cole verified.

"What do you expect?" the teen asked. "You're at a shrine. There are lots of us here today."

"Are they still listening to us?" Cole asked.

"Two of them," the teen said.

"Can we get some privacy?" Cole asked.

"Shoo," the girl said, waving a hand at unseen people.

"Unless you want to materialize and join in, this is my conversation now. Leave us be."

"Are they going?" Dalton asked.

"Yes, though one of them is being grumpy about it." She looked away from Dalton at empty space. "Go on! You can have a turn later if you want." Her gaze returned to Cole. "There. We're alone. How can I help you?"

CHAPTER

2

ECHOES

D o you already know what we're after?" Cole asked.

"You're looking for Honor and Destiny Pemberton," the teen said. She took a step closer and lowered her voice. "And you talked about stopping N-A-Z-E-E-M." She spelled his name instead of saying it.

"What do you know about him?" Cole asked.

"More than I want to know," she said. "Be very careful throwing that name around. His followers are fanatical. Some who oppose him are too."

"Do many echoes follow him?" Dalton asked.

The teen looked uncomfortable. "He has followers everywhere. Plenty in the echolands. New topic?"

"You don't want to talk about N-A-Z-E-E-M?" Cole asked.

"It's a good way to avoid trouble," she said.

"Do you know where we can find Honor or Destiny?" Dalton inquired.

"I didn't know Honor might be in Necronum until you

mentioned it," she said. "There has been a lot of new talk about the Pemberton girls lately. I've heard rumors that Destiny is in hiding here, but I have no idea where."

"Not many people know the Pemberton girls are alive," Cole said.

"We've had those rumors for ages in the echolands," the teen said. "Since before my body died. Of course, not all rumors are true."

"When did you die?" Cole asked.

"Almost twenty years ago," the girl said.

"You were a teenager?" Dalton asked.

"Fourteen," the girl said.

"Your echo doesn't age," Cole noted.

"Not normally," the girl said. "You tend to look how your body looked when it died, though old people almost always appear a bit younger. At least until you move on. Who knows what lies beyond the echolands?"

"You're not in heaven?" Dalton asked.

The girl giggled again. "I sure hope not. You guys really don't know much, do you?"

"Like what?" Cole asked.

"The echolands are only the beginning of the afterlife," the girl said. "Not much more than a jumping-off point, really. Your echo is temporary. You can linger here for a time, but eventually you move on."

"To where?" Dalton wondered.

"I'd have to go there to find out," the teen said. "Nobody returns."

"Why not get moving?" Cole asked.

"Are you trying to kill me off?" the teen asked, mildly offended.

"No," Cole said. "But if you have someplace else to go, why stay?"

"Why do you go on living?" she countered. "You could come here."

"I'm alive," Cole said. "You died. Why not go to heaven?"

She stared off to one side, her gaze slightly skyward. "I could, I suppose. I don't feel ready. I'm not sure what to expect. You call it heaven. Hopefully, that's what it is. You don't learn much just by dying. You become an echo and see there is an afterlife. But nobody here has been beyond the echolands, so everyone is still just guessing. Moving on will mean leaving behind the echo of my body. I feel the call sometimes. It's exciting but also scary. Unknown. I want to wait for my mother to join me. It would be nicer to set off together. But her heart keeps ticking."

"How'd you die?" Cole asked.

"You're nosy," she said.

"You're the one who was spying on us," Cole reminded her.

"It wasn't very nice," she said. "I had a lung disease. In the end I couldn't breathe. I was full of liquid. It felt like drowning."

"That's horrible," Dalton said, scrunching his face.

"It seemed pretty awful at the time," the teen admitted.

"What's your name?" Cole asked.

"I was starting to wonder if you'd ask," she said with a

giggle. "That usually comes before the details of your death. I'm Yeardly. You're Cole and Dalton. I've been listening since you entered the garden."

"You know what we're after," Cole said. "Is there any way you can help us?"

"I've been helping you!" Yeardly exclaimed, sounding a little exasperated. "I felt bad for you. I mean, you're kids! I told you to watch your words because others are listening. Who is Jenna?"

"My friend," Cole said. "We came to the five kingdoms from Outside. Slave traders brought us. I want to find her."

"I hear the Temple of the Still Water is beautiful," Yeardly said. "I've never been there. It's far away."

"Don't you travel?" Dalton asked.

"Why?" Yeardly asked. "I've gotten to know the echoes here, and the lay of the land. I have a good shrine for when I want contact with mortals. And I'm close to my hometown for when Mom crosses over."

Cole spoke quieter. "Is there anybody who might know where we can find Honor or Destiny? Can you point us in the right direction?"

"Somebody might know," Yeardly said. "Hard to say who. I haven't caught wind of any rumors about their locations." She paused. "Tell me about Aaron."

Cole stared at her. She had paid attention to their names. Good thing Hunter had suggested aliases. Aaron was Hunter's middle name and the name of Cole's paternal grandfather. The name Sally for Mira came from an old nickname derived from her middle name, Salandra. Hunter had maintained it was best to use codenames that weren't complete lies, because some echoes were experts at detecting falsehood.

While serving as one of the most feared of the High King's Enforcers, Hunter had typically covered his face with a mask. As a result, to move around anonymously, he could simply dress in normal clothes and let his face show. Cole didn't like Yeardly's interest in his brother. If word got out who he really was, it could bring a lot of trouble. Had they made a mistake? Had Hunter's identity slipped?

"Why?" Dalton asked.

"No big reason," Yeardly said. Her tone was casual, but her eyes showed real interest. "He seemed to be in charge. I like the way he carries himself."

"You like him!" Cole realized.

Yeardly tried to look innocent. "I'm just interested. How about the other one? Jace?"

"I get it," Dalton said. "We're the approachable guys. They're the cool ones."

"You're all great," Yeardly assured him. She couldn't hide a little grin. "But they're a little extra great. Who was that girl with you at the start? Sally? Jace seemed to have eyes for her."

"She's nobody," Cole said. "Jace does like her, but he'd be mad if anybody knew."

Yeardly clapped her hands and grinned with delight. "That's my kind of secret! Do you like her too?"

"Not like a girlfriend," Cole said.

"No," Yeardly said. "But I saw something when you talked about Jenna."

Cole became very interested in a flowering bush off to one side. "Maybe. She's mostly a friend."

"Mostly because you're not sure it's mutual yet," Yeardly said with a giggle, clapping again. "This is a cause I can get behind. Trying to find and rescue the unrealized love of your life."

"I don't know if I'd say—" Cole began.

"Shush!" Yeardly held a finger toward his lips. "Don't spoil it. Listen, if you guys don't wander off too far, I'll do what I can to help you."

"But you don't know anything," Cole reminded her.

Yeardly winked. "Not yet. Hard to say what a curious echo might do if she puts her mind to it."

"We'd appreciate any help," Dalton said.

Yeardly smiled. "Of course you would. Especially if I make no demands in return. Tell you what, when the time is right, I may ask to be introduced to Aaron. Think you could manage that?"

"Sure," Cole said. "Knowing him is no big deal."

Her eyes flashed with interest. "Maybe not to you. Good luck!"

Yeardly disappeared.

Cole looked at Dalton. His friend sighed.

"This is a weird place," Dalton said.

"Not a bad start."

"We should probably split up."

Cole started down the untraveled path to the right, and Dalton proceeded to the left. Soon shrubs, trees, and irregularities in the terrain screened Dalton from view.

Reaching more intersections, Cole took a meandering route beside streams and hedges, then entered a corridor of trellises that arched overhead to create a curved ceiling of flowering vines.

A laughing boy raced through one blossoming wall of the corridor, ran along it for a stretch, then lunged through the other side just as a second boy came into view. Though younger than the first, the second boy dashed after him, plunging through the trellis wall.

Approaching the section where the boys had vanished, Cole found no space through which they could have fit. They had passed through solid wood laced with vegetation. More echoes.

Beyond the corridor, Cole followed a circuitous path of gray pebbles around several mounds where dense, thorny shrubs with dark green leaves flourished. Several little paths branched off, ending abruptly at benches. Near one bench, a dignified man in a fancy coat stood very straight. He had a bony nose and thick, wavy, white hair. He was semitransparent, allowing Cole to view the garden directly behind him almost as clearly as the background to either side.

Gathering his courage, Cole turned down the path that led to the man's bench and stared up at him. He was quite tall. Though the echo had glanced at Cole as he approached, he now acted oblivious to his presence.

"Are you an echo?" Cole asked.

The man glanced down with no hint of a smile. "We both know the answer to that question, which makes it hardly worth asking. Run along."

"I was just trying to start a conversation," Cole explained.

"Your overture was as thrilling as a remark about the weather," the man said flatly, no longer making eye contact.

"I'm looking for information," Cole said.

"I possess vast stockpiles," the man said, examining his fingernails.

"Great."

The man's eyes shifted to regard Cole. "I do not invite common urchins into my confidence. Run along, boy."

"Do you even know who I am?"

The man gave half a smirk. "One of my valets inspected you and your cohorts upon entry. I heard big talk of princesses and Nazeem. You are clearly pretenders." The man drew out a handkerchief and waved him away. "So . . . go pretend."

Cole felt himself getting mad. He knew that probably wasn't smart but couldn't help it. "Shows how much you know."

"Perhaps it does," the man said dryly.

Cole turned away. "Forget it."

"Already done," the man said with relief.

Cole took a few steps. The man made no effort to stop him. He seemed really not to care. Or maybe he was expertly baiting him. Either way, Cole couldn't resist and turned back.

"I've seen three of the princesses," he said.

The stuffy man raised his eyebrows as he polished a cuff link. "Not just one? Three of the five? Extraordinary. And highly credible."

Cole had to bite his tongue to keep from revealing Mira's

identity. That wasn't his secret to share. Maybe leaving was the best option.

"And still you linger," the man said.

"What can you tell me about Nazeem?" Cole asked.

The man huffed. "You're right. Forgive me. Seeing as you have offered definitive proof that you are a close associate of many princesses, I shall now divulge all I know about the most perilous personage in the echolands."

"Nazeem lives in the echolands?" Cole asked.

The man chuckled to himself. "Where did you imagine him? In Necronum?"

"The Fallen Temple."

"Hmmm," the man said. "Not everyone has connected Nazeem to that location. It is hardly common knowledge. The Fallen Temple has a physical counterpart in Necronum, but Nazeem has long dwelt inside the portion in the echolands."

"Nazeem is dead?" Cole asked. That didn't make sense. At the secret meeting in Junction, Nazeem had talked about returning from captivity.

The man narrowed his eyes. "His body may have perished. Nazeem is far from dead. And you would do well to avoid mentioning him. These are not matters for amateurs to discuss."

Cole felt his face flush. "Amateur? I've seen him, mister. Face-to-face. Have you?"

The man looked down his nose at Cole. "I had you all wrong. Clearly, your ignorance is a complex pretense. You are the most remarkable youth in the five kingdoms. Tell me: How was it that you entered and escaped the Fallen Temple?

You are the first I know of to succeed! Did you rescue any princesses along the way?"

"I didn't go there," Cole said. "I saw him at a gathering of shapecrafters. And he saw me."

The man gave a simpering laugh. "You caught wind of that rumor? That much is well done. The gossip in the echolands holds that Nazeem is looking for a mortal boy who roughly meets your description. Am I to believe that the intrepid lad in question is foolish enough to reveal himself to an unknown echo? You are duller than average, my boy, but your audacity almost entertains."

Cole gave a nervous chuckle. Maybe that hadn't been a very smart thing to share. "You're onto me."

"Of course I am," the man said. "Had you ever met Nazeem, he would own you body and soul. Now run along."

Cole walked away. The man seemed to know a lot, but Cole had a feeling that talking more could prove dangerous. Hopefully, the stuffy echo wouldn't rethink his assumption that Cole was an imposter. The man seemed very sure of himself.

After so much success, Cole expected to find another echo around the next corner but was disappointed. He wandered for at least an hour and saw nothing but vegetation and other mortals, including Joe and Hunter.

Later, feeling thirsty, Cole recalled a fountain inside the shrine that people drank from using cups. He steered back toward the main building, crossing little bridges and occasionally doubling back as footpaths wound astray.

As he approached the tall doors to the shrine, he noticed

an elderly man in a large hat and a ragged gray robe sitting in the shadows, knees up, head partially bowed, back to the wall. A deeply tanned hand with dirty fingernails held out a small wicker basket. He didn't glance at Cole or make a gesture, but he was clearly a beggar, and the basket was empty.

Cole fished a spare ringer from his pocket. Hunter had cashed out a bunch of Zeropolitan credits at the train station and given them all a personal stash of ringers, the currency used in the other kingdoms of the Outskirts.

The ringer was silver—worth ten coppers, enough for several good meals. But Hunter was loaded, and Mira had access to big funds too. Even though the beggar wasn't looking directly at him, Cole didn't want to make a show of searching for smaller change.

He dropped the ringer in the basket.

It fell through to the ground.

The man looked up, his toothless smile becoming the widest crease in his seamed face. "Few people notice me. Fewer still make an offering. I'm Sando, young sir, and I hope that I can be of service."

SANDO

I could use information," Cole said.

Sando's smile widened, showing his smooth gums. "That's just the kind of help I can provide." He looked Cole up and down, then squinted, making even more wrinkles gather around his eyes. Sando spoke slower, as if his interest had increased. "There is more to you than greets the eye, young sir."

"What do you mean?" Cole asked.

Sando sprang to his feet. "Pick up your ringer. I can't use it, and there's no sense in leaving silver on the ground. We'll find a private place to get acquainted."

Moving with an easy grace that contradicted his elderly appearance, Sando led the way off the path, skipping over obstacles and sliding around shrubs. Cole tried not to crush any flowers as they followed the outside wall of the shrine, away from the doors. When they reached a shady nook shielded by bushes, Sando sat, crossing his legs. "This will serve."

Cole knelt in front of him. "Are we supposed to be here? When we first arrived, a guy told us to stay on the paths."

"I am seldom noticed, and so easily forget such policies," Sando said. "I would not wish to lead you into trouble. Since we are already here, I recommend avoiding attention. I suppose you could inform any nosy authorities that you were following a wayward echo."

"Okay," Cole said, crouching a little lower.

"I take it this is not the first time you have strayed from a path," Sando said.

"Nobody's perfect," Cole admitted, thinking of some of the rules he had broken since arriving in the Outskirts. His adventure with Mira had begun when they ran away from the Sky Raiders. From the High King's perspective, pretty much all Cole had done since that day was break laws, including when he helped Dalton escape his captors.

"Tell me how I can be of service, young renegade," Sando said, bowing his head slightly. "What information do you seek?"

"Can you tell me about Nazeem?"

Stillness settled over Sando. "You name a dangerous object of curiosity. Surely, there are brighter matters to investigate. How about directions to a stream that appears to flow uphill? I could hum a forgotten melody, popular in bygone years, which you could now revive? I know several rumors about lost treasure."

"I'm interested in Nazeem."

Sando sighed. "What would you have me tell you?"

Cole wasn't sure how much to divulge. Sando seemed

willing to help, but could he be trusted? Cole decided to ask about something that had bothered him when talking to the rude old guy by the bench.

"How can Nazeem be in the echolands but not dead?"

"Many in the echolands are not dead," Sando said. "I am not dead."

"I'm new to Necronum."

"An echo mirrors the physical body, not the spirit," Sando explained. "The echo is not the essence. It is not the lifespark. Like the physical body, an echo is a container for a lifespark. Unlike a physical body, an echo can continue to function without the lifespark. A dead echo can walk and talk without a lifespark."

"So you can be a live echo or a dead echo," Cole said.

Sando gave a nod. "With a dead echo, the essence or lifespark has moved on, leaving the functional shell behind. These dead echoes can move and talk, but they lack a will and have no new ideas. Over time they degenerate into madness. A regular echo like me still has his essence. Though my mortal body has perished, in the echolands I am alive. There are also bright echoes. They form when death weavers temporarily leave their physical bodies behind and cross to the echolands."

"Nazeem is a bright echo?" Cole asked.

"Doubtful," Sando said. "He has been here too long. Any physical body he once possessed should be long gone. He was a being of great power imprisoned long ago for the safety of the entire world. Another topic might be of greater interest. I could divulge the location of a huge abandoned tree house. . . ."

"Nazeem must be a bright echo," Cole said. "How else would he break free and return to the five kingdoms to lead the shapecrafters?"

Sando leaned toward Cole and lowered his voice. "Where did you hear that?"

Cole appreciated that Sando took him seriously. But he worried about revealing too much. "Just rumors."

Sando studied him closely. "Few know of shapecraft. Fewer still know Nazeem believes he can escape confinement in the near future. Where have you learned such rumors?"

"I don't know how much to tell you," Cole said frankly.

Sando fixed him with a searching gaze. "I would like to help you, young sir. But some of what I know could be hazardous. I do not wish to endanger you. How can I gauge how much to share without understanding what you already know?"

"You don't work for Nazeem?" Cole asked.

"Like many echoes, I trade in information," Sando said. "My affiliations and loyalties vary. Had you wanted harmless knowledge, I would have been as free with it as you were with your silver. Nazeem is another matter. We all must speak of him with caution. Are you a shapecrafter?"

Cole blinked. "No."

Sando narrowed his gaze. "I can perceive your shaping power. It writhes like a dozen tangled serpents trying to devour one another. It is maimed. I have observed shapecrafters who tampered with their abilities to achieve unique results."

"My power is a mess," Cole admitted. "Shapecraft was

involved. But it was an attack. I can't use my power any-more." He remembered the time in Junction when contact with the Founding Stone had temporarily reawakened his abilities, but he didn't want to get that specific with Sando.

The beggar winced. "Ruthless and foul. Who had the power to do such a thing?"

"She was called Morgassa," Cole said.

Sando's eyes widened. "You faced Morgassa? And lived?"

"You believe me?" Cole asked.

"I can plainly see that you believe it," Sando said. "I suppose you could be insane or deluded. I had an aunt who held long conversations with her flowers."

"I helped defeat Morgassa," Cole said. "She damaged my shaping power."

"To have challenged Morgassa and lived, you must know the Pemberton girls," Sando said with awe. "You are helping them, I take it?"

"Trying," Cole said.

"I have discovered a young celebrity," Sando said. "You must have some connection to Honor. You're aware that she came here not long ago?"

Cole decided he might as well come clean. "I'm looking for Destiny and Honor."

"Honor is kept, not found," Sando said with a sly grin. "And need we search for destiny? It tends to find us whether we like it or not."

"I'm talking about the princesses," Cole clarified patiently.

"You want to help the Pemberton girls?" Sando asked.

"Yeah," Cole said.

"How did you become involved?"

"Long story."

"You were not born in the Outskirts," Sando said. "You came from Outside."

"You can tell?"

"Experience."

"I hope to get home someday."

Sando hooted with laughter. "No small tasks for you, young sir."

Cole felt his cheeks warm up. "It won't be easy."

Sando pointed at him. "That puts it mildly. You interest me. You are no ordinary boy. Tell me your name."

"Cole."

"You must sleep lightly these days," Sando said. "A knife under your pillow, and a rope by the window. I discern that Stafford Pemberton is not your friend. Nor is Owandell or Nazeem. Who do you serve?"

"The princesses," Cole said. "I got involved with them directly."

"I see now why you desire knowledge of Nazeem," Sando said. "A shadowy subject. His precise origin remains unknown. We're aware that in mortality he was a shaper of extraordinary power. From his place of confinement in the Fallen Temple, he has reached out to humans and taught them shapecraft and has recruited many echoes as well. For an imprisoned being, he wields considerable influence in the echolands and across the five kingdoms. Like you, he intently wishes to find Destiny Pemberton, and her sister

Honor as well. He is also searching for a young man who fits your description. Are you aware?"

Cole's mouth was dry. "Yeah," he managed, sick dread coiling in his gut.

Sando held up a hand. "Do not be alarmed, giver of silver. I trade in information but am happy to guard your secret. Others may not extend the same courtesy. You cannot hide for long. Not in Necronum, where so many echoes prowl. They will notice your deformed shaping power."

"How can I avoid Nazeem?" Cole asked.

"The real question is how to avoid the mortals and echoes who serve him," Sando said. "Nazeem is trapped in the Fallen Temple. You are beyond his physical reach."

"Unless he gets free," Cole said. "Can he come back from the echolands?"

Sando's eyes flashed with interest. "How? It would defy nature. But Nazeem seems convinced he has found a way, and so do his followers. Who am I to name anything impossible? The whispers suggest he expects freedom in the near future. But what does that mean to a being who has been imprisoned for so long? Is the near future later this century? Or next week?"

"From what I heard, it sounded closer to next week," Cole said.

"This could be," Sando said. "I know little more about Nazeem. I suspect you have more intimate knowledge of him than I do."

"Is the Fallen Temple far from here?" Cole asked.

"Very far," Sando said. "If you desire a long and prosperous life, may I suggest you keep it that way? In fact, you might consider departing Necronum. I understand Zeropolis has many conveniences."

Cole shook his head. "I can't. There are things I have to do here."

Sando considered him intently. "What information do you most desire?"

"You can probably guess," Cole said. "Do you know where I can find the princesses? Destiny or Honor?"

"Of course this would be your priority," Sando said, rubbing his hands. "I cannot tell you the present location of either sister. But I do know a place where Destiny has been. You could acquire her trail there. There would be risk involved."

"Everything is a risk these days," Cole said. "Lots of people are after me. The sooner I find the princesses, the less time they'll have to catch me."

Squinting intently, Sando lowered his voice to a whisper. "This is one of my most guarded nuggets of information. I survive by trading knowledge. Would you grant me a favor in exchange for the knowledge you seek?"

Cole fell silent. Hunter had warned him to be very careful bargaining with echoes and to make no binding oaths. What might Sando want? Had everything until now been a setup?

Sando smiled, wrinkles gathering at the corners of his mouth and eyes. "Do not fear a trade! I have not yet spoken my terms. They are very lenient."

"What's the deal?" Cole asked warily.

"I could not keep your silver," Sando said. "Instead, favor me with a different offering. Maintain the silver ringer in your custody, on my behalf, until you give it to the person I designate. While you retain the ringer, I will serve you as best I can from the echolands."

"How will I know who gets the ringer?" Cole asked.

"I'll bind the ringer to both of us," Sando said. "That way, while you retain the ringer, I'll be able to reach your mind."

"I was warned to avoid binding oaths," Cole said uneasily.

Sando waved his hands. "I don't mean a binding oath. Avoiding those is a good policy. Under a bound oath, you would owe me a particular service, with a punishment attached should you fail. This is not my proposal. Not all bindings involve punishments. Some can simply help echoes and mortals find and trust one another. I would bind the ringer to us so I can help you avoid losing it by accident, and so I can tell you who I want to have it."

"Isn't that a lot of trouble just to give somebody a ringer?" Cole asked.

"Donating the ringer will bring me joy," Sando said. "But my motives go beyond generosity. Echoes spend our existence resisting the call of the Other."

"The other what?"

"Just the Other, young sir. The unnamed realms beyond the echolands. They summon us. At first the invitation is easy to resist. But the pull increases over time. I have withstood the call for many long decades. Interaction with the material world helps us resist. Some echoes collaborate with mortals to resolve matters of personal concern. For others, it is a question of survival. In short, having a ringer to give in Necronum will help keep my echo alive."

That seemed like a fair reason to Cole, but he had just met Sando and didn't want to be reckless. "How do I know you're not tricking me?"

"Young sir, what have I to gain from deceit?" Sando asked with a chiding smile. "The binding depends on the quality of my information. If my tip fails to lead you to Destiny's trail, the binding will unravel, as if it never happened. I'm trading a platinum for a copper. Your task is easy, but this knowledge will be most difficult to uncover elsewhere."

"What if you lead Nazeem's people to me?" Cole said.

"As a token of good faith, and to give you maximum assurance of my worthy intentions, I will pledge to serve you and only you until I instruct you to deliver the ringer."

"You can't break that pledge?"

"Absolutely not," Sando said. "I'll bind it. But in return you will need to keep our arrangement secret."

"Wait a minute," Cole said. "That seems weird. I want to check with my friends before I make any deals."

Sando shook his head. "This bargain is not with a group. That gets hazy. This offer is for you and only you, good now or never. The secrecy protects me. Some unscrupulous death weavers use their power to bind and command echoes. You are no death weaver. If you can't talk about me to anyone, no death weavers will interfere with our bargain. Just like you, I deserve to protect myself."

"Will you give me a minute to think?"

"Be my guest, young sir. No need to rush."

Cole folded his arms. Mira and his friends had come here to find information that might lead them to Destiny, and this was a chance to get it. What if one of the others had already learned what Sando would tell him? Or worse, what if somebody else already had a better lead?

Then again, what if the others had learned nothing? Delivering a ringer didn't sound too bad, especially since Sando pledged to serve only him until it happened. The echo seemed knowledgeable and friendly. Who knew when his help might come in handy?

Hunter had warned not to make binding oaths and to be careful about striking bargains. This wasn't a binding oath, and the bargain seemed innocent. Even if one of the others discovered a better lead, Sando's requirement was simple, and the echo could prove useful in other ways.

"All right," Cole said. "How do we make it official?"

"Very good, young sir," Sando said, his head bobbing. "We will make quite a team—I'm sure of it. You still have the ringer you tried to give me?"

Cole hadn't returned it to his pocket yet. He held it up.

"Set it down and tell me that it belongs to me," Sando said.

Cole placed the small silver hoop on the dirt in front of Sando. "This ringer is now yours."

Leaning forward, the beggar waved his hands over the silver ringer, fingers fluttering. "If you take up the ringer again, Cole, you will hold it on my behalf. You will keep the ringer until I designate a recipient. In return, I will tell you about a place Destiny Pemberton visited where you can pick up her trail, though doing so is your task, not mine. You will keep our arrangement secret, including my identity, and I pledge to serve you and only you until I ask you to deliver the ringer. While the ringer is in your possession, it will be bound to you, and to me, so as not to go missing before the conclusion of our arrangement."

Sando stopped speaking but kept stirring the air with his hands.

"What now?" Cole asked.

"If you agree to these terms, pick up the ringer," Sando said.

"What if we don't find Destiny's trail?" Cole asked.

"Then you owe me nothing for flawed information. The binding will not hold."

"What if I mess up?" Cole asked. "What happens if I tell about you?"

"If I hold up my end, you won't be able to dispose of the ringer until I say so, and you won't be able to tell anyone about me."

Cole hesitated. "That sounds like I'll be bound. Are you sure this isn't a bound oath?"

"A bound oath would have a punishment for breaking your word," Sando said. "This binding will simply hold you to what you promised if I keep up my end. And it holds me to what I promised if you keep up yours."

"Sounds like it will control me."

"Control you?" Sando cried with a laugh. "You will have to keep the ringer, and you won't be able to tell my secret. Otherwise, you will be in full control of yourself. If you don't mean to keep the agreement, you shouldn't make it. I intend to fulfill my part and hold you to your promise."

"I don't know," Cole said, wondering how the deal could backfire.

"This is simple," Sando said calmly. "If I ask too much, walk away. You are under no obligation. I see this as a generous offer. I require a minor favor in exchange for very valuable information. If you see it otherwise, good day to you, young sir. May you travel prosperous roads."

"Can't you just tell me?" Cole begged.

"It was my pleasure to provide free information about Nazeem," Sando said. "We could discuss other matters. But I cannot tell you about Destiny for free. I can't divulge such precious knowledge without some form of recompense. Binding myself to the material world is how I survive."

Cole waited.

Sando placed his hands on his knees, as if to rise.

Cole picked up the silver ringer.

CHAPTER

4

KNOWLEDGE

A faint tremor rippled through Cole. Not a physical vibration—more a disturbance of his emotions, intangible but unmistakable. The sensation briefly allowed him to feel his shaping power.

"Good choice, young sir," Sando approved, rocking happily. "Destiny Pemberton visited the Cave of Memory not many months ago."

"Is that nearby?" Cole asked.

"Three days by horse or coach," Sando said. "You seem unfazed. I expected more excitement. How much do you know about the Cave of Memory?"

"Nothing," Cole said.

Sando grinned, gums gleaming wetly. "Certain places in Necronum are woven differently from others. No echoes can enter the Cave of Memory. The interior has no parallel in the echolands. After entering, any mortal who departs the cave leaves behind a lasting impression that functions like a dead echo."

"An echo forms?" Cole asked.

"Not a true echo," Sando said. "An echo only forms once for each person. No second chances. It happens upon death, or earlier if a death weaver crosses to our side and becomes a bright echo. Such echoes remain bright for as long as they can return to their physical bodies. The constructs inside the Cave of Memory are not true echoes. Most call them imprints. They have no physical substance. But they retain the form and memories of whoever they represent."

Cole had gotten used to encountering the impossible in the Outskirts, but this was still hard to process. "Are you saying I can talk to Destiny's memories?"

"In essence, yes," Sando said. "The imprint you meet will look like Destiny and will have the same memories and personality Destiny had when she exited the cave. But the imprint cannot learn or change."

"She'll be like a figment," Cole said. "A semblance made of illusion."

"Similar," Sando said. "Finding Destiny's imprint could be a challenge. The cave is not small. Many imprints have accumulated over the years. All who enter pay the same price."

"I'll leave behind an imprint," Cole realized.

Sando tapped his temple and pointed at Cole. "At minimum, proof you were there. At worst, your imprint could impart secrets to others."

"If I wouldn't tell a secret, would my imprint?" Cole asked.

"Depends," Sando said. "Can you be tricked?"

"I guess."

"If so, your imprint could be fooled as well. An imprint is intangible, so it can't be tortured or threatened. But your imprint also can't learn new concepts. Its only tools would be everything you knew and believed when you left the cave. The imprint can't alter an opinion, develop a skill, or entertain a fresh thought. There is no inspiration for imprints. No new memories. Their nature tends to cause exploitable weaknesses."

"Makes me wonder how much I trust myself," Cole said.

"A sensible concern, young sir," Sando said. "But if you truly wish to find Destiny, the cave will offer you a chance."

"I could probably learn a lot about what led to her current problems," Cole said. "You told me that dead echoes can go crazy over time. Does the same happen to imprints?"

"I understand that it can," Sando said. "The reaction would partly depend on the person imprinted. The imprint would have no physical needs or appetites, but it will be no happier to remain trapped inside the Cave of Memory than you would be. If such a fate would drive you mad, your imprint will have the same response."

"The imprint would have no hope of escape," Cole said. He tried to picture how it would feel to be stuck forever in some cave. "Does the imprint suffer?"

Sando gave a light chuckle. "An imprint might seem to suffer. It could act distressed. But the imprint has no life. No will. It only imitates something that was alive. It's a replica. The imprint can convey information. It can mimic emotion. But its feelings are no more real than those of a puppet or a footprint."

"Is the Cave of Memory hard to find?" Cole asked.

"The location is no great secret," Sando said. "Many could direct you. The closest village to the cave is called Rincomere."

"Well, thanks," Cole said.

"This is not good-bye, young sir," Sando said. "Our partnership is just beginning. Save your farewells for after you deliver the ringer. A final matter. You are traveling alone?"

"No," Cole admitted.

"How will you explain your new knowledge to your friends?"

"That's right. I agreed not to tell them about you. They'll want to know my source."

"Try not to lie," Sando advised. "Falsehoods have a way of unraveling, especially in Necronum. Do your companions know about your damaged power?"

"Yeah."

"Report that you met an old semblance who recognized your mangled power and took pity on you. This is all true. You had desperate need for rare knowledge in my possession. I could have required an exhausting quest. I could have demanded vast treasures. Instead, I made a generous bargain. And if they ask my name?"

"Pretend I don't know?" Cole tried.

"That would be a lie," Sando chided. "Try something like, 'Good question. I should have found out.'"

"I should have and I did," Cole said.

"Imply the lie," Sando said. "Don't state it outright."

"You're good at this."

"I lived a long mortal life, and many years as an echo besides," Sando said. "I've had ample time to practice."

"Cole?" a voice called.

Cole put a finger to his lips so he could listen. It sounded like Joe. He seemed to be a fair distance away.

"Cole! Cole? Come to the shrine. Cole?"

"Your friends are searching for you," Sando said. "Go to them."

On impulse, Cole attempted to drop the silver ringer. He swung his hand forward, but his fingers refused to let go. He tried once more with no success.

"Did you think I was bluffing?" Sando asked.

"I just wanted to see what it felt like," Cole said, pocketing the ringer and then flexing his fingers. They moved fine when he wasn't trying to drop it. "Thanks for the info."

Sando folded his hands on his lap, closed his eyes, and smiled. "We will meet again, giver of silver. May each step bring you closer to prosperity." The old beggar faded and disappeared.

"Cole?" Joe called again, nearer this time.

Cole stood up and peered over the bushes. Joe was coming back toward the shrine along a trail. "I'm coming," Cole answered, dodging around vegetation.

As Cole reached the path, a short woman in a silk robe marched up to him. "Leaving the footpaths is prohibited throughout the garden," she scolded.

Cole considered a joke about going to the bathroom but reconsidered given her stern expression. "An echo led me," he explained. "I'm sorry."

"Any respectable echo knows to stay on the paths," she complained.

"It's my first time here," Cole apologized.

"And your last if you don't watch yourself," she said.

"Is there a problem?" Joe asked, approaching. He was tall and well-dressed, with a stubbly beard. Cole could imagine Joe back home in California, playing with his band. Joe flashed his most disarming smile.

"He's with you?" the woman asked.

"Yes," Joe said. "Thanks for finding him. I'd lost sight of him."

"Don't give me the lovable-scoundrel routine," the woman said. "It carries no weight at the Seven-Cornered Shrine. Is he Cole?"

"That's right," Joe confirmed.

She squared up to face him, hands on her hips. "Please don't raise your voice in the gardens. You were crying out like you would for a dog lost in the wilderness! Have you no sense of decorum? This is a place of tranquility. Be responsible! The boy wandered off the path."

"My apologies," Joe said, placing a hand on his chest. "Won't happen again."

"It won't for sure if I ban you," she said. "Watch yourselves. You've been warned. You're on your way out I hope?"

"You guessed it," Joe said. "Good day."

He laid a hand on Cole's shoulder and guided him along the path toward the shrine.

"Where are the others?" Cole murmured as they entered the ornate building.

"Out in front," Joe said. "Sally got a disturbing tip, so we all cleared out. You were the last."

"Did she get any leads on her sisters?"

"Wait until we have more privacy," Joe said.

A large coach awaited them in front of the shrine. Joe guided Cole to the horse-drawn vehicle, and they both climbed inside the compartment. Cole joined Hunter and Dalton on a cushioned bench facing Mira, Jace, and Joe. Jace drew the curtains closed as the coach started rolling.

"Where were you?" Mira asked Cole. "We looked all over."

"He was right by the shrine," Joe said. "He'd gone off the path into the bushes."

"I needed a restroom too," Dalton said.

"No," Cole said. "I was with an echo."

"How much did you spill?" Jace asked, an edge to his voice.

"I told who I was looking for," Cole said. "I didn't say anything about you guys."

"We can speak freely," Hunter said. "I'm blocking the area inside the coach from echoes."

"Sally learned some scary stuff," Dalton explained to Cole.

"I met a woman from my childhood," Mira said. "Zelna Laperne. She was a maid who spent time with me at the castle. She's been an echo for decades now."

"Did she have any leads on your sisters?" Cole asked, unsure what exactly he hoped to hear. Part of him wanted the info he got from Sando to save the day.

"Zelna could only confirm that Nazeem is looking for them," Mira said. "It sounds like he's hunting you too, Cole."

"He didn't seem happy the last time we met," Cole said.

Zelna warned me that the shrine is swarming with his agents," Mira said. "Nazeem's influence in the echolands has grown really strong almost overnight. Nobody had heard his name until recently. When Zelna recognized me, she made contact to caution me to stay away from shrines. They're being heavily watched. I thought we should regroup before asking more questions."

"I helped Mira round up the others," Joe said. "We told everyone to abort. Nobody gained any vital knowledge about Honor or Destiny, but I don't think we gave ourselves away, either."

"Hard to be sure," Hunter said. "If a friend recognized Mira, an enemy could have as well. Dalton told us that he and Cole brought up the princesses with Yeardly. Any time we tell an echo who we're looking for, we run the risk of getting discovered by Nazeem."

"What were you doing off in the bushes with an echo, Cole?" Jace asked. "How much did you spill?"

"It was an old echo," Cole said. "He was friendly and guessed a lot about me. He could see the damage to my shaping power."

"If he could see your power, he might have targeted you," Hunter said. "Nazeem knows about your damaged power."

"The echo didn't come to me," Cole said. "I went to him."

"If he was any good, he may have positioned himself where you would see him," Hunter said. "In an ambush, you let your prey approach. How nosy was he?"

"Medium nosy," Cole said. "I think I got good info from him."

"What?" Mira asked.

"Destiny went to the Cave of Memory," Cole said, hoping the information would impress them.

"Really?" Mira asked. "How long ago?"

"A few months," Cole said.

"He told you this freely?" Hunter asked.

"I have to do a favor for him," Cole said.

"But no bindings," Hunter clarified.

"Well . . . not with punishments attached," Cole said.

"Wait," Hunter said. "You let him do a binding? I told everybody to avoid bound oaths."

"There was no punishment," Cole repeated.

"I guess, strictly speaking, bound oaths have punishments," Hunter said. "But if this echo connected the favor to a binding, that's almost the same thing. What was the binding?"

Cole found himself unable to explain. After two failed attempts, he managed to reply, "I can't say."

Hunter shared a worried glance with Joe and Mira. "He won't let you tell? That's part of the bargain? Who was this echo? What was his name?"

Once again Cole couldn't get the words past his lips. "I can't say."

"What did he look like?" Hunter asked.

After failing to give details, Cole shrugged. "I can't."

Looking shaken, Hunter wiped his eyes.

"Is this bad?" Jace asked.

"Maybe," Hunter said. He studied Cole intently. "My guess is the binding seemed innocent?"

45

"Yes," Cole said, relieved he could spit out that much.

"Do you see any way it could endanger us?" Hunter pressed.

"No," Cole said, relieved again. "It was a very simple request."

"That's good at least," Hunter said. "Did the binding require loyalty from the echo?"

Cole couldn't answer. He tried to nod but failed. "I can't say."

"You can't give us any details?" Hunter guessed.

"Yes," Cole said.

"But you're confident it can't backfire?" Hunter asked.

"Yes," Cole said. "It seemed like the echo did me a favor."

"We're so doomed," Jace muttered.

"Maybe not," Hunter said. "Cole isn't stupid. Since the binding is keeping him from answering my questions, the info he got has to be solid. The binding wouldn't hold if it was based on a lie."

"But he could have been dealing with an agent of Nazeem," Mira said. "We don't know what Cole has to do. There could be a trap built into the binding."

Hunter looked at Joe, who held up both hands defensively. "I've never been to Necronum. You and Mira know much more than me about this place."

"We could have been exposed at the shrine in other ways," Hunter said. "Mira could have been recognized. We didn't have lots of interactions with echoes, but we already might have accidentally given the wrong hint to the wrong person. At least Cole got a lead. If we want some serious background about Destiny, we know where to go."

"Should we split up from Cole?" Jace asked. "We know to visit the Cave of Memory. We don't need him to get there. Maybe he can go his own way for a while until we see how the binding plays out?"

Cole noticed Dalton looking at him. If they wanted to take off and look for Jenna, this was a golden opportunity.

"Not unless he wants to leave," Mira said firmly. "Cole has saved us more than once. If he doesn't think he left an opening for trouble, that's good enough for me. He may have struck a good bargain. That does happen. And even if he didn't, we'll figure it out together."

"Every minute we're in Necronum, we risk blowing our cover," Hunter said. "The road won't be smooth no matter what precautions we take. We should count ourselves lucky that we know where to start our search. The Cave of Memory is roughly the same direction as Destiny's star. I think we should head that way and find a decent inn."

"Sounds good to me," Cole said, avoiding eye contact with Dalton.

"Nice work, Cole," Mira said. "We didn't expose ourselves too much at the shrine, and we still walked away with new knowledge. Without your binding, we'd know nothing."

"I hope it doesn't get us in trouble," Cole said.

"So do I," Jace said heavily. "So do I."

HORSES

Cole snapped awake, certain he needed to get out of bed. Sitting up, he wiped grit from the corners of his eyes. Orange moonlight filtered into the dim room through the cracks in the shutters. He could hear Dalton breathing evenly.

It looked suspiciously like the middle of the night. He heard no threatening sounds. Why exactly did he need to get out of bed? His bladder didn't feel strained. Had he been dreaming? If so, he couldn't recall any details.

Something felt wrong. He hadn't awakened in a natural way. Cole remembered arriving at the large inn as the brightest stars began to appear in the sky. After a hearty meal of beef ribs, potatoes, and bread, he and Dalton had decided to share a room. Hunter had bunked with Jace. Joe and Mira each had their own rooms.

Was he being paranoid? Should he go back to sleep? The residue of his urgent feeling remained, but Cole slouched onto his pillow. He couldn't get comfortable. He had no desire to close his eyes. An internal tug coaxed him to get up. He stretched one hand toward a far corner of the room. That somehow felt right.

Weird! Was he turning psychic or losing it?

Cole kicked back his covers and slid his legs off the edge of the thin mattress. The far corner of the room inexplicably beckoned.

He got out of bed and crossed to the corner, where he had left his clothes on a chair. Almost without thinking, he picked up his pants and started rummaging through the pockets.

A sense of relief struck as his fingers closed around a ringer. Pulling it out, he found it was silver. Had it been a mistake to leave the ringer in his pants? Did it always need to be touching him?

Cole? a familiar voice spoke in his mind. Even without physically hearing the word, Cole recognized the speaker as Sando.

"Yeah," Cole whispered.

Thank Fortune I could reach you, Sando continued. *Depart the inn immediately. You and anyone in your company. Ride north for now. Stay off the roads. Some local Enforcers have caught wind of you. They're coming your way. Hurry!*

"Thanks," Cole said, crossing to Dalton.

My pleasure, young sir. I'll try to reach you again. Keep our ringer in hand.

"Got it," Cole murmured. He shook Dalton's shoulder. "Get up! We have to scram!"

Dalton gave a soft groan. "Huh?"

"Enforcers are coming."

That grabbed his attention. Dalton lurched from the bed, his hands breaking his fall before his feet followed.

"How much time to we have?" Cole whispered, reaching out with his mind.

"What?" Dalton asked.

"Grab your clothes," Cole said. Clenching the ringer in his fist, Cole whispered, "Can you hear me—"

He meant to say Sando, but the word wouldn't form on his lips. Probably because Dalton was listening. Cole sensed no reply.

"You okay?" Dalton asked.

"I'll explain later," Cole said. He quickly dressed. "Get Joe." Cole dashed to Hunter's room, then knocked softly. Though haste was needed, he didn't want to announce their departure to the entire inn.

Hunter opened the door, squinting, hair mussed. "What's up?" Beyond him, Jace sat up in bed, a dagger in his hand.

"I got a message from the echo," Cole said. "Some Enforcers are coming. He told me we need to get out of here and ride north. He didn't want us on the roads."

Hunter scowled thoughtfully.

"Think it's a trap?" Cole asked.

Hunter gave a quick shake of his head. "If the echo meant us harm, it would be easier to let the Enforcers take us here. There's no point in warning us unless the help is real. We'll have to ditch the coach and steal horses. Wake the others."

Hunter went back into his room. Dalton was talking to

Joe. Cole jogged to Mira's room and knocked gently. After a moment he knocked again.

"Hello?" He could barely hear her from behind the door.

"It's Cole," he said, keeping his voice low.

The door cracked open, showing a sliver of her face, including most of one eye.

"Enforcers are coming," Cole said. "I got a tip from the echo."

"I'll be right out."

The door closed.

Feeling antsy, Cole looked up and down the hall. Dalton had entered Joe's room. Every second seemed precarious. Would Enforcers come pounding up the stairs? If so, Cole and his friends had little to rely on. No gadgets from Zeropolis. No special weapons. Only Hunter could shape here, and he had warned there wasn't much that death weaving could do in combat.

Squeezing the ringer in his fist, Cole tried to reestablish a mental link with Sando. *Are you there?* he thought intently. *Can you hear me, Sando?*

Cole sensed no reply. Apparently, the ringer had limited use as a communicator. Maybe it took a lot of effort from Sando? Or some weaving? Could echoes shape? He pocketed the ringer.

Joe, Dalton, Hunter, and Jace exited their rooms and gathered near Cole.

"What weapons do we have?" Cole asked.

"Your Jumping Sword is in the coach," Hunter said. "Mira's too. I haven't caught up to any of my stashes of

Necronum equipment yet. I have nothing more than knives right now. We were counting on secrecy."

"What are the Enforcers like here?" Dalton asked.

"They use conventional weapons," Hunter said. "Bows, swords, spears—all that. Unless they're very powerful weavers, they tend to be expert soldiers. A lot of them rely on echoes for information. They have echoes follow people or set up invisible sentries."

"Have you been communicating with echoes?" Joe wondered.

"I like to work with certain echoes," Hunter said. "It's been a while since I visited Necronum. I reached out to some of my most trusted contacts but haven't heard back. It can take time. Confiding in random echoes can be risky. After the shrine I thought it best to wait for an echo I really trust."

"Can echoes attack?" Cole asked.

Hunter held out a hand and waggled it. "Not usually in a direct way. They can scare you. They can distract. If you're not careful, they can bind you. But usually the big danger is if they share information you want kept secret. Like your location."

Mira emerged from her room. "What's the plan?"

"A coach is fine for travel but bad for a getaway," Hunter said. "We'll borrow some horses from the stable. I checked when we arrived. There are several."

"You checked?" Dalton asked.

Hunter shrugged. "You didn't? We're on the run! I'll leave money. You've all ridden?"

"Some of us more than others," Cole said. "But yeah."

Hunter led the way to the stairs. "Do we know a time-frame?"

"I was just told to hurry," Cole said.

"Did we pay the innkeeper?" Dalton asked.

"In advance," Joe said.

"Did we leave a letter thanking the cook for dinner?" Jace mocked.

"Let's go," Hunter said.

They moved in silence from the bottom of the stairs across the dim common room. Embers glowing on the hearth provided most of the light. Jace held his dagger ready.

Cole slipped out the front door after Hunter. Stars sparkled in the sky overhead. A dull, red moon shed muted light. Glancing up, Cole shuffled to a stop.

Some of the stars were neatly arranged into words.

The writing was not large but distinct.

NO MORE STARS.

Cole turned to Mira, who was looking up as well.

"Mother," she said. "Honor's and Destiny's stars aren't in the sky anymore. Somebody must have caught on."

"Now all the Outskirts knows," Jace said.

"Almost nobody will get what it means," Mira said. "Mother had to get the message to me and my sisters. Especially to me, so I'd know not to stop looking for Destiny just because the stars are gone."

"What now?" Joe asked.

"We need to get away," Mira said. "The Cave of Memory matters more than ever. It's now our only lead."

"Come on," Hunter said. They trotted across the yard

BRANDON MULL

toward the stables. Hunter first went to where the coach was parked. No horses were currently attached to the vehicle. After scouring the compartment, he handed Cole his Jumping Sword, Mira hers, and passed out knives to Dalton and Joe.

Hunter then entered the stables. He stopped so abruptly that Cole collided with his back.

"Sorry," Cole said, grabbing his brother's shoulders half to keep Hunter from falling and half to steady himself.

"No," Hunter said, ignoring Cole, real despair in his voice. "I don't believe it."

"What?" Jace asked from behind.

"The horses are gone," Hunter said, racing along the row of stalls. He ran outside the building and soon returned. "All of them. The horses for our coach, plus eight others I saw here earlier tonight."

"Sabotage," Mira said. "Are we being watched?"

"At least by echoes," Hunter said, looking around. "Come on."

The inn was situated near a crossroads. Cole followed Hunter to the intersection. Empty roads stretched in four directions. Hunter paused and raised a finger to his lips. The others stopped and listened. The unmistakable rumble of galloping hoofbeats drummed in the distance.

"Not good," Cole muttered, sliding a hand into his pocket to touch the silver ringer. He still sensed no contact from Sando.

"What do we do?" Dalton asked, hysteria creeping into his tone.

"We split up," Hunter said, calmly assuming command. "Two by two. Whoever stays free rescues the others. The riders are coming from the west. Joe and Mira will go south. Dalton and Jace will travel east. Cole and I will head north. Stay off the roads. Eventually make your way toward the town of Rincomere, north and west of here."

After Hunter fell silent, the approaching hoofbeats did all the talking. The riders couldn't be more than a few minutes away. This was bad. They could all go down tonight. Without shaping, Cole and his friends were no match for trained soldiers. Panic threatened to take over, but Cole resisted.

"What if echoes are already tailing us?" Cole asked. "Won't they lead the Enforcers right to us?"

"Let me check," Hunter said. Sitting cross-legged on the edge of the road, he closed his eyes, made fists, and pressed his knuckles together.

Cole shared curious glances with Jace and Dalton.

"Are you praying?" Jace asked.

Hunter gave no reply.

"Maybe Mira and I should get started," Joe proposed.

Eyes still closed, Hunter held up a finger, asking him to wait. Hunter flinched, eyes squeezing tighter. His head jerked a little. He pushed his knuckles together tighter, arms trembling. Then he opened his eyes.

"Okay," Hunter said. "There were a couple of echoes spying on us. I took care of them. Let's hurry. Stay safe!"

"He means die bravely," Cole amended, earning a smile from Jace.

Hunter started running along the road to the north. Cole caught up and ran beside him. Glancing back, Cole saw Joe and Mira racing along the edge of the road in the opposite direction. Dalton and Jace dashed eastward.

"What did you do to the echoes?" Cole asked.

"I confronted them," Hunter said. "After opening my mind to the echolands, I found a couple of echoes there. I worked a weaving on them that forced them to depart. It was the best I could manage. A full binding could have imprisoned them or even destroyed them. But I'm not that good yet."

Cole was already panting. "This is a fast pace."

"We won't outlast horses," Hunter said. "Our best bet is to blow our energy before they get too close and hope they never see us." He veered off the road, running across farmland.

Cole kept up. "What if they find us?"

"If they come this way, we split up," Hunter said. "We have to stay out of their hands."

Cole understood. He and Hunter couldn't hope to out-fight the Enforcers. And if they got caught, who knew what would come next? Owandell led the Enforcers, and he served Nazeem. Cole had made powerful enemies. Would they experiment with his mangled shaping ability? Torture him? Kill him? Anything was possible.

Hunter had been an Enforcer. If they were aware that he had changed sides, who knew what they might do to him?

Cole caught his foot on a clump of dirt and went down hard, tasting soil. He scrambled back to his feet. Cole missed a lot of things about Zeropolis, but having a battle suit enhance his speed and endurance was currently at the top of the list. Hunter slowed until Cole caught up, then poured on the speed again.

They passed a line of trees into another cultivated field. The trees helped screen them from the road. The pounding hoofbeats grew louder.

"The riders turned north," Hunter said. "All of them, I think. Good for the others. Bad for us. Could mean they're specifically after you."

"How would they know I went north?" Cole asked.

"Weaving involves knowing things," Hunter said. "For some weavers, the skill goes beyond using echoes for tips. They sense echoes and people, sometimes across great distances. We call them perceptives."

"You think we have a perceptive tracking us?" Cole asked.

"It would be rotten luck," Hunter said. "We'll know soon."

Cole ran harder, studying the ground in the dull red moonlight, trying not to fall. He gripped the silver ringer in his hand but still received no advice. He wondered if Sando might have been one of the echoes Hunter had driven away.

Hunter shoved the back of Cole's shoulder, causing him to tumble to the dirt.

"Lie still," Hunter commanded in a stage whisper, changing course a bit. "It's your best chance. I'll try to mislead them."

Flat on his stomach, Cole watched his brother sprint away. He supposed staying low was his best bet for hiding in an empty field.

The sound of the hoofbeats changed as the horses left the road, muffled by the softer soil of the field. Beyond the line of trees dividing the field where Cole waited from the next, he detected flickers of motion.

In the other direction, Hunter ran in a crouch. He was almost to the far end of the field.

It didn't feel right to let his brother draw their attention away. Then again, Hunter was a leader among the Enforcers. There was still a good chance none of them knew that he had defected and was helping the resistance. Maybe Hunter could bluff his way out of trouble.

Cole decided to trust Hunter's judgment and stay put. His eyes strayed to the sky. NO MORE STARS.

Six Enforcers galloped past the tree line, drawing his attention earthward. They rode dark horses and wore black armor.

And they came straight at Cole.

Allowing himself a small, whimpering laugh, Cole slid the Jumping Sword from its sheath. Was there any chance of it working? He couldn't feel his power. Should he fight anyhow?

He was still on the ground, but it was clear that he wasn't fooling anybody. As the horsemen slowed and circled him, Cole stood up. The way the six were positioned, he could only see three of them at a time.

"Cole Randolph," one of the Enforcers said.

Cole faced him. "Maybe."

"It wasn't a question," the rider responded. "Lay down your sword."

Cole pointed the blade at the ground between and beyond two of the horsemen. "Away," he said. There was no tug. He sensed no connection to his power.

"This is your final warning," the spokesman called, drawing a longsword.

Cole stood his ground. Where was his ability? It was buried somewhere inside of him. Cole searched desperately, willing himself to feel something, but came up empty.

Power or no power, if they wanted him, they would have to take him. He would dodge and slash at men and horses for as long as he could. In his gut he knew there was no way he would win. He probably wouldn't harm any of them, and the chances were decent he would get killed instead of captured. Still, after all he had been through, and knowing the horrors that captivity would mean, he couldn't just give up.

"Who do you think you serve?" Cole cried.

The Enforcer hesitated, as if trying to discover the trick in the question. "The High King, of course," he finally said.

"Your orders didn't come from Owandell?" Cole asked.

"Naturally, since he leads the Enforcers, under the direction of the High King," the spokesman said.

"I am a servant of the High King," Cole said. It was at least partially true. The High King had asked him for favors when they last spoke. "Stafford Pemberton does not want me captured. The person who wants me is Nazeem, Owandell's real master. Nazeem taught Owandell shapecraft." If he was going down, Cole figured he could at least start some rumors that Owandell and Nazeem would rather keep unspoken.

The Enforcers were looking at one another. Did some of them know that Cole spoke the truth? Any of the experienced shapecrafters probably did. Had some of them heard similar rumors? Nazeem seemed more known in Necronum than elsewhere. Many echoes were clearly aware of him.

"Enough stalling," the spokesman barked. "Take him."

Cole heard pounding hoofs and a piercing whinny. All heads turned toward the oncoming sound. A riderless horse was closing on the group, its dark coat and mane aflame with flickering red highlights. The horse jumped over one of the mounts surrounding Cole, smashing an Enforcer from his saddle in the process. The horse landed smoothly and kept running.

The other horses began to stamp and rear. None of them were nearly as large as the newcomer. The new horse ran wild, leaping and bucking, crashing into the lesser horses and sending their riders flying.

The Enforcers had no answer to the sudden assault. A pair of them who had fallen to the ground were promptly trampled by the fierce horse. Cole held his sword ready, prepared to jump out of the way when the wild horse turned on him, but the crazed steed paid him no mind.

Though the rampaging horse appeared out of control, it soon became clear that it was targeting the Enforcers. Moving like a rodeo cowboy's worst nightmare, the huge steed kicked horse and rider alike, ruthlessly stomping the Enforcers when they flopped to the ground.

Within less than a minute, the wild horse galloped off into the night, spewing clods of soil. Six Enforcers lay motionless, along with two of their horses. The other four mounts can-tered away, empty stirrups flapping.

Cole sheathed his sword as Hunter ran up to him.

"How'd you do that?" Cole asked.

"Wasn't me," Hunter said, surveying the fallen riders. "I could hardly believe my eyes."

Stunned and relieved, Cole found himself laughing. "It was like a tornado."

Hunter laughed too.

Cole walked over to a fallen Enforcer, taking in the dented armor. "No way did that just happen. I was doomed. Do horses get rabies?"

"That wasn't rabies," Hunter said seriously. "That horse was an assassin. I had a great view. It couldn't have taken out those Enforcers more efficiently. And then it stormed off."

"Where'd it come from?" Cole asked.

Hunter rubbed his chin. "Some echoes can influence animals. Maybe the echo you're working with guided it. If so, he's really powerful."

Cole held up the silver ringer. He still sensed no commu-nication. "That makes more sense than some random horse protecting me."

Hunter laughed again. "Those Enforcers had no clue what to do. It caught them totally flat-footed. Not one of them even tried to use their weapons. I can hardly blame them."

"What now?" Cole asked.

"Enforcers tend to work in isolated units," Hunter said. "I doubt they involved legionnaires or guardsmen. I scattered the echoes that were trailing us. The short-term threat might be over. Finding Dalton and the others in the dark will be tricky, especially since they're on the run. Let's get farther from the inn. Tomorrow, we'll buy horses and make our way to Rincomere. The others can catch up with us there. I think all the Enforcers followed us."

They started trotting away from the fallen Enforcers.

"Did the horse look weird to you?" Cole asked.

"While it pummeled those Enforcers to death?"

"Almost fiery," Cole said.

"I noticed. Kind of like fire reflecting off smoke."

Cole nodded at the perfect description. "Yeah."

"The reddish moon is up. Just a trick of the moonlight."

"The other horses had dark coats. But they didn't look like that."

"No," Hunter agreed pensively. "They didn't."

CHAPTER
6

CAVE

Cole and Hunter found Joe and Mira lounging near a well in the town square of Rincomere. Joe stood and waved as they rode up to them.

"What took you so long?" Mira asked.

"We had to kill six Enforcers," Hunter said, dismounting.

"You're not serious," Joe checked.

"There's a story to it," Hunter said. "We'll fill you in later."

Fewer than a hundred buildings formed the village of Rincomere, most of a modest size, with walls of gray stone and roofs of dark shingles. All could have been designed and built by the same team. Every structure looked like it had stood for a long time. Cole noticed swallows flying in and out of muddy nests clustered under many of the eaves.

Weathered flagstones paved the few streets in town and covered the entirety of the square. The whole village had a sleepy feel. Cole had seen a few women sweeping porches and a couple of men leading mules. The square around the well was vacant except for a few scrawny kids playing marbles in one corner.

"No sign of Dalton?" Cole asked.

"Not yet," Mira said. "We got here last night."

"I expected to be first," Joe said. "We swiped a pair of horses from a farm just south of the crossroads. We left more than their value."

"We bought ours the morning after we escaped," Cole said. "No trouble since then."

"When in doubt, steal horses and ride hard," Joe said. "The Outskirts has taught me that much. There are worse lessons to learn, I guess. Rincomere is quiet. A bunch of old folks hang around the two inns. A big ranch just outside of town breeds mules. There is some farming and some sheep-herders in the hills to the east."

Hunter handed his reins to Joe and sat down by the well. Cole swung down from his horse as well, keeping the reins in his hand. Hunter bowed his head and pressed his knuckles together. After a moment he looked up.

"Lots of echoes," Hunter said. "I didn't feel special attention from any of them. They're regulars, I think. Feels like this town has been here for a long time. I'll shield our conversation just to be safe."

"We learned the way to the cave," Mira said. "We just follow a trail outside of town. I think Cole should go inside."

"Won't your sister's imprint be more likely to talk to you?" Cole replied.

"Joe and I talked about it," Mira said. "If I go in, I leave behind proof I was here. That doesn't make sense if we can avoid it. Same with proof of Hunter. We need somebody who can win Destiny's trust and who will leave behind a smart imprint that won't blow our secrets. Joe would do well, but I worry about Destiny trusting a strange adult. She's always been more open to young people. Cole, I think you've proven yourself more reliable than Jace and Dalton for this sort of mission. Jace is brave but not always careful. Dalton hasn't been tested enough."

"I'm pretty great," Cole said, unable to resist a grin. "I get why you would pick me over those wannabes. But don't forget that Nazeem is after me too. An imprint of me could heat up the hunt."

"We thought about that," Joe said. "After your inter-actions at the Seven-Cornered Shrine, your cover might already be blown. We heard all the Enforcers turn north, the way you went."

"Not only that," Hunter added. "They went straight to him. There must have been a perceptive with them. I don't know exactly how the secret got out, but they were after Cole."

"How'd you get away?" Mira asked.

"A wild horse came and killed them all," Cole said.

Joe and Mira exchanged a look.

"Six Enforcers?" Joe verified.

"And two of their mounts," Hunter said.

"A horse did that?" Mira asked. "Working alone?"

"It came galloping out of the night," Cole said. "It went on a rampage and then ran off."

"My best guess is an echo controlled the animal," Hunter said. "Maybe the echo that bargained with Cole."

"That would be one powerful echo," Mira said.

"It's a guess," Cole said. "All we know for sure is it happened. We hadn't seen the horse before, and we haven't seen it since."

"Somebody is on our side," Mira said. "Cole's echo gave us a key tip. The warning got us out of there."

Cole slid his hand into the pocket with the ringer. "It sure seemed like the echo meant to help, whether or not he controlled the horse."

"So will you go?" Mira asked. "Into the Cave of Memory, I mean?"

"If that's what you want," Cole said, not overly excited at a chance to let everyone down. "Are there any secrets that could help get Destiny to trust me?"

Mira beckoned Cole close with her finger. He drew near, pulling his horse as well, until Hunter relieved him of the reins.

Mira whispered, "Tell her about speaking to our mother and knowing that she marks us with stars. Only the most trusted people know about that. Tell her the haystacks have fallen down. That's the master code phrase for identifying a messenger from Mother. Also tell her I'm with you. Mention that I needed to avoid making an imprint. But tell about the time she wet the bed and I threw her underthings and sheets out the window to help her hide it. That didn't work, by the way. She was four, I was six. Remind her of the time her tooth fell out, and she lost it and was sad because she couldn't put it under the pillow for the Toothmonger. I found a little pebble that looked almost like a tooth on the white gravel path in the East Garden. I told her the Toothmonger would accept it. She used it and still got some ringers the next morning."

"Our Toothmonger is called the Tooth Fairy," Cole explained quietly.

"Ours is a hairy demon," Mira whispered. "Yours sounds nicer."

"Ours brings money too," Cole explained. "Same result. Any other secrets or memories?"

"Tessa liked when I sang to her," Mira said, her voice catching. "She was my only little sister. The one I cared for. She could be freaky. She would sometimes say things that sounded way too adult. Or even beyond adult. Mysterious prophesies wrapped up in riddles. She was kind of like a perceptive, but more than that. She said things that she had no business knowing. But then a lot of the time she was just a small girl. My little sister. I sang songs about talking flowers. She loved flowers." A tear slid down Mira's cheek.

"I'll find her," Cole assured her.

"Please," Mira said, nodding and then wiping her eyes. "I don't know if I can handle losing her." She squeezed her eyes shut, but more tears spilled out.

Cole hugged her. "It's okay. Her imprint is just the start. We'll find *her*."

As Mira clung to him, Cole felt his resolve strengthening. Mira had been through a lot. Her little sister obviously held a special place in her heart. There were a lot of things Cole hoped to accomplish, including finding Jenna and getting home, but right now this was the most urgent problem.

They had helped two of the other sisters. He wouldn't blow it with this one.

"Stop traumatizing Mira," Hunter scolded.

Cole realized that Hunter and Joe couldn't hear their whispered conversation. "She's telling me about Destiny," Cole explained. "I have a way with the ladies."

Mira pushed Cole away and wiped her eyes again. "I'm sorry," she said, glancing at Cole and the others. "I don't know what came over me."

"Don't apologize," Joe said. "You're under so much stress."

Mira shook her head. "I can't afford to crack up. Weakness doesn't help anybody."

"You're tired," Joe consoled. "We've been riding hard."

"There is plenty more travel ahead of us," Mira said, looking more or less composed again. "I'm not comfortable sitting still. It's early. Maybe Cole and I can go ahead to the cave? Then Joe and Hunter can catch up after Dalton and Jace get here."

"Be sure to tell Jace that Mira chose me for cave duty," Cole said. "So he'll get why we didn't wait."

"Better yet," Joe said to Mira, "Hunter and Cole can visit the cave while you and I keep watch for the others. Maybe you can sneak in some rest."

"But I should be there," Mira said.

"Sitting outside a cave alone?" Joe asked. "Not on my watch. You're too valuable."

Mira stared at him.

"What?" Joe finally asked.

"I'm trying to decide whether you mean valuable or incompetent," Mira said.

"The revolution depends on you girls," Joe said. "The Unseen tasked me with keeping you safe. I'm doing my best."

Mira gave a single nod. "Cole? Hunter? You up for it?"

"It would be a shame to waste the day," Hunter said.

Cole mustered his most confident tone. "Let's go caving."

The nondescript cave opening looked like a little cleft in the rocks that probably went back no more than fifteen feet. Given the reputation of the Cave of Memory, Cole had pictured something more grand—yawning darkness fanged with stalactites.

"Think that's it?" Cole asked.

"Joe pointed out the trail and told us to go left at the fork," Hunter said. "Looks like the trail ends here."

The leather saddle shifted slightly and creaked as Cole dismounted. The ride from Rincomere had only taken a couple of hours. Staring at the unassuming gap in the mountainside, Cole patted his horse.

A sound from a stand of trees off to one side made Cole turn abruptly. He could make out a vague shape in the trees.

Nudging his horse to a trot, Hunter rode that way. "It's a horse," he soon called. "Wait. Two horses. I don't see riders. They must be in the cave."

"Enforcers?" Cole asked.

"Doesn't look like their kind of mounts," Hunter replied, turning his horse to ride back to Cole.

"Great," Cole said. "I'll have actual people to worry about in there as well."

"It's a little surprising," Hunter said, swinging down from his horse.

"Why? Don't lots of people know about the cave?"

"Sure, but they stay away because of the curse."

Cole stared at his brother. "*Now* I hear about a curse?"

Hunter shrugged. "You already know the basics. Whoever goes in leaves an imprint. Think about the downside. People can figure out you went there. By speaking with your imprint, strangers can find out about you and potentially use the info against you. And bad people have gone inside. You can meet some serious evil in the Cave of Memory. Most people in Necronum have decided the place is bad luck."

"But nobody can touch me," Cole checked.

"Not physically," Hunter said. "You won't get punched or stabbed, unless real people do it. But bad imprints could mess with your head. Watch out."

Cole took a deep breath. Except for meeting live people inside, Cole had thought through these dangers. "I might as well get going."

"I'll be waiting," Hunter said.

Shielding his eyes, Cole glanced toward the sun. It wasn't high enough to be noon yet.

Leaving his horse with Hunter, Cole walked to the gap in the rocks. Cool air wafted out. He had to crouch a little to proceed. The way curved, narrowing somewhat, and looked like it probably stopped just out of sight. But as he crept forward, the opposite happened. The tunnel widened, opening into a vast chamber, the air cool enough that Cole wished he had a jacket. Cole could see where four different tunnels branched out from the large chamber, each lit by a different color—red, blue, green, and purple.

A woman stood on the near side of the chamber. She was heavyset and in her fifties, with short black hair and a long brown fur coat. She held up a hand. "Halt. Do you know where you are?"

"The Cave of Memory," Cole said, holding still.

The woman gave a nod. "All who enter leave behind a permanent impression of themselves. If you come any farther, you will do the same when you leave."

"I know," Cole said.

"Proceed if you wish," the woman said. "You've been warned."

Cole walked over to her. "Who are you?"

She ducked her head and held up both hands. "Not your business. I came here by accident. So I warn people who enter. I spare the unwary from surprises."

"You're an imprint," Cole said.

"You've already come too far," she said. "You'll leave one too."

"Do you mind it here?" Cole wondered.

The woman folded her arms and looked a little puzzled. "Honestly? I got more than I bargained for when I came in. But I can't say I'm suffering."

"Don't you get bored?" Cole asked.

She scrunched her eyebrows. "Funny—I can't recall. I guess that means I don't. I remember coming here with my husband and exploring for a good while. Once we went to exit the cave, it gets fuzzy." She looked around, peering toward the colored passages. "My husband isn't with me. I suppose he wandered off. Not sure how long ago. He always had wanderlust. It was why we stumbled across the cave in the first place."

"How long ago?"

She looked perplexed. "Feels like it's been a while. Maybe not? Time gets funny in here. We learned that we had found the Cave of Memory from some of the imprints while we were still tangible. It was strange to meet the imprints. Watch out. Some aren't all there, if you take my meaning." She pointed a finger at the side of her head and twirled it in little circles.

"Do you miss your husband?" Cole wondered.

She peered around the area again. "I expect I will if he doesn't turn up soon."

"Do many people come into the cave?" Cole tried.

She stared upward in thought. "Hard to say. Not since I've been here at any rate."

"Are there two other people in here right now?" Cole asked.

"That doesn't ring true," she said.

"There were two horses outside," Cole explained.

She shrugged. "Could be I missed them. Doesn't seem likely, though. Looking back, it gets muddy since I exited the cave."

Cole remembered Sando explaining that the imprints didn't learn anything new after they were made. How long had this imprint been here? Years, maybe. Or days. Or centuries. If she couldn't remember, it all might feel the same to her.

Cole gestured toward the colorfully glowing passages. "I didn't think of bringing a light."

"You'll find enough in the cave," she said. "There are some dark places, to be sure, but never for too long. At least in my experience. This is an enchanted place. Strong weaving. Dates back to near the founding of the Outskirts, so I'm told."

"What if I'm looking for somebody?" Cole asked.

"Could take some time," she said. "The cave goes and goes."

"Any tips to keep me from getting lost?" Cole asked. "Do the colors help?"

"We never made complete sense of the colors," the woman said. "We got ourselves good and lost, but an imprint gave us the tip that heading down would generally lead us farther in while trending up would lead us out. Not always true in a cave. But true in this one. It's how we found our way back to the entrance."

"Thanks for the tip," Cole said. He felt like he should get moving. "You stay here all the time?"

The woman shrugged. "It's good to have a purpose."

"Thanks for the warning," Cole said. He glanced over at the colored tunnels. "Any thoughts which I should try first?"

"Far as I could tell, they all lead somewhere."

Cole headed for the passage with the red glow, since the color made it seem warmer. After walking out of sight from the woman, he paused. How long before she would forget meeting him?

He counted to ten in his head, then returned to her.

"What have we here?" she asked, sizing him up. "An imprint, I take it?"

"I'm a person," Cole said. "I just came in. We spoke a short time ago."

The woman broke eye contact and stared at the cave floor. "Did we?" she asked with an embarrassed smile. "Funny how the mind works in here." She gazed at him suspiciously. "I don't recall you."

"It's okay," Cole said, backing away. "I have one of those faces. Very, um, forgettable."

Her eyes narrowed. "Are you pulling my leg? Did we really speak?"

"Sorry," Cole said, not wanting to upset her. "Maybe I'm mistaken."

"Some of you are devils," she replied huffily. "Not fair to play with a person's mind. Not when they're alone in a cave."

"Again, sorry," Cole said, returning to the red tunnel and passing out of view. The ground sloped slightly down ahead of him.

Cole took comfort that the woman wouldn't be confused for long. She would forget him all over again. He tried to imagine how it would feel to forget everything after it happened. Life would be disorienting. Then again, having no sense for how long he had been there would be merciful if he was stuck in a cave forever.

Cole glanced back. Should he be marking his way? Should

he have brought more provisions than a water flask? Maybe some rope. He might not need food if he was quick. If his mission took too long, he could always go back and resupply. And if the woman's trick to find the entrance failed, he could probably get directions from imprints. Determined to find Destiny sooner rather than later, Cole quickened his pace.

CHAPTER

7

MEMORIES

Cole considered some of the benefits of the imprints making no new memories. For one thing, it meant that his conversations would be forgotten. His inquiries would leave no tracks, and if an interaction went badly, he could go away, come back, and have another try.

That meant he was free to ask for help from any imprints he met. None of them would remember any tips they shared. Only the imprint Cole left behind would know about the imprints he met and the conversations they had. Knowing a version of himself would remain behind, Cole resolved that once he became that imprint, he would keep silent to anyone who tried to pry any information from him. When the time came, he would find a secluded corner of the cave and slip into blissful forgetfulness.

Many of the people who entered the Cave of Memory with important information would probably do likewise. They would want to limit the interactions their imprints had with others. He would have to check all the nooks and crannies and follow tunnels to the end.

One big problem was the other live people.

There were almost certainly at least two other humans in the cave. Maybe more—not everyone had to arrive on horseback.

If not for the other people, Cole realized he could shamelessly roam the cave calling out to Destiny. The imprints who heard him would forget before long, and any who might help him would be drawn to him. It could really speed up the search.

Of course, if she was trying to hide, calling to Destiny might drive her away. He had a feeling that whatever tactics he tried, finding her was going to be a chore.

The cavern widened into a long chamber with several branching passages, each lit by a different color, this time orange, green, yellow, white, and blue. The chamber itself was illuminated by the light spilling from the various tunnels. At the far end of the chamber, a man sat on a rock. His black hair was slicked back, forming a slight widow's peak, and a dark, narrow beard followed the lines of his jaw and surrounded his mouth. He had rings on his fingers and elaborate clothes covered by a rich cape. Cole thought he looked like a professional hypnotist.

"Welcome," the man said, as if he owned the place, his voice a resonant baritone.

"Hi," Cole replied.

"You have come seeking my knowledge," the man declared.

"I don't think so," Cole said, drawing closer.

"You know who I am."

"No."

The man's small smile hinted that he doubted Cole but also suggested he was willing to play along. "Then allow me to introduce myself. I am Harvan Kane."

He seemed to be waiting for a reaction.

"I'm Cole."

Harvan gave Cole a shrewd look accompanied by a slow nod. "This is not our first conversation."

"It is," Cole said.

"Then why didn't you shake my hand to check if I'm an imprint?"

"I didn't want to be impolite."

"Nice save," Harvan said, extending a hand.

Cole waved his hand through Harvan's. He felt nothing.

Harvan flashed a wide grin. "I know how this works, Cole. You can talk to me, then walk away and return with a new tactic. I can't form new memories. At least not beyond a single conversation. You've failed with me before. Probably a lot. This time you're playing the role of the one person in Necronum who doesn't know my name."

"I've really never heard of you," Cole assured him.

"Let me save you some time. There are obvious things I must keep hidden, but I am willing to reveal some mysteries." He looked around the stony chamber. "You may have noticed I'm not exactly hiding."

"True." Now that they were talking, Harvan seemed less like a professional hypnotist and more like a guy on an infomercial who was trying to appear successful. "I kind of need to keep moving."

Harvan considered him carefully. "You're good. Who sent you?"

"Nobody."

Harvan laughed knowingly. "Nice try. I find that highly improbable. Why would a child come to the Cave of Memory on his own? However . . . those who are after what I know would absolutely hire a kid to deceive me. They would stop at nothing."

"I'm looking for somebody else," Cole said, taking a step away from Harvan.

"Answer quickly," Harvan challenged. "Who is the Grand Shaper of Necronum?"

Cole paused. "I'm not sure. I haven't asked."

Harvan wagged a scolding finger and smiled. "Not too quick on your feet that time."

"I really don't know," Cole said. "I'm new here."

"You want me disoriented," Harvan said. "You don't want me to know the year."

"I'm from outside the Outskirts."

"What world?" Harvan asked quickly.

"Earth."

"What country?"

"The United States."

"What state?"

"Arizona."

"The territory?"

"It's a state now."

"What's your favorite food back home?"

"Hamburgers, I guess."

"Never heard of them."

"Ground beef on bread."

"Sounds like pig."

"You've been here a while."

Thick rings glinting, Harvan steepled his fingers. "Who is the current High Shaper?"

"Stafford Pemberton."

Harvan squinted suspiciously. "Never heard of him. How long has he been in office?"

"At least sixty years," Cole said. "Maybe quite a bit more than that. He ages slowly."

"What year is it?"

Cole hesitated. "I don't know," he said, mildly surprised that it was true. "It never comes up."

"Sounds like I may have been here for longer than I realized," Harvan said.

"Could be," Cole said. "Especially if you can't make new memories."

Realization dawned on Harvan's face. "You're counting on that. I can't trust a word you say. You're trying to play me. You're no Outsider. You created a false identity through research. Arizona was a nice touch. You must have heard of my interest in the Outside. And you've clearly fabricated an imaginary High Shaper to convince me that I've been here for ages, so I'll let my guard down. Bring better deceptions next time, pup. Or better yet, don't try again. Nobody outfoxes Harvan Kane."

Cole gave no reply. The conversation was going nowhere. He needed to keep moving. Was it rude to walk away from somebody who wasn't really a person? No, right? Especially when the nonperson wouldn't even remember.

"I see I struck a nerve," Harvan gloated. "Better luck next time, young pup. Word of advice—just deal plainly. You won't get anywhere with me using guile."

Cole felt tempted to explain that he wasn't defeated, just sick of wasting time, but stopped himself. He needed to avoid wasting words with every imprint he met or finding Destiny would take days. Maybe weeks.

Cole made his way deeper into the cave. He soon became disoriented among the many forking corridors. The woman at the entrance had noticed no pattern in the colors of the tunnels, and neither did Cole. He supposed if he wrote down the color of each tunnel he took, he could use the colors to find his way back, but he had brought nothing to write with, and he soon became thoroughly lost.

The farther he went, the wetter the cave became. Stalactites dripped onto stalagmites or into puddles, and flowing formations of stone glimmered damply. Clusters of fragile white crystals decorated some areas of the cave, as did groupings of delicate stalactites as thin as soda straws.

Cole met many imprints. A few ran from him. He shook hands with the others, never feeling them. At first he kept his conversations short. There were certain patterns. Whether the person came across as creepy or nice, they were all confused about how long they had been there, and most seemed to be hiding something.

Before long Cole stopped talking to any of them—he just checked to make sure they weren't tangible. There were too many imprints, and he had too much ground to cover. Though the ages varied, he only encountered adults. He needed a nine-year-old girl.

While Cole knelt beside a pool in a roomy chamber with several natural stone columns, a man approached, perhaps in his late twenties or early thirties. Cole filled his cupped hands with cool water. It tasted gritty with minerals. Cole shook a hand dry and held it out. The man offered his hand, and Cole swiped through it.

"You're young to visit the cave alone," the man commented.

Cole had already learned that if you didn't want to get stuck in a conversation with an imprint, you had to keep moving. But the water was refreshing, so he scooped up some more, then paused with it on the way to his lips.

He was really looking at the man for the first time. He was well-dressed and startlingly familiar.

The man seemed perplexed by the staring. "Hello? Are you going to answer?"

It took Cole a moment to place him. The only other times he had seen this person, he had looked much older.

"Stafford Pemberton?" Cole asked.

The man grinned. "You know of me? It must not have been too long since I entered the cave."

"Kind of long," Cole said. "You're older now. And you've lived a long time."

"Have I?" Stafford asked cheerfully. "Can't say I'm sorry to hear that. What exactly am I doing after living for so long?"

The Stafford before him was young enough that he might not yet know what the future held for him. How old had Stafford been when he married Harmony to become king? "You're the High Shaper," Cole said. "And the High King."

"No," Stafford said, flushing. "She said yes? It worked out?"

"You're married to Queen Harmony," Cole said.

Stafford closed his eyes and raised his fists. "Yes!" he exulted. He seemed a lot friendlier and more carefree than the beleaguered king Cole had met. Stafford opened his eyes. "How long have I ruled?"

"Over sixty years," Cole said.

"And I'm a powerful shaper?" he asked hopefully.

"Probably the most powerful," Cole said. "At least you were."

Stafford furrowed his brow. "I was?"

"It's a long story," Cole said.

"Tell me."

"You'll just forget," Cole said.

"I came here with grand aspirations," Stafford said. "This construct of me is stuck here forever. It would be a mercy to know, if only for a moment."

Cole rose from the edge of the pool. He didn't want to list the terrible things the High King had done. This version of Stafford had no daughters yet and seemed nice. "A shape-crafter helped you increase your powers."

"Who?"

"Owandell."

Stafford scowled. "How do you know that name?"

"You already know him?"

"He is very secretive. Things are different in the future?"

"You could say that," Cole said. If he played this right, maybe he could get information about Stafford's past. "He works for you. Kind of."

"Kind of?"

Cole tried to phrase his explanation carefully. "Owandell turned on you. He helped you for a long time, but he was secretly working against you. He works for Nazeem."

"I don't know that name," Stafford said.

"He's an evil guy imprisoned somewhere in Necronum," Cole said. "He taught Owandell shapecraft. Nazeem was a big secret. Only now are people learning about him."

"How do you know so much?" Stafford asked, a faint suspicion in his tone.

"I worked for you," Cole said. "I was one of the royal errand boys. But now I'm here to help your daughters."

Stafford grinned with delighted astonishment. "I have daughters? With Harmony? How many?"

"Five," Cole said.

"And sons?"

"None."

Stafford's face fell. "That's a blow. Is there still a chance?"

"I don't think so," Cole said. "But your daughters are amazing."

"They need help?" Stafford asked.

"Owandell stole their shaping powers," Cole said. "They're on the run from him."

"Running from Owandell?" Stafford blustered. "But I'm High Shaper! What am I doing?"

"Owandell got powerful," Cole said. "He runs a lot of your military. The politics are complicated."

"One of my daughters is here?" Stafford asked. "In the cave?"

"The youngest came here," Cole said. "I'm with some people trying to find and rescue her, including one of your other daughters."

"Incredible," Stafford muttered. He gazed at Cole with real suspicion. "How do I know you're not working for Owandell? Or some other enemy?"

Cole thought for a moment. "I guess I can't prove that. But I'm not. Why are you here?"

"No big mystery since you already know about Owandell," Stafford said. "He sent me here to talk to some people. I need to improve my powers if I'm to win Harmony."

"You talked to them?"

Stafford nodded. "I guess their advice worked if I end up with Harmony." He grinned. "I can hardly believe it. I mean, I have ambitions, and connections, but Harmony is such a long shot. I'm not in a strong position to win the most eligible maiden in the five kingdoms."

His genuine excitement made Cole sad. "Is it about the power?"

"I mean, sure, it would change everything for me," Stafford agreed. "But she's the bigger prize. You've seen her, I take it. She has it all."

Cole thought of Stafford and Harmony living in separate

towers, quietly warring against each other. He reflected on Stafford stealing his daughters' shaping abilities. The Stafford he was talking to didn't act like he would do those things. And maybe he wouldn't at this point. He must have changed.

"What's wrong?" Stafford asked. "Does something happen to her?"

"Harmony is all right," Cole said. "I was just thinking about your daughters. Does Owandell have any weaknesses you know about?"

"I know very little about him," Stafford said. "He is competent and secretive. He has delivered on his promises to me so far. And apparently, he will deliver on the outrageous ones, though I wish I could have known he would betray me."

"I can't help there," Cole apologized. "It's already in the past." He stooped and scooped up another handful of water, bringing the fluid to his lips.

"Hey!" a voice called.

Cole turned to see a young man and young woman emerging from a passage into the chamber. The young woman held a small lantern. The young man had spoken and was pointing at Cole.

"Imprints can't hold water," the young man said. "You're a person. We didn't expect to see anybody else in here."

"Yeah," Cole said, since he had been caught wet-handed. "You're people too?"

"We sure are," the young man verified. He glanced at Stafford. "Is that your brother?"

The couple looked nice. Their clothes weren't fancy, but they were clean. The young woman had a fresh face, and the young man seemed friendly. Hopefully, they weren't murderers or servants of Nazeem.

"He's an imprint," Cole said.

The young man came forward and shook hands with Cole. The young woman as well. They passed their hands through Stafford's.

"You've got guts," the young man told Cole. "A kid coming in here alone."

Cole detected no threat in the statement. "I'm trying to help a friend."

"We wish you luck," the young man said, glancing at the young woman. "Today has been lucky for us."

"Really?" Cole asked.

"Tell him," the young woman said.

"It's kind of a secret," the young man muttered, lowering his voice but not enough to go unheard.

"Oh, tell him," she said.

The young man smiled. "It's a surprise to find anyone here. Not many people brave the caves. But our family has a tradition. My great-great-great-grandfather left an imprint in here. When any of his grandkids choose a spouse, we bring them to meet him. The route is all mapped out."

"If he agrees, you're in," the young woman said. "If not, you're out."

"Sounds like you're in," Cole said.

"He loved her," the young man gushed. "Then again, he's only turned down five candidates since the tradition began."

"Well, that makes me feel special," the young woman said. "At least I'm not one of the five worst."

The young man rolled his eyes. "He was really taken by you. Probably more than any of the others."

She gave him a playful shove. "Now you're laying it on thick."

"I'm serious," he said.

Cole was glad they acted so happy. And unthreatening. "Would you have called it off if he hadn't liked her?" Cole wondered.

"Yeah?" the young woman asked, interested by the question. "Would you have ditched me by the roadside?"

"I knew he would like her," the young man hedged. "Who wouldn't?"

"Good answer," the young woman said. She looked at Cole. "But if Pappy had been against it, we probably wouldn't go through with it. Of the five Pappy didn't like, two went ahead and tied the knot anyhow. Both marriages didn't work out."

"Now everybody is sure Pappy is a prophet," the young man said. "Or at least has sharp judgment. But no worries here. The old guy knows a good thing when he sees it."

"Congrats," Cole said. "I noticed some horses when I came in. Yours?"

The young woman swatted the young man. "I told you people could see them!"

"Off in the trees?" the young man asked.

"Right," Cole said.

"Those are ours," the young man said.

"You may see my friend when you exit," Cole said. "Could you tell him I'm all right?"

"No problem," the young man said, walking toward another passage. "Good luck."

"You didn't happen to see a girl?" Cole asked. "An imprint. Kind of young? Like nine?"

The young man frowned. "No kids. Sorry."

"We saw some weirdo who couldn't stop laughing," the young woman said. "He was skipping around. Didn't need that in my mind."

"Oh, and keep away if you see a guy wrapped in chains with a sack over his head," the young man said. "My brother warned me."

"Thanks for the tip," Cole said, unable to resist a shiver.

The young man and young woman proceeded out of the room along a passage that sloped slightly upward. They kept talking to each other. The conversation became unintelligible as it faded into the distance.

"You are the first person I remember meeting in here," Stafford said. "Now I've met three."

"You remember them?" Cole asked.

"Sure, I can still hear them."

"You'll forget soon."

"So I understand."

"When I'm gone, you'll be back to zero," Cole said.

"I suppose so. And I'll forget that I succeed with Harmony."

Cole looked around the cavern. In one corner he saw a bunch of loose rocks and pebbles. He hustled over there and began arranging pebbles on the cave floor.

"I'm in a hurry," Cole said. "But you were good luck. Now that I've met the other people in the cave, I'm going to risk calling to your daughter. It could save me a lot of time."

"Not everybody who comes here necessarily leaves horses out front," Stafford said.

"Right," Cole said. "But I'm told not many people come here. I'm going to risk it."

He worked in silence for a moment.

"What's her name?" Stafford asked.

"Destiny," Cole said.

"I name my daughter Destiny?" Stafford asked, not delighted.

"Harmony chose it," Cole said.

"Sounds like I'm going to be a pushover," Stafford said.

"You'll hold your own."

Stafford leaned forward. "Let's see. What are you writing? Oh! That's very kind."

Cole stepped back to survey his handiwork. Using pebbles, he had formed the message U GET HARMONY.

Folding his arms, Stafford stared at the pebbles. Tears shone in his eyes. "I'm not sure you know how much that means to me. I know I'm not . . . real, but, it will be a source of comfort and happiness."

"Glad to do it," Cole said. If only Stafford stayed like he was when he was young, the entire five kingdoms might be a different place. Cole would not have been in a hurry to do the older version of the king any favors. In fact, he might have written *U DIE POOR AND UNLOVED.* This Stafford was a different story.

"You know, I come from a noble house," Stafford said. "We're not as ancient or renowned as some, but we have a saying used to reward good service. Tell any member of my household, 'A radiant deed shines forever,' and see what they do for you."

"What if I tell you?" Cole asked.

"All the better," Stafford said. "You'll get a reward that would astound any errand boy. And be assured, it would impress more than errand boys."

"Thanks," Cole said.

"No. Thank *you*. Take good care of my daughter."

"I'll do my best," Cole said. *To protect her from you,* he added silently as he turned and walked away.

CHAPTER
8

IMPRINT

By some Miracle, I was sent to look for my Destiny!" Cole called again. His voice was getting hoarse. He had used that same shout hundreds, maybe thousands of times over the past hours.

Since he had started yelling, he saw fewer imprints. Undoubtedly, many were avoiding him. He sometimes glimpsed figures fleeing down distant tunnels.

Cole continued to test the imprints that came close enough, to be sure they weren't actual people. But he spoke to few, and kept the interactions short, in an attempt to cover as much ground as possible.

As he trudged deeper into the cave, he increasingly encountered dead ends. Each gave him a sense of hope—at least the subterranean labyrinth didn't go on forever.

To spare his voice, Cole began calling less loudly. His cry remained the same. "By some Miracle, I was sent to look for my Destiny." Depending on his position in the cave, the last word would sometimes echo impressively. Cole figured the phrase was a little cryptic if a stranger overheard him, but it should be clear enough to make Tessa curious.

When a young voice finally responded, Cole was in a narrow passage with a dead end in sight. He always walked close enough to the dead end to make sure an unseen corridor didn't branch out. White deposits on one wall bristled with glittering crystals.

"You're not giving up," said a young girl behind him.

Jumping and whirling, Cole found Tessa standing there, looking much as she had when Trillian the torivor sent Cole to a simulation of her castle during the trial to rescue Honor. Tessa looked a couple of years younger than Cole, with straight brown hair and dark, soulful eyes.

"Tessa?" Cole asked. "Destiny?"

"Tessa," she said. "I've been following you." Her expression was serious, her voice grave.

"For how long?"

The young girl shrugged. "Did Miracle really send you?"

"Yes," Cole said. "I even have proof. The first is a code phrase. The haystacks have fallen down."

"Honor knows you," Tessa said. "She thinks I can trust you."

"Honor is here?"

"Her imprint," Tessa said. "She's making sure nobody bothers us."

"Wait," Cole said. "You would have come here before Honor. How can you remember her?"

Tessa glanced over her shoulder. "I can still see her against the wall down there."

"Where?"

"On the left."

"Oh. Yeah, I kind of see her."

"If she passes out of my notice, I forget she's here," Tessa said. "Or so she tells me." Tessa held out a hand. "Don't you want to test me?"

Cole passed his hand through hers. "My job would be a lot easier if this was really you."

"Sorry. We're only imprints. Is Mira okay?"

"She's on the run but doing all right."

"What does she want?"

"We're looking for you and Honor. We're trying to help. Your mom put stars in the sky. You're in big trouble."

"I'm not surprised," Tessa said, shuffling her feet, eyes downcast. "Somebody is after me. Maybe he finally caught me."

"Who is after you?"

"A powerful echo. I don't know his name."

"Nazeem," Cole said.

"Maybe."

"Probably. He's after me and Mira too."

Honor gazed at him. "You don't work for my father?"

"No," Cole assured her.

"Or anyone who wishes me harm?"

"No."

"You're with Mira and you're trying to help me?"

"Yes."

Tessa gave a small smile. "I can tell when people are lying. You're not. At least I don't think so. Can I trust myself as an imprint? I feel normal, but I can't feel my power anymore. Not at all."

"I'm here to help," Cole said, and he meant it more than ever. Tessa was only two years his junior, but her small build, big eyes, and pretty face made her seem even younger. Anyone would want to protect her!

"Father is looking for me too," Tessa said. "I have to be careful what I share. Even when people mean well, they could accidentally give away clues." Tessa looked young, but like Mira, she hadn't aged for more than sixty years. Though still a kid, she had a lot of experience living on the run.

"The real you is already in trouble," Cole said. "You've probably been caught. We're not just trying to find you— we're trying to rescue you."

"Mother sent a young boy to rescue me?" Tessa asked.

"We have an adult with us," Cole explained, trying not to feel inadequate.

"Does that mean there are other kids?" Tessa wondered.

"Well, yeah, three others," Cole said. "Four if you count Mira."

"Who sends kids against soldiers and evil weavers?"

"We're what Mira has," Cole said for want of a better reason. "We rescued Honor and got her power back. Constance too."

"You found Costa?" Surprised joy lit up her expression.

"And restored her power," Cole said. Tessa's excitement at the news helped him feel less defensive.

"All right, I'll talk to you," Tessa said. "Where do I begin? Tell Mira I've been all right. She always worries. After father took my weaving power, I didn't feel like myself for years. I went around in a daze. You know the feeling when you forget something important you want to say? You just had it in mind, but then you can't remember? I felt like that all the time. Something was missing."

"That sounds terrible," Cole said.

"Not too bad," Tessa said. "I just felt . . . off. More annoying than terrible. Anyhow, a few years ago, I started feeling more like myself again. I began to get impulses about where to go and what to do. I started saying things that disturbed people."

"Disturbed people?"

"I used to do it all the time," Tessa said. "I didn't stop to think about what the words meant. They just showed up. That stopped after father took my power."

"Then your power started coming back," Cole said. "It happened to your sisters too."

Tessa puckered her lips off to one side. "I don't feel it now. My power, I mean. Being an imprint. But it was coming back. And people were after us."

"Us?"

"Me and Leo," she said. "My bodyguard. He didn't come in here with me. I hope he's all right."

"Why'd you come here?" Cole asked.

Tessa shrugged. "On a hunch. My hunches saved us a couple of times, so Leo was starting to trust them."

"Where were you heading next?"

"That's the big question," Tessa said. "If you know where I went, you'll run off to save me."

"Is that so bad?"

"Not bad. I want to be saved. I just wish I could feel what would be best for you. And for Mira. And for me, too. The feelings were coming back to me. As an imprint, I don't have the gift at all."

"We'll be careful," Cole said.

"You'll try," Tessa said. "Honor tried too. She had some soldiers with her. If you're here, Honor failed. If Honor couldn't do it, what are Mira and some kids going to do?"

Cole remembered Desmond and Oster, knights from Blackmont Castle who had joined Honor in her quest to find Destiny. "We have to try," Cole said. "We can get more help if we need it. Mira will never give up on you."

"I know," Tessa said. "But maybe she should."

"Not going to happen," Cole said. "We'll just end up looking for you with less information. It'll take longer. Mira will be in more danger."

"I guess," Tessa said reluctantly. "When I first arrived to this cave, I didn't know what I was looking for. That's how it always used to work. I said what I felt, did what I felt, and interesting things would follow. Back home at the castle, I was never in danger, but people around me always told me how what I said or did changed their lives. Sometimes it was good. Saved their marriage. Helped their business. Cured their cat."

"You cured cats?" Cole asked.

"I shared some recipes," Tessa said. "Just don't ask me to remember them. The words spilled out. I didn't know how people would take them."

"Your mom has a gift like that," Cole said. "Knowing things."

"We had some things in common," Tessa said. "But hers was different from mine. Nobody was like me. My gift is . . . weird. Poor Mother."

"Why?"

"I would always say the most dreadful things to her."

"Like what?"

Tessa rolled her eyes and extended her arms like a sleep-walker, then spoke in haunted tones. "You will lose everything you love most. Enemies plot behind every door. Your joy will turn to ashes, your peace to turmoil, your dreams to ruins." She lowered her arms, and her voice returned to normal. "I was fun at parties."

"Those words just came?"

"I couldn't resist," Tessa said. "Mother loved me, I think, but she didn't like speaking to me. She started avoiding me."

"What you told her kind of came true," Cole said.

"Doesn't make me fun to be around. Who wants bad news? Not many people liked speaking to me."

"What about the people you helped?"

"I like to think about them. But my messages didn't always help. What if some girl started telling secrets from your past that could destroy your career? I got people arrested. I ended friendships. I could be scary. What if I explained how your cousin felt when he drowned, though you didn't know what I meant at the time and it didn't happen until the next day?"

"Freaky," Cole said.

Tessa brightened. "Mira liked me, though. I never knew

things about her. Words didn't come when we were alone."

"Never?"

"Not once."

"Did you ever try?"

Tessa's face grew serious. "I never tried. With anyone. I couldn't stop the feelings or cause them."

"Did you miss your feelings when they were gone?" Cole asked, wondering if it might have been a relief.

"I did," Tessa said. "More than I would have guessed. I didn't know how much my power guided me until it was gone. When my abilities started to come back, my life was more dangerous than before. The feelings have helped me."

"What did you learn here?" Cole asked.

Tessa frowned. "Are you sure I should tell you? Mira is with you. My power doesn't work as an imprint. I have no feel for whether telling you will be good or not. It could be so dangerous."

"I told you: we're not going to stop looking for you," Cole said. "You might as well help us."

Tessa covered her eyes with both hands, as if trying to hide. "Have you heard of Gamat Rue?"

"No."

"The old prison? Abandoned centuries ago?"

"I'm new to Necronum."

Slightly lowering one hand, Tessa peeked at Cole. "Once, Gamat Rue held the worst criminals in Necronum. But people haven't used it for hundreds of years. An imprint here told me about an echo imprisoned there."

"It's a prison for echoes?"

"Not at first. But an evil echomancer took it over. The echolands side has lots of prisoners now. That's why it was abandoned."

"What's an echomancer?"

Tessa dropped both hands and stared. "For somebody who wants to save me, you sure don't know very much."

"So teach me."

"Echomancers are echoes with weaving powers," Tessa said. "Your shaping power doesn't usually cross with you into the echolands. Echomancers are the exceptions. The imprint told me the echomancer at Gamat Rue is named Nandavi."

"You needed to find Nandavi?"

"No, I went to find an echo named Ragio that Nandavi holds prisoner."

"You went to the prison?" Cole asked.

"Unless somebody stopped me," Tessa said. "That was my plan."

"How were you going to talk to an echo imprisoned in the echolands?" Cole asked.

"I wasn't sure," Tessa said. "Not exactly. People stay away from Gamat Rue. Not much is known about it. I'm no good at seeing the echolands. But Leo was coming with me, and he's a talented weaver. I hoped he would help me contact Ragio."

"What about Nandavi?"

"Nandavi." Tessa shivered. "I didn't want to meet her. I had no idea how much she could bother us from the echolands. But I'm looking for my shaping power, and when I heard about Ragio, I knew I needed to find him. I felt the tug, so I went."

"Your power told you to go?" Cole said.

"My power doesn't usually explain much," Tessa said. "I get a feeling to say something or do something without knowing what will happen. But I was looking for the rest of my power, and it felt right to come to the cave, and then finding Ragio felt important."

"What did you learn about Ragio?" Cole asked.

"He was a shapecrafter spying for the Grand Shaper of Necronum," Tessa said. "He was caught and killed. The imprint I met here said Ragio was involved with those who were trying to gather and control my power. Ragio's echo ended up at Gamat Rue."

"You could be at Gamat Rue too," Cole said. "That might be where the trouble happened."

"Maybe," Tessa said. "If so, be really careful. Honor might have fallen into the same trap. Don't be the third."

Cole hesitated before asking his next question. "Who is the Grand Shaper of Necronum?"

"Really? You don't even know that?"

Cole winced. "I've only been here a few days. Part of that time has been on the run."

"Prescia Demorri," Tessa said. "My aunt. Mother's big sister. They were never very close. I met her at the castle when I was younger. I haven't seen her since then. She's been in hiding."

Tessa signaled Honor, who came toward them. The imprint looked perfectly like her.

"Hello, Cole," she said.

"Hi, Honor."

Honor reached a hand out to Cole. His hand passed through hers.

"I told him," Tessa said.

"That's hopefully for the best," Honor said. She turned to Cole. "Costa?"

"She's fine," Cole said. "We found her and restored her power."

"That's a relief. I gather events have gone poorly here?"

"Your star is up," Cole said, not wanting to explain why they had recently come down. "Tessa's too. Your mom told me you were in extreme danger."

"You spoke with her?" Honor asked.

"Not too long ago," Cole said. "I took the monorail from Zeropolis to Junction."

"Mira is with you now?" Honor asked.

"Yes," Cole said.

"Don't let her come after us," Honor said. "She is no warrior, and her powers are irrelevant here. I had Desmond and Oster with me. I knew what you know. If I failed, something is really wrong. Who knows what you're up against? Send help, surely, but not Mira. We can't risk losing her. She could do more good by rallying others to help us."

That made sense to Cole. "I'll try to convince her. It isn't always easy."

"I know," Honor said. "I'm sorry this responsibility has fallen to you. I should have found Tessa."

"Don't apologize," Cole said. "We don't even know what happened yet."

"I imagine you are in a hurry," Honor said.

"Actually, yeah," Cole said. "You don't know the way out, do you?"

"I was in a hurry too," Honor said. "The common wisdom has it that you just need to keep going uphill."

"I've heard the same," Cole said. He stared at Honor and Tessa. They looked so real! "Any last requests?"

"Tell Mira I love her," Tessa said. "Tell her to be careful."

"Watch out for echoes," Honor said. "There is a new force at play in the echolands."

"Nazeem," Cole said.

"He has a name?" Honor asked.

"Seems like he has just revealed himself lately," Cole said. "I'll try to be careful."

"Tell Mira I order her not to come for us personally," Honor said. "And that I care for her."

"I'll pass it along," Cole said.

"Thank you, Cole," Tessa said.

"I'll do my best," he replied.

Turning away from them, he hurried back the way he had come. It wouldn't be long before they forgot him. Cole wondered if he would see their faces again.

CHAPTER
— 9 —

SHIVER

Twilight had fallen by the time Cole exited the Cave of Memory. He assumed it was evening but supposed it could be morning. It was hard to be sure how long he had wandered the caverns.

Finding the entrance had been no trouble. He followed upward slopes for less than an hour before he met once again with the imprint of the woman who waited near the opening.

As Cole walked out, he had looked back and seen himself standing near the woman. His imprint had waved. Cole waved as well, aware that his duplicate wouldn't remember the gesture.

When Cole had hesitated to round the bend that would conceal his imprint from sight, his imprint called out, "Go save everybody. I've got this!"

Cole had turned and exited, happy to know he could be so brave about an eternity stuck in a cave. Well, at least he could *act* brave about it.

Cole found Dalton, Jace, Mira, and Joe waiting with Hunter not too far beyond the mouth of the cave, their horses tied up nearby. Cole saw them before they looked his way.

"Dalton!" Cole called. "Jace! You made it!" He jogged over to them.

Jace snorted derisively. "If you made it, of course we did."

"Slower than me," Cole observed.

"Our road from the crossroads took us the wrong direction," Jace said.

"And a guy tried to swindle us when we bought horses," Dalton said. "One of them was basically lame."

"Nothing I couldn't handle," Jace quickly clarified.

"Do you think you showed the guy your freemark enough?" Dalton asked.

Jace shoved him playfully. "At least I wasn't apologizing."

The dynamic between Jace and Dalton seemed friendlier than Cole had seen it. In times past, Dalton's joke would have made Jace genuinely angry. Perhaps the time alone together had been good for them.

"Did you find Tessa?" Mira asked.

"Would I have come out if I hadn't?" Cole replied.

"Maybe if you were hungry," Hunter said. "You didn't bring food. We had some. I called out once I noticed, but you didn't hear."

Cole did feel hungry. Just the mention of food made the void in his belly seem to double in size. But he put on a brave face. "I'm fine. I ate some bats."

"Whatever," Dalton said.

"And a few tarantulas," Cole added. "It's hard to eat something that keeps biting you."

"Gross," Mira said. "So . . . Tessa?"

"And Honor," Cole said. "Can we talk?" He looked to Hunter. "Are there echoes around?"

Hunter nodded at the sky. "Shiver Moon tonight." Cole followed his gaze to a smallish moon glowing a crystalline blue. He had seen it before. Mira had told him the name once. It wasn't in the sky most nights. "That means if you don't see echoes, they aren't around."

"A Shiver Moon makes echoes visible?" Cole asked.

"You can't miss them," Hunter said. "Many in Necronum stay indoors when the Shiver Moon rises."

"Does it let them hurt you?" Jace asked, not quite succeeding at nonchalance.

"No more than usual," Hunter said. "Many people just don't want to interact with echoes. Not without reason. Some mess with your head. Some might haunt you. Lots of people follow superstitions about how to keep echoes away."

"What do they do?" Jace asked casually.

"It varies by community," Hunter said. "Some salt doorways. Others use wind chimes. I've seen offerings like bread or cheese left in yards overnight. Some people live beside or above running water. Others hang signs or post symbols. All of those people would hide indoors during a Shiver Moon."

"Does any of that stuff work?" Jace asked.

"I'm not sure," Hunter said. "I've noticed echoes don't seem to like running water. If it was me, I'd hire a skilled weaver to work protections around my home."

"Will we see echoes tonight?" Dalton asked, eyeing the woods.

"Probably not too many roaming the wilderness," Hunter said. "I expect we'll see plenty when we get near Rincomere."

"We're heading back to town?" Cole asked.

Hunter glanced around. "Unless you want to wander blindly through the forest. Rincomere has the nearest decent crossroads."

"We already have rooms booked," Joe said.

"Where are we going?" Mira asked Cole. "What did Tessa tell you?"

"Honor and Tessa both send their love and say hello. They don't want you coming to rescue them."

"Whatever," Mira said. "Where?"

"When Tessa left the Cave of Memory, her next stop was a place called Gamat Rue."

"The old prison?" Hunter asked.

"You make that sound bad," Jace said.

"It has a terrible reputation," Hunter said. "Some places in Necronum are haunted by bad echoes. Gamat Rue is supposed to be one of the worst. Why would Tessa go there?"

Cole explained about Tessa risking interaction with the echomancer Nandavi in hopes of finding Ragio and learning where to go to fully recover her power.

"You learned more than I knew about Gamat Rue," Hunter said. "I never heard the name Nandavi."

"Tessa felt her power urging her to go there," Cole said.

"She has blind faith in her intuition," Mira said. "Her impulses tend to set things in motion. Not always good things."

"Tessa told me her power has been coming back over the past few years," Cole said. "It's been helping her avoid trouble."

"Trouble obviously caught up to her," Jace said.

"Our job will be to figure out where," Mira added.

"We should get back to Rincomere," Joe said, starting toward the horses. "We'll already be riding in darkness."

"The Shiver Moon will light the way," Hunter assured them.

"And plenty of other things," Jace grumbled unhappily.

They rode slowly by the icy moonlight—single file, Joe in the front, Hunter at the rear. Cole swept the wilderness with his gaze but didn't see any echoes until they neared the village.

In a grove of trees near an outlying farm, Cole noticed a silver-white flicker. Joe reined in his horse to take a look, stopping the other five riders. The figure emerged from the woods, walking toward them. He was an older man, softly glowing a translucent silver.

Nervous tingles ran down Cole's spine as he watched the echo. The somber old guy could have wandered straight out of a ghost story. Cole wondered if this had once been his farm. Maybe he was just roaming.

Dalton looked back at Cole. *Freaky,* he mouthed.

I know, Cole mouthed back.

Dalton pantomimed taking a picture.

Cole decided it was a good wish. How cool would it be to have photographic proof of an afterlife?

"Ride on," Hunter instructed. "Think of it like passing an ordinary person. If you ignore them, they'll generally ignore you."

Joe encouraged his mount to a trot. The others followed suit. The echo watched them ride away before turning back to the grove of trees. Cole glanced back a couple of times until he could no longer see the silvery shimmer.

Looking up, Cole noticed that the written message was gone from the sky. He mentioned it to Mira.

"Mother knows we check every night," Mira said. "I don't expect we'll get any more notes from her that way."

They passed more echoes as they neared Rincomere. Cole did his best not to stare, but it was hard not to sneak peeks. An older woman. Two middle-aged men. A child. Cole rode behind Jace and noticed that his friend never turned his head toward any of the apparitions.

A four-foot-high stone wall surrounded Rincomere— the perfect defense against a horde of raging turtles. If the attack ever came, Cole supposed the reptiles would enter along the road, since there was no gate.

The Shiver Moon hung high and the stars shone brightly as Cole and his group rode into the village. The streets were far busier than Cole had seen them during the day. All the people glowed a translucent silver white. So many echoes were strolling around and conversing that Cole wondered if anyone in Rincomere had ever left after they died.

"Go straight to the inn," Hunter advised from the rear.

Joe stayed at a trot, occasionally passing through echoes as he led the way along the crowded street. Cole made eye contact with several individuals but tried to keep his gaze moving. Their little procession attracted some attention but not the full notice of the crowd. Many echoes went about their business with hardly a glance at the riders.

Cole ended up riding beside Dalton.

His buddy leaned toward Cole and spoke in a loud whisper. "*This* would be a cool Halloween."

Cole chuckled, taking in the ghostly sights. "We finally got our awesome spook alley."

"Not worth it," Dalton said. "We should have bobbed for apples."

"Pretty cool, though," Cole said, staring at a silvery woman holding the hand of a translucent child.

"Way cool," Dalton agreed.

Joe dismounted in the modest courtyard of the Lollygag Inn. An obese echo relaxed on a bench in the yard, stroking his heavy mustache. Cole and the others led their horses to the stable. A dozing stableboy jumped up and offered to help them find stalls. Joe handed the boy some ringers.

Linger at the stable. The words entered Cole's mind without him hearing them. It was undoubtedly Sando. *Don't explain. Just linger.*

Cole offered to help with the horses. Dalton spoke up as well. Jace was the first of the group into the inn.

Each leading a pair of horses, the stableboy, Cole, and Dalton got the mounts settled into stalls. "I'll take it from here," the stableboy said.

"I'll help, if you don't mind," Cole said. "I need to unwind."

"Up to you," the stableboy said.

"Aren't you tired?" Dalton asked.

Cole was exhausted. Keeping his eyes open was starting to make them burn. He was hungry, even though he had grabbed some food from the saddlebags during the ride from the Cave of Memory. He was sore.

"I'm okay," Cole lied. "It's been a weird day. I could use some time to think."

"Can't you think in your room?" Dalton asked, glancing toward the stable entrance. "Lots of echoes out tonight."

"I want to be doing something," Cole said. "I'm good. I'll be right behind you."

"Okay," Dalton said reluctantly. "See you in there."

Cole started undoing his horse's saddle. Dalton was right to encourage him inside. A warm meal sounded heavenly. Who would want to unsaddle their horse after a long day when somebody else had been paid to do it? Especially after so much travel.

Go out to the yard, Sando communicated.

Cole pulled the saddle off and set it aside. "I changed my mind," he told the stableboy. "I'm tired."

"I can't blame you," the stableboy said. "Good night."

Cole went out to the yard. He was alone except for the obese echo on the bench.

Out to the street and left.

Wondering where Sando was leading him, Cole followed the instructions. There were no regular people on the street but dozens of echoes. A tall woman with curly ringlets stared at Cole from behind a fan as she walked by.

Now left down the alley.

Cole paused. The gap between buildings was hardly an alley. He wasn't sure if he would fit without turning a little sideways.

Yes, young sir. That's where I mean.

Leading with one shoulder, Cole entered the gap, dirt and pebbles grinding underfoot. As Cole progressed, he heard squeaking up ahead. He paused, not eager to end the night with rat bites.

Keep coming, young sir. All is well.

"Then why do we need to talk," Cole muttered.

A convenient opportunity, giver of silver. A pleasant moon smiles down. And I have some tidings.

Cole continued forward. The narrow alley intersected another gap between buildings, and Cole found Sando around the corner, seated, his body translucent silver, his hat mostly hiding his face.

"That hat is almost an umbrella," Cole said.

Sando looked up, eyes crinkling as he smiled. "Quite so, young sir. You had some success at the Cave of Memory."

"I guess you would know," Cole said.

"Yes, I do," Sando agreed. "I prefer for my tips to deliver results. I could not sense you while you were inside the cave, but I heard what you shared with your friends afterward." He shook his head and his expression grew serious. "Gamat Rue is no place to visit. Mortals should stay away. Echoes too."

"We have to go there," Cole said.

"So I gather," Sando said. "Be wary. There are a few places

where echoes can directly harm mortals. Gamat Rue is one."

"Can we protect ourselves?" Cole asked.

"Easy," Sando said, grinning toothlessly. "Don't go there."

"And if we have to go?"

"Send somebody else."

"Are you volunteering?" Cole asked.

Sando laughed. "You are funny tonight, young sir. I am no adventurer."

"Thanks for the help back at the other inn," Cole said.

"Thank the horse," Sando said.

"Did you send it?" Cole asked.

Sando snickered. "I did not directly control the animal, if that is what you mean. Did I play a role in the mare being there? Yes, indirectly. I have news."

"You want me to give away the ringer?"

"In due time. Other news."

"Don't tell me we have to run again," Cole said, unsure if he could endure another night in the saddle.

"Not yet," Sando said. "If you were less tired, perhaps. Enforcers are coming. Rest tonight. Start early. There is a little-known trail that leads into the hills. It will keep you out of sight and serve as a shortcut if you intend to visit Gamat Rue."

"How do I find it?"

"I will guide you in the morning. Just keep the ringer in your pocket, young sir."

"What if they have a perceptive?"

"These do not," Sando said, head bobbing. "A prudent concern, though."

"How do I reach you if I need you?" Cole asked.

Sando made a sour face and scrubbed his hands together. "This would be difficult for you, young sir. You are no weaver. If we must talk, I will contact you. It is no small feat, but I will. The ringer helps. The Enforcers will arrive tomorrow afternoon. Depart long before then."

"We will," Cole said.

"Sleep well," Sando said.

"Any tips on Gamat Rue?"

"Only the one, young sir. Don't go. Some places are best left alone."

"Could the girl we're looking for be there?" Cole asked.

"If she went there, she could certainly still be there," Sando said. "But I know of few foolhardy enough to go after her."

"You know me," Cole said.

"Not for long, maybe," Sando said. "I will try to label you brave instead of foolish. But honesty is always a consideration."

"I'll tell the others about your warning," Cole said.

"Multiple warnings," Sando replied. "Go rest."

Cole hurried back the way he had come and caught up with the others just as the food was arriving. Day-old bread and oily stew never tasted so good.

CHAPTER

— 10 —

TUTO

Sando's trail was very well hidden. It didn't connect to any road. As the sun came up, Cole led the others into a pathless forest and over a couple of ridges before finding the trailhead near a large pond.

As promised, young sir, Sando spoke to Cole's mind. *One last time, I ask you to reconsider your destination.*

"This is it," Cole said.

"Good," Hunter said. "This route is sneaky." He climbed down from his horse and unbundled some rolled blankets. "I did some buying in the small hours. There are ways to get shops to open."

"Were you pretending to still be an Enforcer?" Dalton asked.

"I'm not sure I have to pretend. I haven't been discharged. I wore a disguise." He handed Joe a sword in a sheath, then gave Jace a crossbow and a small quiver with six quarrels. Dalton received a short sword, and Hunter strapped on a sword of his own. "Considering how I got these weapons,

I didn't want to show them on the way out of town. We should be fine now."

"These don't happen to work on echoes?" Jace asked, aiming his crossbow at a tree.

"That would be nice," Hunter said. "I expect they'll prove more useful against Enforcers and legionnaires. Do you know how to use it?"

"The basics," Jace said. "I practiced with one like it at the Sky Raiders."

"Cole and Mira already have their Jumping Swords," Hunter said. "No need to turn them into walking armories."

"Riding, not walking, thank goodness," Mira said.

Cole rubbed the hilt of his Jumping Sword. It had a good blade, but its real value was dormant in Necronum unless he could get his power back. As he reached for his ability, he felt no glimmer of it.

"My echo friend told me the ride should take about five days," Cole said. "The trail ends like it starts—without connecting to a road. But if we continue straight past the end, we'll reach roads that connect to a town called Houndsborough. I guess it isn't far from there to Gamat Rue."

"We could last comfortably for a week on our provisions," Hunter said. "Let's ride."

Cole spent the day glancing back, especially whenever they crested a rise and a view spread out behind them, but he never saw pursuers. The deeper they journeyed into the forested hills, the calmer he became. Sometimes he slipped a hand into his pocket, but he received no further communication from Sando, which hopefully meant they got away clean.

That evening after making camp, Cole went with Mira to refill their flasks from a stream. He had been waiting for a chance to talk to her alone. She chose a spot where the water flowed swiftly. She knelt beside the stream in the fading light. Deep circles stood out under her eyes.

"Long day," Cole said.

"It doesn't stop," she said, her voice a little numb. "We scramble from one danger to another. It's all we do. You're crazy for staying with me."

"Don't worry about us," Cole said. "You have enough stress."

She paused and looked at Cole. "Have you ever been to the seashore?"

"Yeah," Cole said. "A couple of times."

"Once, I was at the beach, and I swam out to play in the waves. It was fun. I was a few years younger than I am now, so it was a very long time ago. I would duck the waves, or go over them, or brace myself and let them break against me. Until a big one got me. Playtime ended immediately. It had full control, holding me under and shaking me. And that wasn't the worst of it. The wave was the first in a series. I got my head above water to take a breath as another one was breaking. It was relentless. I tumbled blindly. Salt water burned in my nostrils. I couldn't breathe. I felt like I had no control over my body. I couldn't influence the outcome. I kept struggling mostly by instinct, but at some level I knew it was just a matter of time. I was going to die."

"You didn't die," Cole pointed out.

"One of our bodyguards came and got me," Mira said. "Without him, who knows?"

"That's why you keep good people around you," Cole said. "We help one another."

"This is different," Mira said, her eyes haunted, her voice trembling. "We can't get away from these waves. There's no shore. They keep coming, bigger and stronger, swallowing everyone I care about."

"I know you're worried about Tessa," Cole consoled.

"Not just Tessa," Mira insisted. "You. Jace. Dalton. Hunter. Joe. Honor. Costa. Ella. My mother. Twitch. Skye. Your poor friend Jenna. So many people. And it keeps getting worse. How much longer can we keep coming up for air? How long before the whole world gets swallowed?"

"You're tired," Cole said.

"Not just tired," Mira said. "I'm worn out, Cole. I don't know how much more I can take. I used to hate being the fourth daughter of the High King. I felt like a useless mascot. I also hated living anonymously in exile. But give me either of those lives! Anything but this."

Cole had never seen Mira let her guard down this completely. She had seemed more frayed lately. Her worries about Tessa were pushing her toward the edge.

"We'll save your sister," Cole said.

"Will we?" Mira asked. "None of us have any idea how to go up against an echomancer."

"I've meant to talk to you about that," Cole said. "Your sisters didn't want you to go after them. Not you personally, at least. They didn't think the risk made sense. They want you to send people. The echo who helped us gave me the same advice. He said nobody should go to Gamat Rue. Maybe we should recruit some help."

Mira set down her flask and smoothed her hands over her shirt. Her expression grew calm before speaking, but Cole had a feeling she was exercising restraint. "Thank you, Cole. I appreciate your concern. It makes sense to try to get help. Maybe we can find somebody. I wasn't saying that I'm giving up." Tears came to her eyes. "Or maybe I was, a little. Cole, part of me wants this to end at Gamat Rue, just to be done. I want this to be over. But it isn't fair to take everybody with me. And it isn't fair to give up on Tessa! Why'd she have to get drawn into this?"

Mira buried her face in her hands and shook with sobs. Cole wasn't sure how to respond. He drew near and put an arm around her. She leaned into him, which he took as a good sign.

As Mira continued to cry, his heart ached. He felt bad for her, and for Tessa, and for himself, and for Jenna. Things really were terrible. But you couldn't just sink to the bottom! You had to keep coming up for air.

"Nobody is leaving you," Cole said.

Mira brought her sobbing under control. Leaning away from Cole, she wiped snot from below her nose. "You know where to find Jenna. We're going the wrong way."

"I'll worry about Jenna later," Cole said. "She's not in immediate danger."

"If you get killed, who helps her?" Mira asked.

"Dalton."

"What if you both get killed?"

"I don't know," Cole said, not wanting to face the question. "She'll do her best. Nazeem wants me. What if I lead him to her? We'll take care of your stuff first. If we beat your dad and Nazeem and Owandell, then I can really work on helping all the kids who were taken."

"That's a lot of optimism."

"I'm not saying we'll succeed," Cole said with a laugh.

She laughed too.

"It's the plan that makes the most sense to me," Cole said. "If we're drowning, it seems like the shortest distance to the surface."

"I guess," Mira said.

"At least right now we're between waves," Cole said, looking around. "We can breathe tonight, right?"

"Can we?" Mira asked. "I mean, mentally it doesn't stop. So many people are after us. Terrible things are ahead of us. The stars are gone. Who knows how Tessa is suffering?"

"You weren't like this before," Cole said. "You're extra worried about Tessa."

Mira squinted and teared up. "She's so little. Thinking of her in hiding was all right. She doesn't deserve to be hunted. Nobody ever really treated her like a person. Because of her gift, you know? I think I was her only friend. My poor little sister."

"I'll save her, Mira," Cole said. "I promise." The words brought a feeling of irrational bravery, like when he had jumped at the cyclops or charged the Rogue Knight. Something about protecting people brought out the best in him.

Mira looked at him through her tears. "I hope so. You're a good friend."

"You're a good sister," Cole said. "Now wipe your face before Jace decides I'm abusive."

"I'm not a crier," she professed.

"Obviously," Cole joked.

"Save it," Mira said, her normal personality returning a bit. "Not a word to anybody."

"As long as you think about sitting this one out," Cole said.

Real anger entered her eyes. "Cole, all I have is saving my sisters. It's my fight, and it's all I have. Do you think I care about surviving? I haven't cared about that for a long time. I only worry about failing them. I could get captured or killed just as easily in hiding. If I go down, I want to be helping them."

"Die bravely," Cole said.

"The Sky Raiders had some things right."

"Too bad our Jumping Swords don't work. I'd feel a little braver."

"Get your power back," Mira encouraged.

"I keep trying. Still nothing."

"We'll find a way."

Cole smiled. "Look at you being optimistic."

Mira shrugged. "It beats crying into our water flasks."

A tidy cottage came into view the third day on the trail. Joe spotted it first, a few hundred yards ahead, halfway up the next incline, nestled among lush evergreens. Before they could move out of sight, a figure came to the porch and waved at them.

Joe lifted a hand in reply. "We're in the middle of nowhere," he said. "Hopefully, this person won't be trouble."

"Stay ready for anything," Hunter said. "Necronum draws some strange hermit types. They live lonely lives muttering to echoes. Not always healthy for the sanity."

Cole and the others rode up to the cottage. A man awaited them on the porch, his long, graying hair fastened back in a single thick braid. Several sets of wind chimes dangled from the eaves. Without a breeze they hung limp.

"I only get visitors out here during Shiver Moons," the man greeted. "I seldom see flesh-and-blood people—let alone a band of mostly children. What brings you so deep into the wild?"

Mira and Joe whispered together.

"You have some marks of the Unseen on your walls and on that rain barrel," Joe said.

The man smiled. "I live far from regular roads. I should have suspected you might be fellow radicals."

"Do you have the latest code phrase?" Joe asked.

"Probably not the latest," the man replied. "If you hear it twice?"

"It might be an echo," Joe said.

"Three times?"

"Kids chanting rhymes."

"Four?"

"A bore. That's an older one but it was accurate."

"I don't get much contact out here," the man said. "I remain a sympathizer, but I've been inactive for some time. I go by Tuto. My given name is a tongue twister."

"Let's hear it," Cole said.

"Tutoulohavanook," the man replied. "You must be weary. Let me open my home to you for the night, humble though it may be."

Joe turned toward Mira. "It would mean stopping early."

"You're a weaver?" Mira asked.

"Guilty as charged," the man replied.

"Talking to a friendly weaver would be worth the time," Mira said.

Tuto placed a hand on his chest. "I'll help however I can. I remain devoted to the cause. Please, come inside."

After tying up the horses, they joined Tuto in his cozy cottage. A footstool and a cask were used as extra chairs. Cole thought Tuto seemed a little overwhelmed by all the people, but he remained good-natured as he gave them water to drink and bowls of what tasted like cool, creamy oatmeal.

Jace left his bowl untouched while he lingered by a wall where a variety of medallions hung on pegs. "Do you make these?" he asked casually.

"I do," Tuto said. "They ward off echoes."

"Do they work?" Jace asked.

"Some shysters sell cheap trinkets," Tuto said. "These are all made with strong weaving."

"I might be interested," Jace said, fingering a pendant made of wood, bone, beads, and leather. "We should talk later."

Tuto turned to Mira. "You wanted to talk to a weaver. How may I be of service?"

"We have to go someplace dangerous," Mira said. "Gamat Rue."

Tuto's jaw dropped. He looked at the others, as if to make sure they were all in agreement on such an absurd idea. "The accursed prison?" he finally asked. "Why?"

"To save somebody," Mira said.

Tuto sucked in a lot of air through puckered lips and shook his head. "Anybody who got lost there is not coming back. Let it be."

"We know she went there," Mira said. "And we know she isn't dead."

"How can you be sure?" Tuto asked.

"There are ways to know things," Mira replied evenly.

Tuto considered her closely. "There are ways, I suppose. You are sure about your ways? This girl is definitely alive? And definitely at Gamat Rue?"

"She was definitely alive a few nights ago," Mira said. Cole knew Mira meant the last night they had seen Tessa's star. "And I know she went to Gamat Rue. She may not still be there. If we can't find her, we need to talk to a certain echo named Ragio."

Shaking his head, Tuto rubbed his thighs. "You are determined?"

"Completely," Mira said.

"This person is special?" Tuto asked.

"You have no idea," Mira said.

"Important to our cause?" Tuto wondered.

Mira glanced at Joe, then over at Cole. "We really need help, so I'm going to tell you a secret. Will you keep it?"

"Yes."

"You're a weaver," Mira said. "Swear by the strongest oath you know."

"That's a lot to ask," Tuto said.

"It's the price of knowing," Mira insisted. "It's a secret vital to the rebellion. Just keep the secret, and the oath won't matter."

"All oaths matter," Tuto said. "But I sense sincerity, and frankly, I'm curious. If I divulge this secret, may my bindings never hold and all my weavings be undone. May all echoes dominate me and the echolands provide no refuge."

Mira glanced at Hunter.

"Sounds strong to me," Hunter said.

"The girl in danger is Destiny Pemberton, daughter of Stafford Pemberton," Mira said.

"Her echo?" Tuto asked, marveling.

"Maybe, but she's alive," Mira said. "A strange type of shaping called shapecraft stopped her from aging when her father took her powers. Now her power is returning, and she is on the run."

"Your words carry the power of truth," Tuto said somberly. "This is . . . beyond belief. A surviving heir could change the entire complexion of the rebellion."

"Exactly," Mira said. "We have to rescue her. How can you help?"

"You give me much to ponder," Tuto said. He folded his arms and tucked his chin down. When he spoke again, the words came slowly. "A man prepares his whole life for an opportunity like this, never knowing if it will come. A chance to put his principles into action in a way that could make a real and lasting difference. A test of his abilities greater than he would undertake except at extreme need." He looked to Hunter. "You have weaving abilities, young man?"

"I have some experience," Hunter said.

"Your power burns bright," Tuto said. "I've not seen such variety. But your weaving is less developed than some of your talents."

"I've had less experience in Necronum than other kingdoms," Hunter said.

"Yet you can see across to the echolands," Tuto said. "And you can weave there. Have you stepped across?"

"Not yet," Hunter said.

Tuto nodded. His gaze returned to Mira. "You need the help of an experienced weaver. If you desire, I will come with you to Gamat Rue."

Mira smiled. "Thank you. We'd love extra guidance. Have you been there?"

"No, but I have visited some unsettling haunting grounds. I will develop a strategy to get us in and out with the lowest possible risk." Tuto's gaze took in everyone in the room. "I cannot guarantee the safety of any who venture there. It is a very real possibility that none of us will survive. Your life could be lost and your echo trapped. The price of failure could be paid not only in this world, but for eons in the afterlife."

Jace had no color in his face. "The echoes at Gamat Rue can hurt us?" he asked.

"Some powerful echoes can exert their power over a

place," Tuto said. "At the shrines and temples, the weavers of Necronum dedicate spaces where the echolands draw near. At haunting grounds, mighty echoes pull the physical reality of Necronum close to their realm. At Gamat Rue, echoes could harm you, and quite possibly kill you, taking your echo prisoner for ages untold."

His posture rigid, his eyes not quite hiding the horror inside, Jace nodded. He cleared his throat. "So, how much did you say those pendants cost?"

CHAPTER
11

GAMAT RUE

The ruins of the ancient prison crowned a huge, brushy hill surrounded by dense woods. All roofing had caved in long ago, and many walls had collapsed into grassy heaps of rubble. The irregular fins of stonework that remained rose from the brush in bewildering shapes, leaving the design of the original structure unrecognizable. A few empty windows still contained rusty bars, giving the only clue that the broken ramparts once contained prisoners.

The midday sun glared down from almost directly overhead as Cole and the others gathered at the base of the hill near the edge of the woods. Each of them wore one of Tuto's pendants, though he had warned that most of the protection would be forfeited by knowingly entering the haunting ground. Jace wore three.

The journey from Tuto's cottage to Gamat Rue had provided no difficulties. Only forcing their way through the untamed forest around the hill had really slowed them.

"The timing could not be better," Tuto said. "Here in

physical Necronum, the powers of Nandavi should be at their lowest ebb under the noonday sun."

"So we better get up there," Jace said, trying to sound relaxed.

"We don't want to wait too long," Tuto agreed.

"Somebody should stay with the horses," Cole said. They had led their mounts through the woods around the hill. "I vote for Dalton."

"Why me?" Dalton asked, not without some hopefulness.

"In case things go badly, you can go help Jenna," Cole said.

"Not everyone needs to do this," Mira said, looking up the long, gentle slope. "Cole? Hunter? Jace? Joe?"

"You should stay," Jace told Mira. "You're not a weaver. Why risk it? The revolution could be ruined without you. The rest of us can look for Tessa and Ragio just fine."

"I'm going," Mira said resolutely. "That's final."

"Then I'm with you," Jace said without hesitation, though one hand strayed to a feathered pendant.

"I won't leave your side," Joe said.

"Me neither," Cole added.

"I'd love to watch the horses," Hunter said. "But I'm the only other person with some weaving skills. I better come."

Dalton looked uncertainly at his horse. "We leave the horses tied up all the time. It won't be that long."

"You're not only watching the horses," Cole said. "This is for Jenna. And if none of us return, maybe you can find rescuers."

"Stay," Mira encouraged. "It makes sense."

"All right," Dalton said. "But come back. I don't want to try to lead seven horses through those woods."

"Weapons?" Jace asked, hefting his crossbow.

"We're dealing with echoes," Tuto said. "Normally, there would be no reason to involve tangible weapons. But at a haunting ground, sometimes echoes can take material form and interact with the matter of the physical world. In such cases, they may become temporarily vulnerable to physical weapons."

"They can fight us?" Jace asked.

"Potentially," Tuto said. "An echo might hurl a stone, or knock over a wall, or even push you directly."

"He's right," Hunter said. "I've heard stories."

Jace looked a little peaked. Cole clapped him on the arm. "At least we might be able to stab them. Better than nothing, right?"

Face valiantly composed, Jace gave a nod.

"Stay near me," Tuto said. "We should do this together. There is some strength in numbers."

They hiked up the hillside. Cole could picture that in the dark, the eroded remains of the ancient prison could be scary. But under the sunlight, walking with friends, it felt more like a field trip.

Tuto halted a few steps downhill from the first broken wall. Scarred blocks littered the brush ahead of him. Tuto pointed at a timeworn chunk of carved masonry.

"The area is marked," Tuto said. "It's a warning that we are entering haunted ground. Such a warning further limits our protection. We are knowingly trespassing."

"So why tell us?" Cole asked.

"There are other warnings around the site," Tuto said, scanning the area. "Some written in plain language. You'll feel the difference when we enter the former boundaries of Gamat Rue. Your senses will warn you to depart."

"What's our strategy?" Jace asked, trying to sound business-like, but failing to mask his uneasiness.

"Stay strong," Tuto said. "The echoes here will take what you give them. Your fear or uncertainty will only encourage them. They may ask for things. They may harass you for trespassing. Agree to nothing. We will collectively maintain that we have a right to be here because they may have harmed Destiny. We will not accept their claim to this place. We will not admit to being trespassers. Standing firm on those issues will make it harder for them to bother us."

"Can they sense if we're secretly afraid?" Jace asked.

"Our thoughts and emotions will be at least partially exposed to the echomancer," Tuto said. "But what you claim to believe still matters. Acting confident carries weight no matter how you privately feel."

"Could Destiny actually be here?" Mira asked.

Tuto shrugged and raised both hands. "I don't see any other people around. I suppose there could be unseen dungeons where live prisoners are held. We'll know more once we enter Gamat Rue."

"If we can't find Destiny, we'll want to learn what Ragio knows," Hunter reminded everyone.

"As soon as we enter, I'll start looking for him," Tuto

pledged. Shielding his eyes, he glanced upward. "The sun can't get much higher. Shall we proceed?"

Now that the moment had arrived, Cole felt deep reluctance. He touched the ringer in his pocket. There had been no word from Sando since the morning they left Rincomere. The old echo had already made it clear that visiting Gamat Rue was a bad idea. The prospect of finding out how bad made Cole a little nauseated. He noticed Jace's tight grip on his crossbow.

"Let's get this over with," Mira said.

Tuto moved as if to continue up the hill, then hesitated and looked over his shoulder. "Take care with your weapons. Without caution, the chances are greater of us hurting one another than damaging any echoes."

Cole took his hand off the hilt of his Jumping Sword. He noticed Jace engage the safety on the crossbow.

Staying near the others, Cole weaved between low piles of rubble and passed the first crumbling wall of the prison. As he stepped beyond the wall, an immense feeling of dread took hold of him. Something was not right here. The temperature noticeably dropped, and the air became clammy. Suddenly, the daylight felt wrong, almost as if he had put on tinted sunglasses—the light seemed a bit dimmer, and the colors were off. His instincts screamed for him to run.

"Feel it?" Tuto asked. "This is our warning." His voice was too muffled, as if speaking from another room.

Cole's skin rippled into goose bumps, and the hairs on his arms and neck stood tall. Beside him, Jace breathed shallowly, wide eyes darting. Cole nudged him with his elbow. "Scared?" Even from his own lips, the word seemed distant. Cole remembered words sounding like this once when he took a flight with a cold and his ears were slow to pop.

Focus returned to Jace's gaze. He clenched his jaw and gave Cole a scowl, his thumb on the safety of his crossbow.

"This way," Tuto said, walking briskly.

The top of the hill was either naturally flat or else had been leveled to accommodate the prison. As Cole advanced, he found the perspectives confusing. There were more walls and pillars than it appeared from down the hill, and the distances between them were disconcertingly unpredictable. A stony barrier looked ten paces away, but he would reach it in three. Another appeared five paces away, but it would take fifteen steps to get there. He got the feeling that when he wasn't looking in a particular direction, the ruins were shifting position, only to hold mockingly still when his gaze returned.

Stepping carefully around a heap of broken slabs, Mira quietly drew her Jumping Sword. Joe stayed at her side. Jace pointed his crossbow toward the ground and released the safety, his finger near the trigger.

Hunter came closer to Cole. He muttered something inaudible, then raised his voice. The words were still almost too soft to hear. "This place is crammed with echoes."

"Yeah?" Cole asked.

"I haven't looked across. But I can feel them."

"I can feel something," Cole said. The dread inside was

mounting. He wasn't sure if it was appropriate to talk. He felt like a mouse sneaking through a room full of sleeping cats.

"Stay calm," Hunter said. "Hopefully, we can get this over with quickly."

The air was unusually heavy and still. It seemed reluctant to fill Cole's lungs, reluctant to carry words, reluctant to part for intruders.

Tuto led them purposefully to a circular clearing at the center of the ruins. Unlike elsewhere, no brush or weeds grew inside the circle. No walls or rubble interrupted the naked expanse of rock and dirt, though plenty surrounded it.

Give the ringer to Jace, a voice instructed in Cole's mind. The words came clearly—apparently, the drowsy atmosphere of Gamat Rue didn't interfere with mental communication.

"Now?" Cole asked, the whispered word barely making it past his lips.

Tuto instructed them to gather in a ring.

Yes, immediately, Sando replied in his mind.

Cole formed a circle with the others, Hunter on one side, Jace on the other. Wasn't this a suspicious time for Sando to make this request? Couldn't it wait until they got out of the prison? Was he up to something?

We had a deal, Cole, Sando insisted. *Deliver the ringer now, or you break your promise. You don't want to do that in a place like this. I've been helping you. Quick. Do it now.*

Cole's hand went to his pocket, and his fingers easily found the ringer.

"Jace," Cole murmured. His friend didn't hear, so he repeated it louder.

Jace glanced at him.

Cole held out his hand, the silver ringer pinched between his thumb and forefinger.

Looking a little bewildered, Jace extended his hand.

Cole set the ringer on his palm.

And Sando appeared in the middle of the circle. "Hold them," the wiry beggar commanded, his voice unusually resonant.

Tuto began gesticulating, hands describing fluid patterns as he crouched and swiveled. Cole's head was tugged upward, his muscles tensing in unison, and suddenly, he couldn't move. Even his eyes were locked in place, though he could see the others around him, at least peripherally. They all held their chins up and stood very still.

Tuto continued to pivot and pose, as if demonstrating a martial art.

"Greetings," Sando said with a toothless smile, eager eyes taking in the entire group. He looked perfectly tangible. "I am the echo who helped you elude capture twice. Cole was kind enough to complete our bargain and release me from my promise to do no harm."

Cole couldn't move, but everything inside of him withered. Here was the real price of Sando's help! The moment Cole handed over the coin, the old beggar had been freed to turn on them precisely when they were most vulnerable. And Tuto was clearly an accomplice. In complete stillness, Cole battled fruitlessly to move. He had failed to foresee how delivering a coin could lead to serious trouble. He had made the wrong deal with the wrong echo. Consequently, he and his friends were doomed.

Hunter collapsed. Cole tried to turn his head, or at least his eyes, but could do nothing more than pay extra attention to his peripheral vision.

"I see you mean to rush this," Sando said irritably. "Tuto, permit all but Mira and Cole to speak. I need volunteers to cross to the echolands. Without other offers, I take Mira."

"Me," Jace said immediately.

"No, me," Joe volunteered right after him.

Cole tried to speak, but his vocal chords refused to respond. He couldn't even grunt. The only action he could manage was to breathe very slowly.

"Nandavi?" Sando called, pointing at Jace. "Him."

Jace flopped to the ground. Cole could only see him in the corner of his vision, but after hitting the dirt, Jace looked very still. Cole didn't see Nandavi anywhere. If she was present, she wasn't visible.

Cole lurched and lunged and thrashed and screamed, all without budging an inch or making a sound. He couldn't even go limp. Every muscle remained tightly fixed in position.

Then Sando pointed at Joe. "And him."

Joe crumpled as well. Cole could see this better, since Joe was across from him.

Cole exerted himself violently but again failed to even twitch. His friends were dying! It was his fault! And there was nothing he could do.

Sando grinned at Mira. "I neglected to clarify that even

with those volunteers, you will still come to the echolands. My preference would be to keep this tidy. Mira, I will claim Cole unless you volunteer. Tuto, let her speak."

"Will he live if I volunteer?" Mira asked sharply.

"I will not take him to the echolands if you come now," Sando said. "Hurry. The offer won't last."

Cole tried to scream *No!* Nothing came out. Not a squeak. Not a whimper.

"You won't take him to the echolands?" Mira asked. "Or he will live and go free?"

Sando wrinkled his nose. "Fine. Yes. Cole will live and go free."

"All right," Mira said.

"Nandavi?" Sando asked, indicating Mira.

She dropped like a marionette with her strings cut. Mira didn't just look unconscious. She looked dead.

Cole no longer tried to thrash. He seemed to shrink. Jace, Joe, and Mira? Just like that? He couldn't sag. He couldn't cry. He couldn't blink. He could only stand there with his chin up, his muscles frozen, and his heart desolate.

Sando glanced at Tuto, who continued to flutter his arms and fingers. "This got a little messier than I would have preferred. The boy Dalton stayed behind, and Cole must be monitored—"

Hunter appeared. Cole felt confused. Hunter was slumped on the ground on the opposite edge of his vision from Jace. And yet he had just materialized between Cole and Sando.

The Hunter who had just appeared dove toward Jace, snatched the crossbow, rolled, and aimed. The quarrel hit Tuto in the chest.

And suddenly, the stretched feeling in Cole's neck ended. His other muscles relaxed as well. He could move!

Without pause, Cole drew his sword and charged Sando. The elderly beggar snarled and shuffled away from him. Reaching into his loose sleeve, Sando withdrew a knife, the blade much shorter than the Jumping Sword.

Cole didn't slow. He hacked at Sando's neck, but the beggar ducked and slid away, swinging his knife but not quite reaching Cole's belly. Hunter had his sword in hand and quickly looped around behind Sando. The beggar noticed and lunged toward Cole, trying to stab him, but Cole knocked the blade aside with his sword, then slashed Sando's arm with a return stroke.

Sando vanished with a shrill yelp.

Hunter disappeared as well, his sword falling to the ground.

Tuto lay in the dirt, a shaft jutting from his ribs, chest hitching as redness gurgled from his lips. His eyes were tightly closed, his face scrunched in agony.

Cole ran to Mira. Her hair lay across her face. He hesitated to touch her. She wasn't just asleep. Her body looked lifeless. He brushed the hair away and felt for a pulse in her neck. She wasn't breathing. He could find no pulse. How could she really be dead? This was a nightmare!

Hunter's body sat up, the abrupt motion drawing Cole's eye.

"She's gone," Hunter said urgently. "Bring her body. I'll grab Jace."

"Wait, how are you back?" Cole asked, looking to Jace, Joe, and Mira, wanting to see them stir. "What about them?"

"Nandavi didn't steal my lifespark," Hunter said. "I crossed over on my own and stayed free. They're stuck there. Hurry."

Hunter rushed to Jace, reached under his arms, and started pulling. Cole seized Mira the same way and walked backward, her legs dragging. He kept his head turned to monitor where he was going, which carried the benefit of letting him avoid looking at her.

But it was impossible not to feel her limp weight. Cole tried not to think. He was carrying Mira. She was not breathing. And it was his fault.

Hunter was moving faster. Cole managed to speed up a little but couldn't keep pace.

"What did you do?" Cole called, his words dampened by the oppressive atmosphere of Gamat Rue.

"I crossed over to the echolands," Hunter said.

"Was that when you collapsed?" Cole asked.

"Yeah," Hunter said, hauling Jace around a damaged fortification. "After a minute, I tried what the toothless old echo did. I brought my echo to the material world. I used the crossbow and chased your echo friend."

"Sando," Cole said, guilt writhing in his gut, shame tearing at him. "The echo is named Sando." His lips now spoke the name without difficulty. Arrangement fulfilled, Cole supposed.

"Yeah, well, when he retreated to the echolands, I went after him, but I wouldn't have lasted against him and Nandavi, so I returned to my body."

Cole focused on Hunter rather than the shifty ruins. They had almost reached the outermost wall.

"I didn't know you could do that," Cole said.

"Neither did I," Hunter replied. "First time." Hunter passed the outermost rampart and raised his voice. "Dalton! Get up here! Bring a horse!"

CHAPTER
— 12 —

BODIES

Cole positioned Mira beside Jace, and Hunter crouched between them, his hands on their foreheads. Hunter bowed his head.

"Can you help them?" Cole asked.

"Shhh," Hunter hissed.

Cole tried to steady himself. Now that he was beyond the boundaries of Gamat Rue, it seemed like a regular day again. The temperature had warmed up. His voice sounded right. The sunlight had the correct brightness and color.

His head gently throbbed in sync with his heart. He was out of breath, sweaty, and still trying to shake off the effects of panic and shock. Otherwise, things were back to normal.

Except for his motionless friends sprawled in the brush.

"I should be able to keep their bodies stable," Hunter said finally. "You and Dalton need to get Joe quickly."

Dalton was on his way up the slope astride his horse.

"Wait," Cole said. "They're alive?" Could he have been mistaken? Could Mira just be unconscious?

"They're in longsleep," Hunter said. "The body can't live without the lifespark. But when the lifespark is removed before the death of the physical body, a faint connection remains. If that connection is strengthened by weaving, the body can be preserved. As long as the connection persists, they're not fully gone. In Necronum, an empty body can survive in stasis while the lifeforce is away. It's how I left my body to slip into the echolands when Tuto bound us. It's how mortal weavers visit the echolands without truly dying."

"Should I try some CPR?" Cole asked. "Blow in their mouths?"

"We can't restore the lifespark that way," Hunter explained. "The body didn't die. The spark was removed. But I can keep the bodies from rotting and help maintain the connection to their sparks. The heart barely beats, the lungs barely breathe, but the body can still accept the lifeforce if it returns."

"We can still save them?" Cole asked desperately.

"There's a chance," Hunter said.

"I don't get how their sparks left."

"Nandavi did it," Hunter said. "She ripped their lifesparks from them. Back home we might say she took their spirits. There was no physical damage. If Sando or Tuto had stabbed them, there might not be a functional body left behind."

Dalton reached them, reining in his horse and dismounting.

"What happened?" he asked.

"Ambush," Cole said. "Tuto turned on us. My echo friend too. Mira, Jace, and Joe are basically dead."

"Dead?" Dalton exclaimed.

"Not completely," Hunter said. "But we can't revive them without finding their echoes. You and Cole bring Joe here. We still might be able to save him too. I should stay with these bodies."

"All right," Cole said.

"Take off the pendants," Hunter said. "Tuto was using them against us."

Feeling angry and stupid, Cole pulled the pendant over his head and tossed it aside. Dalton chucked his in the opposite direction.

"The Gamat Rue echoes will harass you guys," Hunter said. "It could get ugly. Don't agree to anything if they try to communicate. If they become tangible and attack, defend yourselves. Get Joe."

Cole and Dalton ran back into Gamat Rue. As soon as he passed the remnant of the outermost wall, Cole found it became much harder to sprint. The air didn't want to part for him or fill his lungs, and gravity seemed to increase. The disorienting tricks of perspective started to make him feel dizzy. Cole slowed to a quick walk, and Dalton did likewise.

"Everything feels off," Dalton said, the words weirdly muffled.

"This place is wrong," Cole said. "Let's get Joe and get out."

Cole ground his teeth. This was an emergency! Why was he walking? In defiance of the sluggish atmosphere, Cole upped his pace to a jog, and Dalton matched him.

The barren circle soon came into view. Sando looked

tangible again, kneeling beside Tuto. The beggar looked over his shoulder and saw Cole, then rose, knife in hand. Blood dripped from the blade.

Cole drew his Jumping Sword and rushed toward the echo. Dalton brandished his short sword. Sando glanced at Joe's fallen form, then disappeared.

Tuto still had the arrow in his chest, but he was no longer wheezing. He lay still, his throat cut.

"Did he . . . ?" Dalton asked.

"Looks like it," Cole said. "Sando probably wanted to hurry Tuto to the echolands. Joe looks untouched. Grab a leg."

Keeping his sword out, Cole gripped Joe by one ankle and Dalton grabbed the other. They pulled him as quickly as they could manage.

"Going so soon?" asked Sando.

Glancing up, Cole saw that the beggar had reappeared in the barren circle. Cole scowled. Why did the echo's voice carry so well here when everyone else sounded far away?

"Keep going," Cole grumbled to Dalton.

"I have Miracle, you know," Sando said. "Reborn as an echo. Along with Jace and the fellow you're dragging."

"Congratulations," Cole yelled, pulling as hard as he could.

"Perhaps we could discuss—"

"No deals!" Cole shouted.

"You really should—"

Cole dropped Joe's ankle, spun, pointed his sword at Sando, and cried, "Away!"

The sword did not pull him forward. He hadn't felt his power, but he had so desperately wanted it to work that he thought maybe it might.

Sando chuckled through a grin. "You have some fire in you, young sir. I see why you amuse Nazeem. But that power of yours is a disaster. I could take a closer look if you wish. Make some recommendations?"

Cole took hold of Joe's ankle again and continued pulling. The beggar made no move to give chase. As Cole and Dalton progressed, a broken wall blocked Sando from view.

"You keep that body," Sando said, no longer visible but his voice still plenty loud. "You deserve a souvenir. I will see you soon, maybe. Why pursue what wants to find you?"

"Want to go get him?" Dalton asked.

"Yes," Cole said. "But he'll just disappear."

A blunt blow struck Cole on the shoulder, making him drop his sword and Joe's leg, then an invisible force shoved his chest, and he stumbled over some rubble and fell. Dalton staggered away from Joe as well. Cole rose, and a rock the size of his fist flew by his head, brushing his ear. An invisible blow struck him behind the knees, and he was back on the ground.

"Stop it!" Cole yelled, punching and kicking the air around him, striking nothing.

One of Joe's legs lifted, and an unseen force started dragging him. Dalton lunged at Joe, swinging his sword at the air above the raised leg, and the blade seemed to connect with something. The leg fell.

"Hurry," Cole said as he raced to Joe, picked up the Jumping Sword, and grabbed an ankle.

Waving their swords at the empty air around them, Cole and Dalton scrambled as fast as they could with a grown man in tow. A rock thumped painfully against Cole's back. Dalton grunted as a stone pelted his side.

Up ahead, past the final rampart, Cole saw Hunter pulling Jace down the slope. Mira already lay far beyond them.

"Almost there," Cole encouraged. He dodged a rock that came from the side, then ducked one that sailed at him from up ahead.

"Keep going!" Hunter called as they passed beyond Gamat Rue and the air returned to normal.

"That's better," Dalton said.

Back in regular atmosphere, they both picked up the pace. A couple of rocks flew by to either side. One struck Joe's thigh. As they proceeded down the slope, they moved out of range. Rocks stopped flying.

They halted when they reached Hunter, who crouched between Mira and Jace, his hands on their foreheads. Dalton's horse roamed off to one side, farther down the slope, grazing in the tall grass.

Hunter hurried to Joe, hunching over him and cupping his face. "He's not completely gone."

"That's something," Cole said with relief. Reaching behind himself, he tried to rub his back just to the side of his spine, where the rock had hit. He couldn't reach the spot very effectively. It sure ached.

"Should I go after my horse?" Dalton asked.

"Wait," Hunter said. "It's not running off. We have more horses than riders now. I need to catch you guys up."

"I still don't really get what happened," Cole said. "Why didn't Nandavi just kill us too?"

"Let me guess," Hunter said. "Jace and Joe volunteered somehow."

"Sando told them he would take Mira to the echolands if they didn't," Cole said.

"And didn't mention he would still take her even if they volunteered," Hunter concluded. "They were brave but stupid. It would have been a lot harder to hurt them if they had kept quiet. We might have all escaped."

"I tried to volunteer too," Cole admitted.

"That's because you're brave, and you didn't know enough about the echolands," Hunter said. "I imagine they kept you frozen, so you couldn't speak."

Cole nodded.

"Sando played us from the start," Hunter said. "I've actually heard of that guy. And that isn't a great sign, because I haven't spent tons of time in Necronum. He's a trickster. One of the worst. Known for getting things done."

"That's on me," Cole said, staring at Mira's body. The guilt hurt a lot worse than his back. He felt like he might puke.

"You got played," Hunter said. "We all did. He's a pro. All Sando asked you to do was hand over that ringer?"

"Yeah. I had to give it away at his command." It was weird that the words came out so easily now.

"Seemed so innocent," Hunter said. "Keep this ringer for me, and I promise to help you until our bargain is over."

Cole nodded again.

"He used the ringer to track you and spy on us," Hunter said. "He helped us get away from Enforcers but led us to a lonely path that went right by a weaver he liked to work with. I bet he set it up with Tuto before we got there. Probably taught him the outdated Unseen code words. Then when he wanted to turn on you, Sando had you give the ringer to Jace, and we were in trouble."

"Why lead us away from the Enforcers?" Dalton asked. "They could have caught us days ago."

"Sando probably wanted credit," Hunter said. "And he may have wanted us in a place where our lifesparks would be extra vulnerable. He might have planned everything from the start. He might have known we'd end up at Gamat Rue when he first contacted Cole back at the Seven-Cornered Shrine. He probably could have guided us directly here. He might have just used the cave to build trust and put us off our guard. Or to get us close to the road that would lead us to Tuto. The way he did it was cleaner than armed Enforcers. Less risk of Mira getting physically hurt. I'm sure he wanted her body intact. Probably yours, too, Cole."

"I'm an idiot," Cole said.

"You couldn't have known," Dalton said.

"Don't blame yourself," Hunter agreed. "The deal you made seemed safe. You got good info in return for a small favor. We knew there might be a catch. We tried to be ready for it. I thought we were being careful, but we got burned."

"Not just burned," Cole said, tears stinging his eyes. His breathing became irregular as he tried not to burst into sobs. He waved a hand at his fallen friends. "Look at them."

Hunter held up a finger. "We're in Necronum. Their bodies are whole. You know, beyond getting scratched up from being dragged around. Don't forget there's still a chance we can save them."

That helped Cole feel steadier. "You really went to the echolands?"

"Sando didn't know my level of weaving talent," Hunter said. "He didn't expect me to cross over."

"That was when you first collapsed," Cole said.

"When my body was frozen, and I saw what was going on, I crossed over," Hunter said. "It's important that I'd never done it before. You only get one echo. Once you have one, you can only cross over when you're near it. Same if you're trying to get back to your physical body."

"Had you deliberately saved crossing over for an emergency?" Dalton said.

"Yep," Hunter said. "I never had a dire need before. Why waste your easiest trip?"

"How'd you know you could pull it off?" Cole asked.

Hunter shrugged, one hand still on Joe. "I wasn't sure I could. I knew the theory, and I'm pretty good at all things shaping. It's why people were scared of me as an Enforcer. Anyhow, I went for it, and it worked."

"What was it like?" Cole asked.

Hunter blanched. "Not good. I'd heard of the music in the echolands. It penetrates you more deeply than the music we know here. You don't just hear it. You feel it. When I went over, it seemed like I'd dropped into some freaky video game level. The music was seriously scary, and I was in this dark castle. Or maybe a fortress."

"A prison?" Dalton asked.

"Sort of. It didn't seem quite like a prison on that side. I've looked across a lot. Things don't always match up like you might expect. Anyhow, Nandavi was there, but she was busy helping Tuto with his weaving. I went unnoticed at first. So I reached out for Ragio with my weaving and found him."

"No way!" Cole said.

Hunter smiled. "Clutch performance, right? I connected with Ragio mind to mind. He was someplace nearby. I hunkered down in a quiet corner. We didn't have long, but I got the basics."

"Do they have Destiny?" Cole asked.

"Nandavi tried," Hunter said. "Tessa came here. But she got away alive. Her bodyguard wasn't so lucky."

"Honor?" Cole asked.

"Same story. She came and went. But a guy with her, Oster, died here."

"I knew him," Cole muttered, remembering the knight who had led him and a bunch of friends out of Blackmont Castle. How long before everyone he knew was dead? Jace, Mira, and Joe lay motionless. They'd survived some hardships together, but it felt like things were unraveling. His darkest worries were coming true.

Hunter snapped his fingers. "Cole? You with me?"

Cole realized he had zoned out. "Yeah. Sorry." His gaze strayed to Jace. Then Mira.

"We can save them," Hunter reminded him. "Focus on that."

"Right."

"Did you find out where Destiny went?" Dalton asked.

"She learned from Ragio that her stray power was being gathered in the echolands. So she went to the best place in the area to cross—the Temple of the Robust Sky."

"They were collecting her power in the echolands?" Cole asked.

"A place called Deepwell in the Hundred Forests," Hunter said. "I don't really know the geography of the echolands. Ragio was a shapecrafter working on the project to capture Destiny's power. He died and continued with the project as an echo. I guess Destiny's power was the hardest to gather. They were trying to shapecraft it at Deepwell. Ragio had a change of heart and ran away. They eventually caught him and brought him to Gamat Rue."

Cole didn't want to ask his next question. He really didn't. "Is Destiny in the echolands?"

"We don't know," Hunter said flatly. "Maybe she never crossed over. Maybe she crossed and already returned. Maybe she's on the other side. The only way to find out is to go to the Temple of the Robust Sky. Do we still want to go after her? Things are kind of a mess after today."

"Mira would want us to find Tessa above anything," Cole said.

"What about Mira?" Dalton asked.

"That's where this gets tricky," Hunter said. "The only reason I survived the echolands version of Gamat Rue was because Nandavi was concentrating on you guys. And there seemed to be some other commotion. I heard people yelling about an attack at the gates."

"Who was attacking?" Dalton asked.

"I don't know," Hunter said. "I was just glad the echoes seemed distracted. I focused on my conversation with Ragio. I only knew Nandavi had taken Joe, Jace, and Mira when I came out of my hiding spot and they were there."

"You saw their echoes?" Dalton asked.

"Sure did," Hunter replied. "While Tuto was holding our physical bodies with his weaving, Nandavi bound the echoes created when Jace, Joe, and Mira crossed over. Sando must have struck a bargain with both of them. I wish I had thought of going tangible earlier. I knew that if I returned to my body, Tuto would have me frozen again. But at a haunting ground, echoes can become physical, like Sando did. I'd never had a chance to try it, but Sando had done it, so I gave it a shot, and it worked. First I took out Tuto to free Cole. When Sando jumped back to the echolands, I followed, but Nandavi wasn't as focused on you guys anymore. Her will was hard to resist. I barely made it back to my body."

"They have your echo," Cole realized.

"Yes," Hunter said.

"What can they do with it?" Dalton asked.

"Imprison it," Hunter said. "Or destroy it."

"Your soul?" Dalton exclaimed.

"Not my soul," Hunter said. "My lifespark is here in this body, or I wouldn't be talking. My echo is a new body in the echolands. To us it seems like a ghost. They have my echo. If they destroy it, my spark would skip the echolands entirely when I die."

"You keep calling it a spark," Cole said.

"It's the local lingo. Lifeforce. Soul. Spirit. Whatever. In Necronum, a lot of people call it your lifespark, including the people who trained me. Or just your spark."

"What do we do about Mira?" Cole asked.

"Right now?" Hunter replied. "Nothing. Nandavi has my echo. I can't risk crossing over again. I must already be imprisoned. And you guys can't cross here. I don't have enough weaving skill to send you."

"Who can send us?" Cole asked.

"Our best bet is the same place Tessa went—the Temple of the Robust Sky," Hunter said.

"That makes sense," Cole said. "We should follow her trail."

"Exactly," Hunter said, looking at Cole steadily.

"That's where I'm going," Cole said.

Hunter patted Joe. "Our other priority is getting these bodies someplace where a more skilled weaver can put them into a stable longsleep. Until then, I have to stay with them, weaving constantly, or they could lose their connections to their lifesparks. Somebody needs to go fetch an expert weaver. I won't be able to move them without one. If we try to haul them out of here on horseback ourselves, I'm worried the bodies will get spoiled for revival. I have a weaver in mind, in the town of Dobson. If we keep the bodies close together, I should be able to sustain them until the weaver arrives."

"Cole and I can find the weaver," Dalton said. "Then we can all go to the temple once they're settled."

Hunter watched Cole, saying nothing.

"I don't know if we can afford the time," Cole said. "I'll ride ahead to the temple. Maybe you guys can follow me. Or maybe Dalton should go after Jenna."

"Alone?" Dalton asked, his voice squeaking.

"Maybe," Cole said. "This is falling apart." He paused, trying to think clearly despite his anxiety. "Jenna deserves somebody to come for her. So does Tessa. Mira too. I'll try to find Tessa. Then I'll go after Mira. You save Jenna."

"If you cross to find Destiny, I can't follow," Hunter said. "My echo is compromised. Maybe Dalton should follow you. I could go after Jenna."

Tears clouded Cole's vision. They weren't for himself, though he worried it looked that way. "No," he said. "You should go with Dalton. Stabilize the bodies, then help Jenna together. I don't want Dalton stuck in the afterlife. If it comes to that, I'll go alone."

"Do you have to go after Tessa?" Dalton asked. "We could send somebody."

"We'd have to find somebody," Cole said. "We'd lose too much time. And we might not find the right person. If Tessa went to the echolands, I'll go after her." He had promised Mira he would save her little sister. His blunder had led to Mira getting taken into the echolands. The least he could do was fulfill her last wish. Maybe he could save them both. And Jace. And Joe. That possibility was the only prospect that made the pain bearable. "Then I'll save Mira."

"You get that Mira won't stay here," Hunter said, jerking his head toward the ruins.

"Well, no," Cole replied.

"Sando is probably working for Nazeem," Hunter said. "If so, Mira will most likely be brought to him. The same would have happened to you. The others might remain. Depends on the arrangement with Nandavi."

Anger and fear warred inside of Cole. For the moment, anger had the upper hand. "I better go."

"Tessa went to the temple alone," Hunter said. "Her bodyguard didn't survive to help her. She was only here a few weeks ago. You may not be too far behind her."

"Got it," Cole said. "You two can handle the bodies?"

"We'll figure it out," Hunter said. "When you get to the temple, insist on talking to the prelate."

"The who?" Cole asked.

"The head cleric," Hunter said. "The weaver in charge of the temple. Destiny would have gone to the top. In Necronum, the prelates mostly side against the High King. If I remember right, the prelate at the Temple of the Robust Sky is a woman loyal to the rebellion. I don't recall her name."

"Good to know," Cole said. He knelt beside Mira, reached inside her collar, avoided Tuto's pendant, and unclasped the slender chain he found. An engraved golden disk dangled from the chain—the royal seal. "I'll use this to help prove whose side I'm on."

"Should we take off Tuto's pendants?" Dalton asked.

"Not a bad idea," Hunter said.

Cole removed Mira's and Joe's pendants and chucked them into the brush. Dalton did likewise with Jace's.

"Here's a thought," Hunter proposed. "Once we get the bodies settled, Dalton and I will follow you to the temple, to check what's going on. Maybe Tessa didn't cross. Or maybe she already crossed and came back. If she isn't in the echolands, I can help."

Dalton stared down at Mira. "Or both of us can help. I care about Mira too, you know. And Jace and Joe. It's not like I want to ditch them." He looked at Cole. "But part of me wonders if other people could help better."

"I worry too," Cole said. "How am I supposed to save them? But don't forget all we've accomplished. And remember that getting home is a long shot. So is saving Jenna or anyone else from back home unless we help Mira defeat her dad and Nazeem."

"He's right," Hunter said.

"Should I even go after Jenna?" Dalton asked.

"I think you should at least make contact," Cole said. "She deserves to know she isn't forgotten. You can see how well she's doing there and play it by ear."

"We'll see," Dalton said. "First things first. We'll take care of the bodies, then follow you to the temple."

Cole gave Dalton a hug. "Be safe. See you soon."

"Don't jinx us," Dalton said. "Die bravely."

Cole gave a nod, not trusting his voice.

Hunter rose and hugged him.

"You were awesome today," Cole said. "You saved us."

"You're awesome too," Hunter said. "We've got this. Go find Tessa."

Cole let go of his brother and ran down the slope toward the horses. He tried not to think about the bodies of his friends. It felt good to be moving. For now he could concentrate on getting to the temple and pretend he could outrun all that had happened today.

CHAPTER
— 13 —
TEMPLE

Despite having plenty of money, Cole slept on the ground and ate mostly from his provisions while traveling to the Temple of the Robust Sky. The practice freed him to stop for the night just about wherever he desired, whether or not a city was near. It also allowed him to avoid drawing attention by staying at an inn alone at his young age.

He could have made up excuses to pay for a room, but he wasn't in the mood to be around people and didn't particularly want to be comfortable. His best friends were on the brink of death. What right did he have to a soft bed and warm food? Better to get in some extra miles and hopefully make it to the temple in three days instead of four.

Throughout his lonely journey, Cole fought to ignore a host of questions. He did his best to concentrate on riding, caring for his horse, and preparing simple meals. He tried to look ahead to how he would find Tessa.

But the questions persistently leaked through his defenses. Why had he made that bargain with Sando? After accepting the deal, why hadn't he departed from the group? Why hadn't he seen the tragedy coming? Why had they trusted Tuto? Why had so many of them entered Gamat Rue? Why hadn't they at least insisted on Mira staying behind? Why had Jace and Joe volunteered to die?

He wished he could go back and make different choices. Destiny and Honor had tried to warn him! Even Sando and Tuto had offered clues! Why hadn't he seen the signs?

At his most rational, Cole knew he couldn't change what had happened. But it was hard to stay sensible. He spent long stretches of his ride stewing over the fatal mistakes that had culminated at Gamat Rue.

The Temple of the Robust Sky came into view on the third evening after leaving the ruined prison. Spired buildings loomed atop a terraced ridge, with staircases descending to numerous gardens and smaller structures at lower elevations. A dark gray wall around the base of the modified ridge enclosed the massive complex.

Cole reached a large gate in the wall as the last embers of sunset dwindled on the horizon. The great doors stood open, but a pair of uniformed guards asked him to halt.

"Can I come in?" Cole asked.

"Riding alone?" one of the guards inquired, a bald man with a tiny mustache.

"I'm catching up to my parents," Cole said, hoping the lie would help avoid further questions.

"Then I expect they already made your donation," the guard said. "You're staying the night?"

"I think so," Cole said. "I'm not sure where to go."

"You would be in the family dormitories," the guard said. "North side of the temple grounds, lowest level. Your first stop should be the north stable."

"Thanks," Cole said.

"Proceed." The guard waved him forward.

Cole rode through the gateway, feeling quietly pleased. He was getting better at acting casual. Jace would approve. Cole tried not to picture his friend's lifeless body sprawled on the hillside. Too late. The image took center stage in his mind.

Cole knew he needed to emphasize the positive. Jace was an echo someplace, probably trapped, but not completely gone. There was a chance he could be restored to life.

Night deepened as Cole made his way around the long ridge toward the north side. Light seeped from windows and glowed from street lanterns, all of it dim.

Cole needed answers. What made a temple different from a shrine? This one clearly had more buildings. Could some of the people he saw be echoes? Or did that only happen in certain areas? What did it take to access the top of the ridge? Those buildings were the largest and looked the most official. How late could he go up there? Figures were still visible on the stairways and roaming the terraces.

And of course the big question for now—how could he get in front of the prelate?

Cole reached the north stable and paid to have his horse kept there for a week. The stablehand, a lanky fellow with crooked teeth, seemed friendly enough, so Cole tried to mine some information.

"This is my first time here," Cole mentioned after paying the man. "How late is everything open?"

"Don't you know?" the stablehand replied with a chuckle. "This is the only temple open all hours. It's hard to stargaze in the day or watch the sun and clouds at night."

Cole nodded. The temple was named for the sky. And it covered a tall ridge. People used it like an observatory. "Is it hard to meet the prelate?"

"Elana Parson? What do you think? She oversees the whole temple. Unless she's giving a speech on a holiday, not many people see her besides the clerics."

"Makes sense," Cole said, a plan already forming. "Do you know where I could find writing supplies?"

After hearing the answer, Cole rushed off.

Night had fully fallen by the time Cole climbed the stairs, a rolled message in his hand. Addressed to the Honorable Prelate of the Temple of the Robust Sky, the missive was sealed with wax bearing the imprint of the royal seal he had taken from Mira.

When Cole finally reached the ridgetop, the muscles in his legs burned. He turned, pausing to enjoy the view. From the high vantage, the horizon seemed low, opening up an unobstructed panorama of blazing stars. No moon had risen, and the dim lanterns used throughout the temple grounds created little light pollution. Not only did uncountable stars of varying brightness gleam in diverse shades, but even the luminous clouds of nebulae and the swirly smudges of galaxies stood out against the unfathomable blackness.

Cole lingered. The staggering view made him feel small and large at the same time—small because of the vastness represented by the spectacle, large because at the present moment, it was all on display for him, as if he had found the aquarium that held the universe.

"Keep moving, please," a voice prompted from behind him.

"Sorry," Cole said, turning. "It's just so spectacular."

He now faced a man in a dark robe with short blond hair. "No quarrel on that point," the man said. "But the walkways are for traveling. We have many viewing areas for stargazing."

"Maybe you can help me," Cole said. "I'm new here, and I have a message for the prelate." He held up the rolled missive but didn't offer it for examination.

The man held out a hand. "I can see that it finds her."

"Sorry," Cole said. "I'm a royal errand boy, and this carries the royal seal. I'm under orders to personally deliver it."

The man heaved a sigh that conveyed the absurdity of protocols. "Very well. Come with me. I'll introduce you to Ingrid. She has access to the prelate. No promises that you can gain audience this evening."

"As long as the prelate knows that the message came a long way," Cole said. "And that the Crown considers it a high priority."

The man gestured for Cole to follow. Cole felt he had sounded official. His brief time spent as an actual royal errand boy had given him some lingo to draw from and knowledge of certain procedures. He had an explanation ready for why he wasn't dressed in livery, but since the subject didn't come up, he didn't want to oversell his cover story.

Some of the buildings atop the ridge had no roofs. Many featured porches and balconies where people gathered to gaze heavenward.

"This is beautiful," Cole commented as they walked along.

"If you appreciate the sky, before you depart, try to take in the view from the Tower of Eternity. Many viewing areas offer generous vistas in certain directions, but only from the summit of the tower is the fullness of the firmament exposed no matter where you turn."

"Sounds incredible," Cole said sincerely.

"Normally, an appointment is required, but if the prelate appreciates your message, Ingrid could make arrangements."

They found Ingrid inside a brightly lit, windowless room within one of the larger buildings. Her brown hair was pulled back in a small, tight bun, and she wore dark robes like her colleague. Outside, Cole had thought the material was black, but now he could see it was a very dark blue.

"May I inspect the seal?" Ingrid asked after Cole explained his intention.

Cole handed over the rolled message. She took a close look.

"This comes from the High King, you say?"

"It's either his seal or his chamberlain's, I think," Cole said. Actually, he wasn't sure if Mira's seal was the same as the High King's or anybody else's, so he was trying to be vague.

"We seldom get direct messages from the High Shaper," Ingrid said. "I suppose the prelate will want to see it."

Cole held out his hand, and Ingrid returned the message. "Wait here." She left the room.

"May I be excused?" the man asked. "I have duties elsewhere."

"Sure," Cole said.

Cole waited alone for several minutes before Ingrid returned. She gave him a nod. "This way."

Ingrid led him down some hallways with intricate carvings on the walls and stopped in front of a large door made from dark red wood. After knocking briefly, Ingrid opened it.

They stepped through the doorway into a sizable residence. The ceiling, walls, and floors were composed of dark gray stone, brightened by patterned rugs and tapestries. Some of the tables and chairs incorporated the same dark red wood as the door.

A woman sat regally in a high-backed chair facing the door. She looked stern, and a little defiant, with streaks of silver in her wavy black hair. Cole guessed she was a little older than his mom.

"Pardon the interruption, Madam Prelate," Ingrid said. "This errand boy claims to bear a message from the High Shaper."

"You may approach," Elana said.

Cole noticed from the imprints on the rug that the chair had been recently repositioned. The prelate must have wanted it to feel more like he was entering a throne room. He crossed to Elana and handed her the rolled message. She inspected the seal, then stared at him.

"I'm supposed to watch you read it," Cole said.

The prelate broke the seal and unrolled the message. Cole couldn't see the words, but he knew what he had written.

Dear Prelate Elana,

On my honor, I am looking for my destiny. The seal is royal, but not from the person you might think. It's a miracle I'm here. Could we please speak in private? I have news, and I need information.

Many thanks,
Cole

He had done his best to communicate indirectly in case somebody intercepted the note. But he had also wanted to make sure she would understand what he meant. He watched her scan the words.

Elana looked up from the message, her eyes first fixing on Cole, then Ingrid.

"I wish to interview this messenger in private," Elana said.

"As you will," Ingrid said, withdrawing from the room.

Elana's eyes softened. "You poor boy. I'm sorry for the cold reception. The High Shaper is not a favorite of mine. I try to turn a brave face in his direction. Who are you?"

"I work with Princess Miracle," Cole said. "We know Destiny is in trouble. We think she came here."

"Where is Miracle?" Elana asked. "Is she well?"

"We ran into trouble," Cole said. "Her echo was captured."

165

Elana closed her eyes briefly and gripped the arms of her chair. "Dire tidings. Where will it end? Her body?"

"Other friends were stabilizing her when I left," Cole said.

"Good news has become a rarity. I take it you want my help?"

"My mission is to find Destiny."

Elana shook her head. "These are grim times in Necronum. Even grimmer in the echolands. You are not a weaver."

"My shaping power is weird," Cole said. "And damaged. But I have to help Destiny."

"You're so young, dear."

"I already helped Mira get her shaping power back, and Honor, and Constance."

"All three?" Elana asked, impressed. "And here you stand. Constance is well?"

"Last I saw," Cole said. "Not too long ago."

"I can see that you believe your words," Elana said. "I also see your horrendously mangled shaping power. What happened to you?" Her concern seemed genuine.

"An evil shapecrafter attacked me. We defeated her, but my power doesn't work anymore."

"What a world. So harsh. So violent. You are weary. Can I offer you a refreshment?"

"I'd rather find out about Destiny. Did she come here?"

Elana gave a small nod and stood. "Follow me."

She led him to a different room. Cole noticed a large balcony outside the room, offering a magnificent view. He wanted to go take a good look, but she turned away from the balcony, pulled back a tapestry, inserted a key, and opened a hidden door.

Cole followed Elana down a steep, winding stairwell with bright lanterns on the walls. "We're dropping deep into the ridge to my most private chamber," she explained. "My quarters are protected against eavesdropping, but our destination is even more secure."

"I noticed you don't have guards," Cole said.

"Not all guards are visible, dearheart," Elana replied. "Especially in Necronum."

The observation left Cole pensive. And a little creeped out. He peered ahead and behind with greater attention. How many unseen echoes were watching him right now?

"Careful, these steps get steeper and narrower and are not entirely even," Elana said. "They may one day be the death of me."

Cole took her advice and stepped cautiously as the curving stairs became more precarious. By the time they reached the bottom, the temperature was much cooler. A short hall gave access to an iron door recessed in thick stone.

"Open for the prelate and her guest," Elana demanded, and the door swung inward without her touching it.

They passed into a hall, through another door, down another long stairway, and stopped before a heavy door of dark red wood, expertly carved with a host of human faces the size of golf balls. Muttering words that Cole didn't catch, Elana pressed two of the faces, one high on the right, the other low on the left, and twisted them in opposite directions.

The door swung open.

"After you," Elana invited, taking a lantern from a hook on the wall.

Cole entered but stayed ready to dive backward in case she tried to slam the door behind him and lock him inside. Recent events had taught him to be a little paranoid. Instead of springing a trap, Elana followed him in and closed the door.

The same dark red wood as the door paneled the fairly large room. The lantern's light revealed a table and chairs, a writing desk, and four cots against the far wall. Three of the cots were occupied.

"Tessa!" Cole cried in surprise, dashing forward. Tessa lay on one cot, Honor on another, Desmond on the third. Cole had recently spoken with the imprints of Honor and Tessa, but he hadn't seen the former knight of Blackmont Castle since they had parted ways after fighting Morgassa. Their eyes were closed. They didn't appear to breathe.

Cole turned to Elana. "Are they . . . ?"

"In longsleep," Elana said. "Destiny came here alone, and I helped her cross over at her insistence. Imagine my surprise! I had no idea the daughters of Stafford Pemberton had survived. I assumed the rumors were idle speculation. Some days later, Honor arrived with Desmond. I helped them cross to the echolands in search of Destiny."

Cole buried his face in his hands. Why couldn't he get a break? They had all gone to the echolands. If he was going to go after them, he would have to become a ghost too. The prospect made him queasy. He had secretly hoped that maybe he would find Destiny in hiding. But she and Honor were both in the same realm as Mira.

"You can't wake them up?" Cole asked.

"Not unless their echoes return to the temple," Elana said.

"Would you know if they returned?" Cole asked.

"That's my job, dear," Elana said. "I supervise the affairs of the temple on both sides."

"Oh," Cole said. "Any news about them?" He gestured at the bodies on the cots.

"Not since they left," Elana replied. "I'm sorry. I know it's distressing. I've been worried myself."

Cole gazed at the still forms of Honor, Tessa, and Desmond. Was Mira resting on a similar cot somewhere? Jace? Joe? Did they look this peaceful? The daydream of them in repose on cots was much preferable to his memories of them discarded in the weeds.

"Can you send me?" Cole asked.

"Yes," Elana said hesitantly. "But *can* and *should* might be separate matters."

"Not today," Cole said. "I have to go after them."

"You've never been to the echolands?" Elana asked.

"Never."

"And I gather you're new to Necronum?"

"A couple of weeks," Cole said.

Elana wrung her hands. "I wasn't sure whether to obey Destiny and send her. She is so little! But she has lived more years than her appearance suggests, and she described dangers too profound to ignore. Now another child wants my help to start a perilous road. You can't possibly fathom the danger involved."

"Story of my life since coming to the Outskirts," Cole

said. "I'm not excited to do this. I know it isn't safe. I know I may never return. But I have to try. I promised Mira. It's my duty."

Placing her hands on her hips, Elana considered Cole thoughtfully. "A strong sense of purpose can go far on the other side. Still, you only get one echo, dearheart. If it perishes, you move on permanently. Worse, an echo can be captured and bound. Time works differently in the echolands. You could be imprisoned for a duration that we can't comprehend from a mortal perspective."

Cole didn't like the implications. At least in a normal prison, you knew that one day death would free you. But Tessa was already facing the danger of being captured forever. So was Mira. "You have an empty cot."

"It's no accident," Elana replied. "Destiny told me that three others would come looking for her. She expressed that I needn't bother to send additional rescuers. Honor came here with a single companion. The other fell at Gamat Rue. I assumed that Destiny had failed to predict his demise and got two rescuers instead of three. But here you are. Alone."

Her words gave Cole tingles along his spine. It also helped strengthen his resolve. Destiny had real power. If she had seen a third person coming after her, and he had found his way here, it meant this could be part of a grand design.

"What do I need to know?" Cole asked.

"Destiny went in search of her power," Elana said. "Besides predicting that three others would come after her, she revealed no details. Honor was searching for her sister. She didn't disclose any specifics."

"I think I know where Destiny was going," Cole said.

"So did Honor," Elana said sadly. "The echolands are in a state of turmoil not seen in many lifetimes. If not for Destiny's prediction, I would not send you."

"I'd just find somebody who would," Cole said.

Elana considered him with pity. "That won't be necessary. Are you ready to cross?"

"No point in losing more time. My brother might come along with a friend. If so, could you let them know where I went?"

"I'll watch for them," Elana said. "Would you please recline on the empty cot?"

Cole got settled. After sleeping on the ground for the previous several days, the simple bed felt comfy. "Any tips?"

"I'll greet you on the other side and advise you there," Elana said. "May I have permission to disconnect your lifespark from your corporeal body?"

Cole studied her warily. "Does that give you power to do what you want with my spark?"

"Only to send it to the echolands," Elana said. "This being your first visit, an echo will form to house it."

"Do I have to do anything?"

"Just grant me permission."

Hunter had heard that Elena was one of the good guys. And she had greeted Cole harshly when she thought he represented Stafford Pemberton. That was a plus. Also, she had been watching over Destiny and Honor. He had to trust somebody and probably wouldn't find a better candidate. "Okay. Go for it."

A wave of energy surged through Cole, saturating him with sensation. In a single burst he saw light, darkness, and every color of the spectrum. He smelled numerous fragrances—sharp, sweet, and foul. Diverse sounds assailed his ears—loud and quiet, jarring and melodic. He tasted sweetness, saltiness, sourness, and bitterness. Over his entire body he felt pain, pleasure, heat, cold, and a gut-clenching jolt of electricity.

The sensory overload left him shaken. He lay still, eyes closed, recovering, until a hand took his and helped him to his feet.

Elana looked the same, except her skin had a gentle glow, as if more light were striking her than anything else in the room. The chamber looked basically the same, except the stone of the walls and floor was now white, and all four cots were empty.

CHAPTER

—❧— 14 —❧—

DUSKDAY

A re we there?" Cole asked.

"Welcome to the echolands," Elana said.

"You got here quickly."

"I instructed a colleague to bring my echo to this room."

"When?" Cole wondered.

"As we spoke."

"With telepathy?"

"Mind to mind, yes."

Cole shook out his arms and alternated kicking his legs. "I don't feel different."

"You're still you," Elana said. "The echolands have substance. The material here is just more refined than in the physical world you know."

Cole nudged the cot with his toe. It felt normal. He pinched his wrist. That felt normal too. He noticed that his hands had an extra glow to them. "Am I shining?"

Elana smiled. "We're called bright echoes when we're still connected to a living body in the mortal world. The extra light makes us stand out a little, but also carries some advantages." She gave a perplexed scowl. "You still have your sword."

Cole drew his Jumping Sword. The blade had a faint gleam similar to the subtle shine of his skin. "Is that weird?"

"Duplicate versions of your clothes appear to cross over. But no other items. Not unless you've put some of yourself into them."

"The sword came from Sambria," Cole said, sheathing the blade. "I used my shaping power to make it work in Elloweer."

"Interesting," she said. "The action must have forged a personal bond with it. You'll notice that not many people carry weapons in the echolands. But considering your mission, you might be happy to have one."

"Do people get killed here?" Cole asked.

"Come with me," Elana said, leading him from the room. The stone in the hall had also brightened from gray to white. "We'll talk as we walk. Echoes can die. But not typically in combat. Death by physical trauma requires a lot of damage. Echoes don't bleed. They don't suffer from sickness or infection."

"Is my sword useless?" Cole asked.

"Not completely," Elana said. "In a pinch, you could hurt or kill an echo with it. But consider the weapon a last resort. You'll find different social patterns here than in mortality. There is a camaraderie like you might expect among castaways. They've all left their former lives behind. They're clinging to this phase of existence, or else they would move on. There is no shortage of food or shelter to motivate crime, and most echoes lack many of the drives and passions inherent in our physical bodies, which tends to make them gentler. How do you feel, Cole?"

Now that she mentioned it, he felt better than he had in days. "Really good, actually. I was pretty tired, but I feel refreshed."

"The physical needs of an echo are different from a mortal body," Elana explained. "Before you crossed over, your body was tired and hungry, but you left those needs behind. You don't require sleep here. Or food. Or water. At least not how a physical body needs those things. You won't age. But there are some new challenges. Your echo won't naturally heal. And your energy can fade." She stopped at a door. "Do you hear the music?"

Cole recalled Hunter describing the disturbing music that greeted him when he crossed over at Gamat Rue. Bowing his head, Cole listened. Barely audible, as if originating several rooms away, gentle strains reached his ears. Or was the music playing in his imagination? Long, slow, rich chords gradually evolved. No individual instruments stood out. He felt the emotion of the tune as much as he heard it. "Faintly."

"The music is seldom softer than when you're inside a temple," Elana said. "Everything in the echolands has music to it. The places, the land, the vegetation, every animal, every person. Some of the music is easy to discern. Some takes great talent and practice to recognize."

"Do I have music?" Cole asked.

"Yes, you poor boy," Elana said, stroking his hair. "The

specific music of a person can be tricky to apprehend. It takes practice. Yours is confusing and discordant."

"Why?"

"Your shaping power is in disarray."

"That comes through?"

Elana nodded. "Some weavers devote their entire effort to reading music. The most skilled can apprehend surprising details without ever seeing you. They can judge your mood or uncover a lie. They can also locate a person across great distances. But you don't need to worry about any of that yet. You must first learn to beware the music of the Other."

"That's what lies beyond the echolands," Cole said.

"The echolands are a way station," Elana explained. "This is only the first stage of the afterlife. None can say how many stages lie beyond. At least one. Some have taken up long-term residence here with considerable success, but they can only do so by resisting the call of the Other. The more time you spend in the echolands, the more beguiling that invitation becomes."

"Is the call quieter in the temples, like the music?" Cole asked.

"That's one advantage of the temples." Elana opened the door, revealing a staircase that wound upward. This looked different from the way they had come down. "They protect you from being summoned into the next phase of existence."

Cole followed her up the steps. "Are there tricks besides hiding in temples?"

"Don't be caught by surprise. The music of the Other tastes like home. You'll know it when you sense it. At different times, that particular music calls to different individuals at varying intensity. No other music in the echolands is as beautiful or as alluring. Eventually, it becomes irresistible. Unless you wish to move on, the music of the Other is the greatest threat in the echolands. It claims far more lives than any other hazard."

"How do I resist?" Cole asked.

"Being a bright echo helps, especially at first. You should be almost completely immune for a time. It helps to stay where the music is quieter, or in places with strong enough music to overpower the call. It helps not to stray to the fringes of the echolands. It also helps when you have reasons to remain. More than a few echoes make bargains with people in Necronum primarily to anchor themselves against the call. Of course, whenever possible, you should stay away from the channels."

"Channels?" Cole asked.

Elana shook her head. "You're so new here. So underprepared. It was criminal of me to let you cross over."

"It's not your fault. I insisted. So did Destiny. I can learn. Tell me what I need to know."

"Channels are like rivers," Elana said. "They're also unlike rivers."

"What do you mean?"

"Channels sometimes correspond to rivers and streams in physical Necronum," she said. "But the substance flowing through them is not water. We call it ether. It moves quickly, a wild hybrid of wind, water, and music, and always flows away from the Source at the center of the echolands, out toward the fringe. The music of the ether harmonizes with the music of the Other. If it draws you in, you'll be swept away."

"So don't wade in the rivers," Cole said.

Elana smiled sadly. "That's putting it lightly. Flowing ether is nicknamed a slipstream. If you enter, you won't come out."

"They all start at one place?" Cole asked.

"There is a churning fountain at the center of the echolands called the Source," she said. "Channels of ether large and small flow away from it."

They reached an iron door flanked by two guards in dark blue robes. Their skin didn't glow like Elana's. They silently opened the door and let them pass. Elana led Cole down a few corridors. They went through another door and started up another stairwell.

"Do you have normal rivers?" Cole asked.

"Water is a rare resource here," Elana said. "Fortunately, it's not needed. Your echo doesn't even need air to survive."

"I'm breathing," Cole said.

"I breathe too," Elana said. "And you can eat and drink, if you choose. Go ahead and try not breathing."

Cole held his breath as they climbed the stairs. She was right. As the seconds ticked by, the need to exhale never increased.

"Weird," he finally said.

"No harm in breathing," Elana said. "No harm in losing the habit. Echoes who have been here for centuries do it both ways. Eating is another matter. Your echo can survive without eating, but food can be helpful, as well as subtly harmful."

"How?" Cole asked.

"We don't bake in the echolands. We don't eat meat. But you will find abundant fruit and vegetables. Consuming these in moderation can help replenish your energy. It can improve focus. We don't sleep here, but we can slide into trances. Keeping your energy up with occasional meals helps you avoid accidental trances."

"Are the trances bad?" Cole asked.

"They can have benefits," Elana said. "Trances rest the mind much like sleep does. They occur as you get lost in certain music. If you slip into a trance here at the temple, chances are you will simply meditate. But if you are drawn into a trance while listening to the call of the Other, you could end up wandering off toward the fringe or into a channel."

"How can food be harmful?"

"If you eat too much, you can become more susceptible to unwanted trances. Consume too little, and your energy can seep away with similar consequences."

"How do you get it right?" Cole asked.

Elana gave him a pitying look. "This is one of many reasons I'm worried about you exploring this place on your own. The echolands are riddled with unique perils. It takes time to learn how to survive here."

"Doesn't everyone come here when they die?" Cole asked. "Aren't people getting used to it all the time?"

"Many only visit briefly," Elana said. "They often move on to the Other before long. There are debates regarding the purpose of the echolands. I believe they are a landscape of forgetting—a place to shake off your attachments to mortality, especially to let go of your heartaches and regrets. The more time you spend here, the more distant you will feel from your former life, causing less reluctance to proceed to the Other. If you want to last in the echolands, it takes effort. If you come here as a bright echo, once your lifeforce goes to the Other, your physical body will truly die."

"At least this proves there's life after death," Cole said. "I used to worry about that a lot."

"It's a consolation, but beware of that mindset," Elana said. "Accepting death can give the music of the Other extra power over you. The certainty of life after death doesn't mean we need to rush through any of the previous phases. It's a comfort to know the Other is there. We'll head that way when the time comes, but why pass on before we must?"

"Makes sense," Cole agreed. They were still going up. "Lots of stairs."

"Are you tired?" she asked.

"Not a bit," Cole realized.

"Physically, you could keep going forever," Elana said. "The key is maintaining the energy of your will."

"Tired or not, I could just get sick of climbing stairs."

"Exactly. A strong will is your best weapon in the Outskirts. It can protect you from the Other and from those who seek to control you. Here we are!"

The stairway ended at a room with a ladder that led up to a hatch in the ceiling. Elana climbed up and opened the hatch, revealing a deep blue sky. Following her, Cole emerged onto the flat top of a lofty tower edged with low golden railings.

Cole slowly turned in a circle, trying to absorb the stunning view. It was a duskday—all horizons were aglow as if multiple suns were poised to rise, but the colors looked richer and brighter than any duskday he had seen, and the higher regions of the sky were a deep blue that seemed more appropriate for gemstones. Not a single cloud trespassed in the vivid firmament.

But the sky wasn't the most striking surprise.

Cole could hardly believe the color and beauty of the land visible in all directions—gleaming channels, lush lawns, splendid trees, colorful shrubs, and abundant flowers all vied for attention. Only some scattered boulders and buildings lacked vegetation. He saw no empty dirt and no dead plants. For miles around, the terrain appeared immaculately landscaped.

He glanced between the sky and the ground. The glorious horizon shed a warm, even light from all directions, virtually eliminating shadow. The vibrant colors reminded Cole of something. . . .

It came to him in a flash. The Red Road at the Lost Palace! After he crossed into Trillian the torivor's prison, the Red Road had seemed redder than any red he had ever witnessed. The colors arrayed before him had that same quality—bluer than blue, greener than green, whiter than white. They were the familiar colors he knew, but intensified to a degree that he had not known was possible.

"It's paradise," Cole marveled.

"More or less," Elana said. "It's inarguably beautiful."

"Shouldn't it be nighttime?" Cole asked.

"It's always like this here," Elana said. "No sun in the sky. No moon, no stars. Just an endless duskday."

"How do you keep track of time?" Cole wondered.

"When you crossed over, you took a big step away from time and toward eternity," Elana said. "Time is chiefly relevant in the echolands as it pertains to the physical Outskirts."

"How do you make appointments?" Cole asked.

Elana laughed, and there was music in it, a light melody Cole felt more than heard. "That can be a problem. There are still some elements of time. At the temples, for example, we use hourglasses to stay aware of the time in Necronum. We don't have sunrise, or sunset, or seasons. Nothing really ages or dies, except for the occasional new fruit or plant growing to replace something that was removed. But feelings and attitudes still change. And people grow more susceptible to the music of the Other. Wherever you can find change, there are elements of time."

"Too deep for me," Cole said. "How do I know when to eat?"

"Eat when your energy gets low," Elana said. "One item is usually enough—an apple or a carrot. Avoid eating for the pleasure of it. Eat to replenish."

Cole looked down on the other brilliant white buildings and spires of the temple. No other structure rose high enough to obstruct their view of the sky or the landscape. "Is this the Tower of Eternity?"

"Yes," Elana said. "I have visited the other temples, and this is my favorite place in any of them."

"The echolands are big," Cole said, scanning the horizon and trying to imagine what lay beyond.

"Much bigger than Necronum," Elana said. "The echolands stretch on and on, with no known end, though if you venture too far from the Source, you will probably not return."

"Do you eventually reach the Other?" Cole asked.

She shrugged. "Could be. None who got near enough to know have returned to tell. And nobody has deciphered any clues in the music."

"I think I heard your music when you laughed," Cole said.

"That could be," Elana said. "Yours became more fluid when you first gazed at our surroundings. Cole, I hate to pry, but I wish you would tell me where you are going. I could at least steer you in the proper direction."

Cole considered her offer. He would have to ask directions from somebody. He should be able to trust Elana more than some stranger. "Will you keep it a secret?"

She gave a knowing smile. "You want a pledge from me? Are you sure you're new to Necronum?"

"I've already been burned."

"I hope it served as a learning experience. I will not share your secret, if that is your wish."

"It's called Deepwell. In the Hundred Forests."

By the way she inhaled, Cole could tell it wasn't good. "I see."

"Scary?"

"Unsafe," Elana said. "There are regions in the echolands where the music becomes . . . unsavory. Like the discord of your mangled power. Gamat Rue is such a place. Some of these tormented locations are ancient. An alarming amount are new. Deepwell is such a place. We blame the followers of a new power in the echolands. A power that recently assumed a name."

"Nazeem," Cole whispered.

"Speak of him sparingly, even in the safety of a temple," Elana said. "I have feared he might be involved with the princesses."

"He taught the people who stole their abilities," Cole said. "His followers want to take control of their shaping powers."

"They practice a strange art that predates weaving or shaping as we know it."

"They call it shapecraft."

"It threatens the very fabric of our reality," Elana said. "Should this art continue to spread, I'm not sure the Outskirts will survive."

"He plans to escape his prison soon," Cole said.

"Where did you hear this?"

"I snuck into a secret meeting of shapecrafters."

Genuine fear filled her eyes. "How?"

"In Junction," Cole said. "Long story."

"Did he know?"

Cole nodded. "He's after me."

She raised her fist to her mouth and bit her knuckle. "He is like no power we have known. You should not have come here, Cole. I should return you to your body and you should get far from Necronum."

Cole tried not to let her concern become contagious. He already knew Nazeem was dangerous. "I have to find Destiny. She told you three people would come after her. Our enemy wants her power. I have to find her first."

"What if he already has her?" Elana asked.

"Then I have to save her."

"Such courage," she murmured. It sounded less like a compliment and more like she pitied him. "What is to be done? I'm tempted to offer you a guide, but I'm unsure who I can fully trust, and I worry about tampering with Destiny's instructions. Her gift is authentic."

"Just show me the right direction," Cole said.

She pointed into the distance. "That way. It can be difficult to stay oriented. You'll need help. You did well playing a messenger. I take it you actually are a royal errand boy?"

"The Unseen helped me become an errand boy to meet the queen," Cole said. "How could you tell?"

"Lies are conspicuous in the echolands," Elana said. "They come through as disharmony in your music. I only caught the smallest whiff of falsehood when you delivered your message to me. It was so faint that I dismissed it as accidental. You really were an errand boy. The message really had a royal seal. And you were confident that Princess Miracle would have wanted you to reach me. Your ruse worked. So you will deliver a message for me."

"Okay," Cole said. "Do I get a horse?"

Elana gave a small frown. For a moment, Cole caught the bittersweet music of the emotion. "You have so much to learn. Animals seldom dwell for long in the echolands. They swiftly move on to the Other. They can't be compelled to remain. Only a very special bond will keep an animal in the echolands, usually associated with a specific companion."

"Everybody just walks?"

"Almost all of us. Some clever weavers have designed alternate means of transportation. And a few echoes have animal companions. The lack of mounts makes long-distance travel a chore. Or so I understand. I've never tried it. Let's make this official. I hereby commission you as an errand boy of this temple. I will give you a message to deliver to Lottie Natt of the Sweet Channel Charnel House. It is the most reputable destination near the Hundred Forests. This way you can ask for directions without appearing to look for Deepwell. Once you find Lottie, you can get her advice on reaching your actual destination. The message will introduce you to her and urge her to offer assistance. She is an old friend."

"That's a great idea," Cole said.

"I'll place a weaving on the message that should help mask your personal music. Many will be searching for you. The weaving will help protect you from all but the most careful scrutiny. When you reach Lottie, she can give you an even more disruptive talisman. Such items are a specialty of hers. I'll solicit one for you in the message."

"Thank you so much," Cole said.

Elana took his hands in hers. "I wish I could do more. My heart aches to think of the danger you will face. You have a mission, Cole. At this moment, you see it clearly. Fight to maintain that clarity. You must succeed. Survive for those you need to help. Survive for the good of all the Outskirts. Survive to return to your loved ones. Hold true."

"I will," Cole said.

"Echoes may try to trick you into deals. Make no bargains. Never surrender your will. That may sound easy now, but it can get complicated. Cling to your duties, Cole. They can save you. Cling to life."

Her earnestness was a little unnerving. "Okay."

"As you travel the echolands, heed the music. It can serve as a compass, guiding you to comfort and companionship and warning you away from danger. Whenever possible, avoid music that makes you uncomfortable. The only alluring music you must shun is the call of the Other. You will know that song when you hear it."

"Are you sure?"

She nodded. "We all know it. The call feels like home, and an end to everything else. You won't go because you're deceived. When we move on, we go willingly."

"That's almost scarier," Cole said.

"Exactly right."

ECHOLANDS

Beyond the temple walls, Cole experienced the music of the echolands unmuted. Throughout his life, during movies or on audio devices, he had listened to music that conveyed certain emotions—sadness or excitement or anger. But here the emotional nuances came through much more precisely, sometimes ahead of the audible cues.

Cole couldn't discern individual instruments in the music, and it was hard to pick out melodies that he could hum, but the enchanting euphony brought profound feelings of refreshment, tranquility, wonder, and grandeur. Outside the gates, the music specific to the temple also gained clarity. Though wordless, it sounded more like human voices than the other music around him, transmitting a sense of importance and solemnity.

Some other echoes came and went from the gate, a couple of them bright. None showed particular interest in Cole. As he moved away from the temple, he soon found himself walking alone.

Cole knew that danger awaited him. The beauty around him concealed hidden perils. But as he marched across the springy grass, enveloped by sublime music, he couldn't suppress his high spirits. This wilderness looked like what gardens aspired to be but never quite achieved. The uniformly green turf would be the envy of the most exclusive golf course. Shrubs, flowers, and trees were artfully grouped, all their blossoms in full bloom, every color resplendent beyond description. There were no dead branches, no fallen leaves. Nothing was wilting or drying out. Everything in view was gloriously thriving.

The farther he hiked, the more Cole felt like he was on a stroll in the world's largest and most immaculate park. Despite plentiful groves of trees and extensive flower beds, with a little zigzagging he never had to leave the flawless grass. No natural wilderness could feel this orderly. Wherever he looked, Cole found ideal spots to spread out a quilt and enjoy a picnic lunch. He had a hazardous mission to fulfill. Destiny, Honor, and Mira were in trouble. But it required effort to sulk when everything looked and sounded so heavenly. Whenever he let his guard down, feelings of serenity and wonder soothed his heart.

Cole didn't want to get too relaxed. He needed to stay ready. No matter how pretty the echolands were, no matter how inspiring the music felt, Sando was out there somewhere, along with other servants of Nazeem. Cole drew his Jumping Sword but soon felt ridiculous. What was he going to stab? The tree with the gorgeous apples? The enormous rosebushes? There was nothing to fight. Not even weeds.

Though constant, the music stopped short of becoming intrusive. As he grew used to the complex harmonies, they receded into the background, though certain details came through more clearly if he paid deliberate attention. When Cole paused to admire a field ablaze with wildflowers, the gentle music specific to the flowers became more prominent. Apparently, in the echolands you didn't just stop and smell the roses—you could listen to them as well.

The temple shrank in the distance. Soon Cole found he could only hear its music if he stared at it and focused. It was strange how the level of his attention altered the volume. He experimented with emphasizing certain trees, or a hill, along with just soaking in the broader soundscape.

He began to notice the absence of animals. Cole had journeyed a lot in the Outskirts, and there were always insects buzzing, little critters rustling in the brush, birds on limbs or in the sky, and occasional larger beasts spotted from a distance. But here there was no animal life—no birds, no rodents, no bugs. The companionship of the music helped mask their absence, but the lack of other people and animals started to make the breathtaking beauty seem a little more sinister. There was a difference between an enormous beautiful garden and an enormous beautiful *deserted* garden.

Everywhere except right by the gate to the temple, Cole also found no roads or paths. Before he departed, Elana had mentioned the general lack of roads. Without horses, carts, wild animals, or many traveling echoes, how could trails form? Since the landscape tended to be easy to cross, the sparse travelers weren't funneled along a particular route.

Having too many convenient, grassy ways he could turn became a problem. Cole tried to watch landmarks to keep his path straight, but once the temple was out of view, the task got more difficult. He hoped he wasn't curving away from the direction Elana had indicated.

The temperature remained the kind of comfortable that drew little attention. Not too hot, not too cold, no breeze. Ideal for walking. Or sitting. Or hiking forever.

It took some time for Cole to really grasp that the day was never going to end. All horizons shed their constant light. No cloud intruded on the empty sky. Hills and groves and fields came and went. He knew he had gone farther than he had ever walked all at once. Some instinct kept suggesting he should find a place to make camp, but that impulse came from habit rather than exhaustion. His mind felt clear, his muscles unfatigued. The changing sights coupled with the stirring music kept boredom away. And the light never dimmed.

So he walked. And walked. And walked.

Only when Cole saw an elderly woman in the distance did he alter his pace, slowing almost to a stop. The woman saw him as well and veered away. Apparently, she didn't want company. He supposed that made sense, since he was a stranger.

After seeing the woman, Cole felt more alert. Had he been slipping into a trance? If so, it hadn't been hard to snap out of it when the woman came into view. Maybe his mind had just been relaxing.

He had grown accustomed to the harmonies and emotions

of the forests and fields, but from up ahead, he heard something new—rushing, whistling music like an orchestrated windstorm. Curious, Cole quickened his pace in that direction.

Coming over a shallow rise, he got his first close look at a channel. The strange river looked like dense, silver mist whipping along at the speed of a gale. As he focused on the ether, the symphonic whistling drowned out the rest of the music around him.

Cole hurried to the bank of the channel. The slipstream was broad enough that only his best throw would put a stone across it. As Cole studied the rushing current up close, he found streaks of every shade of gray between brilliant white and deepest black.

He felt tempted to crouch down and touch the rapidly flowing surface. Would the ether feel wet or windy? More like a waterfall or a tornado? How high would it spray if his hand interrupted the flow? But he recalled being warned that if he fell in, he would be swept away to the Other, so he decided against experimentation.

When Elana had told him there were infrequent paths in the echolands, she had also informed him there were many bridges over the channels. Looking left and right, Cole saw no sign of a bridge. But while his gaze lingered to the left, Cole thought he caught a hint of some unusual though not unpleasant music, so he set off in that direction.

Cole stayed away from the brink of the channel as he walked but felt invigorated by the hustle and fury of its spirited music. Eventually, the other music he had heard became clearer, conveying a sense of safety.

Soon a white stone bridge came into view, spanning the channel in a single broad arch. As Cole approached the bridge, he saw a man standing off to one side, toward the center of the span, peering over the edge at the frantic slipstream below.

On the older side of middle-aged, the man was fairly tall, with a long face and the rugged overalls of a farmer. As Cole started across the bridge, the man edged closer to the low railing at the edge of the span, eyes downward.

Curious what exactly the man might be staring at besides the slipstream, Cole sidled up to him. Gazing down with blank eyes and slack features, the man began to tip forward. Cole grabbed his overalls and yanked him back from the edge.

The man jerked, glanced down at Cole without recognition, then hastily checked his surroundings. Stepping away from Cole, he brushed at his overalls. "Thank you, young man," he mumbled absently. "Don't know what came over me."

"You were staring over the side," Cole said. "You started to lean like you were going to tip."

"I suppose I must have," he replied, seeming flustered and embarrassed. "Can't be too careful about the homesong."

Looking over the side, Cole listened to the whistling music. "That sounds like home to you?"

The man gave a soft chuckle. "New to the echolands, are you?"

"Pretty new."

"I can see the glow on you," the man said. "Hard to hear

193

the homesong at first. Especially as a tourist. Slipstream just sounds like a pretty blizzard."

Cole thought that was a good description. "Were you in a trance?"

The man put his hands on his waist. "I suppose so. I've been trying to hold out until my youngest brother comes across. Been coming to listen by the channel more and more the last while. Woke up on the bridge not too long ago. I was alone that time. Here I am again."

"Maybe you should stay away from the channel," Cole suggested.

Hooking his thumbs in his pockets, the man squinted at the countryside beyond the bridge. "I could maybe last a bit longer if I went far away. Someplace loud. But I'm expecting my brother in yonder township any day now. I don't want to wander off too far. When I'm alone, I hear the call wherever I go. That's how Ainsley, my wife, got before she moved on."

"Your wife already . . . ?"

"We were here together a good spell. She started getting dreamy. I don't blame her. Hard not to around here. I blame myself. I got distracted with word of Hank about to cross and lost track of her. Off she went. And now I catch myself lingering by the slipstream."

"I'm sorry about your wife. Isn't it dangerous to hang around here if you want to see your brother? Don't you want to wait for him?"

"Mostly I do. In theory, yes. Be good to see Hank. Show him around. But this place . . . I don't know, young man. A body couldn't rightly demand more beauty, but it's not really a place for living. Take my meaning?"

"I think so."

The man smiled. "I'm Clint."

"Bryant," Cole said, using his middle name.

"Thanks for tugging me back," Clint said. "Just prolonging the inevitable, I expect, but it was a neighborly gesture. I would have gone in headfirst without a helping hand."

"No problem," Cole said.

"If you don't mind my asking, what brings a live boy your age to a place like this?"

"I'm delivering a message from the Temple of the Robust Sky," Cole said.

Clint shook his head. "Wicked if you ask me, sending a young person to a place like this. Piece of free advice— deliver your message and get out. You have a body on the other side? Go use it. Save this place for when the time comes. It's meant to be temporary. You don't want the homesong to claim you before your time. And you don't want to get comfortable here. I haven't met a single soul who makes a career living here that seems right in the head."

"Thanks," Cole said.

"I mean no offense," the man added. "You hauled me back from the plunge. Just returning the favor. Know where you're going?"

"I'm trying to find the Sweet Channel Charnel House. Sort of near the Hundred Forests."

Clint puckered his face in thought. "Don't know those names. Might be far off. Can you hear the township?"

Cole listened. He mostly heard the bridge and the slipstream, along with a little of the countryside beyond. "Not really."

The man extended an arm. "That way. You'll hear it when you leave this ruckus behind. Somebody in the township can steer you."

"Do you want to come with me?" Cole asked.

Clint gave a nod and started walking toward the far side of the bridge. Cole joined him.

"It's just a matter of time," Clint said.

"What?"

"Before I move on. Nothing wrong with taking the next step. This place is just an echo of really living."

"I guess that explains the name."

Clint frowned. "It's no place to live. I don't know how much longer I can hold on."

"But you want to see your brother."

Clint rubbed his nose. "Yes and no. What kind of welcome is diving in the slipstream? My days are numbered. Might be kinder just to let him hear about it. Less dramatic."

They reached the far side of the bridge and started walking on grass again. A grove of tall trees with coppery bark and purple leaves sang off to one side.

"Won't he be sad you didn't wait?" Cole asked.

"Hank'll want to see me, sure. But I'm afraid I won't be good company. Might be best to meet up in the Other. I wouldn't mind seeing how Ainsley is getting on."

Cole wasn't sure what to tell him.

"Know what, Bryant? You go on ahead. Being in town makes me itchy of late. I'm going to sit a spell."

Cole hesitated. "What about—"

Clint held up a hand. "I'm not saying I'm going for a swim. I make no pledge that I won't, either." He sat down on the grass, knees bent. "I just want to turn a few things over in my mind. You did a good deed. I was lost in the home-song, sure enough. You pulled me back in case I wasn't in my right mind. I thank you for the courtesy. People move on from this place all the time, son. You did your part. Run on ahead now."

Cole still wasn't certain what to do. "Are you sure?"

Clint gave a small smile. "You're very new here. Make every stranger with an ear for the homesong your burden, and that message may never get delivered. I'm in my right mind. No trance. I have no current plan to ride the channel. I just need to sit a spell. Maybe I'll listen a bit and head back to town. I've done it before."

"All right," Cole said.

"Head between those hills," Clint said, extending an arm. "Can't miss it."

Looking that way, Cole heard hints of new music. "Okay. Bye."

Clint gave an acknowledging grunt.

Cole started walking. He checked over his shoulder a few times. Clint still sat there, hands on his knees, gazing out over the channel.

As Cole went up the shoulder of the hill, he glanced back again to see Clint stepping up onto the railing of the bridge. He must have started moving just after Cole last glanced back. The distance made the man less than an inch high. Panicked, Cole considered the distance. Was there any chance he could make it back in time?

"Clint!" Cole called.

Eyes on the slipstream, Clint lifted his arms above his head.

Cole dashed toward the bridge.

Clint toppled forward into the ether. When he hit the surface, a brief, yearning melody tugged at Cole's heart. Then the tune was gone.

Clint's body rushed along the channel at a good pace, but not as quickly as the slipstream seemed to flow. Still, there was no chance of catching up to him from where Cole stood. Clint wasn't struggling. In a few moments the man passed out of view.

Cole stared at the channel, an empty feeling in his gut. Should he have tried to drag Clint back to town? How could he have done it? Clint was a lot bigger than him. And he had acted intent on staying.

Cole reminded himself that Clint was already dead. Who knew how long he had been in the echolands? He probably missed his wife.

One thing Cole now knew for sure—the call of the Other was real and deadly. He might not hear it yet, but he would need to keep his guard up. There was a lot of living he hoped to do before leaping into a slipstream.

CHAPTER
— 16 —

FOLLOWED

Golden ivy smothered the houses in the little town, and bright gardens bloomed on the rooftops. The playful, welcoming music set Cole at ease. If the music could be trusted, he figured this should be a good place to ask for directions.

Narrow roads crisscrossed the town. The people on the streets meandered and conversed. Nobody drove a cart or manned a stand or carried a load or hammered a nail.

It didn't take long for Cole to notice a sizable crowd around one of the larger homes. He went to see what was happening.

At the edge of the crowd a balding man with a bulbous nose and a saggy gut came up to Cole. "What's your interest, tourist?" he accused.

"Just curious," Cole said, keeping his tone light and friendly. "What's going on?"

The man folded his arms. "Fun to come see the real echoes in action?"

"Lay off, Stu," a woman scolded. "He's a kid."

"All the more reason he belongs back in the real world," Stu said.

"The echolands are just as real," the woman said.

A cheer went up from the group.

"What happened?" Cole asked the woman.

"A fellow just crossed over," she said.

"To stay," Stu grumbled. "Not a vacation."

"Hank?" Cole asked.

"I think that was the name," the woman said.

"Yes," Stu said. "Hank Groat. How'd you know?"

Cole winced. "His brother just jumped into the channel."

Head pivoting, Stu searched the crowd. "Clint's not here?"

"It was Clint," Cole said.

Stu gave a scathing laugh. "I bet you loved that! Little tourist gets to watch the echo ride the slipstream?"

Cole didn't appreciate his tone. "I found him on the bridge and pulled him back before he went over the side. He told me to go on to town. He insisted. When I looked back, he . . ." Cole found the words too hard to say.

The woman pushed Stu in the chest. "Shame on you. Look at the boy! He didn't take it lightly."

Cole tried his best not to cry. Echoes might not have blood, but he could feel they had tears. He managed to keep his from spilling down his cheeks.

Stu heaved a sigh. "Happens sometimes. People take the plunge right before a loved one comes across."

"That's right," the woman said. "Clint had been dwelling

on the homesong for a good while. And his wife went not too long ago."

The crowd shifted to accommodate a moving center of attention. Stretching tall, Stu craned to see. "You got me gabbing and now I'm missing the brother." He shouldered his way closer to the center.

"How'd you know he was coming?" Cole asked.

"In a slow death, the music can signal a new arrival well before the end," the woman said.

"Why so many people?" Cole asked.

The woman smiled incredulously. "Why attend a funeral? Or a birthday? We all lived in Weatherby. Friends, relatives, acquaintances. I never knew Hank well, but his sweet mother was a friend, on the other side and here as well. Several boys in that home. Five or six. Don't know how she did it."

"Have you been here long?" Cole asked.

"Longer than most in town," the woman said. "The homesong still doesn't hold much appeal. I'm Nina."

"Bryant."

"Do you live near Weatherby?"

"No, I'm passing through."

"What prompts a healthy young man to roam the echolands?"

"I'm a messenger for the Temple of the Robust Sky."

"I see," Nina said. "Is the message for anybody here-abouts?"

"No," Cole said. "I'm looking for the Sweet Channel Charnel House, near the Hundred Forests."

"Never been friendly with geography, even in Necronum," Nina said. "Less here. But Lister will know."

"Would you introduce me?"

"Why not? Wait here."

She walked away. The crowd was moving down the street, presumably with Hank at the center. Cole couldn't get a good look at him.

As he watched the crowd progress along the street, Cole noticed a woman staring at him. She was not older than thirty, with Asian features. She stood off to the side of the group, near the corner of a house. When his eyes met hers, she glanced away and stepped out of view.

He suddenly felt on edge. Had he caught a jangle of unsettling music? Or were his instincts just warning him that she had glanced away too quickly and slid out of view too smoothly?

"This is Lister," Nina said from behind him, making Cole whirl in alarm.

An older man with a bushy gray mustache stood beside Nina. "Feeling jumpy?" Lister asked.

"A lady was staring at me," Cole said.

"We don't get many strangers," Nina said. "Especially not young ones, and especially not tourists. I'm sure more than one person was looking your way."

Cole didn't want to elaborate that something about her had felt suspicious.

"You're looking for the Hundred Forests?" Lister asked.

"And the Sweet Channel Charnel House," Cole said.

"You have a long way to go," Lister said. He pointed. "Leave town going that direction."

"Do you travel much?" Cole asked.

"More than some," Lister said. "Less than others. You're new to the echolands?"

"Pretty new," Cole admitted.

"Staying oriented can be a pain," Lister said. "Helps if you know what to listen for. The sound of the Source, of course, and the direction the channels are flowing. The music of the standard landmarks. Some study of maps doesn't hurt. It takes time to learn to navigate these parts. Some never get the hang of it."

Cole mimicked where Lister had pointed. It was not the way he would have instinctively headed. "That way."

"That's right. Until you gain some experience, listen for towns and keep asking."

"Are there many towns?" Cole asked.

"Enough," Lister said. "Just don't hop into any channels or follow unpleasant music. Hunger and exposure can't touch you here."

"Thanks," Cole said, starting down the street in the general direction Lister had indicated.

"You're welcome," Lister said.

"Go in peace," Nina added.

Cole glanced past them to where the Asian woman had disappeared. He saw no sign of her. But he didn't think it would be a bad idea to hurry out of town.

Cole glanced back several times after leaving the town. Each time he was greeted by a vacant, beautiful landscape. Could those idyllic shrubs and groves be hiding enemies? The music of the town faded until he could no longer detect it even when he strained.

Long after he no longer heard the town, Cole looked back and saw a figure coming his way across a long stretch of vivid grass. The sight startled him. It was clearly the Asian woman from the town.

She didn't try to hide when he looked her way, so Cole waited for her. She didn't speed up but came straight toward him.

"Hello," Cole said once she was about fifteen paces away. "Why are you following me?"

"You're interesting," the woman said, still closing the distance.

"Why?" Cole asked. She was now less than ten paces away. He couldn't sense her music, but Cole didn't have a good feeling about her.

"We seldom get travelers," the woman said. "The echolands can be dull that way."

When she was five paces away, Cole set a hand on the hilt of his sword. "That's close enough."

She stopped and grinned. She wore a gray dress topped by a red shawl. "Do you greet everyone while touching your sword?"

"You were watching me back in town."

"You're a stranger," she said.

"So why follow me?"

Her smile held little warmth. "Maybe I'm lonely."

"I don't think so."

The smile faltered. "Where are you going?"

"I'm a messenger."

"With a message that masks your music?" she asked innocently.

Cole wasn't sure how to respond.

"You should come with me," she said, and Cole caught a hint of chilling music.

"Who are you?"

"Call me Keko," she said. She held out a hand. "Take my hand, and I'll reveal your fortune."

Cole drew his sword. "Leave me alone, lady."

Keko pouted. "This is not how to make new friends."

Cole felt awkward. Keko appeared to be unarmed and had made no aggressive moves. But he knew she was up to something. "Please leave me alone."

"You're that boy Nazeem wants," Keko said.

Cole gave no reply.

Keko giggled. "It's all over your face, and it just peeked through in your music. The message is well done, by the way. Excellent weaving. If you want to survive out here, you're going to need my help."

Cole started walking backward. "I'd rather be alone." He couldn't ignore the scary impression from when he first noticed her staring at him, or the hint of menacing music he had recently heard and felt.

"What if I want to go the same way you're going?" Keko asked, walking to stay near him.

"I'll pick a new direction," Cole said.

Keko produced a small carved piece of wood about the size of a pencil. "Take this. It will help you on your journey."

"No thanks."

She tossed it to him, and he knocked it aside with his blade.

"How rude!" Keko huffed.

"Stop following me," Cole said.

"They'll nab you without my help."

"I bet they'll catch me even faster with your help. Are you honestly telling me you want to protect me?"

"From them," Keko said.

"Only so you can catch me," Cole said.

She gave a little shrug. "I'd love to travel with you."

"To Nazeem," Cole said. "I get it." He swished his sword through the air a couple of times and backed up some more. "Have you heard the one about the echo with no arms and no legs stranded in the wilderness?"

Keko stopped walking. Her face contorted in outrage. "Are you threatening me?"

"Lady, you started it," Cole said. "Go away."

She made complicated gestures and started muttering. Cole heard her chilling music more clearly, and suddenly, his arms wouldn't move. His feet felt rooted to the ground. He managed to keep holding his sword.

Fingers making spidery motions, Keko drew closer, chanting under her breath.

Panic threatened to turn his mind blank. Cole resisted and tried to think. This reminded him of being immobilized at Gamat Rue, except he didn't feel as tightly held. He could pivot at the waist and move his head and eyes. Most of his muscles could flex to some degree, but his arms and legs remained locked in position.

Keko was almost close enough to reach out and touch him. His arms trembled. He could feel the invisible hold weakening, his arms and legs twitching a little more with each effort. Growling, he bent his arm at the elbow, and suddenly, he was free. Cole swung his sword at Keko. She lunged away just in time.

Cole didn't pursue her. "Do that again and I really will attack."

Keko glared at him, panting. "You're not worth the trouble."

She turned and started walking back toward the township. Cole watched her go with mixed feelings. It was a relief that she was leaving, but what if she returned with reinforcements? Should he chase her? What would he do if he caught her?

"Keko," Cole called, trotting after her. "Promise me you won't come after me."

"I owe you no pledge," she said without looking back, and he felt another hint of her unnerving music.

"But I want one," Cole said.

"You go your way. I'll go mine."

He stopped chasing her. He couldn't chop her with his sword. Not with her walking away. He turned and walked at his fastest pace.

For the next long while, Cole kept checking behind him, but he saw nobody. The music of the gorgeous landscape eventually helped calm him. Maybe Keko was really gone.

He didn't like how she was able to partially freeze him. What had made him vulnerable to her? Had he accidentally made some kind of bargain? Or was that kind of attack just part of life in the echolands?

Cole had been walking for some time when he noticed ominous music up ahead to the right. It sounded a little discordant and made him feel upset, like after losing an argument he should have won. Cole curved far enough out of the way that he never saw what the music represented, but he was glad to leave it behind. He had encountered enough trouble for one day. Of course, you could cram a lot into a day when it never ended.

A large hill rose into view as Cole walked toward it. Covered in waist-high ferns, it didn't look hard to climb, and Cole thought it might give him a chance to study his surroundings. The summit was easily the highest point in sight.

The lush ferns on the hill parted easily for him, gently brushing his legs and waist as he plodded upward. The climb required him to be more careful with his footing but didn't tire him more than anything else.

When he reached the top, Cole took in the panorama of grassland, flowering fields, stands of trees, and a distant channel crossing his path. Staring back the way he had come, he felt a jolt of panic when he noticed a distant figure following him. As he scanned the area, Cole began to notice other figures—eight total. Two traveled alone. The others moved in pairs. The nearest had to be twenty or thirty minutes away. They were fanned out behind him and off to either side. All were coming his way.

Cole took off down the far side of the hill at a sprint. Scanning up ahead, he noticed no other people. But additional enemies could be hiding almost anywhere. There was plenty of cover. Halfway down the hillside, Cole tripped and fell flat, sliding a good distance over crushed ferns.

After scrambling to his feet, Cole kept up his quick pace. He hadn't run in the echolands before now. He found that though he could remain at a sprint without tiring, his mind became a little foggy, and the music started to sound slightly out of tune.

Not only was he not panting, but he experimented with holding his breath and found that breathing was still not necessary. He remembered Keko breathing heavily after he broke free of her control. That might have been a response to a different kind of exertion.

Cole ran into a grove of plum trees and yanked a piece of fruit from a limb without breaking stride. It looked perfect—no wormholes or signs of decay. He hadn't eaten anything in the echolands yet.

He bit into the tender, juicy flesh, and flavor flooded into his mouth, accompanied by a surge of exhilarating music. His senses enlivened, Cole took another bite and soon finished the delicious treat.

By the time he tossed the pit aside, Cole felt largely replenished. His focus was sharp again, and the music sounded clear. He kept running, reminding himself that if he started to feel unfocused again, he would need to eat something.

Should he have attacked Keko? Maybe. His pursuers were probably working with her. So many were converging that she must have contacted them. And that meant more were probably on the way.

What if they could all immobilize him as Keko had? What if some were more powerful than her? Even if they weren't, Cole knew he wouldn't be able to resist so many.

He drew his sword. The blade glowed with a soft light. He hadn't tried using his power here. What if being an echo helped him rekindle his abilities?

Searching inside, Cole couldn't feel his power. Undaunted, he pointed the Jumping Sword up ahead and shouted, "Away!" The sword offered no forward tug. He tried a few more times with no result.

Why couldn't he access his ability? It was there someplace. He had used it when touching the Founding Stone. If only he could use his sword to bound across the echolands, Keko and her friends would have no chance of catching him.

Cole wondered if they had spied him on the hilltop. Since he had seen them, the reverse was probably true. At least one of them must have spotted him. None had appeared to be running. If he kept a good pace, maybe he could out-distance them through sheer willpower.

Or maybe they hadn't run because others were up ahead.

The thought made him slow to a jog. Were they driving him toward danger? Was he being corralled? Would it be smarter to hide and hope they passed him by? Keko had sensed the message that cloaked his music. If he hid, would she lead everyone right to him?

Cole passed groves of trees and some lower hills. He stayed away from high ground for fear of being spotted. He vigilantly did his best to look and listen in all directions.

He saw no people. It became hard to gauge how long he had been running. The sky remained the same. Landmarks came and went.

From up ahead, he heard the whistling music of a slipstream. He listened for a bridge but didn't hear one. When the channel came into view, there was no bridge in sight. This slipstream was narrower than the other channel, but Cole's best jump would barely get him a third of the way across the skinniest stretch he saw.

Once again Cole looked inside for his power. The Jumping Sword could save him if he got it working. The power was in him somewhere, blocked, hibernating. There had to be a way to awaken it. Unfortunately, he had no idea how to even try. Searching intently in his desperation, he still perceived no hint of his ability.

As Cole drew near the channel, he pointed the Jumping Sword at the far side. "Away!" he cried, to no avail. He mustered all his need, all his will. "Away!" The sword did not react. His efforts amounted to nothing more than heartfelt wishes.

Cole reached the streaming ether and strained his ears for music like he had heard at the previous bridge. Sensing nothing, he turned right, running hard.

After a few minutes he heard the reassuring sound of a bridge ahead. The welcome music cheered him onward.

When he finally saw the bridge, four people were waiting

for him. They stood on the near side of the span. Looking back and off to the side, Cole saw another five people run into view, including Keko. Legs pumping, she grinned wildly.

Cole drew his sword.

As Keko and her friends closed on him, Cole ended up with his back to the slipstream and a semicircle of enemies confronting him—five men and four women. "Put the sword down, kid," Keko said.

Cole shook his head. "Back off, guys. I don't want to hurt anyone."

"We don't mind if you try," one of the men said.

Cole glanced over his shoulder at the blurred rush of the slipstream. "Might be better to just take a dive," he said, hoping to stall them.

Several of the people began gesturing, and Cole couldn't move. This time his attempted struggles did nothing. His toes, his head, his eyes—everything was firmly locked in place.

"We're not going to hurt you," Keko said. "You can't get away. You may as well come quietly."

Cole couldn't move his lips to reply. He was out of options. He had already failed! Maybe if he played along he could eventually find a chance to escape.

"Free his head," Keko said.

Once again Cole could move his eyes and his lips. "You're making a big mistake. You should let me go."

The man who had spoken earlier held a finger to his lips. Everyone fell silent. At first Cole heard nothing. Then came the distant drumming of galloping hooves. A whinny reached them, just loud and shrill enough to be heard above the nearby music.

Several of the people exchanged glances and started muttering.

"Is it . . . ?"

"Couldn't be."

"What do we do?"

Keko waved her arms. "Stay calm!" She neither looked nor sounded calm.

The pounding hooves came rapidly closer. Cole began to hear thrilling music, evoking a potent blend of excitement and danger.

Keko's companions stopped making gestures and chanting. Most of them scattered. Cole found he could move again.

And then the horse burst into view. The enormous steed had a coat like thunderclouds. Whether it was the way the muscles rippled as the horse ran, or how the hair caught the light, the coloring of the coat seemed to be in motion, highlights shifting like smoke in the wind.

"Good luck!" Keko shrieked at Cole as she ran off to one side.

The thrilling music surged as the horse chased the fleeing echoes, running them down with ease. The animal bumped a woman into the slipstream and trampled two men. The echoes fled in all directions.

Cole gaped at the rampaging steed. Could it be the same horse that had helped him back in Necronum? What could it be doing here in the echolands? Might there be a team of horses mysteriously on his side?

The horse did not pursue all the fleeing echoes. As they got farther away and spread out wider, the horse circled back to Cole. He sheathed his sword.

The horse came and stood before him. Cole's head was lower than its back. Even with the horse up close and standing still, its hair flowed and swirled like churning clouds. The large head bent down to Cole and nudged him with its nose.

Cole hesitantly petted it.

The horse nudged him again, then turned sideways.

Was he supposed to get on?

There were no reins, no saddle. How was he supposed to ride a horse so mighty and fierce without any equipment? How was he even supposed to climb up?

As if reading his mind, the steed crouched. Cole saw that some of the fleeing echoes had slowed and were looking back at him.

Cole swallowed. This was his only chance. Stretching to grip the black mane in one hand, Cole jumped and pulled and managed to swing a leg over the top. The horse straightened, and Cole found himself sitting much higher than he ever had astride a horse, legs forced wide by the broad back. He stroked the horse's meaty neck. The coat felt soft and smooth beneath his palm.

The horse trotted away from the slipstream. A trot was typically a bouncy gait, but this horse made it feel like gentle rocking. The animal turned and charged the channel. Made breathless by the sudden acceleration, Cole squeezed with his knees and gripped the silky mane with both hands.

Was the horse insane?

They cleared the channel in a fluid leap that temporarily made Cole feel he had mounted Pegasus. Air rushed over him, and his stomach tingled. The landing hardly jounced Cole, and at a full gallop the powerful horse felt unbelievably stable beneath him, bobbing mildly.

Glancing back, Cole watched the channel rapidly recede and saw Keko and her friends beyond it. Ahead, more paradisiacal gardens awaited.

"Where are we going?" Cole wondered aloud.

The horse just kept running.

CHAPTER
--- 17 ---

HALL OF GLORY

Cole had galloped on a horse before but felt sure he had never gone half this fast. It was as though he had only driven go-carts, and suddenly, he had a sports car. No, a bullet bike.

Except he wasn't really driving.

This was more of a levcar experience.

With a lot more wind in his face.

Where had this horse come from? Where was it taking him? When a similar steed had rescued him in Necronum, Cole had suspected it might have been sent by Sando. If so, he could be in serious trouble. Was it possible that Sando wanted to free Cole from Keko so he could catch him personally?

Wherever the huge, powerful animal was taking him, there wasn't much Cole could do about it. If the horse bucked or reared, Cole would go flying. To jump off at this speed would be suicide, and the horse never slowed.

"I'm trying to go to the Hundred Forests," Cole exclaimed. "To the Sweet Channel Charnel House."

The horse gave no indication of hearing him and didn't change course. If they were going in the wrong direction, Cole would have a lot of ground to make up. At least he hadn't been captured. That was something.

Cole held on and tried to enjoy the ride. The exhilarating music of the tireless horse gave him hope that it meant no harm. Judging by what he heard and felt, the horse might not be safe, but it also didn't feel evil. Nothing in the music suggested that anybody was controlling it. One of the main emotions that came across was fierce independence.

"Thanks for rescuing me," Cole said. "I don't know if you can understand, but I appreciate it."

The horse gave no response.

"Can I call you Thunder?" Cole asked. "You look like a storm cloud."

The horse raised no objection.

They galloped onward. Forests and fields came and went. Hills rose into view only to shrink behind them. Cole occasionally glimpsed towns and villages. He caught distant fragments of unusual music both pleasant and threatening. They crossed several channels, jumping the narrow ones, using bridges when the slipstreams were too broad, always at a relentless gallop.

When Thunder finally slowed, it took Cole by surprise. He had grown used to the rhythm of the hoofbeats, the steady wind in his face, and the vegetation blurring by.

The horse came to a stop. Cole patted the muscular neck. "Do you need food?"

Thunder gave no answer.

"Is this where I get off?"

Thunder snorted, head bobbing.

Cole slid off to the ground, stumbling because of the height of the drop. Thunder took a couple of steps away, looked back, whickered softly, then stormed off.

"Thank you!" Cole called.

As usual, Thunder made no reply.

Cole watched the horse until it galloped out of view. As Thunder's music faded, Cole noticed other unusual music, like the fanfare he might hear at the start of a big event or perhaps announcing the arrival of royalty. The bold music promised splendor and spectacle and called strongly to his sense of adventure.

He paused. Could it be the homesong? Elana had told him he would know the call of the Other when he heard it. This music didn't feel like leaving the world behind, nor did it make him feel entranced. He could go toward or away from it as he chose. The music was about participating in the world, not leaving it.

Unsure which direction would take him toward the Hundred Forests, Cole followed the grand music. The clearer the music became, the more he wanted to participate in whatever was going on. It was the most appealing music he had heard in the echolands so far. He started to run for fear of what he might otherwise miss.

As he came around a stand of tall trees, a sprawling building appeared, filling most of the valley before him. The white stone masonry and shining gold accents gave it the feel of a flashy mansion. Cole had seen no larger structure in his life, including the First Castle, as well as shopping malls back home. Ranging from a couple stories to several stories tall, the irregular monstrosity just kept going and going, as if an architect had designed the biggest building ever and then added several other huge buildings for good measure, connecting everything with walls and walkways and courtyards.

Cole jogged down into the valley, heading for a large set of golden doors. A pair of soldiers stood out front, a man and a woman, dressed in showy golden breastplates and helmets, each holding a spear. Cole slowed as he reached the steps leading up to the doors. The powerfully built guards stared out beyond him. The exciting music blared louder than ever.

"Can I come in?" Cole called.

The female guard looked down at him. "You hear the music."

Cole chuckled. Her comment seemed like a joke because it was so loud. "Hard to miss."

"To those who hear it," the male guard replied. "Enter, friend."

Cole climbed the steps and paused at the doors. Both guards stood much taller than him. "You have weapons," he said.

"Such is our honor," the female replied firmly.

"What is this place?" Cole asked.

"Its music tells the tale better than any name," the male said. "Most call it the Hall of Glory. You are young and bright to hear its song." He saluted with his spear.

"Is my sword a problem?" Cole asked.

The female grinned. "It's an endorsement. Wear it well."

One of the two doors stood a little ajar. "Thanks," Cole said, and pushed through.

The music and feel inside were completely different from outside, the brash fanfare giving way to calm, soothing tones. He entered a vast chamber with a high ceiling of stained glass. A fountain burbled in the center of the room—an obvious luxury in a land with little water. Soft snatches of conversation rebounded in the cavernous space. Men and women mingled in diverse attire—some dressed like knights, others in fine clothes or more common outfits. He saw one man wearing a dark blue United States military uniform.

A gentleman in a white wig and tricornered hat wandered up to Cole. He removed his hat and bowed. "Hamilton Hayes, at your service," the man said. "What brings a young, bright echo to our hall?"

"The music," Cole said. "And I'm looking for directions."

Hamilton gave an easy chuckle. "You've come to the right place, my boy. I don't know much about the local geography, but the combined knowledge of those assembled here could map out more than one world for you. Somebody will know."

"Who comes here?" Cole asked.

"You already know the answer," Hamilton said. "Those who hear the clarion call of glory. The boldest and most heroic men and women, whose hearts are acquainted with passion and sacrifice."

"Not everybody hears the music of this place?" Cole asked.

The man gave a little frown. "Many are quite deaf to it, I'm afraid." Then he smiled and clapped Cole on the shoulder. "But others hear the summons loud and clear. Count yourself fortunate to stand among them. There is an entire wing of Vikings who believe this is their final destination. A rowdy but jovial crowd."

"Where are you from?" Cole asked.

"I hail from Virginia," the man answered.

"America?" Cole asked.

"You know it? I had you pegged as a local—Necronum or Elloweer."

"I came from Arizona."

The man chuckled. "I've heard of it, though it was not a state in my day. To think our modest colonies expanded from ocean to ocean! You will find folk from various worlds here. The echolands are a crossroads." Hamilton tipped his hat forward and wandered off.

Cole watched him walk away. How long had that guy been here? Since Colonial times? Cole wanted to ask more questions, but Hamilton seemed to be on his way somewhere.

Cole started roaming. All the rooms were beautiful. Many were enormous. The more Cole paid attention, the more he found little rooms and yards hidden here and there. Most rooms had sparse furnishings, but some of the smaller ones were cozier. Many rooms had tables set out with fruit and vegetables on them. Cole found greenhouses and lush, open-air courtyards.

The diversity of echoes continued to impress. Cole

could have been behind the scenes at a movie studio where a variety of period films were simultaneously in production. Rugged mountain men chatted with Romans in togas. Primitively dressed tribesmen walked alongside military nurses. Some outfits looked completely foreign. A few echoes had the heads of wolves or cats.

Down one hall Cole spotted a short echo with grasshopper legs and translucent wings. Thinking of Twitch, Cole ran to catch up.

"Excuse me," Cole said when he got close.

The slender man turned. "What is it?" He sounded defensive.

"You're one of the grinaldi!"

The man blinked. "Are you also from the Ellowine wetlands?"

"No, but I'm friends with one of your people. Twitch."

The man appeared thoughtful. "I'm not familiar with the name. Might be from before my time. I died a short while ago in the Battle of Kasori."

"When the swamp people took over?" Cole asked.

"No, lad, when the Halfknight helped us reclaim our villages."

"Wait," Cole said. "You met the Halfknight? Then you must have met Twitch. He would have brought the Halfknight to Kasori. I was with him when he met Minimus."

Realization dawned on the man's face. "You mean Ruben," he said. "Twitch must be a nickname."

"That's right," Cole said. "He got Twitch from the Sky Raiders."

The man shook Cole's hand. "I'm Zig. Any friend of Ruben's is a friend of mine. He and Minimus saved us!"

"Tell me what happened," Cole said eagerly. "I never heard."

Zig smiled warmly. "It was beautiful. You've heard of Renford and the swamp folk?"

"The basics," Cole said. "They defeated your champions, took over your villages, and managed them poorly."

"It was a grim day when that scoundrel came to town," Zig mourned. "He and his lot kept inventing new ways to degrade our community. Good fields went to waste, productive live-stock were mismanaged, stores we had built up over years were raided, and our people were basically enslaved. It was horrible."

"But Twitch came. I mean Ruben."

"Twitch will serve, if that's how you know him. He shows up unannounced one day with a tiny knight claiming to be the champion of Wenachi, the one grinaldi village too remote to earn the attention of the swamp folk. The grinaldi are not large in stature, but this knight in full armor was at least a head shorter than all but our children. Imagine our surprise when he marches up to Renford and challenges him for the championship."

"Renford was champion of all your neighboring villages," Cole recalled. "If Minimus beat him, you were all free."

"Aye, that was the notion," Zig said. "I heard Renford talking before the duel. He didn't like the high quality of the Halfknight's armor. His own equipment was mismatched and incomplete. But he was confident that his size would take the day. Was he ever wrong!"

"Minimus won?" Cole asked.

"Handily! The fight ended almost before it began. Quick and bloody. Renford hardly knew what hit him. It was almost enough to make a man pity the brute."

"You mentioned a battle," Cole said.

Zig gave an uneasy chuckle. "The swamp folk had made themselves quite comfortable. They weren't ready to quit the good life over trifles like fair play and honor. Renford's cousin immediately challenged Minimus to a duel."

"That was against the rules," Cole said.

"You bet it was!" Zig exclaimed. "Since Renford justified his first challenge by claiming to be champion of the swamp folk, Minimus had not only won control of our villages but was champion of the swampies as well."

"Did Minimus accept the challenge?"

"The little knight dispatched the challenger as swiftly as he killed his cousin," Zig said with a giggle. "As the Halfknight wiped the gore from his sword, he invited other challengers to apply. The silence was deafening. With their two top fighters dead in the mud, bested without inconvenience, nobody was in a rush to volunteer."

"I can imagine," Cole said. "I've seen Minimus in action."

"When nobody stepped up, Minimus ordered them to return to the swamp and to never again set foot on grinaldi property. Some of the older ones conferred, and then they all attacked."

"You were right," Cole said angrily. "No honor."

"Most of them rushed Minimus," Zig said. "They would have had better luck leaping into the mouth of a volcano.

All who charged him were just lining up for the slaughter. There was a terrible beauty to it—that tiny knight tirelessly carving up so many villains twice his size. Of course, not every swampie went for Minimus. Some attacked the nearest grinaldi."

"Is that how you got killed?" Cole asked.

"We hopped away at first, mostly avoiding them. Twitch rallied us. He charged into battle boldly, cutting down Renford's younger brother. With Minimus dispatching them so readily, they were distracted and off-balance. We wiped them out. Three of the grinaldi fell, and a half dozen were wounded. Renford's father got me from behind with a hoe."

Cole winced. "I'm sorry."

Zig shook his head. "Don't be. I was avenged many times over. It was a glorious day. We worked for generations to build those communities. The swamp folk had stolen everything. We had no hope for the future. But we got it back. My wife and children will have the lives I hoped for them."

That pricked Cole's heart. "You're a good man."

Zig smiled, eyes twinkling. "I must have done my part if they let me in here. I didn't die immediately. I lived to get word that Minimus had purged the other villages of any lingering swampies. Your friend Twitch survived without a scratch. There was no hope in sight, lad, then all of a sudden the world was set aright. Goes to show you—never give up."

"I guess it does," Cole said.

"I would have rather lived," Zig said wistfully. "I had plenty of good years left in me. But what we were doing before Minimus came to our rescue was not living. Given that we drove the swamp folk away, I wouldn't change a thing." He looked around. "I had no suspicion that a place like this might await me."

"It's amazing," Cole agreed.

Zig looked Cole up and down. "You've got a glow to you, lad. You in love or something?"

Cole laughed. "My body isn't dead yet."

"You're fooling me," Zig cried. "Then how are you here?"

"It's part of the weaving they do in Necronum," Cole said.

"I never heard of such a thing," Zig said. "Nor have I seen an echo with your particular . . . sheen. But I'm new here. Plenty to learn."

"Thanks for telling me about Twitch," Cole said. "I'm sorry you got killed."

Zig waved it off. "Don't mourn for me. The rest of my kin will be along in due time. It's the one certainty. We're all headed this way sooner or later. It's not so intimidating once it happens."

"I'll see you around."

Zig gave a little bow and moved on.

Folding his arms, Cole leaned up against a wall. It was good to hear that Twitch had succeeded in his quest to save his people. Just knowing his friend was out there someplace, having achieved what once seemed like an impossible goal, gave Cole hope and motivation.

The Hall of Glory was a big place full of diverse people. Surely he could find somebody to steer him in the right direction.

CHAPTER
— 18 —

GUIDANCE

As Cole continued to wander, he began to realize that bright echoes must not visit the Hall of Glory very often. Not only did he get a lot of stares, but several echoes approached to ask his business. He stuck with his story of being a messenger and fished for information about where he could find the Hundred Forests. None of the echoes who approached him knew the geography of the echolands well enough to help.

While strolling past a glass wall that looked out on a modest orchard, Cole noticed a man with bushy gray sideburns roaming the grassy area. Not immediately seeing a way into the courtyard, Cole rapped on the window until he caught the man's attention. It was Durny—the old shaper who had bought him for the Sky Raiders and who had protected Mira until getting killed by an enormous spider at the proving grounds.

When he recognized Cole, Durny first looked stunned, then delighted. He gestured to the right and hustled that way himself. Durny had lost his limp but wore the same shirt, jacket, and trousers from the day he died.

"Look at you!" Durny exclaimed when they met at the door. He stepped inside, shook one of Cole's hands with both of his, then pulled him into a hug. "We meet again! You're bright, aren't you?"

"Yeah," Cole said. "Still alive."

"How is Mira?"

Cole looked around. "Can we talk here?"

"Come into the courtyard," Durny said, leading Cole under the shade of the fruit trees. "This entire compound is shielded from outside scrutiny, but out here we won't risk other guests of the hall eavesdropping."

"Mira's in the echolands," Cole said. "Not dead. Her body is in longsleep. An echo captured her."

"Oh no. What about her power?"

"She got it back."

"Outstanding," Durny enthused. "That could not have been easy. But now she's in trouble. You're looking for her?"

"And her sister Destiny," Cole said.

Durny placed a hand on Cole's shoulder. "I'm deeply impressed, Cole. You promised me you would take care of her. You've clearly taken that vow seriously."

"I'm trying," Cole said. "Honor is somewhere in the echolands too."

Durny gave a slow nod. "Three of the five trapped in the afterlife."

"I want to save them," Cole said. "Last we knew, Destiny

was heading to a place called Deepwell in the Hundred Forests. I'm trying to get there, but I'm on my own."

Durny rubbed his chin. "I don't know the lay of the land here. Some in the Hall of Glory could help us. Most are more familiar with places besides the echolands."

"How come?"

"When I died, I found myself traveling along a white, misty passage. From off to one side I heard this bombastic music. Following it, I entered the echolands near the Hall of Glory, and the bombast lured me inside. I haven't left. The vast majority of those who come to the Hall of Glory make their way directly here and never depart to explore. Word has it this is the safest, most comfortable haven in the echolands. For those who decide to move on, there is a channel nearby. Tell me all you know about Miracle and her sisters."

Cole related how Sando had tricked him and the suspicion that he was working for Nazeem. He summed up how he and his friends had previously helped Honor and Constance and shared what he knew about Destiny.

Durny listened solemnly. When Cole finished, the old man folded his arms and stared at the ground. "I may not know my way around the echolands. But I might know just the man to help you."

"Really?"

"He can be fickle. But I expect this scenario will intrigue him. He's one of the few who comes and goes around here. Something of a folk hero. He should be able to steer you right."

"Can we tell him everything?"

"I talk to him about Stafford and the princesses all the time. He works with the Unseen. He's as reliable an ally as you're likely to find. He's been my best source of news. I already knew Nazeem was searching intently for Tessa, for example. But I didn't know about Mira and Honor crossing into the echolands."

"Where can we find your friend?"

"Come with me."

Cole waited outside a door while Durny checked with his contact. After a few minutes Durny came and retrieved Cole. He followed the old shaper into the room.

Two men awaited them. A handsomely dressed man sat in a red leather chair. A stockier, balding man perched off to the side on a stool.

Cole recognized the man in the chair! His clothes were different from during their previous encounter, but the rings and cape looked the same. His face appeared a little older, but his carefully shaped beard remained black. "Harvan Kane!" Cole exclaimed.

Harvan grinned. "Always a thrill to meet an admirer. And you are?"

"Cole Randolph."

Harvan bowed his head in greeting. "All those stories you've heard about me? Understatements."

Cole couldn't help laughing at the casual cockiness. "We've met."

"Have we?" Harvan asked, squinting. "Set aside the message, Cole, I can barely get a read on you."

Cole glanced at Durny, who held out a hand. Cole passed him the message, and Durny set it on a table. Now Harvan would be able to hear his actual music.

"I'm normally good with faces," Harvan apologized, one dark eyebrow raised.

"We met indirectly," Cole said. "In the Cave of Memory."

"Ah," Harvan said. "My imprint. Was I helpful?"

"You were guarding a secret," Cole said. "I was there looking for somebody else."

Harvan rubbed the dense, sculpted fur on his chin. "I remember the secret. I hoped my imprint would protect it. How'd I do?"

"You told me nothing," Cole said.

Harvan pumped a fist. "More than a hundred years later, still going strong."

"Although you let him know you had a secret," the guy on the stool pointed out. "That's only one step away from revealing it."

"We all have secrets," Harvan replied dismissively. "Especially anyone in that cave." He jerked a thumb at the man on the stool. "This is Winston. On a good day, he's more useful than annoying. I was a capable weaver in my time, but he's the better weaver in the echolands."

Winston folded his hands on one knee. "And why is that?"

Harvan shrugged and shared an uncomfortable smile. "Because I can barely weave anymore."

"Barely?" Winston inquired.

"Not at all, really," Harvan admitted.

"My power is blocked too," Cole sympathized.

Harvan squinted at him. "Blocked? More like destroyed!" He glanced at Winston. "You ever see such a mess?"

"It's not pretty," Winston said.

"How'd you manage that?" Harvan asked Cole.

Cole glanced at Durny. "Can I talk in here?"

"Speak freely," Harvan said. "Nobody can spy on us. Winston sees to that."

Durny gave a nod.

"I fought a shapecrafter named Morgassa who was terrorizing Elloweer," Cole said. "She attacked my power as we defeated her."

Harvan laughed and smiled, rubbing his hands briskly. "My kind of guy! See what I mean, Winston? You haven't really taken a stand until you get your hands dirty. The kid has battle scars."

"I'm sure you can provide him with more," Winston replied dryly.

"Maybe," Harvan said with a chuckle. He refocused on Cole. "I'm to believe you've met four of the Pemberton girls?"

"Miracle, Honor, and Constance," Cole said. "I helped all of them regain their powers. I've only met Destiny's imprint."

Harvan leaned forward. "Your music sounds truthful, and I have an ear for it. Winston?"

"Agreed."

"This guy vouches for you too," Harvan went on, jerking his chin toward Durny. "You want directions to the Hundred Forests? You're hoping to catch up with Destiny?"

"Yeah," Cole said. "Do you know how to get there?"

Harvan rolled his eyes. "Cole? Please."

"Does that mean you do?" Cole said.

"He doesn't know the stories," Winston said.

"Stories?" Cole asked.

"He's arguably the greatest explorer the Outskirts has known," Durny explained. "Harvan Kane stories have expanded into folk tales."

"They haven't grown that much," Harvan protested.

"You had others write your autobiography so they could embellish," Winston said.

"It's tedious to transcribe events you lived," Harvan said. "Writing produces grotesque oversimplification. The verbal history has been accurate enough."

"The one about Mount Fairview?" Winston prompted.

"The highest peak in Sambria," Harvan said. "I reached the summit."

"Defeating an army of yetis?" Winston pressed.

"There were yetis," Harvan maintained. "They tried to kill me. Avoiding is basically defeating."

"With a magical spear?" Winston pursued innocently.

"I found a spear," Harvan asserted. "Some details improve with any retelling."

"The one about the witch?" Winston went on.

"Enchantress, witch," Harvan said. "She had powers."

"Turned you into a frog, did she?" Winston asked.

"I had huge warts," Harvan said. "And I couldn't speak."

Winston shook his head.

"Harvan's renown is well deserved," Durny inserted.

"He was a legitimate hero, or he wouldn't be in the Hall of Glory. And unlike many, he continues to explore here in the echolands."

"This is just my base of operations," Harvan said. "I interact with a few of the top Unseen weavers. I know quite a bit about the Pembertons. I'm concerned about this new fellow, Nazeem."

"I think he's been around for a very long time," Cole said.

"So it seems," Harvan said. "But his name has only recently surfaced. He remains shrouded in mystery."

"I met him," Cole said.

Harvan's jaw dropped, and he stared with undisguised astonishment. "In the flesh?"

"I snuck into a secret meeting beneath the First Castle," Cole said. "Nazeem used the Founding Stone to communicate with his followers. He was speaking from the Fallen Temple."

"There have been theories . . . ," Winston mused.

"The Fallen Temple?" Harvan checked. "You know this for certain?"

"I was in the meeting when Nazeem spoke," Cole said. "He noticed me. Now he's hunting me."

Harvan covered his mouth. "You're the boy in the recent reports. Yes, you match the description. No wonder he wants you. Cole, nobody knows Nazeem resides in the Fallen Temple. In Necronum and the echolands, we all keep our distance from that accursed place. For centuries, nobody has laid eyes on the temple and survived to tell the tale."

Cole held up a finger. "People have been there. They just know how to keep a secret."

"What people?" Harvan asked, almost hesitantly.

"Owandell, for one," Cole said.

Bringing his fists to his temples, Harvan reeled in his seat, as if Cole had struck him. "I feared as much. What do you know of the shapecrafters?"

"Nazeem taught Owandell shapecraft," Cole said. "The shapecrafters all follow Nazeem."

Grimacing, Harvan nodded. "Owandell used shapecraft to strip the princesses of their abilities and empower Stafford."

"Right," Cole said. "Now Owandell and his followers expect Nazeem to return. Nazeem acted like it would happen soon."

Harvan slackened, his eyes gazing vacantly. "Funny how some mistakes never stop haunting you."

"What mistakes?" Cole asked.

Winston shook his head. "We can discuss other—"

Harvan held up a hand. "No. The boy is embroiled in this. Like so many others, he is paying for my faults. He deserves to hear it."

Cole listened.

"I knew Owandell. Long ago. He was a companion on several of the adventures toward the end of my mortal life. We became friends. Younger than me, he was smart, fearless, and full of ambition. I should have heeded the warning signs."

"You couldn't have known—" Winston began.

Harvan held up a hand again. "We shared some similarities. Both of us wanted to go places nobody had ventured. We wanted to behold unexplored regions of the five kingdoms. But while I avoided the known strongholds of great evil, he displayed an unhealthy interest in them. I could never tell him enough about the Lost Palace, the Forsaken City, or the Fallen Temple."

"I went to the Lost Palace to rescue Honor," Cole said.

"Nobly done," Harvan said. "You were fortunate to escape with your life and your sanity. Would you have gone there out of curiosity?"

"No," Cole said.

"This is where you and Owandell differ," Harvan said. "And where I am unlike him as well. He was absolutely fascinated by knowledge and power, regardless of the source. His own shaping abilities were nothing extraordinary, but his ambition knew no boundaries. He was very patient. Despite many hints of his true character, I didn't take him seriously until it was too late."

"What happened?" Cole asked.

Harvan heaved a remorseful sigh. "Though most of my explorations happened in the physical Outskirts, I was a weaver. Over time, Owandell showed increased interest in mapping the echolands. At first we crossed over together, but my primary interests involved exploring the physical world. I figured I would have time to explore the echolands after I crossed over."

"Sounds like you have," Cole said.

"More than most," Harvan said. "Owandell, however,

remained intent on mapping the echolands as a bright echo. Due to his persistence, I eventually let him cross alone while others watched over his body in longsleep. He undertook several such journeys. I was courting a magnificent woman at the time, the Grand Shaper Denshi Ridal. I had resisted marriage for years, but her charms overwhelmed me. I was utterly distracted, and for the first time, seriously considering an end to my bachelorhood."

Harvan covered his eyes with his hands but kept speaking. "The day after Owandell returned from a lengthy trip to the echolands, Denshi lost her shaping powers. She came to me, blaming Owandell. In her sleep, she had felt his violent presence, and she awoke with her shaping disabled. There was no hard proof, and Owandell gave a virtuoso performance of baffled innocence. I honestly believed there had to be some other explanation."

Harvan uncovered his eyes. Tears shone in them. "I went to the Cave of Memory. I spoke with one of the ancient Grand Shapers and learned that on rare occasions, individuals had developed the ability to shape the shaping power, always after a trip to the echolands."

"Was that your secret?" Cole asked.

"A grave one at the time," Harvan said. "Nobody in my day had considered the possibility of altering the shaping power. Such attempts could undermine the very fabric of the Outskirts. Over the years, the Grand Shapers had succeeded in quietly eliminating those with such abilities for the public good."

"That must be why the latest shapecrafters stayed so

secretive," Cole said. "They had been wiped out before. Nazeem would have known that."

Harvan let out a bitter chuckle. "You're not slow, kid. I began to examine Owandell's fascination with the arcane in a new light. His recent visits to the afterlife became a cause for real concern. If he represented the rebirth of this ability to reshape shaping, he would have indeed had the power to strip Denshi of her abilities. The imprint of the Grand Shaper I spoke with could offer no alternate explanations."

"What happened?" Cole asked.

"I should have gone straight after Owandell," Harvan said, teeth gritted. "I should have attacked out of hiding. I also should have warned others, but the Grand Shaper in the cave really wanted to keep the possibility of tampering with the shaping power a secret. In the end, I was overconfident."

"You're admitting to hubris?" Winston exclaimed. "Can I get that in writing?"

"Anybody can make a mistake once," Harvan said with a faint smile.

"Got it," Winston said. "Your one mistake ever."

Harvan waved away his reaction. "I went straight to Denshi and told her all I had learned. She was so happy I finally believed her. Owandell had gone into hiding, but we started planning how to flush him out and deal with him. Little did we know he had poisoned our supper."

"Really?" Cole exclaimed.

Harvan smiled ruefully. "That was our last night in mortality. But it gets worse. Owandell had used my time away to prepare. Not only did he assassinate both of us, but he had weavers lined up who bound and imprisoned our echoes."

"No way," Cole said. It was too terrible to be true.

"Some lessons come at great cost," Harvan said. "I wasn't kept with Denshi. I didn't escape for over fifty years. It took outside aid. By the time I was free, Owandell had helped Stafford steal his daughters' powers and fake their deaths. I started working with the Unseen, and I searched for Denshi. Before I could find her, another freed her, and she went straight to a slipstream. I couldn't blame her, but I was devastated. I spent some time in the Hall of Glory trying to recover. I considered moving on, but felt I had introduced too much evil to the world to leave before the situation was resolved. Instead, the horizon continues to darken."

"I've seen evidence of that," Cole said.

Harvan studied Cole, then glanced at Durny. "Please keep the end of my life a secret. Very few know the full story."

"Others might tell it and triple the heroics," Winston said.

Harvan glared at the man on the stool.

"Sorry," Winston said. "I know the rule. No joking about your death."

"It's a horrible story," Cole said.

Harvan grinned. "The price of fame. Gripping stories and a painful life go hand in hand. Enough about me."

"Is it ever enough?" Winston asked.

"Enough for now," Harvan said.

"I need to get to Deepwell," Cole said. "You can give me directions?"

"Directions aren't much use in the echolands," Harvan said.

"Especially if you're untrained in the music. You're new here. Fresh and bright. Can you even hear the call of the Other?"

"Not really," Cole admitted.

"How about the Source?" Harvan checked.

"I don't think so."

"He heard the song of glory," Winston noted.

"Which makes him cool," Harvan said. "We get very few bright echoes here. But it doesn't mean he can navigate the endless garden."

"Heading off in the right direction would be a start," Cole said.

"But not much of one," Harvan said. "You'd be roaming in circles before you knew it. I mean no insult. The best of us have done it."

"Meaning Harvan has done it," Winston interjected.

"You've circled too," Harvan shot back. "And countless otherwise brave and enterprising echoes. The misdirection creeps up on you. Look! More grass! Hey, big surprise, trees and flowers! You can pass the same location many times without realizing it. Time and practice are required to learn to keep your bearings."

Cole felt daunted by how hopeless Harvan was making it sound. "I don't have time to waste. At least if I start in the right direction from here, I can keep asking as I go."

Harvan steepled his fingers, rings glittering. "Why do you wish to find Destiny Pemberton?"

"To help her get her power back," Cole said. "I promised her sister I'd do it. The princesses are the key to the revolution."

"Durny informed me that Honor and Miracle are in danger too," Harvan said.

"They're both here in the echolands," Cole said. "Mira was captured for sure. Maybe Honor as well. Mira is probably at the Fallen Temple, or else on her way. And Nazeem thinks he'll be free soon."

Harvan rubbed his beard. "Could Nazeem's physical body still be awaiting him at the Fallen Temple in mortal Necronum? It would be an unprecedented longsleep, but this guy apparently knows how to bend the rules."

"Speculation," Winston said.

"Durny mentioned that Sando was the echo who apprehended Mira," Harvan said.

"That's right," Cole answered, the familiar nausea of guilt filling his gut.

"He's a wily one," Harvan said. "Been around a long time. He's never shown any true loyalty. But he likes catering to the biggest fish. Right now that seems to be Nazeem. What do you plan to do about Mira and Honor?"

"I'll help them next," Cole said. "One disaster at a time."

Laughing, Harvan looked over at Winston. "He's the best, right?"

"Great kid," Winston agreed.

"You have a sword," Harvan mentioned, pointing at it.

"Jumping Sword," Cole said. "From Sambria. I made it work in Elloweer. I think that somehow connected it to me."

Eyebrows raised, Harvan looked at Winston. "Now do you get his music? That's the mysterious undercurrent."

"Yep," Winston said.

"No wonder Nazeem wants him," Harvan said. "No wonder they carved up his power."

"What?" Cole asked.

"You're aware that your power is unusual," Harvan said.

"Yeah," Cole said.

"It transcends normal categorization," Harvan said. "Works in every kingdom. Challenges the established boundaries."

"Seems that way," Cole said.

Harvan gave a low whistle. "A sure way to attract the attention of shapecrafters. Nazeem is a lethal enemy."

"Letting him win won't make him less dangerous," Cole said.

Harvan laughed and slapped his thigh, glancing at Winston again. The man on the stool gave a nod.

"Look, Cole," Harvan said. "You know I still care deeply about events in the Outskirts. I'm partly responsible for what went wrong. I believe in the mission of the Unseen. I detest Stafford Pemberton and what he represents. You can imagine how I feel about Owandell, Nazeem, and the shapecrafters. The Pemberton daughters are probably the most valuable assets in this war. I don't want to send you off with directions. I want to come with you. Winston too. So much depends on this mission. We'll guide you and help you succeed."

It was more than Cole had dared to hope. Wandering the echolands was confusing and intimidating. And being alone with so much responsibility felt terrible. He gave a relieved laugh. "Seriously?"

"You have your sword," Harvan said, standing up. "I have

my walking stick." He picked up a sturdy carved staff from where it leaned against the back of his chair. "It's been with me through many of my journeys, both here and during mortality."

Cole looked to Durny.

"You should absolutely use his help," Durny said. "I had hoped he might offer. Harvan can navigate the echolands better than anyone I know."

"Do you want to come too?" Cole asked.

"I would," Durny said. "But I'm also concerned about Mira. What if I start working on that problem?"

"Could be a big one," Cole said.

"All the more reason to get started," Durny said.

"Cole still hasn't officially accepted our offer," Winston pointed out.

"How about a one-day trial?" Harvan suggested.

Cole grinned. "The day never ends here."

Harvan grinned back. "Then it'll be a thorough practice run."

"I'd be glad to have your help," Cole said. "I honestly don't know if I'd make it alone. I got chased not long before coming here. A bunch of people were converging on me."

"Your message didn't conceal you?" Winston asked.

"I went through a little town to get directions," Cole said. "The message made some lady curious. She followed me out of town, figured out who I was, and then called in reinforcements."

"How many?" Harvan asked.

"About eleven," Cole said. "Maybe more."

"How'd you give them the slip?" Harvan pursued.

"No skill of mine," Cole said. "They had me pinned up against a channel. A big horse showed up and started trampling them. I rode away on it."

"A horse?" Durny asked.

"We've been hearing tales of a mystery mare," Harvan said. "No bridle or saddle. No rider. Shows up unannounced and leaves just as quickly."

"That fits," Cole said.

"You rode her?" Winston asked.

"I didn't catch her or anything," Cole clarified. "I'm no cowboy. The horse came up to me and let me climb on. Then it dropped me off not far from here."

"You're an interesting kid," Harvan said.

"That's high praise," Winston said. "He bores easily. Of course, when Harvan gets interested, violence usually follows."

"A desperate mission," Harvan said. "The fate of the world in the balance. A hurricane of enemies swirling around us. It's almost enough to make a guy feel alive again."

COMPANY

Cole sat alone at a table, thumbing through an art book. The painted birds inside helped distract him from his racing thoughts.

After it had been settled that Harvan and Winston would join him, they wanted to make ready to depart. Harvan explained that he had some people in mind who might join them on their mission, and Cole waited while he went to find them. Durny left as well, hoping to locate a guide who could escort him to the Fallen Temple.

Durny returned first and sat down by Cole.

"Any luck?" Cole asked.

"Not yet," Durny said. "Not many people leave the Hall of Glory except to ride the slipstream. And even fewer want to head toward the Fallen Temple."

"What will you do?"

"I'll strike off on my own if necessary," Durny said. "There are still more people I can approach, but I didn't want to miss your departure."

"We're alone," Cole said quietly. "You're sure about Harvan?"

Durny smiled. "He likes to talk and can come across as too proud and intense. I didn't take him seriously at first. Some people never do. But he's the most reliable echo I've met. You're in good hands."

"Do you know the people he wants to join us?" Cole wondered.

"I'm not sure," Durny said. "Trust his instincts. He's your best chance."

Before too long Harvan returned with a pair of men. One had flat features. Long black hair hung past his shoulders, with part of it rolled up at the base of his neck. He wore a loose brown robe and moccasins. The other had more conventional clothes, short hair, an average build, and a friendly bearing.

"Let me introduce a pair of echoes who didn't live in the Outskirts during mortality," Harvan said. "This is Drake, son of Hessit, of the Amar Kabal." The man with the long hair placed two fingers on his chest and gave a small bow. "And Ferrin, son of Baldor, a displacer." The other man nodded.

"I'm Cole Randolph," Cole said. "Son of Bryant and Elizabeth."

"Drake and Ferrin never lived in the Outskirts," Harvan said. "They never wandered the echolands except to come here. Neither man can have been corrupted by our enemies. Get to know them. If you're in agreement, they're ready to join us. Durny, would you come with me for a moment? There is somebody I want you to meet."

"Excuse me," Durny said, exiting with Harvan.

Cole found himself alone with the two men. "Where are you from?" he asked.

"We lived in a land called Lyrian," Ferrin said. "We both died of the same disease. Drake caught it early, seemed cured, then suffered a fatal relapse. I came down with it late in life, and it wasted little time in destroying me."

"What disease?" Cole asked.

"Heroism," Ferrin said.

Cole chuckled. "I guess a lot of the people here caught it."

"There are worse ways to go," Drake said. "We're all headed for the same end. I've died many times. There is a certain wholeness and comfort that comes from dying for what you truly feel is right."

"Died many times?" Cole asked.

Drake rubbed the back of his neck. "I'm a seedman. My people are the Amar Kabal. When we die, a seed detaches from the back of our necks. If planted, we regrow and are reborn, along with all of our memories. The last time I regrew, my seed was deformed. And so I finally get to see the afterlife."

"Does your echo have a seed?" Cole wondered.

"No," Drake said. "Just a little lump where the amar should be. I'm not destined to spend multiple lifetimes here."

Ferrin removed one of his hands, tossed it into the air, and caught it on his wrist. The hand fused back to his arm without leaving a mark. "I'm a displacer. My kind can pull ourselves apart and then put ourselves back together. My echo works the same way."

"That's bizarre," Cole said.

Ferrin removed his head and held it while speaking. "I knew two kids from Earth who felt the same way. If you can get used to this, we should be fine."

Cole stared with a mix of curiosity and horror. "I can live with it. How'd you meet kids from Earth?"

"How did you come to the Outskirts?" Ferrin replied. "There are ways between the worlds. Not many from Earth make it to Lyrian, but the two I met were outstanding people. I understand you're not truly dead. A bright echo, they call it."

"That's right," Cole said. "I still hope to make it home."

"We want to help you," Drake said.

"Were you and Ferrin friends in Lyrian?" Cole asked.

Ferrin and Drake glanced at each other, as if sharing a joke.

"More like mortal enemies," Ferrin said. "Seedmen and displacers have never mixed well. But since our deaths, we've come to an understanding. Long story."

"Some of our other friends came here as well," Drake said. "There was a war. Many people died bravely. Our friends have all moved on. Ferrin and I were thinking about doing the same. But the prospect of one last adventure beforehand appeals to us."

"You can count on us," Ferrin asserted. "Both of us have seen our share of mayhem without losing our heads." He placed his head back on his neck. "I could use another good deed or two before going onward to whatever comes next."

"You know it could be dangerous," Cole said. "Very

powerful people are after me. Our echoes could get imprisoned."

"We know the risks," Drake said. "We've faced evil before."

"Some of us may have lived in one of evil's pleasure palaces," Ferrin said with a crooked smile. "Or even worked for evil directly."

"Seriously?" Cole asked.

Ferrin shrugged. "Mistakes are how we learn. Drake and I wouldn't be here if we hadn't decided to hold true to what we thought was right. It's what all the echoes here have in common—they were willing to sacrifice for their beliefs. Some were even on opposing sides of the same conflict."

"But all were striving to help others in some way," Drake said. "I've investigated. Nobody got here chasing their own interests. It's no refuge for the selfish."

Cole thought of when he had attacked the cyclops to save Mira. Had that been his ticket into this place? Or maybe his showdowns with Carnag, Morgassa, and Roxie.

"You're wondering how you qualified," Ferrin said. "I can see it in your eyes. I think everyone here wonders to some degree. I did plenty of terrible things during my life. Lies, betrayals, you name it. I was a spy. It was my job. I'm proof you don't need to be perfect to hear the hero's music."

"You've risked your life for a good cause?" Drake asked.

"Yeah," Cole said.

"That seems to be the ticket inside," Drake said.

"And it's why you can trust us," Ferrin said. "We've proven we know how to stick to our word, or we wouldn't be here. And we give our word that your cause is our cause. Harvan explained about Stafford and Nazeem. We'll stand with you against them."

For a moment Cole caught a hint of thrilling music. He sensed that Ferrin was sincere. "You're not from here. Why are you willing to help me?"

"If we were ready to move on, we would have already gone," Ferrin said. "Could be we're bored. Could be we're curious. Could be we have fond memories of those kids from Earth. Could be Harvan amuses us. Could be we can relate to the need to overthrow evil. Could be we really could use a few more good deeds to take with us wherever we go next."

"Once you come down with heroism, it can be a tricky illness to kick," Drake said.

Harvan returned to the room, smiling and spreading out his arms. "Cole, what do you say?"

"I think you found good guys," Cole said.

"We're lucky to have them," Harvan agreed. "So many people at the Hall of Glory just want to rest. They're letting go of heartache and horrors and getting ready to move on. Not us. We're just getting started. Trust me. These two are seasoned, and they're willing to help. We'll need strong wills on this mission. I can hear it in their music."

"Will we need weapons?" Drake asked.

"They're difficult to obtain here," Harvan said. "Swords and spears probably won't decide this."

"Is there any point to my sword?" Cole asked.

"Just one," Ferrin replied. "At the tip."

"Beat me to it," Harvan said, snapping his fingers in

disappointment. "Cole, carrying a weapon in the echolands can be useful for intimidation. And you could physically destroy an echo with a sword—just not as easily as a mortal body."

"The battles here aren't won by physical combat?" Drake asked.

"They can be," Harvan said. "But often stealth can be more useful. Or cunning. Or strength of will. There are dark forces in the echolands that can ensnare you. Treacherous echoes will try to trick you into a bargain. They also might try to bind you with their wills."

"I think that happened to me," Cole said.

"Couldn't move?" Harvan asked.

"Once at Gamat Rue," Cole said. "They froze my actual body there. Not just my echo. I couldn't even wiggle a finger. I was frozen another time here in the echolands. I couldn't move at first but broke free."

"Good illustrations," Harvan said. "There are different types of bindings. If a weaver is helping your enemies from the other side, or if you've made a bargain with them, or if you're at a location controlled by their music, their power to bind you increases. If they just try to bind you out in the open, it's basically their will against yours. Refuse to submit and you'll break free. With a little practice, a strong will can shake off bindings quickly. The more abruptly you do it, the more you'll stun the binder."

"There was one other time I got frozen in the echolands," Cole said. "A group bound me."

"If they attack in large numbers, it can be your will against many," Harvan said. "Having five of us together will help offset that risk. Also, enemies could try to physically restrain us and throw us into a slipstream or a holding pit."

"Is it bad that I want somebody to try to control me?" Ferrin asked.

Harvan shook his head. "Confidence will go a long way against bindings and anything else they throw at us. Just don't go looking for trouble."

"Fair enough," Ferrin said.

"Cole, fill these guys in on where we're going," Harvan said.

"They know about the princesses?" Cole asked.

"The basics," Drake said. "We're looking for Destiny?"

"Last we heard, she was heading for a place called Deepwell," Cole said. "It's where they were trying to control her shaping power. Which could mean there is some sort of monster there. The shapecrafters do bad things with these powers."

"So off to Deepwell," Harvan said.

Cole picked up the message from the table. "The prelate of the Temple of the Robust Sky asked me to deliver this to the Sweet Channel Charnel House. But the echo who figured out who I was got curious about me because the message was masking me."

"The message works great," Harvan said. "Elana Parson knows her craft. I take it the echo who found you out was up close?"

"Yeah," Cole said.

"From a distance the message will mask you just fine," Harvan said. "It's good work. Winston will be masking himself, me, and you as well. We don't need to hide Drake or Ferrin. They have no history here. Their presence will make us look like a random group of echoes to all but the most-skilled observers."

"Won't the skilled ones be the most dangerous?" Ferrin asked.

"True, but also the least frequent to encounter," Harvan said. "We'll avoid populated areas. Cole, should we deliver the message? The Sweet Channel Charnel House isn't far from our destination, and right on the way."

"The prelate wrote a real message," Cole said. "She told me her friend Lottie Natt would help me and can give me a better disguise."

"Then we have a destination," Harvan said. "The temple prelates are among the best weavers in Necronum. I don't know Elana Parson personally, but we don't want to overlook her advice."

"What exactly is a charnel house?" Cole asked.

"In the echolands, it's a place to bring dead echoes," Harvan said. "They dump them into a channel. The house is typically insulated against the call of the Other."

"Dead echoes can still walk and talk," Cole said.

"To different degrees," Harvan said. "For example, if you return to life, your echo will linger and remain as lively as a dead echo can be. It won't learn, but it won't get any more susceptible to the homesong than you were when you departed. If at all possible, your echo will await the return of your lifespark. Once your lifeforce moves on to the Other, if the dead echo is not washed away in a slipstream, it will linger and gradually darken. Some become catatonic. Some grow violent."

"Do echoes ever die outside of the channels?" Cole asked.

"Some people hear the call of the Other so strongly they simply leave their echo behind," Harvan said. "No slipstream, no wandering off into the fringe—the lifeforce just goes. It seems to happen more frequently to those who cross over at a very old age. Sometimes a powerful weaver or echomancer can cause your lifespark to leave your echo, but usually only if you allow them power over you. And if an echo takes enough physical damage, it can die, freeing the lifeforce."

"If we get imprisoned, can we let our lifeforce go?" Ferrin asked.

"I was once bound for many years," Harvan said. "I wanted to move on. It would have been a welcome release at the time. But I couldn't. If we get captured in certain haunting grounds or by a skilled echomancer, they can block the effects of the homesong. If that happens, you can end up trapped for ages."

"The worst thing would be getting caught by Nazeem," Cole said.

"True," Harvan agreed. "He remains somewhat in the shadows, but what I know of his abilities exceeds much of what I believed possible. We're talking about the inventor of shapecraft. Yet falling under his power is the reality our princesses are facing."

"We have to save them," Cole said.

"We'll do it," Ferrin said.

Drake confirmed with a nod.

CHAPTER
20

CHARNEL HOUSE

Walking away from the Hall of Glory, Cole felt much better than he had so far in the echolands. He wasn't alone! Four seasoned adventurers strode at his side, ready to guide and protect him. Sure, they were ghosts, but so was he for now, so why complain?

Cole was the shortest of the group by a good margin, followed in height by Winston, Ferrin, Drake, and finally Harvan. Nobody else had a sword, but Cole suspected Harvan had thumped people with his heavy walking stick before, and it was a comfort knowing Winston could weave.

The exciting music of the Hall of Glory trumpeted loud and clear, causing Cole to pause and gaze back at the sprawling building. They were leaving behind the safest refuge in the echolands. He could picture the lavish rooms and courtyards full of relaxed heroes. Harvan came up beside him.

"Feel the pull?" Harvan asked.

Cole especially noticed the draw now that Harvan had put a name to it. The farther they had walked from the comfortable oasis, the more reluctant Cole had felt about departing. Even though he knew they needed to find Destiny, it seemed like they were missing something big. The music beckoned brashly. Couldn't they go back and rest a bit longer? What was the rush? Would a few hours make much difference?

"Yes," Cole said.

"Feels like something is about to start," Ferrin said. "Some rousing event that we never experienced during our long stay. Seems like if we hurry, we might get there just in time."

"Then you arrive, and it's the same people lounging around the same rooms," Harvan said. "I've come and gone a lot."

"Even knowing why we must go, the music is beguiling," Drake said. "Emotion can be stronger than reason."

"The summons is strong," Harvan agreed. "It helps lure people from various worlds to the echolands. I have seen many attempt to depart the hall only to return minutes later."

Ferrin detached one arm just above the elbow and held it out toward the Hall of Glory. "Maybe I can leave a little piece of myself."

Cole couldn't help laughing. Ferrin grinned as he reattached his limb.

"Come on," Harvan said, walking again. "The pull will fade after we get far enough away."

"Who comes to the echolands?" Cole asked. "Everybody in the Outskirts? Everyone on Earth? How many other worlds?"

"Far as I can tell, just about everybody from the Outskirts makes a stop here," Harvan said. "The echolands only get a sampling of people from other worlds, often drawn by a big landmark like the Hall of Glory or the Catacombs of Regret."

"Those catacombs sound like loads of fun," Ferrin said sarcastically.

"I've visited," Harvan said. "The Hall of Glory is more pleasant, but the catacombs serve a purpose as well. The echolands are a way station—a pause on the journey to higher planes. The interruption can be helpful for some. I am benefitting from my time here. Yet, I assume many from different worlds move on to the Other without this interlude."

They climbed out of the valley that contained the Hall of Glory. A panorama of lush hills, thriving forests, emerald lawns, and blooming fields spread out before them.

"It's beautiful," Drake said reverently.

"We didn't get much of a view on the way in," Ferrin explained, looking around. "We entered these lands right by the Hall of Glory, and its presence controlled our attention. Look at the colors! Are you guys sure this isn't heaven?"

"Much of it can be a paradise of sorts," Harvan said. "But trust me, I've encountered plenty of places and people here that nobody would confuse with heaven."

"I had no idea this splendor awaited," Drake said. "I would have left the hall long ago."

"Outdoorsman?" Winston asked.

"Some of my favorite years were spent alone in the

wilderness," Drake said. "But even after wandering far and wide in Lyrian, nothing could have prepared me for this. The sounds alone!"

"The music is incredible," Ferrin said. "Just as Harvan promised."

"What is that most lovely, longing melody in the distance?" Drake asked, his eyes losing focus.

"That would be the call of the Other," Harvan said.

Drake shook his head briskly and blinked. "I see now why people go willingly," he said.

"I don't hear it," Ferrin said. "There's a lot of nice music, but only the hall back there is calling me."

"I don't hear it either," Cole said.

"Don't be in a hurry to discern it," Harvan said. "At least not until you want to move on. Try not to dwell on the call, Drake. Let it exist in the background, a far-off promise to be fulfilled one day."

Drake smiled. "I know how to be patient."

"Patience has never been my best virtue," Harvan admitted. "Any objection to running? It takes a little more concentration and energy, but you won't grow tired. We have some distance to cover. It can save loads of time."

"Lead on," Ferrin said.

They sped up to a quick jog. After a few minutes Cole wondered why he hadn't done this before he was chased. He could have covered much more ground. Thinking back, he supposed the echolands had all been so new, and he had worried about getting lost. Walking had just felt appropriate.

Cole wondered where Dalton and Hunter could be right

now. Had they found his body at the Temple of the Robust Sky? Were they on their way to Jenna? Had they already found her? What would they think of the echolands, with the vivid colors and music everywhere?

He thought about Jace, Mira, and Joe as well. Could they hear any nice music where they were being held? Could they see any beautiful gardens? The imagined deprivations made Cole better appreciate the sights and sounds before him.

From time to time Harvan mentioned that he heard dead echoes, or a village, and would swerve off in one direction or another. The first time they reached a channel, they arrived directly at a bridge. And again at the second channel. And the third. Cole realized that Harvan could hear the bridges long before they came into view.

After some time Cole found himself running beside Winston. Not having spoken in hours, he decided to strike up a conversation.

"How'd you meet Harvan?" Cole asked. "Did you know him when you were alive?" He found it wasn't difficult to talk and run. He wasn't out of breath at all.

"I was born after he died," Winston said. "But I knew his stories. We met in the Hall of Glory. He needed a weaver, and I thought it would be fun to explore the afterlife with a legend."

"Has it been fun?"

"Sometimes. And scary. But worth it."

They mostly ran without conversation. Occasionally, Harvan explained a shift in direction. They traversed a region with many large hills, and then a flatter expanse, with sparse trees. They crossed several channels, some wide, others narrow. A few of the channels seemed to flow uphill. Apparently, streaming away from the Source toward the Other trumped pesky laws like gravity.

They saw no lakes or deserts or true mountains or deep canyons. A few areas had some boulders, and towns were sometimes glimpsed in the distance, but for the most part they were exploring enormous, verdant parkland.

"Out here you notice the single day more," Ferrin commented. "I keep waiting for the light to fail."

"The endless sunrise," Harvan said. "You never get fully used to it. You think your shoes will wear out, but they don't. Your clothes never get smelly. You can eat or not, but you never have to use a bathroom. Everything has a different rhythm here."

"I tried eating once," Cole said. "It was good."

"I avoid it when I can," Harvan said. "I think eating the food gives the echolands a stronger hold on you. That can be good if you want to apprehend the music with greater sensitivity but bad if you don't want to heed the call of the Other."

"If your focus falters, you should eat," Winston said. "I think Harvan fasts too much."

"When in doubt, starve," Harvan said.

"Doesn't the food help keep trances away?" Cole asked.

"It can," Harvan said. "But trances can have benefits, as long as they don't lead you into danger. You've probably experienced light trances as we've been running. Trances can rest the mind kind of like sleep, and they keep boredom away."

"We wouldn't want to get bored," Winston said.

"Tedium gnaws at some of us more than others," Harvan replied. "Anyhow, it's true that if your concentration gets muddied, food can help, effectively substituting for healthy trances."

"How can you tell a good trance from a bad one?" Cole asked.

"You retain your awareness in the good ones," Harvan said. "You can snap out of them at will. If you start experiencing blackouts, you're in danger."

"You just might wake up falling into a channel," Winston said.

"Or getting captured," Harvan added.

"My people don't sleep, even in mortality," Drake said. "This concept of using trances to rest and revive the mind seems perfectly natural."

"I like running without tiring," Ferrin said. "Though horses would be nice."

As Cole continued to run with the others, he lost track of time. He would see hills ahead in the distance, shaggy with trees, and eventually, they would be in the distance behind him. As he enjoyed the steady exertion of running, and the soothing music around him, Cole supposed he might be slipping into trances, but he never lost his awareness.

And then Harvan called a halt at an overlook. "That, my friends, is the Sweet Channel."

The fairly narrow channel ran in nearly a straight line. A stone building spanned the slipstream.

"Is that the charnel house?" Cole asked.

"Unless my ears are deceived," Harvan said. "And they aren't."

"Does this mean we're near Deepwell?" Cole asked.

"Not too far," Harvan said. "We can probably learn more from your contact."

They jogged to the stone house and knocked on the door. A beefy man answered, not fully opening the door. He eyed the group.

"I see no dead echoes," the man said. "How can I help you?"

"I have a message for Lottie Natt," Cole said.

The man looked at him suspiciously, glanced at the Jumping Sword, then held out a hand. "I can see she gets it."

"I'm supposed to deliver it personally," Cole said. "It comes from the Temple of the Robust Sky."

The man gave a soft grunt. "How about this? Each of you tell me whether you sympathize with Nazeem. Go."

"No," Cole said.

One at a time the others also gave negative answers.

"Do you mean any harm to any who dwell here?" the man followed up.

Again they all answered in the negative.

The man gave a nod and pulled the door wider. "Come inside."

The ground floor of the building was a single long room. Another door awaited on the far side, presumably offering access to the other shore of the channel. Doors on the other walls led to walkways overlooking the slipstream. Stacked barrels and crates filled in the spaces between the doors.

Winches stood beside a pair of large trapdoors in the floor. In one corner a flight of stairs granted access to a second story.

A woman bustled toward them, short and pudgy with her cinnamon-and-sugar hair wound into an enormous bun. She wore a brown dress and a big white apron. "Ernie, are you admitting strangers without dead echoes? Did we not have this conversation?"

"They have a message for you," Ernie said. "They passed the questions."

The woman stood before them, hands on her hips. "The young one is bright. The rest look like hooligans."

"You have a sharp eye," Harvan said smoothly.

"Don't sass me or I'll drop you through an etherhatch," she snapped. "Who is the message from?"

Cole took it out. "Are you Lottie Natt?"

"I better be or I'm in the wrong house," Lottie replied.

"It's from Elana Parson," Cole said, handing it over.

"Elana? Really?" Lottie said, inspecting the seal. "So it would seem, and so the weaving suggests. My word, your power is damaged. You're sure you don't serve Nazeem?"

"Positive," Cole said. "Bad things sometimes happen to those who fight him."

Lottie clucked her tongue. "Join him and your power gets maimed. Resist him and you can expect the same. How do we win? Ride the slipstream?" She opened the message and scanned the words.

"You drop bodies into the channel through the hatches?" Cole asked, unable to resist his curiosity.

263

"Dead echoes, yes," Lottie said, still reading. Her eyes rose to reconsider her visitors. "Do you realize half the inhabitants of the echolands are looking for either this boy or his quarry?"

"We intend to protect him and find Destiny," Harvan said with a slight bow.

"And who might you be?" Lottie asked.

"Harvan Kane," he replied. "Perhaps you've heard of me?"

"Catchy name," Lottie said, rolling her eyes. "And these gents are your muscle? A weaver and two Outsiders."

"The weaver will help us hide," Harvan said. "And the Outsiders can't have been corrupted."

"Careful with your assumptions," Lottie said. "Nazeem is infecting the echolands faster than the common cold. But you seem to be right. I don't sense his influence in them."

"Neither do I," Ferrin said.

"Are you all cheeky?" Lottie complained.

"It's a good sign," Ferrin said. "Our spirits are high despite plenty of danger and a long run."

"Straight from the Hall of Glory," Lottie said. "You still have traces of it. Coming out of retirement? That's the safest haven we've got around here. You can't earn a better one."

"We're trying to reach Deepwell," Harvan said.

"That will be markedly worse," Lottie assured him. "You're good at reading music or you wouldn't have made it here. Nazeem has a host of agents looking for that boy. I've never seen anything like it. Three separate search parties have dropped in on me during the past week."

"It's one big day," Ferrin pointed out.

"Some of the more civilized among us keep time as reckoned in Necronum," Lottie whispered, as if sharing a secret.

"So many?" Harvan asked. "All looking for the boy?"

"And the girl," Lottie said. "Destiny. It's ludicrous. A month ago nobody had heard of Nazeem. Now half the echoes you meet are working for him. That sort of following develops over time. Never has it been accomplished so quietly."

"He's based out of the Fallen Temple," Harvan said.

Lottie paled. "That explains some of it." She confronted Cole. "Boy, you're bright. That much is plain. But you're not smart. What smart person would be in your position? Your mortal life hasn't ended. Shouldn't you return to your body and get as far from Necronum as possible?"

"Not without Destiny," Cole said. "I have duties."

Lottie looked unconvinced. "It's hard to be the rescuer and the quarry. If this Nazeem gets hold of you, I expect you'll rather you had dropped through my etherhatch and sped off to the Other."

"We'll have to avoid getting caught," Cole said.

"Isn't he great?" Harvan said with a smile.

"The perfect target for an opportunist," Lottie said. "A willing victim."

"We're not using him," Harvan said, sounding offended.

"He's a kid," Lottie said. "He has no business playing hero in the afterlife. Certainly not with Nazeem hunting him."

"I came to them," Cole said. "Without Harvan I'd be doing this on my own. I can't run from Nazeem. It doesn't matter where I go. He has people everywhere. And I'm not abandoning my friends. The only way I win is if Nazeem loses."

Folding her arms, Lottie shook her head and clucked her tongue. "I'll work up something to mask your identity. Then you had best be on your way."

"Thanks for the hospitality," Harvan said lightly.

"Mind your manners," Lottie said, pointing at him. "You shouldn't stay anywhere for long, no matter how you're disguising yourselves. We haven't seen anything like Nazeem before. Your best bet is to keep moving. A sprint is the right pace."

"Thank you," Cole said.

"Any word of activity near Deepwell?" Harvan asked.

"Plenty until recently," Lottie said, going to a table and snipping a piece of yarn. "A strange lot was taking up space there—bright echoes, weavers, and shapecrafters. Plenty of activity on both sides. The commotion has quieted over the past couple of weeks."

"Does that mean the trail will be cold?" Drake asked.

"Could be," Harvan said. "We'll know soon."

"Let me concentrate for a moment," Lottie said, closing her eyes and rolling the yarn between her thumbs and fingers.

"Weaving with yarn," Winston said. "I like it."

Lottie opened one eye. "Hush. But thank you." She closed her eye again.

They waited and watched. Cole didn't think it looked like much was happening.

Lottie opened her eyes. "Keep this in your pocket. It'll help shield you from scrutiny."

Cole accepted the orange strand.

"That's good work," Winston said.

"It really is," Harvan agreed.

"What?" Lottie asked. "You didn't expect to find a skilled weaver in a charnel house? We all have different callings. I like helping dead echoes move on."

"Have you been here long?" Harvan asked, real curiosity in his tone.

"Longer than any of you," Lottie said. Then she shrugged. "Of course, it's all just one big moment, so who am I to brag? Ironic when you ponder it. I send thousands of dead echoes off toward the Other, but hesitate to pass that way myself."

"It's very quiet in here," Winston said. "I can't hear the Other, or the slipstream, or any music besides our own."

Lottie winked. "Might be part of the reason I've hung on so long. You should go."

"Any tips on how best to approach Deepwell?" Harvan asked.

"Don't follow the channel," Lottie said. "You'll hit a town. Not a very friendly one. Go out the opposite door from where you entered. Loop around. Keep to the trees. The Hundred Forests has plenty. Stay away from everyone. But you know that."

"What else do you know about Deepwell?" Harvan pressed.

"It has still water," Lottie answered.

"That's the one thing I knew," Harvan said.

"It was once a little village, but now it's more of a compound," Lottie said. "It's heavily shielded against using weaving or songreading to spy."

Harvan fingered his beard. "We have to get inside.

You're a very talented weaver. Could you disguise our music to match shapecrafters?"

"You're taking the boy Nazeem wants to find *into* Deepwell?" Lottie asked.

"It's our best chance of finding Destiny," Cole said.

Lottie tossed up her hands in surrender. "I suppose you'll have a better chance of survival with decent disguises. Very well. I've recently had some shapecrafters come knocking. Their music is fresh in my memory."

"You're no echo," Harvan said. "You're an angel."

"How often do you use that line?" Lottie asked.

"Only on extraordinary occasions," Harvan said. "About those disguises . . . my face is fairly recognizable. This would work best if we had something to *shroud* our appearances. New clothes are so hard to come by in the echolands. . . ."

"Are you fishing for burial shrouds?" Lottie asked.

Harvan looked surprised, but Cole thought it came across a bit forced. "Do you have some to spare? Are they hooded?"

"I can spare some," Lottie said. "I have a reliable supplier. I'll weave the music directly into the material. They'll only disguise you if you're wearing them."

"That would be outstanding," Harvan gushed. "Can you do one extra? In case we find somebody? And make the smallest a bright shapecrafter to better match the boy?"

"Shall I bake you a cake as well?" Lottie asked. "Any favorite toppings?"

"We so appreciate your aid," Harvan said, striding over to Cole and putting an arm around him. "This little fella may owe his survival to you."

"Ernie," Lottie said flatly. "Help me retrieve some shrouds."

He lugged a few bulging sacks to her and started opening them.

"These will do well," Lottie said, holding up a cowled robe.

"Perfect," Harvan agreed. "Nazeem tends to segregate his people. Most are strangers to one another. With our music disguised and the right story, we may be able to walk right into Deepwell."

"Sounds ideal," Ferrin said. "Especially if they also let us walk right out."

They waited as Lottie worked her weavings on the shrouds. Eventually, she folded them and stuffed them into a coarse sack. Ernie delivered it to Harvan, who nodded at Winston. The shorter man stepped forward and accepted the gift.

"You just saved our lives," Harvan said graciously.

"Glad to be of service," Lottie said. "Any friend of Elana Parson deserves a good turn."

"A thousand thanks for your aid," Harvan said with a bow.

"Off with you, Mr. Slick Beard," Lottie said. "You look out for this boy."

"We will," Ferrin assured her.

"Thanks," Cole said.

Lottie laid a hand on his arm. "Don't stay in the echolands a minute longer than necessary. Find that girl and get out."

"I'll do my best," Cole said.

"And don't lose that yarn," Lottie said. "Your true music will be naked without it."

Cole patted his pocket. "Got it."

"But leave the yarn behind if you use a shroud," Lottie clarified.

"Will do," Cole said.

Ernie opened the far door, and music flooded into the room, allowing Cole to better appreciate how quiet it had been. They gathered near the doorway.

"Are we running?" Ferrin asked.

"You had better," Lottie said.

"You heard the lady," Harvan said, breaking into a sprint.

Cole chased them out the door.

CHAPTER
—— 21 ——

DEEPWELL

Running among the trees was a different experience from running over the grass. The forests had their own music, more stately and enduring than some of the other themes. Amid the trunks, under canopies of leaves and needles, the songs of the fields and sky became muted. Without much underbrush, and with no dead leaves, branches, or trees crowding the forest floor, their way was hardly more obstructed than on the lawns. Instead of a natural forest, they might have been dashing through a many-pillared woodland temple.

For the first while after leaving the charnel house behind, Cole felt an added weight of worry. Lottie had confirmed suspicions that Nazeem had many echoes looking for him. No matter Harvan's skill, how much longer could they expect to elude pursuit? And once they were found, how much better would five be than one against the combined forces of the shapecrafters?

But hours under the trees helped allay his fears. Harvan

continued to veer in different directions as he sensed the music of other echoes or settlements. Cole took hope that they wouldn't need to outrun the servants of Nazeem forever—just long enough to accomplish their mission.

If Destiny was at Deepwell, part of his mission could be over shortly. Then he would just need to find Honor and Mira. And Jace and Joe. Hopefully, some of them had already found one another or were being held together.

From up ahead unsettling music began to interrupt the song of the trees. Cole instinctively wanted to steer away from that direction, but they weren't turning. "Is that Deepwell?" Cole asked.

"Not friendly music," Harvan said. "But it happens to be our destination."

"Should we put on our shrouds yet?" Winston asked.

"You're just tired of carrying the bag," Harvan said.

Winston shifted the sack to his other shoulder. "And I'm wondering if a group of shapecrafters approaching Deepwell might attract less attention than five anonymous echoes."

Harvan slowed to a walk, then stopped, hands on his hips. "I see the sense in that."

Winston opened the sack and began dispensing the shrouds, giving the smallest to Cole. "We have one extra," Winston announced. "I'll bring it."

"I'm no expert, but the music seems conspicuously dark," Ferrin said. "Why don't they mask it like we're doing?"

"Disguising music is tricky," Harvan said. "Something small like a person is easier than something large. Also, the music of a place is the result of the fundamental nature of the place. If they masked the song too well, the place would no longer be suited to their purposes. Believe it or not, some people find this music inviting."

"You think they'll just let us in?" Drake asked.

"It'll take some persuading," Harvan said. "It helps that the shapecrafters haven't been organized as a group for long. Most have been operating solo. Nazeem kept his people separated. Military procedures are new to them. I've been doing this for some time, so I know some of their protocols and passwords. I'm also pretty good at stretching the truth."

"Truer words were never spoken," Winston muttered.

"It's difficult to lie in the echolands," Harvan said. "That reality can leave guards with a false sense of security after a few simple questions, if you manipulate the details correctly. The music of our shrouds should help, since they will partly conceal any falsehoods. Very few echoes have the talent to weave such effective disguises. But be ready for us to fail. We may have to fight our way out."

The robe was a little long on Cole, the hem dragging, the sleeves covering his hands. "What should I do with my yarn?" Cole asked. "Lottie said not to bring it once I put on the shroud."

Harvan held out a hand. "It will interfere with the music of the shroud. Let's leave it here." He placed it at the base of a tree. "We'll return to this spot and retrieve it."

"Will you be able to find it?" Ferrin asked, scanning the area.

"It has a certain music all its own," Harvan said. "Knowing what to listen for, I can get us back here. On we go."

Before too long they reached a break in the trees and had their first view of Deepwell. The village of squat stone buildings had a stone wall around it. Unlike several towns Cole had seen in the echolands, no vegetation grew on the walls or rooftops. A narrow channel ran along the far side of the town, its whistling music mostly eclipsed by the sinister song of Deepwell.

"There really is a well of still water here," Harvan said. "Calm water is a rarity in the echolands."

"Does it carry benefits?" Drake asked.

"Nothing so grand as the scarcity suggests," Harvan said. "Like the fruit, it replenishes energy. And it's nostalgic."

"Have you considered leaving Cole outside of the town with a guard or two?" Ferrin asked.

Harvan turned to Cole. "What do you think?"

"I'd rather help find Destiny," he said without hesitation.

"It's probably the right move," Harvan said. "These sur-roundings have to be heavily monitored. No matter how your music is concealed, if you wait here for long, you'll arouse suspicion. Plus, when we leave, it might be in a hurry. I think we should stick together and remember that protect-ing Cole is our top priority."

"Might be hard to protect him if they capture us," Drake said.

Harvan raised an eyebrow. "Simple. We don't let them take us. Remember, strong wills. Don't let them push us around. Follow my lead." He flipped up his hood. The others did likewise.

Harvan marched away from the cover of the trees,

advancing like he owned Deepwell and wanted to make sure there had been no nonsense in his absence. The others hustled to catch up.

Cole felt tense inside. Harvan seemed overconfident. Maybe that was part of the ruse? Acting certain so the guards would accept him? Cole hoped he knew what he was doing.

If they were captured here, Cole might never see Dalton or Hunter again. Was he crazy to believe they still might make it home? He was currently in the afterlife of another world. Home felt a billion miles away. And it might actually be farther than that.

Hopefully, Dalton and Hunter were having better luck than him. Hopefully, they were eluding pursuit and finding Jenna. It helped to picture somebody happy. He tried not to dwell on Mira, Jace, and Joe, trapped somewhere in the echolands.

The only gates in the wall were closed. As they approached, Harvan raised his voice. "Open up—we've had a long journey."

"Who goes there?" called a guard, just his head appearing over the top of the wall.

"Who do you think? Five who know the source of unmentionable power."

"That's well and good," the guard responded. "But how about names or passwords?"

"We have Drake with us, and Ferrin. The other names are our own. As for passwords, we've been on assignment. How about 'slumber long no more'? Or the one about skies and hills."

"Over sky and under hill," the guard supplied. "Both of those are old."

"Unlike cozy guardsmen, we've been out chasing leads," Harvan said impatiently.

"Who is your master?" the guard asked.

"Nazeem directly controls our fate," Harvan answered swiftly. "Right now, you're our master until that gate opens."

"I'm not trying to be difficult," the guard replied. "You know the routine."

"Yeah, yeah, you're very dutiful," Harvan said.

"I don't suppose you want to show your face?" the guard asked.

"You have your rules—we have ours," Harvan said. "Our identities are to remain guarded. You know how Nazeem can be. We need to interview your prisoners and hurry onward."

"Won't take long," the guard said. "We only have the one. You'll have to talk to Ryger to get access."

"Can somebody show us the way?" Harvan asked.

The gates opened. "Katka will guide you," the guard called down.

A woman approached, tall with narrow features. The sides of her head were shaved, the hair on top black and combed sideways. Her skin had the unmistakable glow of a bright echo.

"You look shiny," Harvan said. "Let me guess. You're the mediator meant to verify our true identities?"

Katka held out a hand, and he shook it. "I don't have to guess to know your robe is a disguise."

"I'm not supposed to reveal my true identity," Harvan said. "Orders from the top."

"Like all primary mediators at secure locations, I represent Nazeem," Katka said. "You will all reveal your identities to me."

"Naturally," Harvan said. "But not here. Far too many eyes and ears. Perhaps we can visit Ryger? He'll want our identities confirmed as well."

"Very well," she said. "Follow me."

She led them down a cobblestone street away from the wall. Cole tried to keep his face as deep in the hood of his robe as possible. Unlike at the Hall of Glory, entering Deepwell didn't quiet the music. If anything, the disturbing cacophony had become even more invasive.

Cole didn't like how many echoes he saw roaming the village. At least twenty men and women. There had to be more inside the buildings. Every step away from the gate was a step they might be losing for a retreat. How would they fight their way past so many enemies? The bluffing had to hold.

Harvan fell into step beside Katka. "You won't share our identities with anyone besides Ryger," he said.

"Only if they have premiere clearance," Katka assured. "Your identity could not be safer than in my care."

"I love the hair, by the way," Harvan said.

She ran a hand across the short bristles. "You talk a lot for somebody trying to go unnoticed."

"I love being noticed," Harvan said warmly. "I just prefer to remain unknown."

"Your friends don't talk much," Katka said.

"Our spokesman does plenty of talking for twice our number," Ferrin said.

"That I believe," Katka said. "What's with the little one?"

Cole didn't like her attention swinging his way. He already felt out of place because of his stature. There were no kids in view. He kept his eyes off Katka's face and did his best to stand up straight.

"He's actually a giant," Harvan said. "Best disguise in the group."

Katka laughed a little.

"Are you on this side often?" Harvan asked.

"Lately, as we head into the final phases," she replied. "I heard you back at the gate. Are you having any luck with the hunt?"

"So many leads," Harvan said. "Too many, sometimes. False trails. We still haven't puzzled everything together. We're hoping your prisoner might help us explore some theories."

"Not willingly," Katka said. "You'll have to be in top form. I can tell you're good with people."

"That's quite a compliment, considering your area of expertise," Harvan said.

"Sure, I read people," Katka replied. "They can't hide from me, especially here. But you're a charmer."

"Who is the prisoner?" Harvan asked in a conspiratorial whisper.

"You're not that good," Katka said. "We need permission from Ryger before we delve into details. And before that happens, I need a look under your hoods."

A guard at a door stepped aside, and they entered one of the larger buildings in the village. It looked to have once been an inn. The tables and chairs were all cleared off to one side. A man at a desk blocked the way to the kitchen, and another obstructed the hall that led to the rooms.

Katka led them to the man blocking the kitchen.

"You have quite an entourage today, Katka," the man said.

"We need to see Ryger," she replied.

"And if he's busy?" the man asked.

"We'll wait," she said.

The man stood up and stepped aside. "He's available. You know the way."

As Cole walked past the man into the kitchen, he pictured fighting his way out. The chances of escaping if somebody raised an alarm were feeling slim. He tried to thrust away his fearful thoughts. They were here. The task at hand was convincing Katka they belonged. He had to act natural. Once again he hoped Harvan knew what he was doing.

They descended a flight of stairs from the kitchen down to a stone-lined storeroom. Katka approached a door and knocked.

"Enter," came a surly voice from inside.

Katka opened the door and admitted them to a spacious room where a heavyset man with a dark unibrow reclined on a bed, fingers laced behind his head, potbelly projecting upward. There was no other furniture in the room.

"Hello, Ryger," Katka said.

He moved his eyes to regard them without shifting his head. "So many visitors? And so mysterious with the hoods?"

"They're under orders to remain anonymous," Katka said. "We're about to find out who they are."

"Have you figured out how to sleep?" Harvan asked.

"I find a bed more comfortable," Ryger said.

"We need to talk to your prisoner," Harvan said.

"That would explain your presence in the dungeon," Ryger said. "Are you stalling?"

Katka approached Harvan. "Lose the robe, mystery man."

"Okay," Harvan said with a nod. Pushing off against Katka, he sprung to the bed and cracked Ryger over the head with a sudden and vicious blow from his walking stick.

Winston extended his hands toward Katka. "Hold her," Harvan said. "Don't hurt her."

Drake and Ferrin raced forward, taking Katka by each arm as Winston chanted and gestured.

As Ryger tried to roll off the bed, Harvan smashed him on the head again. And again. He kept trying to rise. After the third blow, Ryger stayed down.

"I've got her," Winston said.

"Hurry," Harvan ordered, still wailing on Ryger. "You saw the keys?"

"Yes," Ferrin said, leaving Katka to lift the large key ring off the knob at the head of the bed.

"Fetch the prisoner," Winston said, his voice a little strained. "I have her."

As Cole rushed to the door with Drake and Ferrin, he glanced back to see Katka standing as still as a statue. Setting his walking stick aside, Harvan had crouched down and put Ryger in a headlock.

Back in the room that led up to the kitchen, there were two other doors. One was ajar. Ferrin raced to the other, found it locked, but chose the right key on the third try, revealing a hallway beyond. And a guard with a mustache.

"Who are you?" the guard asked.

Ferrin flipped back his hood. "Ryger sent us to interview the prisoner," he said casually.

Considering the clawing panic he felt inside, Cole could hardly believe how calm the displacer sounded.

The guard scowled. "He would have joined you or sent another guard."

"Those rules don't apply in a nightmare," Ferrin said, removing his head.

The astonished guard never saw Drake coming. The seedman hit him low and hard, tackling him to the floor, then straddling him and pummeling him.

"Come on," Ferrin said, head back in place. There were several doors on either side of the hall beyond the guard. Ferrin raised his voice. "We're here to rescue you! Where are you?"

A muffled thumping commenced a few doors down on the right, along with stifled cries of "Here! Here!"

Ferrin started testing keys. There were twelve on the ring. It took five attempts.

The door swung open to reveal Desmond, dressed just how Cole had seen him on a cot beside Honor and Destiny back at the Temple of the Robust Sky. The knight withdrew a couple of paces from the doorway. "Who are you?" he asked warily.

Cole realized his hood was hiding his face. He flipped it back. "We're here to get you out," he said.

Desmond looked like he was trying to say something.

"Yes?" Cole asked.

Desmond shook his head. "Later. Good to see you, Cole. Your escort is on our side?" He jerked a thumb at Ferrin.

"Yeah," Cole said. "Let's go."

PRISONER

Good to meet you," Ferrin said with a nod. "We should run."

"Yes," Desmond agreed.

"Leave the door open!" Harvan called.

Cole turned to see Harvan entering the hall of cells, dragging Ryger, the thickset man still in a headlock. Drake had his guard pinned to the floor.

"We'll lock them in here," Harvan said. "The prison doesn't allow for external spying or mental communication. Let's use the weaving that protects this place to our advantage."

"What about Winston?" Ferrin asked.

"Could you go lend him a hand with Katka?" Harvan suggested. "Is this the prisoner? No princesses?"

"Sorry," Desmond said.

"He's Desmond," Cole said. "He was with Honor. He used to serve under the Dreadknight at Blackmont Castle."

"Desmond, help Drake drag his man to the cell," Harvan said.

Cole held the cell door open while Harvan manhandled Ryger into the small room. Drake and Desmond came next with their guard. Then Ferrin returned to the hall, carrying Katka, who remained rigid. Winston followed, still muttering and gesturing.

"Katka isn't close enough to her physical body to return to the other side," Harvan said. "It came through in her music. Once I heard that, I knew we had a chance."

After Ferrin set Katka in the cell, Harvan flung Ryger to the floor, and Drake abandoned the other guard. Desmond, Ferrin, Drake, and Harvan raced out of the cell, and Winston quit chanting to help Cole slam the door, then made sure it was locked.

"That should hold them for now," Harvan said. "Come on."

They ran out of the hall and closed the door. Harvan dashed to the room where they met Ryger, retrieved his walking stick, and grabbed a sack, which he tossed to Winston.

"We entered as five," Harvan said. "They'll notice us leaving as six. Do we care?"

Winston pulled the final shroud from the sack and chucked it to Desmond, who immediately started to put it on.

"I'll go over the wall on my own," Ferrin said.

"Can you make it?" Harvan asked.

Ferrin cracked his knuckles. "In my sleep. It's not very high. And the security isn't heavy. I'll meet you back in the woods by where we left the yarn."

"If they try to freeze you, be strong," Harvan said.

"Count on it." Ferrin turned to Winston. "Nice job controlling Katka."

Winston gave an embarrassed smile. "It wasn't the feat it might have seemed. They gave up much of their protection by inviting us inside. I have no doubt she is a talented mediator. But she's not much of a shapecrafter. Many mediators have very sensitive perceptions without powerful wills."

"This is why people will never hear stories about Winston," Harvan complained. "He just held a master shapecrafter in suspension on her home turf, and he made it sound boring."

"What about the guy blocking the way upstairs?" Cole asked.

Harvan stroked his beard. "He will have counted that five entered. But there are no alternate routes past him."

"I've got it," Ferrin said, bounding up the stairs. They could hear his urgent voice after he passed out of view. "Ryger says to come quick! The prisoner is missing!"

The guard came thumping down the stairs. Waiting off to the side, Harvan greeted the guard with his walking stick. The man stumbled under the blows but got a hand up, temporarily freezing Harvan, who remained still for barely a second before breaking free.

Desmond and Drake grabbed the man and hauled him to the hall with the cells. Cole brought the keys over and started testing them one by one, trying to open the door to the hall.

Suddenly, he couldn't move. He exerted his will, but the grip was pretty secure. Drake slammed the guard against the wall and started punching him, and Cole was no longer immobilized.

He found the right key.

Behind him, Ferrin wrestled another guard down the stairs. Harvan helped drag the second guardsman into the hall of cells.

Cole went to the cell where they had left Ryger, Katka, and the other guard.

"Different cell," Harvan said. "They could be ready for us."

Cole moved one door over and found the correct key on the second try. They deposited the men in the cell and secured the door.

"Should be clear sailing now," Harvan said, running down the hall of cells. Everyone else followed in a hurry. They pounded up the stairs, through the retired kitchen, and into the empty common room.

"Now we walk," Drake said, slowing down at the door.

"Exactly," Harvan agreed.

They exited to the cobblestone street. Harvan led them toward the gate where they had entered. Ferrin went in the opposite direction.

"Walk quickly," Harvan whispered. "I have an excuse."

Cole tried not to look around too much. Or too little. Many men and women moved about in the walled village. He waited for a scream from behind. Somebody would call out an accusation at any moment, and then they would be running.

How long before an echo went into the prison to find it unmanned? Would that person sound an alarm immediately or first go searching for Ryger, Katka, and company?

Cole tried to trust his disguise. And his comrades. He fought to slow his breathing and calm his racing heart.

They reached the closed gate.

"Back so soon?" the same guard asked.

"Like you said," Harvan replied jovially, "one prisoner."

"Did you find what you were looking for?" the guard asked.

"Not exactly, but he accidentally presented an interesting lead," Harvan said.

"You seem in a hurry," the guard observed.

"Exactly right," Harvan said. "We're eager to act on this new knowledge. Our quarry is highly prized by Nazeem."

"And Katka?" the guard checked.

"We left her with Ryger," Harvan said.

The guard put his fists on his hips. "She's supposed to walk you out."

"She and Ryger got into some kind of disagreement," Harvan said.

With us, Cole added in his mind.

The guard held up a hand. "Do you mind waiting while I send a runner?"

For the first time, Harvan sounded unpleasant. "Actually, yes. Katka had plenty of time to report to you while we spoke with the prisoner. Instead she got tied up with Ryger." He went from unpleasant to angry. "We came here to verify vital intelligence, with favorable results, but the situation is extremely time sensitive. If that gate were open, we would be running." Harvan moved beyond angry to furious, though he didn't shout. "You are obstructing our investigation. What is your name? Must I take off my hood and pull rank?"

"Open the gate," the guard said. He waved them through. "She should have reported back first thing," the guard apologized. "We'll check it out."

"Good choice," Harvan said, breaking into a sprint.

Cole and the others followed. As he ran, Cole found himself holding back laughter. He managed to contain it with the thought that it could only be a minute or two before the guards found out what really happened and came in pursuit.

"Mask our conversation?" Harvan asked.

"Done," Winston said.

"You came here with Honor?" Harvan asked Desmond as they dashed toward the trees.

"Yes," Desmond answered.

"Where is she now?" Harvan asked.

"They took her to Gamat Rue," Desmond said.

"Interesting," Harvan said. "Not the Fallen Temple?"

"There was talk of that," Desmond said. "But they settled on Gamat Rue in the end."

"Did you guys find any leads on Destiny?" Cole asked.

"Nothing," Desmond said. "I don't think she ever made it to Deepwell. If so, she went in and out without getting caught. This was a dead end for us."

"Disappointing," Harvan said. "What would you suggest we do?"

"If you're looking for Destiny, keep up the hunt,"

Desmond said. "I can't recommend how. I'm going to find Honor. I should have never lost her."

They reached the trees. Looking back, Cole saw nobody in pursuit yet.

"Going to Gamat Rue would lead us backward," Harvan said. "But finding Honor is a priority for us as well."

"Leave it to me," Desmond assured him.

"Gamat Rue will be much more formidable than Deepwell," Harvan said. "You'll need help."

"Should we split up?" Drake asked. "I could join him."

"Would you be willing?" Harvan asked.

"I'll do whatever would most benefit your cause," Drake said.

"There is a powerful echomancer at Gamat Rue," Harvan said. "Nandavi. You could get permanently trapped there."

"I could get trapped with you as well," Drake said. "I've accepted the risks."

"I largely brought extra manpower in case we needed to divide our efforts," Harvan said. "Cole, what do you think?"

"Destiny is my mission right now," Cole said. "But some of my friends might be at Gamat Rue. Joe, Jace, and possibly Mira. I'd love to send help."

They raced through the trees in silence for a time.

Harvan stopped at a tree and crouched to pick up a piece of yarn. He handed it to Cole, then started taking off his robe. "The echoes at Deepwell know us by these disguises. Now would be an opportune time to shed them."

Cole pulled off the robe and pocketed the yarn. Winston took Cole's robe and Harvan's and stuffed them in the sack.

"Are you still shielding us from scrutiny?" Harvan asked Winston.

"The best I can," the other man replied.

"I sense Ferrin," Harvan said. He turned to peer out into the trees.

A moment later the displacer ran into view.

"How'd it go?" Harvan called.

"I didn't get away clean," Ferrin said. "But clean enough. Sorry I was a little slow. I looped around wide to hopefully lead them off course. Are we abandoning the robes?"

"Take it off," Harvan said. "But keep it."

"Where are we heading?" Ferrin asked.

"Away from Deepwell for starters," Harvan said. "We can't accomplish anything if we get captured. Desmond wants to visit Gamat Rue to help Honor and perhaps some of Cole's friends. Cole and I must stay after Destiny."

"Do you know where to go next?" Ferrin asked.

Cole watched Harvan with great interest.

"I have an idea," Harvan said. "But I only mean to share it with those who accompany me."

"I offered to join Desmond," Drake said.

"I could do that too," Ferrin said. "Should I?"

"Let's move," Harvan said. They all started running together. "It might be most effective to part ways. The princesses are our top priority. I can't pursue multiple princesses at once."

"Drake and I would be happy to join Desmond," Ferrin said.

"You may want to seek other help before invading Gamat

"Rue," Harvan said. "It will be no small chore. The princess will be extremely well guarded."

"Let us worry about that," Drake said. "Others can direct us to Gamat Rue?"

"Many know the location," Harvan said.

Desmond came alongside Cole. "I have a message from Honor to Destiny. Would you mind bringing it to her?"

"Of course not," Cole said.

Desmond produced a small, tightly rolled scroll.

"A written message?" Harvan asked. "They didn't confiscate it?"

"The message was disguised with weaving," Desmond said. It seemed he was trying to say something else, but nothing came out.

"You tried to tell me something when we first found you," Cole said.

Desmond attempted to speak again but failed.

"He's bound somehow," Harvan said. "Is that right?"

"Yes," Desmond said. "I know certain things about Honor that I can't express."

"Do you know anything about Destiny's location?" Harvan checked. "A clue you can't reveal?"

"No," Desmond said. "As far as I know, her whereabouts remain a complete mystery to everyone. I wish I could better explain why I can't speak."

"Does your silence have to do with the message?" Harvan asked.

"It's related," Desmond said. "The message was written by Honor and is meant for Destiny's eyes only. I vowed not to read it or share anything I know about what it might contain."

"Should we read it?" Harvan asked. "We made no oaths."

"I cannot entrust the scroll to another unless they vow not to read it," Desmond said. "I don't think my binding will let me give it away unless the recipient promises sincerely."

"Honor couldn't have bound you," Harvan said.

"An agent of hers did it," Desmond replied. He tried to say something else but failed. "It's hard to find words I can utter."

"Happens to the best of us," Harvan assured him. "Would it be dangerous for us to accept the message?"

"I don't think so. But bringing the message to Destiny could be very important for Honor."

"Up to you, Cole," Harvan said. "Sounds like you'll need to promise not to read the message and mean it."

Cole hesitated. He hadn't thought carrying around the coin for Sando would be dangerous either. He knew too well that bindings could carry hidden threats. But just because he had been burned didn't mean it would happen every time. Desmond didn't seem to think it was too risky. And besides, this binding had been performed by an agent of Honor's! It was probably just a precaution to keep the message safe. Since Desmond was returning to Honor, if Cole refused, the letter would go undelivered. What if it had information vital to Destiny's protection? He had to accept whatever risk the binding might involve.

"I'll take it," Cole said. "I promise not to read it."

Desmond handed over the little scroll. Cole tucked it away.

They ran in silence for a time, enveloped by the music of the forest. Part of Cole wanted to go with Ferrin, Drake, and Desmond to help his friends at Gamat Rue. It would be nice to have a known destination, and such a relief to see Jace and Joe. If Nandavi and Sando were holding Honor there, was there a chance Mira remained there as well?

But what if Desmond had faulty info? What if both Honor and Mira were already at the Fallen Temple with Nazeem? What if postponing his search for Destiny let Nazeem claim her? Cole had promised Mira he would find her younger sister. If Harvan had a possible lead, they needed to pursue that first.

"If we're going to split up, sooner would be better than later," Harvan said. "It will confuse those from Deepwell who are trying to follow us."

"I have to go to Gamat Rue," Desmond said. "My sworn duty is to rescue Honor. I'd welcome any help."

"What do you say, Cole?" Harvan asked. "Should Drake and Ferrin join him?"

Cole appreciated Harvan asking his opinion but also felt a little intimidated. It was a big decision. Lives were at stake. "How much will we need Drake and Ferrin as we hunt for Tessa?" It was still a novelty to converse while sprinting without feeling winded.

"The next phase of our search for Destiny will rely more on stealth," Harvan said. "I'm convinced that nobody has found Destiny, meaning we're trying to find her rather than steal her back. Going forward, I don't expect numbers to be as important as they were at Deepwell."

That helped solidify Cole's opinion. "Then if Drake and Ferrin are willing, I'd feel better knowing they were helping Honor and maybe Mira."

"Sounds like a decision," Ferrin said. "We'll go to Gamat Rue with Desmond."

"My other friends are a kid named Jace and a man named Joe," Cole said. "They're bright echoes, held at Gamat Rue."

"I remember them," Desmond said. "We'll do our best to aid them."

"In the town of Duplan, not far from Gamat Rue, you can find an echo named Giselle," Harvan said. "She is connected to the Unseen and will undoubtedly help you. Tell her I sent you."

"Much obliged," Desmond said. "We'll make for Duplan first. Gentleman, thank you for springing me from my incarceration. Would you be so kind as to point me in the correct direction?"

"That way," Harvan said, gesturing off through the trees to one side. "Asking directions to Duplan shouldn't arouse much suspicion."

"It was good traveling with you," Ferrin said. "Perhaps we'll meet again."

"I hope so," Cole said. "Say hi to my friends."

"Safe journey," Drake said.

Desmond veered off in the direction Harvan had indicated. Drake and Ferrin followed. Before long, trees screened them from view.

CHAPTER

23

DEADLANDS

"So where are we going?" Cole asked after running in silence for a good while.

"Any guesses, Winston?" Harvan asked.

"It better be good," Winston replied. "We just lost some capable men."

"No guess?" Harvan checked.

"Should I know?" Winston asked.

"It would require an intuitive leap," Harvan said.

"I'm at a loss," Winston admitted.

"Music to my ears," Harvan gloated with a smile.

"You got me," Winston said. "I'm not a mind reader. Congratulations."

"Any chance of us being overheard?" Harvan asked.

"I'm shielding us," Winston said. "You'd know more about pursuers."

"They're a good ways back," Harvan said. "Some went after the others. They're not very organized. I'm taking us into the deep woods. Lonely country with few echoes they could communicate with to coordinate a hunt."

"So we're getting away?" Cole asked hopefully.

"Looks that way for now," Harvan said. "If we keep up the pace, I think we'll win our way clear. Nobody would be eager to follow us."

"We're going someplace dangerous?" Cole asked.

Harvan glanced at Cole. "If you could speak to anybody in the echolands right now, who would you choose?"

Winston gasped. "You know how to find her?"

"Winston may have guessed it," Harvan said.

"Destiny?" Cole asked.

"That would be better," Harvan conceded. "I mean somebody you don't know."

"You kept this from me?" Winston asked, annoyed.

"People tell me secrets because I keep them," Harvan said.

"Until now," Winston said.

"It's an emergency," Harvan said. "I'm hoping she'll agree."

"The Grand Shaper?" Cole guessed.

"Well done," Harvan approved. "Prescia Demorri."

"Mira's aunt," Cole said.

"How long have you known?" Winston asked.

"I explored these lands long before we met," Harvan said.

"Where is she?" Winston asked.

"Near the heart of the Deadlands."

Winston slowed.

"Keep running," Harvan said. "They won't be any less perilous if we delay our arrival."

"What are the Deadlands?" Cole asked. The name didn't sound very inviting.

"You know how we generally avoid disturbing music?" Harvan asked.

"Yeah," Cole said.

"We're about to do the opposite."

"You've been there?" Cole asked.

"Twice," Harvan said. "Alone."

"What's it like?" Cole asked.

"Dead echoes gather there," Harvan said. "The kind that are lost and confused but still functional."

"In enormous numbers, if I understand correctly," Winston said.

"There are no channels in the area," Harvan said. "Efforts have been made to purge the Deadlands in the past. To help the dead echoes find rest. But there are too many of them, and they are too far gone."

"Will they want to hurt us?" Cole asked.

"Some will try," Harvan said. "We'll avoid them."

"We'll run for our lives is more like it," Winston grumbled.

"We're already running for our lives," Harvan said. "Think of it as a change of venue."

"How can Prescia help?" Cole asked.

"My highest hope is that Destiny might have found her way there," Harvan said. "Wouldn't that be splendid? If not, consulting with the most powerful living weaver can't hurt."

"She's been hiding in the Deadlands all this time," Winston murmured.

"She had to hide somewhere," Harvan said. "She built a refuge for herself. We'll be secure once we find her."

"If you say so," Winston said. "I can't believe we're running *toward* the Deadlands."

"It'll take some time," Harvan said.

"If I had any sense, I would have gone with Desmond," Winston said. "Gamat Rue doesn't sound so bad all of a sudden."

"The unknown always gets to you," Harvan soothed. "I've been there. Trust me."

"Nice try," Winston said. "You've used that line one too many times."

Harvan glanced at Cole. "You're going to spook the kid."

"I'm okay," Cole said. "When you can't avoid something like this, all you can do is be brave and get it over with."

Harvan laughed. "Hear that, Winston. Best. Kid. Ever."

Cole turned his head to conceal his proud smile.

At length they left the woodlands behind, returning to endless vistas of lawns and gardens. Time lost meaning as they sprinted under the unchanging sky. Cole tried not to worry about the Deadlands. If Harvan had survived the place twice, why not a third time?

Harvan continued to direct them around towns and any echoes he sensed, and as a consequence, Cole never saw anybody. After crossing several channels, slipstreams became less common as well. Only the passing hills and fields marked their progress.

Eventually, the landscape started to look less groomed.

There still wasn't any dead vegetation, but Cole began to notice bare patches of ground and craggy ridges. The trees were less clustered, the grass wilder and longer, the way a little less smooth.

"We haven't seen a slipstream in a while," Cole mentioned.

"We're now heading almost directly toward the fringe," Harvan said. "Since we're traveling away from the Source, we're running parallel to most of the channels rather than crossing them."

"The fringe is bad, right?" Cole checked.

"It's less of a paradise," Harvan said. "More hazardous. But there are fewer towns, and fewer shapecrafters, which we don't mind. And it's how we reach the Deadlands."

"It's bad," Winston translated.

"Do the Deadlands reach all the way around the echolands?" Cole asked.

"Oh, no," Harvan said. "They just cover this part of the fringe. There are many other areas, good and bad, depending on which direction you go."

"Have you explored a lot of the fringe?" Cole asked.

"Not as much as I would like," Harvan said. "If you venture too far, you don't come back. I've seen why. As you get out there, the shift in the music is subtle, but pretty soon it lures you along, farther and farther, and all the music behind loses its savor. Everything starts to blur into the call of the Other."

"Sounds like you've gone out far," Cole said.

"Farther than most who managed to return," Harvan said. "I'm curious to go farther, but I know eventually I'll pass a point where return becomes impossible. I long to discover what the Other offers, but if I go there too soon, I may miss many explorations in the echolands. The Other will always be waiting. Who knows if I'll ever get a chance to pass this way again?"

As they proceeded, the patches of dirt or rock became larger and more apparent. They weren't ugly—they just didn't look like part of a meticulously cultivated garden. The music of the empty patches was slower and heavier.

But their pace remained quick. As they progressed, they no longer saw groves of trees, just isolated loners here and there. The fields had a lower density of flowers, and the grass grew in patches. There were still no dead plants or leaves, but lots of soil, lots of stone.

The music up ahead became foreboding. It produced emotions like loneliness and despair, a soundtrack tailored for feeble wanderers crawling through the desert, deliriously looking for the right place to collapse.

"Is that it?" Cole asked.

"We're getting close," Harvan said.

"Should we eat?" Winston asked. "I see some carrots."

"Might not be a bad idea," Harvan said. "We'll want to be at our best."

They paused, and Winston uprooted a trio of carrots. Cole accepted one and took a bite. Crunchy and sweet, the first bite brought a surge of alertness.

"Wow," Cole said. "I feel more awake."

"We've run a long way," Winston said. "It depletes energy and focus. You don't tend to notice until it gets dire."

They finished their carrots.

Harvan placed his hands on his hips. "The dead echoes up ahead are drawn to live echoes. I expect them to be extra captivated by Cole, since he's bright. We don't need to treat them with courtesy. They are the shells of echoes. Their lifesparks moved on long ago. Our goal is avoidance."

"What will they try to do to us?" Cole asked, unsure whether he wanted the answer.

"They want what we have," Harvan said. "They want to feel alive again. Something about the Deadlands amplifies those desires. They came to the Deadlands because at some level they're dissatisfied with their lifeless state. Some dead echoes can function normally for a long while. But if they avoid the channels for long enough, eventually they deteriorate and end up in places like this."

"They'll attack us," Winston translated. "They'll keep coming until we're as dead as they are."

"So we'll be running," Cole said.

Harvan winced. "Probably. But not at first. The echoes of the Deadlands seem drawn to motion. In previous visits, they mostly walked as long as I walked, and it seemed to curb their interest. Once I started running, they did too. We'll see how long we can hold to a slower pace." Harvan brandished his walking stick. "Once we speed up, don't be shy about using that sword."

Harvan started sprinting again. Cole ran at one side, Winston on the other.

"When do we walk?" Cole wondered.

"You'll see," Harvan replied.

As the depressing music up ahead gained dominance, the vegetation dwindled. The bare landscape became gnarled and craggy, dipping and rising haphazardly. Cole didn't like how the contorted terrain limited his line of sight. Dead echoes could be lurking around the next rock pile or beyond the next incline.

Harvan slowed to a walk. "I hear some dead echoes. Not too many yet."

The desolate surroundings looked empty to Cole. He could only hear the dismal music inherent to the landscape.

They advanced at a casual pace over dirt and stone. The uneven ground forced Cole to pay more attention to where he stepped than he had since arriving in the echolands. Harvan began turning a lot more sharply and frequently. Now that the dreary music fully enveloped them, Cole had to fight the urge to sit down.

"Are you guys tired?" Cole asked.

"It's the music," Harvan said. "The fatigue is in your mind, not your muscles. This music demands surrender. Resist."

They weaved around stony projections and plodded across sandy stretches. Nothing grew here.

"Don't be alarmed," Harvan said. "Just follow my lead."

Two men and a woman walked into view from off to one side. Cole was expecting the dead echoes to appear disheveled, like zombies, but these three looked normal.

"Excuse us!" the woman called, her voice a little too strident. "Could we have a word with you? I think we took a wrong turn."

"Don't answer," Harvan muttered.

"Are you ignoring us?" one of the men called. "Are you turning your backs on us?"

"Keep walking," Harvan said. "There are more coming. We don't want a stampede."

Others came into view from a different direction.

"You're a cute one," an older woman called, her eyes on Cole. "I bet the girls won't leave you alone."

Harvan increased his pace a little. Cole matched it. "Stay calm," Harvan murmured.

They came around the side of a low ridge to find a mob of more than twenty people jostling toward them, men and women. They didn't look dead. They weren't decomposing, and their clothes were presentable. Cole found all eyes on him.

"There are more behind us," Harvan said. "We're accumulating a lot of admirers from many directions. More than I ever did alone. Maybe it's having three of us together. Maybe it's Cole's brightness. They're gathering fast. We don't want to get surrounded."

Up ahead Cole saw a gap in a steep wall of rock. The mob off to the side was picking up speed, not fully running yet, but trying to outpace one another.

"So much for walking," Harvan said, breaking into a run. Cole stayed with him. Winston was a step or two behind.

The members of the mob started running as well, moving on a trajectory to cut off escape through the gap. Risking a look back, Cole saw more coming from directly behind.

It was now a footrace. As the gap neared, so did the fastest members of the mob. Harvan clobbered a man in the head with his walking stick, Cole slashed a woman's outstretched arm, and then they were in the gap. Glancing back, Cole saw Wilson right behind him, and many people beyond him, running intently.

Emerging from the gap, Cole saw more scattered echoes ahead, all coming their way. Harvan weaved for a time, trying to keep the dead echoes from effectively converging. It took some artful maneuvering because the dead echoes approached from many directions.

Looking back, Cole saw the echoes behind them losing ground. They sprinted in bursts, but seemed to lack the determination to keep up a long chase. Some who had pursued them through the gap had already lost interest.

Harvan made it a priority to avoid groups, sometimes charging an individual echo to bash the person aside and create a new path. Cole ran hard and kept his sword ready.

There was never a break. At best, three or four echoes would remain in view. At worst, Cole saw more than a hundred. Survival would have been impossible without tireless legs.

Cole tried to shake his sense of desperation, but it was challenging. Time and again it looked like they might not make it around the next group.

Cole didn't have to use his sword too often. When necessary, Harvan reliably toppled echoes with his walking stick.

The dead echoes routinely cried out. Some sounded desperate.

"Help! Don't leave me! Come back!"

Others were strangely polite.

"A moment of your time? Excuse me? Just a moment, please?"

Some got angry.

"Don't you run! Where are you going? Stop this instant! Do you hear me? Don't you dare run!"

Cole did his best to block out the voices and also tried to ignore the melancholy music. The constant threat of attack kept him focused despite the interminable running. Cole felt like he had the football, and a couple of teammates to help block, but the field went on forever, and the other team had an endless supply of players.

An element of sameness pervaded the relentless chase. There were new rock formations to navigate, and new faces to evade, but the dynamics of the danger stayed fairly constant. They either had to run at top speed, using good angles to elude dead echoes, or else get gang-tackled.

Cole didn't suffer physically. His muscles never burned. His lungs didn't strain. But the constant threat of capture was mentally grueling. As the wild run dragged on, to help manage his frustration, Cole quit hoping for the chase to end. Better to grimly pretend there was no finish line. This was his life now.

Harvan did a superb job of avoiding critical threats like narrow places and large groups of dead echoes. Without his guidance, Cole doubted he would have lasted more than a few minutes. But Harvan had a knack for anticipating the positions of the dead echoes and reading the upcoming terrain. As long as Harvan, Cole, and Winston stayed at a full sprint on relatively open ground, the dead echoes lacked the endurance and the teamwork to entrap them.

"Do you know where we're going?" Cole finally asked.

"We're getting closer," Harvan said. "It may get a bit worse before it gets better."

Before long, not only did Harvan have to use his walking stick twice, but Cole hacked a pair of dead echoes with his sword. The echoes scrambled back up after getting slashed aside, but by the time they recovered, Cole, Harvan, and Winston were out of reach.

Near misses became more frequent. Cole regularly had to help Harvan with his sword. He found that striking the head worked best. Sometimes Winston threw punches.

"Good job, Cole," Harvan said after a particularly fierce flurry of fighting. "How are you holding up?"

"I'm okay," Cole said.

"I'm fine too," Winston said. "Remember me? The guy taking on hordes of echoes without a weapon?"

"You could pick up a stick," Harvan suggested.

"Unless we find a really good one, I'll punch and weave," Winston said.

"You're both doing well," Harvan said. "We're almost there. The biggest mob yet lies ahead of us, hundreds strong, right between our current position and our destination. I've been avoiding high ground so we don't get surrounded." He pointed to a ridge up ahead. "But I think we need to break that rule. I'm hoping that if we go up that ridge, we'll draw the big group toward us and we can try to go around."

"Toward us," Winston said. "I love it."

"It should make them clump together more," Harvan

said. "Right now they're too spread out. I don't think we'd make it around them."

"You can hear all that in the music?" Cole said.

"With surprising detail," Harvan said. "I can sense the shape of the terrain too. It's all there if you learn to read it."

"He does have his uses," Winston said.

They raced up a rocky slope. Cole used his free hand to help climb as it grew steeper. The higher they got, the farther Cole could see. The dead echoes in the area seemed to take renewed interest as Cole and his companions gained altitude. Many who had stopped chasing them purposefully began heading their way again.

"We're drawing a crowd from behind," Winston warned.

"We have to be quick or we'll get trapped up here," Harvan said.

Cole found it extra weird to rush up the steep slope without getting winded. With his normal body, just walking up this incline would have made him tired.

When they reached the flat top of the ridge, Harvan hurried with them to the far edge. Cole's stomach dropped when he saw the multitude of dead echoes amassed up ahead. It looked like a sprawling crowd waiting for an outdoor rock concert. Beyond the throng Cole saw what had to be their destination—an oasis of tall fir trees and green grass.

"No," Winston complained. "Seriously?"

The mass of echoes began to drift toward them. Some at the perimeter of the crowd were walking more quickly.

"We've got this," Harvan said. He cupped his hands around his mouth and shouted. "Hi, friends! We should talk!"

That did the trick. The crowd broke into a run, surging toward the ridge.

"Go," Harvan said. "I'll keep their attention here for a minute. Head around them to the trees. I'll catch up."

Winston patted Cole. "He means it."

From behind them, on the other side of the ridge, echoes began to climb into view, most staring earnestly at Cole.

"They're coming from behind," Cole warned.

"I know," Harvan said. "Run."

Winston and Cole started scrambling down the side of the ridge. Though Cole could no longer see Harvan, he heard him shouting, "Come on, hurry up! I have so many questions for you! And so many answers!"

Cole concentrated on not falling. This side of the ridge was steeper than where they had climbed. Loose pebbles skittered underfoot.

Glancing back, Cole saw Harvan following them recklessly, taking huge leaps. His haste was necessary. Many dead echoes were right behind him. There would be no doubling back.

Cole and Winston reached a ledge above a drop taller than the high dive at the town pool back home. Maybe fifteen feet!

"Jump!" Harvan called. "No time."

Winston sprang, landing in a wild tumble on the rocky incline below. Cole tried to leap but couldn't. It felt like suicide!

"Jump!" Harvan insisted, closer now.

Cole had the Jumping Sword in his hand. What if it worked? He needed this. It had to.

He pointed the blade at a point farther down the slope and called, "Away."

There was no tug from the sword. No hint of his power.

So he jumped.

The ground rushed up to him, and he flopped forward, rolling violently. The impact should have snapped half the bones in his body. Instead, it didn't even hurt that much. He was shaken, but as he rose, he could feel that nothing was broken. Nor was he bleeding. Just kind of sore. He had dropped his sword. He retrieved it, and Harvan landed nearby.

"You're tougher than you think," Harvan said, rising. "Keep going."

Cole picked up his pace, descending the ridge more rapidly now that he knew a fall wouldn't hurt as it should. The dead echoes close behind added plenty of incentive.

"Don't try that off a giant cliff," Harvan said as the ground leveled out. "Echoes are more durable than physical bodies, but not indestructible. And they don't heal."

"What about soreness?" Cole asked. It was weird to be running for his life and not be gasping.

"Soreness will usually fade," Harvan said. "Any actual damage won't. Okay. Top speed."

Cole dug deep and sprinted with everything he had. From their lower vantage, he couldn't see the huge crowd of dead echoes blocking the way to the trees. But the memory was scary enough to make him push his limits.

The echoes behind them began to lose steam, but new echoes up ahead forced them to swerve quite a bit. When the big crowd came into view, Cole could appreciate the brilliance of Harvan's plan. The echoes were grouped much tighter and had gone close enough to the ridge that Cole, Harvan, and Winston had a real chance to race around them.

But the horde of echoes was coming fast, voicing a tangle of shouts. Some of the faster outliers still had a chance to cut them off from the green oasis.

Cole could tell he was forcing Harvan to run slower than he otherwise would. With his shorter legs, Cole simply wasn't going to outrun a healthy grown man.

"Are the trees safe?" Cole asked.

"Yes," Harvan said. "Once we're on the grass, they won't follow."

The greenery drew nearer, as did the dead echoes. A few of the fastest echoes managed to intercept them.

"One last brawl," Harvan said, smashing an echo in the face.

Cole chopped an outstretched hand, then dodged a young woman who lunged at him. The evasion slowed him a bit, allowing an older man to dive and seize his ankle.

Cole went down. He tried to kick free, but the man held fast. Cole slashed the echo's wrist, and he finally let go.

Cole looked up to see a flood of echoes descending on him, arms outstretched, faces crazed. Before he returned to his feet, he would be mobbed.

Then Harvan and Winston jumped in front of him. "Go!" Harvan roared, swinging his walking stick in huge, sweeping arcs. Winston lowered his shoulder and rammed an echo in the chest. The nearest echoes were driven back by the violence of the attack, causing those behind to stumble to a halt.

It was a momentary lull, a minor wave moving against the encroaching tide, but the pause let Cole return to his feet and sprint to the grass. The instant he passed from the dirt to the lawn, the music changed, the despairing strains of the Deadlands completely replaced by the refreshing refrain of grass and trees.

The difference was so abrupt that for a moment Cole felt disoriented, like he had awakened from a nightmare. Then he turned to look back.

Harvan fought off a couple more echoes and hauled Winston to his feet. As the dead echoes surged forward, Harvan and Winston bashed their way to the lawn, shaking off grasping hands, fighting for every step. With a final burst of effort, together they staggered onto the grass.

PRESCIA

R elieved that Harvan and Winston had made it, Cole stepped forward, ready to defend them with the Jumping Sword, but the dead echoes acted like an invisible wall shielded the lawn. They pressed up right to where the grass began, but not a step farther.

"That was close," Harvan said, leaning on his walking stick. "Let's get away from the edge. No reason to tempt fate."

The crowd of echoes milled about, yelling and complaining.

"Come back!"

"Don't go there!"

"We need to talk!"

"You're a very special boy!"

"It's been so, so long!"

Cole hurried after Harvan, passing between fir trees, happy when the disgruntled echoes were screened from view. Before long they could no longer be heard, either.

"Thanks, guys," Cole said wholeheartedly. "I was a goner."

"I need a sword," Winston murmured. "At least a stick."

"Happy to help," Harvan said. "You did great, Cole. It's hard to believe you're so young. You have the composure of a real professional."

The compliment helped dispel some of the embarrassment Cole felt for getting tripped. "Are we safe now?" he asked.

"Until it comes time to leave," Harvan said.

"I can't wait," Winston grumbled.

"Let's hope our visit with Prescia will justify the trouble," Harvan said. "It isn't far now."

By unspoken agreement, they walked. Cole basked in the gentler music, gratefully inhaling pine resin. Though he wasn't physically tired, it was a luxury not to be running. Nobody was chasing him.

"This place is big," Cole said after they had walked for a few more minutes.

"Not tiny," Harvan said. "Not enormous. We're almost there."

Between a pair of tall fir trees, a low cottage came into view, the walls composed of long, pale slabs of stone. As they drew near, the front door opened and a tall woman stormed out, slender with angular features. "Traitor!" she cried vehemently. "How dare you!"

"There's a good explanation," Harvan replied.

"You promised!" she accused. "Can nobody be trusted? You swore!"

"Not a bound oath," Harvan said.

"I tried!" she yelled, no longer drawing closer. Hands on

her hips, she waited for Harvan to approach. "You wouldn't let me!"

"I don't like entanglements," Harvan said. "Trust me. This is a good thing. Once you hear me out, you'll be glad I brought them."

"Hear you out? How about see you out! Be gone!"

Harvan walked up to her. Cole and Winston hung back. "Prescia," he said calmly. "You're more beautiful than ever."

"Sweet talk?" she cried. "Don't even try, Harvan. When has flattery been anything but camouflage for a trap?"

"When it's sincere," Harvan said, taking her hand swiftly and giving it a slow kiss, his eyes on hers.

"I have gone to extreme lengths to protect this hideout," Prescia said with a little less agitation. "How could you?"

"This is Winston Proust, my longtime associate and most trusted companion. The boy is . . . well, examine the boy and you'll understand why we're here."

Prescia narrowed her eyes at Harvan, then turned her gaze to Cole. "Come forward, lad. What is your name?"

"Cole Randolph."

"Give me your hand."

Cole extended one arm. Her veiny hands had long fingers with short nails. Up close, she smelled like spices with a hint of smoke. The skin of her face looked stretched and shiny.

"You're alive," Cole said.

"A bright echo, yes," she replied. "I'm not a former Grand Shaper yet. I'd like to keep it that way."

She traced his palm with her fingers, turned his hand over, then turned it back. Crouching, she gazed into his eyes. Hers were long, the outside corners tilting slightly up. He studied the rings and flecks of color in her amber irises.

"You've met a version of Dandalus," Prescia said, surprised.

"The guy in the Founding Stone," Cole said.

"How is that possible?" she asked.

"Owandell was using the Founding Stone to communicate with Nazeem," Cole said. "I snuck into their secret meeting, but they found me. When I touched the Founding Stone, Dandalus helped me escape."

Prescia ran a fingertip from Cole's palm to his wrist. Suddenly, she gripped his hand tightly, and her head turned to Harvan. "He's had contact with the Mare! Why didn't you tell me?"

"Showmanship," Harvan said simply, giving a toothy smile. "Are you less angry?"

"Possibly," Prescia said, her eyes returning to Cole. "How did you encounter the Mare?"

"She saved me," Cole said. "Twice. Once in the normal world, once here. At least I think it was the same horse. Both times she drove away bad guys who were trying to capture me. In the normal world, she looked a little fierier, but that was at night. Here she let me ride her."

Prescia gasped. "She did? Yes, she did. Interesting. What do you know of the Mare?"

"I thought it was weird she could be in the afterlife and the normal world," Cole said. "Could one be her echo? Also, the colors of her coat kind of flow like smoke."

"You have no notion how she came to be?" Prescia inquired.

"Not really," Cole said. "But she's my favorite horse ever."

"Why are you here in the echolands?" Prescia asked.

"I'm looking for Destiny," Cole said.

"Destiny tends to find us all," Prescia said.

"Your niece Destiny," Cole clarified.

Prescia looked at Harvan, who appeared smug. "Yes, I see," she said. She released Cole. "Winston, your hand."

Winston complied. She examined it front and back. "You can weave here."

"I have some talent for it," Winston said.

She stared into his eyes. "Will you divulge my whereabouts to anyone?"

"Not under torture," Winston said. "Not if imprisoned for a thousand years."

She threw his hand down. "He means it. But how can one ever be sure? People mean what they say until they have reasons to change their minds. Everyone disappoints. Everyone fails you."

"Not us," Harvan said.

Prescia swiveled toward her doorway. "Is that so? Come on, you dashing ignoramus. Let's move this discussion indoors."

Cole followed her into the cottage. A bedroom was visible through an open door. The tidy living room had a bench and a wooden rocking chair. Prescia gestured at the bench and claimed the rocker. Cole sat down beside Harvan and Winston.

"You are damaged, Cole," Prescia said.

"My power was attacked by Morgassa when we defeated her," Cole said. "Can you fix it?"

"No, my boy, the damage exceeds anything I could remedy," Prescia said. "You're from Outside. You wish to return home."

"Yeah," Cole said. "How'd you know?"

"It's what she does," Harvan said.

"Not that anyone bothers to listen," Prescia said. "Want to know the quickest way to deafen people? Tell them the truth."

"Do you know where we can find Destiny?" Cole asked.

"What about finding your way home?" Prescia countered.

"Time for that later," Cole said. "One crisis at a time."

"After you find Destiny?" Prescia asked.

"No, then I have to find Honor and Mira and help them defeat Stafford and Nazeem." He didn't even mention the part about saving Jace and Joe from whatever they were currently facing. It was embarrassing to admit how much trouble his mistake with Sando had caused, and how many people he needed to save in order to make up for it.

"Tell me about Honor and Mira," Prescia said.

Cole explained how Honor and Mira had ended up in the echolands. He told about Durny looking for Mira. And he shared how Desmond, Ferrin, and Drake had gone in search of Honor.

"There is much work ahead of you," Prescia said. "You are not new to aiding the princesses."

"I've been working with Mira," Cole said. "We got her power back. Honor's and Constance's too. Now we just need to help Destiny and Elegance."

"You've met Harmony," Prescia said.

"Yeah," Cole said. "She's who told me Honor and Destiny were in trouble."

"I tried to admonish my younger sister about Stafford," Prescia said. "I didn't know the particulars, but I felt this coming. I knew her children and the kingdom would suffer. Of course she didn't believe me. Any true prophet knows the experience—we sense the future, we offer accurate warnings and guidance, and none will heed us. Sometimes I wonder if it would be better not to know. It would certainly cause me less anguish. In Harmony's defense, Stafford was a different man when she wed him."

"Is Destiny here, by chance?" Harvan asked.

"Wouldn't that be nice?" Prescia said. "You'd be the last man I would tell, even with a bound oath, you scoundrel."

"Didn't I have a good reason to bring them here?" Harvan asked.

"Defendable reason or not, you broke my trust," Prescia said. "Cole, you wish to find Destiny?"

"Yes," Cole said. "I promised Mira."

"Destiny is not here," Prescia said.

"Do you know where I can find her?" Cole asked.

"I am the most gifted living weaver in Necronum," Prescia said. "Destiny is my blood relative. And I have no idea. Neither, thankfully, does Nazeem, Stafford, or any of the others hunting her. Part of me wonders if they understand who they are chasing."

"What do you mean?" Cole asked.

"I do not pretend to love my sister," Prescia said. "I did

however feel some affection for my nieces. Until Destiny. That child frightens me."

"Why?" Cole asked.

"She is by far the most powerful of Harmony's daughters. And her gift is the rarest. Some weavers have a knack for cajoling knowledge from echoes. Some weavers have a higher power—the ability to simply know things about the past, present, and future. But Destiny leaves us all behind. The best of us only see bits and pieces. I know of none who see like Destiny. She is less a girl with power, and more like power in the form of a young girl."

"Didn't she lose her power?" Cole asked.

Prescia laughed bitterly. "Only the greatest fool would attempt to steal so prodigious an ability. Enter Stafford and Owandell. Yes, they stripped her power. But the imbeciles sought to control it. Harmony is not without her gifts, with the names of her children as the best evidence. How do you outsmart destiny itself?"

"You don't?" Cole guessed.

"Exactly," Prescia said. "The shapecrafters tried to channel Destiny's ability into a chosen vessel, a very gifted young shapecrafter. Instead, the power entered one of their horses."

It took a moment for the implications to sink in. "The Mare?" Cole guessed.

"Very good," Prescia said. "You were rescued by Destiny's power. You rode Destiny's power. And this is why I suspect you are destined to find my niece."

"Maybe I didn't betray your trust," Harvan said excitedly. "I may just be a humble servant of destiny."

"Nice try," Prescia snapped. "If I were you, Harvan, I would stop reminding me you are present."

"That's a tall order for him," Winston murmured.

"Let's just see how he does with it," Prescia said.

"Will the Mare help me find Destiny?" Cole asked.

"The Mare is an embodiment of Destiny's formidable power," Prescia said. "We can all be grateful for any help we receive from the Mare, but to expect her assistance would be foolhardy. You may very well never cross paths with the Mare again."

"Is that a prophecy?" Cole asked.

"Just common sense," Prescia said.

"I call the horse Thunder," Cole said.

"I call her the Mare," Prescia replied.

Cole stared at Prescia. "You can't help me find Destiny?"

"I never said that," Prescia said.

"She only said she doesn't know where Destiny is," Harvan reminded everyone.

Prescia stared at him coldly. Winston nudged him. After a moment Harvan folded his hands in his lap and bowed his head.

"You can help?" Cole asked.

"Can and will," Prescia said. "I know an opportunity when I see it."

"An opportunity I provided," Harvan grumbled, eyes on the floor. Winston nudged him harder.

"How can you help?" Cole asked.

"By following Harvan's example," Prescia said.

Harvan looked up, smiling.

"Not by breaking a trust," she stated emphatically.

Harvan dropped his head again.

"But by sending you to consult with one who knows more than I do," Prescia said.

"Aren't you the best weaver?" Cole asked.

"In Necronum, yes," Prescia said. "In the echolands, not even close. I recommend you visit She Who Stands at the Summit."

"She's a myth," Winston said, then covered his mouth with both hands.

"A myth I have conversed with," Prescia said.

Harvan looked up, eyes bright. "You know how to find her?"

"I do," Prescia said.

Harvan pumped a fist. "Spectacular."

"The journey will be fraught with peril," Prescia warned, glaring.

"Naturally," Harvan said. Then he pantomimed locking his lips with a key. "I'll keep quiet."

"How do we find her?" Cole asked.

"She stands atop the Farthest Mountain, deep, deep in the fringe," Prescia said.

Harvan drummed the bench between his legs, a huge grin on his face. Winston slumped.

"Do you know how to get there?" Cole asked Harvan.

"No idea," Harvan said cheerfully. "Always wanted to try. Figured I should wait until I was ready to move on to the Other."

"These two can accompany you to the base of the mountain," Prescia told Cole. "They can even go up part of the way with you. But you must scale the summit alone."

"Why?" Harvan asked.

"If more than one person tries to approach her, she will cast you all from the mountain," Prescia said.

"Can I go after he finishes?" Harvan asked tentatively.

Prescia shrugged. "If you must. But accessing She Who Stands at the Summit is no small task. Few find their way to her mountain. Most fail to reach the top. You must pass whatever test she deems appropriate."

"Do you think I can do it?" Cole asked.

"I know of no other way you could find Destiny," Prescia said. "If you are indeed meant to locate my niece, you will find a way to reach the summit."

"The lady at the top will know?" Cole asked.

"She Who Stands at the Summit is wise and powerful beyond reckoning," Prescia said. "She will be able to guide you."

"How do we find the mountain?" Cole asked. "Harvan doesn't know the way."

Prescia stood up. "Wait here."

She walked into the bedroom.

Harvan put an arm around Cole and squeezed him. "What did I tell you?" he whispered. "Isn't she great?"

"She's not too happy with you," Cole replied quietly.

"It'll pass," Harvan said. "Point is, we have a lead now. Not just a lead—an epic adventure!"

"He gets like this," Winston said, arms folded.

Prescia returned carrying a shuttered silver lantern. "See this, Cole."

"Is that . . . ?" Harvan asked.

"The Weaver's Beacon," Prescia said. "An heirloom passed down from one Grand Shaper to the next. Our guiding light in the echolands."

Harvan's eyes widened. "Does that mean Cole is the next—"

"Of course not," Prescia snapped. "I'm loaning it to him."

"Doesn't the Weaver's Beacon make this oasis possible?" Harvan asked.

"It does," Prescia said.

"Then how will you preserve your refuge if Cole takes the beacon?" Harvan asked.

"I won't," Prescia said simply. "I'm returning to Necronum. I mean to go help your other friends rescue Honor. She was always my favorite."

"What should I do with the Weaver's Beacon?" Cole asked.

"You should not lose it," Prescia said. "Can you please repeat that back to me?"

"I shouldn't lose it," Cole said.

"Keep it with you at all times," Prescia said. "Go on, repeat."

"I'll keep it with me at all times," Cole said.

"You don't lend it to these clowns or anyone else," Prescia said. "Understood?"

"Yes," Cole said.

"I told the beacon where you mean to go," Prescia said. "It

will not mislead you. Trust it over your senses, or Harvan's. Far out in the fringe, sweet music can be as dangerous as foul."

"How will I know where it wants me to go?" Cole asked.

"Take it," Prescia said, holding it out.

Cole grabbed the lantern by the handle on top. It was lighter than he expected. The lantern did not hang straight down. It tilted, gently pulling in a certain direction.

"Feel that?" Prescia asked.

"Yes," Cole said.

"Let the beacon guide you," Prescia said. "You won't have to cut back across the central echolands. You're on the proper side to continue out into the fringe. The light of the beacon will drive away dead echoes. And help conceal you from enemies. And it will maintain your energy better than food. Those who rely on tampered shaping or who embrace dark energy and music will find its purity disruptive."

"Thank you," Cole said, amazed.

"Don't forget to open the shutter," Prescia said.

"We can just walk out of the Deadlands?" Winston checked.

"Time is short," Prescia said. "I suggest you run. But the dead echoes will not harass you."

"I'm speechless," Harvan said.

"And yet you're talking," Prescia replied.

"It's an incredible gift," Harvan continued.

"It's a loan," Prescia reminded him.

"We can never repay you," Harvan said.

"I require no payment," Prescia said. "My duty is to

protect Necronum. I have bided my time long enough. Now is the hour to make my move. We are fellow soldiers in the same campaign."

"If you're going after Honor, don't you need the beacon?" Harvan asked.

"Not as much as Cole does," Prescia said, concern entering her gaze. "He will not find She Who Stands at the Summit without it. My instincts tell me it's up to him to find Destiny. The Outskirts have never faced greater peril. Dire forces are in motion. If I can't trust my instincts, I may as well go ride a slipstream."

"We won't fail you," Harvan said.

Prescia took a step toward him. "You had better not. You brought this boy here, Harvan. He is your responsibility. He must succeed. You and your sidekick pay whatever price is necessary to protect him."

Harvan saluted. "It was already my intention."

"This could be your finest hour," Prescia said. "Your greatest story. Or it could negate all the others."

Harvan hesitated, as if trying to resist speaking, then went ahead with it. "People will still tell the stories either way. They're pretty ingrained."

"Not if there is no Outskirts," Prescia said. "And now, I must away. I suggest you do the same."

"Hey, you know?" Harvan said with a chuckle. "If you're abandoning your refuge, I guess it doesn't really matter that I told these two the secret."

"You still broke your promise," Prescia said. "Don't forget that I'm abandoning the refuge because you brought them here. But if you succeed in your mission, all will be forgiven." She winked at Cole and disappeared.

"Is her body nearby?" Cole asked.

"It must be," Harvan said. "Not sure what the Necronum side looks like right here. Probably not very hospitable."

"That's all the rest we get?" Winston asked.

"We came here looking for a reason to run," Harvan said, rubbing his hands together. "Now we have it. Ready, Cole?"

Cole held up the lantern and opened the shutter. A mellow white radiance shone forth. "I think so."

"Good enough," Harvan said. "Let's find out if the Farthest Mountain lives up to its name."

CHAPTER
— 25 —

FARTHEST

The Weaver's Beacon kept dead echoes away as promised. Cole saw plenty, but the lifeless echoes acted like Cole and his companions were invisible.

As they ran, Winston kept staring at the lantern. After some time he spoke up. "I'd almost rather have to run from the dead echoes."

"How come?" Cole asked.

"You're holding the fate of Necronum," Winston said. "It's the Grand Shaper's most storied talisman. And we have it!"

"Of course we have it," Harvan said. "Name a hero more worthy."

"Prescia Demorri," Winston said.

"She gave it to us," Harvan said. "So we must be worthy."

"Or she's horribly desperate," Winston said. "What if she gave us the keys to the kingdom because it's burning down?"

"Of course the kingdom is in peril," Harvan said. "It's our job to save it."

"No pressure," Winston said.

"I'm glad we're not being chased," Cole said. "The beacon wasn't doing much good just hiding her. Now she's joining the fight, and we have a better chance of fulfilling our mission."

"See, Winston?" Harvan said. "What do I keep telling you? Best kid ever!"

Cole smiled, then cringed inside—was it wrong of him to accept all that praise when his actions had endangered his friends, especially when he didn't know whether he could repair the damage? Mira, Jace, and Joe were suffering while he got applause. Harvan had it wrong. Worst kid ever. Most gullible kid ever. As always, Cole did his best to push those thoughts away.

Running with the lantern was a little awkward, but not too bad. Just like his legs and lungs didn't tire from running, his arm didn't tire from holding it, though he switched hands from time to time for variety. The trickiest part was getting used to not swinging his arm as he sprinted.

Without being chased, the Deadlands went by calmly, though the people roaming around still seemed kind of creepy. They all acted so lost. Cole kept reminding himself that they were just shells of people, like imprints.

Beyond the Deadlands, vegetation returned, though not as orderly as the gardens of the central echolands. None of the vegetation was sick or dying. No leaves had fallen; no grass was dry. But the shrubs and trees were more spread out and random, and there were less frequent flowers. Still, Cole was relieved to see plants again and thrilled to escape the depressing playlist of the Deadlands.

"How far will it be to the Farthest Mountain?" Winston asked.

"Better not to wonder," Harvan said. "I've traveled more than most, and I'm prepping my mind for a long run."

"I'm starting to question if I'm doing the afterlife all wrong," Winston grumbled.

"Are you serious?" Harvan asked. "What would you rather be doing? Lounging around the Hall of Glory? *That's* monotony. At least out here the scenery changes! We'll get to see distant reaches of the fringe that few ever lay eyes on. And we're still involved in world events."

"See how I get suckered into these things?" Winston asked Cole.

"He makes a good argument," Cole said.

"Right," Winston replied. "Then before you know it, you're running for your life from countless dead echoes across a nightmare landscape. Next thing you know, the fate of the world is on your shoulders as you're hunted by the forces of evil. Who wants to be that guy?"

"Somebody has to do it," Cole said.

"Exactly," Harvan enthused. "So it might as well be somebody competent."

Winston moaned.

Cole laughed.

They kept running.

Eventually, the music ahead shifted, growing darker and more mysterious. The lantern pulled Cole toward it.

"Have you heard that before?" Cole asked.

"I'm blazing new trails here," Harvan said. "It's new to me."

"Me too," Winston added.

After topping the next rise, a black-sand desert spread out before them, a dark ocean of rolling dunes.

"You sure that beacon isn't broken?" Winston asked.

"It's pulling that way," Cole apologized.

"It doesn't sound evil," Harvan said. "Just . . . ancient, and full of secrets."

The sand turned out to be exceedingly fine. With each step their feet plunged in almost to the ankles. Their running strides kicked up shadowy plumes behind them. Going up the dunes, Cole felt like he lost half a step for each one he took. Running across the sand would have worn him out in minutes in the mortal world, but he still didn't tire. It was just frustrating to have his pace slowed.

The dunes went on and on, rank after rank. They climbed and descended, climbed and descended, climbed and descended. A few times Cole slipped running down the far side of a dune. With each fall he strove to protect the lantern. Though it got jostled, the light continued to glow, and it didn't show any damage.

After a great while, the dunes flattened into a sandy expanse, and then the music began to change as the sand gave way to what looked like gray fragments of pottery. The angular fragments rattled and snapped underfoot but offered a bit more support than the sand, and the music became less ominous.

At one point they spotted a distant tower with hopeful music. Harvan mentioned that it might be worth investigating, but as they moved in that direction, the beacon tugged them away.

The terrain became orange dirt, interrupted by steep ridges and small, sparse trees with golden foliage. The music held an edge of danger but was also fairly majestic.

The dirt gave way to a surface of hard, flat stone, white with gray swirls. It made for easy running, but after some time only white flatness was visible in all directions. With no landmarks, Cole began to lose the sense that they were making any progress. The subtle, soft music was the closest to an absence of sound Cole had experienced in the echolands.

From the distance, Cole began to notice hints of a sweet melody. Only catching it in snippets, he strained to hear it better. The little he could discern seemed to be the prettiest, most welcoming music he had ever heard. And the beacon was taking them in that direction.

"Do you guys hear that pretty music?" Cole asked. "Kind of far off?"

Harvan laughed. "You're finally starting to apprehend it? I wondered how long it would take."

"The homesong has never been more distinct," Winston said.

"You guys have been hearing it?" Cole asked.

"For a long time," Harvan said. "It's much louder than the music of this emptiness."

That wasn't true for Cole. "I can barely hear it," he confessed.

"That's why we didn't mention it," Harvan said. "We were glad you were deaf to the summons. The call of the Other is probably the biggest threat out here on the fringe.

When it gets hold of people, they wander off in a trance, never to return."

"What I hear sounds beautiful," Cole said.

"Try not to focus on it," Winston said.

"Like it or not, you'll hear it more clearly over time," Harvan explained. "It will only get harder to resist."

"The beacon is dampening the effects," Winston said. "Even so, I've never heard the homesong this powerfully."

"Think of your duty," Harvan said. "Don't let your mind get drawn away."

Cole tried not to listen to the call. He still caught little snatches.

"I'm curious how strong the homesong would be without the beacon," Harvan said. "Should Cole shutter it for a moment?"

"Are you mad?" Winston asked. "The call might grab all three of us. Plus, the beacon conceals us."

"You're right," Harvan said. "I just get curious."

"You want to hear the music more distinctly," Winston said. "You want to wallow in it. You want to gargle it without swallowing. I don't blame you. So do I. But that's a deadly game."

Cole wanted to hear it more clearly too. "Are you guys going to be all right?" he asked.

"We both have a good deal of experience resisting," Harvan said. "If we start to wander off course, snap us out of it. We're not just going to disappear."

"Our lifespark could escape," Winston said.

"Not if our minds hold firm," Harvan said. "Destiny needs us. Prescia trusted us. The world could fall without us."

They kept running. Cole tried not to listen as the call of the Other rang out more clearly. Between the unchanging landscape and the unchanging sky, Cole lost all sense of time. He thought back to other places he had been—the orange terrain, the black-sand desert, the Deadlands, the paradise of the central echolands, Necronum, Junction, Zeropolis, Elloweer, Sambria, and Arizona. He needed to remind himself that there was more to existence than running across this changeless expanse.

Finally, little bumps began to take shape on the horizon before them.

"You two see those hills?" Winston asked.

"Yes," Harvan confirmed.

The hills gradually came closer, rising higher. Beyond them, a lone mountain began to take shape, dark, steep, and surreally tall.

"Now that is a mountain," Winston said.

"I've never seen its equal," Harvan said. "I know of no serious mountain in the echolands."

"The beacon is pulling straight at it," Cole said.

"Hear the music yet?" Harvan asked.

"A little," Winston said.

"Not yet," Cole said.

"You'll like it," Harvan said. "The sound fits."

As the foothills approached, Cole began to hear their music. At the beginning of the hills, the song of the mountain came through, its magnificent music dramatic and powerful.

"I hear it now," Cole said as they started into the hills.

"Impressive, right?" Harvan said. "I think we've made it."

"How long have we been running?" Cole asked.

"I usually have some sense of the passing time," Harvan said. "I'm at a loss now. Many days. Possibly weeks. The black dunes threw me. And the white plain was worse."

They continued across the foothills, the forbidding mountain looming above them. Cole considered the steep stone surfaces, angular and raw. The lofty summit appeared unreachable.

"We're going to climb that?" Cole asked.

"Keep trusting the beacon," Harvan said. "We'll go part of the way with you."

"Wait," Cole said, "what will you do when I take away the beacon?"

"We'll do as we've always done," Harvan said. "We'll hold on."

"The music of the mountain is strong," Winston said. "It might help counter the call of the Other."

"We'll test it at the base of the mountain," Harvan said. "Not by closing the shutter. We'll walk away and see how we fare."

"Not a bad idea," Winston said.

Compared to crossing the white plain, the mountain drew rapidly nearer. The hills became darker and stonier, piling up against the base of the mountain itself.

Harvan halted. After going nonstop for so long, the absence of running felt very strange to Cole.

Hands on his hips, Harvan looked around. "I'd say we're on the shoulders of the mountain now. Should I walk away?"

"Go ahead," Winston said.

"Sit tight," Harvan said, jogging away from them.

The music of the mountain now saturated Cole enough that he could no longer hear the beckoning melody of the Other. Hopefully, that was a positive sign.

Harvan kept going until he looked to be about an inch tall. After a few minutes he returned.

"Wow," Harvan said. "It won't be easy. I didn't intend to go so far, or stay away so long. It wasn't easy to return. I focused hard on our mission, and the music of the mountain, and I barely made it back."

"Should I try it?" Winston asked.

"Don't go as far as I did," Harvan said. "You'll feel it after about ten steps."

"Ten paces," Winston said resolutely. He then took ten steps away counting each one. He stopped. Then took another. And another.

"Winston?" Harvan called.

Winston turned, his eyes closed, his mouth bent in a dreamy smile. He swayed.

"We're going to lose him," Harvan muttered. "Winston! Return at once!"

Winston started walking away.

"Stay here," Harvan said to Cole. He ran after Winston and shook his shoulder. Winston shrugged away from him, so Harvan grabbed an arm and pulled. By the time they reached Cole, Winston was blinking and looked disoriented.

"I've never felt anything like that," Winston said.

"Did you try to focus on the mountain?" Harvan asked.

Winston shook his head. "I had no control. I was gone. Our mission dropped out of my mind. The homesong never claimed me like that before. I didn't hear the mountain. I didn't hear my own thoughts. I was too . . . relaxed. Blissful."

"What do we do?" Cole asked.

"We'll climb part of the way together," Harvan said. "When you go on ahead, I'll take responsibility for Winston. I'll pin him down if I must. The duty might actually help my focus."

"I'll try harder," Winston said. "Maybe it'll help that I know what to expect."

Cole stared at the two men. What if he returned from the mountaintop and they were gone? It would be awful!

Harvan held up a finger. "Hear that?"

"What?" Winston asked, cocking his head.

Harvan looked around. "Someone is coming. Fast. Too fast." He looked up, then pointed. "There!"

Cole followed his finger to five specks in the sky coming their way. "Birds?" Cole asked.

"Wind riders," Harvan said. "I've heard rumors. Never actually seen any. What are they doing out here?"

"Coming toward us," Winston said.

Cole squinted. The specks were drawing rapidly nearer. He could now make out wings.

"How'd they find us?" Winston asked.

"Maybe they noticed us when we walked away from the beacon," Harvan said.

"Why are they anywhere near this place?" Winston asked. "We're way off the map."

"Could they be good guys?" Cole asked.

"Shapecrafters," Harvan said. "I hear their music."

"Do we hide?" Cole asked.

"No point," Harvan said. "They've already spotted us. They're coming right at us. Cole, if I say the word, you run for it."

"But—"

"No argument, Cole," Winston said.

"All else aside, we can't let the Weaver's Beacon fall into their hands," Harvan said. "Let them land. I'll talk to them. We'll find out what they want. If it turns into a brawl, Cole, you run up that mountain as fast as your legs will carry you. Strong wills, gentlemen. Don't let them bind you."

As the shapecrafters flew closer, Cole could see that they were men with gliders on their backs. They swooped down and landed perhaps a hundred yards away. They wore the wings like backpacks and shrugged out of them after landing.

Cole recognized one of them. "Sando," he said.

"Really?" Harvan asked. "That guy is everywhere!"

As the five shapecrafters came closer, Cole saw that one was a woman. Sando took the lead, revealing his bare gums with a wide grin.

"Young sir!" he called. "I thought our paths might cross again! And not a moment too soon! You have strayed too close to the Other."

"Come no closer," Harvan said firmly, stepping in front of Cole.

"Back away," Winston suggested to Cole out the side of his mouth.

Cole retreated several paces.

Sando came to a halt ten yards from Harvan. "You are in terrible danger, young sir. This mountain is haunted by a vicious fiend. Very little lies beyond this accursed place. Let us carry you to safety."

"How did you find him, Sando?" Harvan asked.

"It helps to anticipate where your quarry needs to go," Sando said. "Young sir is looking for someone. The fiend of this mountain has considerable knowledge. Let's keep this civil, Harvan Kane. You don't want to meet your end here. Who would tell the story?"

"What do you expect us to do?" Harvan asked.

"What any reasonable person does when outnumbered and outclassed," Sando said. "Surrender."

"Is that my reputation?" Harvan asked. "Reasonable?"

Sando pointed at Harvan with two fingers. The four shapecrafters flanking Sando began gesturing and chanting. Suddenly, Harvan and Winston were not moving. Harvan trembled. Winston stayed still as a statue.

Cole felt nothing. He drew his sword. "Get out of here, Sando." He stepped closer to Harvan and Winston, bathing them more fully in light from the beacon. Both men shook off their paralysis.

Sando glared at the female shapecrafter. "The boy," he murmured.

"I've never felt such a slippery target," she complained.

Sando narrowed his eyes. Then they widened. "You have an interesting lamp, young sir. Unusual craftsmanship. It resembles one that is meant to stay safely hidden. Surely you have not brought it into jeopardy at the periphery of the echolands?"

Harvan twirled his walking stick and looked over his shoulder at Cole. "Time for you to go."

"Let me help," Cole said, holding the beacon higher in one hand while swinging his sword with the other.

Harvan glared at him. "Don't worry about me. I live for these moments. We all have a part to play. Go. Now."

Cole stared at Sando, whose trickery had led to the capture of Mira, Jace, and Joe. At the moment he wanted nothing more than to find out how many chops it would take to physically destroy an echo.

Sando grinned even wider. "Come, giver of silver. I believe you have a grievance to settle with me. We can talk of your squealing little friends."

"Cole," Harvan said, his voice hard. "Now."

"Listen to him," Winston said.

Cole turned and ran. Tears stung his eyes. Harvan and Winston were right. It was his duty to run. But it still felt cowardly.

He glanced back. Winston wrestled with a shapecrafter. Harvan thumped a man to the ground with his walking stick, then immediately fell back. He wasn't attacking. He was maneuvering to keep himself between the shapecrafters and Cole. At least they weren't paralyzed.

Cole stumbled, dropping his sword to catch himself. He kept the beacon from touching the ground. He picked up the Jumping Sword and sheathed the blade, then sprinted with all his might, following the tug of the lantern.

The lantern wasn't just leading Cole up the mountain, but around it as well. He climbed diagonally, stealing glances back as best he could without slowing down. His last view of the fight involved a pair of shapecrafters holding Winston down while another pair grappled with Harvan. Sando stood off to one side, watching the brawl.

The old beggar didn't look up at Cole.

Nobody was coming after him yet.

Would they give chase once Winston and Harvan were entirely subdued? Could they use their gliders to catch up? Would they simply wait for him to come down?

All Cole knew for sure was that his current job was to charge up the mountain. Harvan and Winston had provided an opportunity. To waste it would make their sacrifice meaningless. Cole needed to protect the Weaver's Beacon. He needed to make it to the summit and discover how to find Destiny. Then he could worry about the rest.

He ran hard, his path snaking ever higher over smooth,

dark, angular rocks. Every upward glance made him uneasy—cliffs on top of cliffs stretched to stratospheric heights. If looking up felt intimidating, how would it be to look down? Cole had always been good with heights, but unclimbable precipices were another matter. He had no reason to believe he could access the colossal peak except for the lantern pulling him forward.

What would happen to Harvan and Winston? Was there a chance Harvan and Winston would overpower the shapecrafters and fight their way free? What if they couldn't? Would the shapecrafters march them away from the mountain until they were entranced by the call of the Other? Or might Sando take them prisoner?

Cole tried to console himself that both men were already dead. The thought wasn't very comforting. Neither man was ready to move on. If they were forced out of the echolands, wasn't that basically a second death?

The Weaver's Beacon led Cole onto a narrow path. Sometimes it vanished, only to reappear a few hundred yards later. He began to find stone steps chiseled into the rock. Maybe there was a way up after all!

Cole stayed at a run. Who knew when Sando and his henchmen might come after him? His duty was to give them as little chance as possible to stop him.

The path wound higher up the mountainside. The lantern followed the trail perfectly, curving through switchbacks and guiding Cole across barren areas where the path became hard to discern. Sometimes the path went into little tunnels or along deep clefts in the rock. The way became ever steeper. Some of the stairs were stacked so vertically that Cole felt like he was climbing crude stone ladders.

Cole tried not to look down, but every so often, moving along ledges or clifftops, he glimpsed arresting drops. As the way became almost constantly steep, he was unable to maintain a pace equal to running, but he climbed as quickly as he could.

After a long while he reached a wall where the stone steps dwindled to nothing more than handholds gouged into the rocky face. There was no way Cole could proceed with the Weaver's Beacon in his hand, so he looped the handle over the hilt of the Jumping Sword at his waist. The comfortably spaced handholds were shaped for easy grabbing, but Cole still felt nervous. Even without the panic of vertigo, a serious drop awaited if he slipped. Cole didn't care how tough echoes were—a fall from this height would be deadly. The danger demanded respect.

Higher and higher he climbed, the Weaver's Beacon wobbling at his waist. Every so often he would scan the sky, but he saw no gliders, or anything else for that matter. He was so close to the mountain that it was hard to gauge how far he was from the summit. He would reach the top of one precipice to find another awaiting above it.

The ascent began to feel like crossing the black-sand desert or the plain of white stone—he climbed without ever expecting to stop. The summit was up there someplace, but actually arriving seemed unrealistic. Perhaps the mountain was growing taller at a faster rate than Cole could climb. It sure seemed that way as one steep ascent followed another. Cole would not have been surprised to look down and see stars.

At long last he reached a broad ledge. The beacon at his waist pulled him toward a neatly carved staircase. This one wasn't crude like the previous stairs. It looked like it belonged in a castle.

As Cole approached, a voice filled his mind, accompanied by fierce music drenched in power.

Who dares to scale my mountain?

Cole paused, then spoke aloud. "My name is Cole. I need your help finding someone."

On your knees, then.

Cole obeyed.

Close your eyes.

Again he complied.

Lie down.

He did.

Awake.

Opening his eyes, Cole froze.

He was no longer on a mountain.

He was under a black curtain, on a cool concrete surface.

He had lifted the fabric just enough to see out. He was in a basement. *The* basement. The supposed spook alley where Jenna, Dalton, and so many others were taken to the Outskirts by slavers.

There was Jenna now! Heading down the hole in the floor. He wanted to call out before her head ducked out of sight, but slavers were everywhere, and it all felt too real. If he cried out, he would be captured as well. The last of the kids followed Jenna down, some shrieking as they dropped from the final rung.

Was this real? It sure felt authentic. But he was actually somewhere else, wasn't he? This had happened months ago. He was already in the Outskirts. Where? Sambria? No, Elloweer had come after that, then Zeropolis, then Necronum. That was it! Necronum.

But where in Necronum?

And why had he returned to the basement? Could he have gone back in time?

This didn't feel like a dream or a memory. He felt the weight and texture of the curtain. His senses were alert, his conscious mind active. He felt awake.

There stood Ansel in his wide-brimmed hat and long weathered duster, checking his pocket watch. Secha was beside him, squat and swarthy, her clothes like layers of tattered rags.

"Excellent timing, Ansel," she said. "This was a good plan."

"Think we found what we were looking for?" Ansel asked.

Cole closed off his view. He had heard these words before. Why was he here, now, hearing them again? Could his time in the Outskirts have been a dream? No way. Too much had happened. It had all felt so vivid! But it seemed hazier now, many of the details slipping away.

He heard people walking around. The slavers were packing out the last of their stuff. He knew what they were doing. He knew what they looked like. He had seen it all before. Cole had no doubt about what was going to happen. Secha and Ansel would be the last to leave. They would speak one more time. He couldn't recall the exact words, but he knew basically what to expect.

Could he change how things happened? The kids were already down the hole. If he came out now, he would just get caught. Ansel had his sickle.

If this had happened before, how was it happening again? If the Outskirts had been an elaborate dream, why did he know what was coming next?

"Are we finished?" Secha asked.

Cole raised the fabric enough to see.

Ansel was checking his pocket watch. "Just over six minutes left." He gazed around the room. "Doesn't matter how we leave the place. Nobody can follow us. We're done here."

Secha climbed down the manhole, and Ansel followed. "Do we cover it?" her voice asked from out of sight.

"No need."

Cole knew they were gone. Nobody else was in the room except for a little girl dressed like an angel, hiding under a different curtain.

He knew about the girl because this had all happened before. Had he really gone back in time? Was this a chance to change the outcome?

Last time he had followed his stolen friends down the manhole. And he had ended up in the Outskirts. Before long he was enslaved alongside them. So many adventures had followed. But he was stuck there, risking his life day after day. His chances of getting home were bleak. Nobody even knew he was missing. Everyone had forgotten him. And supposedly, even if he made it home, he would soon get drawn back in.

In a far corner of the room the little girl crawled out from under a heap of curtains. She was small and skinny, with wavy auburn hair and freckles. Cole remembered her angel costume, down to the crumpled wings and the tilted tinsel halo.

The girl looked around furtively. She approached the manhole cautiously and peered down. Then she turned to the stairs.

"Hey," Cole called. "Delaney!"

The girl whirled and jumped, wide eyes searching for who had spoken. "Hello?" she asked hesitantly. "Do I know you?"

Cole came out from under his curtains. "Don't be afraid. I was hiding too."

"I saw you guys come in," she said. "I was part of another group."

"You hid behind the curtains and got covered when they came down," Cole said.

The girl gave him a strange look. "Yes. How did you know?"

"I bet you wanted to warn us, but they would have just sprung the trap earlier and caught you, too."

"Are you psychic or something?" she asked.

"Just a good guesser," Cole said. "Our friends are in huge trouble. You should climb out a window and go for help. Break it if it won't open. Get the police."

"Aren't you coming?" Delaney asked.

Cole folded his arms and stared at the hole in the floor. That was the question. He supposed he could do whatever he wanted. Was this really a second chance?

"I don't know," Cole said.

"Are you thinking of following them?" Delaney asked, her inflection implying it was a bad idea.

Cole gazed at one of the basement windows. His family was that way. He could go home and see his mom, dad, and sister. He could be there in less than ten minutes. He could help explain what happened to Dalton and Jenna. Would anyone listen to him? Would anyone believe him?

"Are you all right?" Delaney asked.

"Just thinking," Cole said.

Would Dalton and Jenna be any worse off if he didn't go after them? Dalton would wind up working at the Silver Lining in Merriston. He would probably be safer at the confidence lounge than fighting the High King and Nazeem. They hadn't found Jenna, so she would presumably remain at the Temple of the Still Water in Necronum.

But what about Mira? As his mind turned to her, memories came flooding back. Would she have been taken by the legionnaires at Skyport? Maybe. No, wait, she would have probably died at the proving grounds. The cyclops would have gotten her. What about Honor and Constance? Who would stop Carnag? Morgassa? Roxie? Would any of the princesses get their abilities back?

"Hello," Delaney whispered, waving a hand in front of Cole's face. "We need to get out of here. What if somebody comes down from upstairs?" She glanced at the hole. "What if some of those guys come back?"

Cole looked at the window. It would be such a relief to go home. But could he live with knowing his friends were trapped? Could he live with Mira getting killed? Or if she somehow survived, getting captured by her father? Could he live with the princesses never regaining their powers? With Carnag and Morgassa and Roxie running wild? All the Outskirts could be destroyed. That included Dalton, Jenna, and all the others.

"I'm going to follow them," Cole said. "I'll be careful. Tell the police what happened."

"Are you sure?" Delaney asked. "They're fast and strong. They might catch you."

"They have my friends," Cole said. "It's what I'm doing. My name is Cole Randolph. Try to remember me. Try to remember us. Please tell our parents what happened. You better go."

"Be careful," she said.

"You too," Cole replied. "Hurry!"

Delaney moved toward the window, and Cole went to the hole and started down the metal rungs. Soon his foot couldn't find the next one. Darkness yawned below.

Cole took a deep breath. "Here we go again," he murmured, stepping off the rungs and plunging into the darkness.

His eyes snapped open.

Cole was not falling.

He was not newly arrived in the Outskirts, seated on

scorched dirt, surrounded by a symmetrical ring of twelve stone pillars.

He was in his bed.

At home. His real home, where he lived with his parents and sister.

It was morning.

Cole sat up. He wore his standard sleep uniform—a T-shirt and basketball shorts.

Had that all been a crazy dream? It must have been. It had even started repeating at the end.

Wow. It had felt very real.

His Halloween costume rested on the chair in his room. He was going to be a scarecrow that got used for archery practice. The tips of the arrows were broken off so he wouldn't be bringing weapons to school.

Cole got out of bed.

What was going on? Had it really all been a dream? Had he not yet gone to school on Halloween? Had Jenna not been dressed as Cleopatra? Had Dalton not yet been a sad clown? Had they not gone to a haunted house in a basement?

What about Mira? And Jace? And Twitch? And Joe? And Honor? And Constance? And . . . Hunter?

Wait a minute.

In his dream he had a brother.

A brother who had gone to the Outskirts a couple of years before him.

A brother who had supposedly occupied the spare room across the hall.

Cole turned away from his door. He was scared to look.

What if the spare room was full of stuff that belonged to Hunter?

No. That was crazy. It had all been a dream.

It was no big deal to go look.

Except it was.

Because Cole had broken out in a cold sweat. Deep inside lurked an unsettling certainty that none of it had been a dream.

He had to walk across the hall and see.

Cole went out into the hall.

The door to the spare room was closed.

What was it supposed to look like inside? Cole could not form an image of the spare room in his mind. Surely he had gone in there. But as he thought back, he couldn't remember any specifics.

He opened the door.

Cole felt like he had been punched in the gut. No, worse, stabbed in the gut. And the knife was twisting.

The bed was unmade, like somebody had slept in it and left in a hurry. There were some clothes on the floor. Jeans. Shin guards. A light layer of dust covered everything.

On the dresser by the door stood numerous soccer trophies. And a framed team photo. An individual photo of Hunter Randolph sat beside it, the brother from the dream. His name was on the trophies too.

Cole backed out of the room.

He didn't want to see any more.

Cole returned to his bedroom.

He had forgotten his brother. His parents had forgotten

his brother. His sister had forgotten him too. Cole hid his face in his hands. His time in the Outskirts wasn't a dream.

What was he doing here? Why was he home?

He had to get back.

His friends would not be captured and taken there until this evening. But could he now keep Dalton and Jenna from going there? What if he brought police officers to the house where Ansel was trapping kids? What if he helped catch the slavers?

But then what about Mira? And her sisters, and all the people in the Outskirts? And Hunter, who had been so thoroughly forgotten by the family that his messy bed remained untouched two years after he had vanished?

Cole had to let it all happen. There could be no police, no warnings. He had to let the same kidnappings transpire. If he changed things, it might not turn out right. He might not help Mira escape Skyport and beat Carnag. He might not save Honor and stop Morgassa and defeat Roxie and go to Necronum.

Necronum.

Where Mira, Jace, and Joe were taken to the echolands. They had been taken, and it was his fault. He had made a deal with Sando. He had to save them. And he had to help Tessa. It was what Mira had most wanted. He had promised.

He had been doing his best. He had crossed over to the echolands at the Temple of the Robust Sky.

And eventually, he had met Harvan, Winston, Ferrin, and Drake.

And Prescia.

He had gone to find Destiny. He owed it to Mira.

That was his current mission.

He wasn't really in his bedroom. This was some kind of dream. This was an illusion.

He was really on a mountain.

"I have to find Destiny!" Cole yelled, heedless of what his mother, father, or sister might think.

He remained in his room.

"Get me out of here!" Cole shouted. "There isn't time for this! I have to find Destiny!"

Everything went black.

Cole was lying on his side.

He could feel the rock beneath him.

He opened his eyes.

Chapter
— 27 —

SUMMIT

Cole was back on the mountain, the stairs before him.

Come. The word penetrated his mind, reverberating with power.

Cole stood, facing the stairs. He unhooked the beacon from his hilt so he could hold it in his hand. Before he started up, Cole peeked over his shoulder.

He was high!

The echolands spread out behind him forever, looking like a map or a model from this altitude. How high was he? Was any mountain on Earth this tall?

Come.

Cole rushed up the stairs two at a time.

The steps ended at the summit.

There wasn't much more space at the top than in his bedroom. A woman stood there, clad in dark gray robes, turned so he was looking at her profile. Her eyes stared into the distance, long black hair tumbling almost to her waist, her skin as pale as moonlight. She was of medium height and quite lovely. Her throbbing music was imbued with deep mystery and sorrow and, at this proximity, overpowered the song of the mountain.

"Cole Bryant Randolph," she intoned, her voice resonant and solemn, her eyes staying fixed on the horizon.

"That's me," he said.

"You have traveled an improbable path to reach me," she said.

"I guess so," Cole said. "What are you staring at?"

"I gaze out beyond the fringe, awaiting the supreme evil that departed ages ago. One day it shall return. We will destroy each other, and I will at long last leave the echolands behind. Until then, I assist where I am able."

"Can you help my friends?" Cole asked. "I left them at the bottom of your mountain."

"The attack occurred beyond my reach," she said. Her words remained in a solemn monotone. "Your assailants seemed to know the irregular boundaries of my influence. Your friend Harvan has been taken. The strain was too much for the other one, Winston. His lifespark has fled to the next phase. The shapecrafters kept his lifeless echo."

Cole bowed his head and fell to his knees. Winston was already gone? And Harvan was captured! Everything kept getting worse!

"I understand your grief," the woman said. "Your comrades sacrificed much to deliver you to me."

Cole looked up at the woman. Her face remained impassive. Her eyes gazed into the distance.

"You never look away?" Cole asked.

"The evil I await will come swiftly," she said. "I must never divert my attention."

"You've been doing this for a long time?" Cole asked.

"Since not long after the Outskirts began," she replied.

"Who are you?" Cole asked.

"You already know," she replied. "I am She Who Stands at the Summit."

"But who were you before?"

"I am one of a small number who framed the Outskirts," she said.

"You helped shape the Outskirts? Did you know Dandalus?"

"You met a shadow of him connected to the Founding Stone," she said. "He was the greatest of us."

"He told me his job was to make the Founding Stone," Cole said.

"Which also meant his job was to physically create the Outskirts," she said. "The Founding Stone initiated the process."

"You must be powerful," Cole said. "I know you're waiting for some evil, but there are already lots of problems in the Outskirts. Before long there might be nothing left to protect."

"You wish for my direct intervention," she said. "Even if I would risk turning my back on the evil I await, I cannot leave this post."

"Why not?" Cole asked.

"I wield considerable power," the woman said. "But no matter how great your power, there is a price to remaining in the echolands. I have lingered for a very long time. I established a sanctuary here upon this mountain. Were I to depart, the call of the Other would immediately claim me."

"You?" Cole asked.

"The call accumulates influence over time," she said. "The echolands were never meant as a permanent home for anyone. This is a place of transition, a place to let go of one existence and move on to another. Your comrade Winston has graduated to a wondrous realm. We will all eventually follow."

Cole stared at the woman. "Do you know where I can find Destiny?"

"I do not. But I know who can provide the information you seek."

Cole pounded his fists against his forehead. "No offense, but do you know how many times I've heard this?"

"I know all that you know. Knowledge is power in the echolands. Few endeavors can benefit you more than finding those who guard it. You hoped to find Destiny at Deepwell. Harvan took you to Prescia in search of an answer. Prescia referred you to me. My Weaver's Beacon enabled you to reach this summit."

"*Your* Weaver's Beacon?"

"As the first Grand Shaper of Necronum, I created it long ago."

Cole held up the lantern. "Well, good job. Thanks."

"You're welcome. It was made to be used. Now you have one last person to visit. He will have the answers you desire."

"He'll know where to find Destiny? For sure?"

"He knows where to find her. He can reveal how you might return to your home. He can advise you on how to confront Nazeem."

"That sounds worth the trip," Cole said. "But what can you tell me?"

"You have not yet realized the nature of your enemy," she said.

"Nazeem? I saw him."

"But you do not yet comprehend his identity."

"Should I?"

"You have sufficient clues to understand."

Cole thought for a minute. "I know Owandell works for him. I know Nazeem taught people shapecraft. I know he kept himself a secret for a long time. I know he's imprisoned at the Fallen Temple. I know he wants the princesses and is also after me. I know he plans to break free soon. Do you know more?"

"I am one of the six who imprisoned him long ago," she said, unblinking eyes staring into the distance.

"You imprisoned Nazeem?"

"With the help of the other founders of the Outskirts."

"What do you know about him?"

"You have met the only other of his kind in this world," she said. "We imprisoned him as well."

Cole's jaw dropped. "Trillian? Wait a minute. Nazeem is the other torivor?"

"He has not always used the name Nazeem. When we faced him, he went by Ramarro."

Cole's mind raced. It made sense. Trillian didn't know the fate of the other torivor, only that he must have been captured. Trillian could shape differently and more powerfully than anyone Cole had met. Trillian had believed the rules of shaping could be changed. And that's what shapecraft did—shape the shaping power.

Of course Nazeem was the other torivor! The Fallen Temple was equivalent to the Lost Palace. Like Trillian, Nazeem had been manipulating people from within his prison. If Nazeem got free, it would be like Trillian getting free. It would mean the end of the Outskirts.

"You are reaching the correct conclusions," the woman said.

"We're in the echolands. Is Nazeem an echo?"

"He is not, though we imprisoned him here. Thankfully, we did not confront the torivors at the same time. We went up against Nazeem first, in Necronum. The battle was close. We had practiced our craft for centuries, and Nazeem was new to this world, or else the outcome might have been different. We managed to lure him into the echolands and imprison him here."

"So if he gets out, he can come back to life?" Cole asked.

"If he can find a way beyond the barriers that imprison him and cross to the other side, yes, he could fully return to life. He brought his physical body here. His body and lifespark are joined in a way I do not understand. We tried to imprison Trillian in the echolands as well, but he refused to cross, and the six framers together lacked the power to force him. We settled for entombing him beneath the Lost Palace. Similar barriers that hold Trillian contain Nazeem."

"Can Nazeem defeat your barriers?"

"The two torivors are the most talented natural shapers we have ever encountered. Given enough time, anything is possible, no matter how securely we bound them. Our top priority must be to keep Nazeem imprisoned. If he breaks loose, no power in this world will be able to stop him."

Cole thought about that. "Supposedly, he's almost free. What should we do if he gets out?"

Her voice remained solemn and calm. "We could fight and perish. Or we could surrender and watch as he remakes the Outskirts according to his desires."

"You don't sound too bothered by that," Cole said. "Or anything, really."

"Do not mistake my focus on the distant evil for indifference," the woman said. "I have suppressed much of who I was to stand at this post."

"What evil?" Cole asked.

"A fiend unconnected to the torivors," she said. "Something older, inherent to the echolands. Only I can stop it. Harbor no concerns. I will do my duty."

"Did you have a name?"

"Once, long ago. Perhaps I will again after I finally move on. Until then, I am She Who Stands at the Summit."

"There isn't a way to destroy Nazeem?" Cole asked.

"If we knew how to destroy him, we would have done it without hesitation."

Cole considered what else he needed to know.

"I have compassion for you, Cole," she said. "I understand what you have lost. I know what you hope to regain. I can see your memories as if I lived them, including the lost memories of your brother, Hunter."

"I still have those memories?" Cole asked.

"Yes. They are veiled from your conscious mind, but they remain. I used them to show you his room."

Cole took a deep breath. A small corner of his mind had patiently waited for Hunter's identity to be an elaborate hoax. He believed Hunter was his brother, it had to be true, but he couldn't help leaving some defenses up in case it was all a ruthless trick. It was nice to have Hunter's identity confirmed from an outside source.

"Was that a test?" Cole asked. "Making me choose to come to the Outskirts again?"

"I had to confirm your level of commitment," she said.

"What if I had failed?"

"I could have sent you to the Other. I could have sent you down the mountain. I could have still permitted you to speak with me."

"It felt so real," Cole said.

"In some of the ways that matter most, it was real," she intoned.

"Trillian sent a message to me that the Outskirts might fall without my help," Cole said.

"I'm aware."

"Was that true?"

"The torivor cannot lie. He believed what he told you. Given all you have achieved, and your presence here, it seems he could be right."

"He also thought I could get my power back."

"You have a unique and remarkable talent," she said. "I am sorry it was desecrated by Morgassa. You hope that I can heal you, but I cannot."

"What about the guy you're sending me to visit?"

"If anyone can help, he can."

Cole frowned. "Prescia said you were the wisest person in the echolands."

"Very few know about the Warden of the Light. His existence is perhaps the greatest secret in the echolands. I only send you to him because of the import of your mission."

"What if he sends me to some new secret person?" Cole asked, feeling frustrated again. "Somebody you don't know. How many mountains am I going to climb?"

"As many as you must," she answered. "But I do not believe he will send you to another. He will help as he is able. Normally, he permits three questions. Hopefully, it will be enough."

"Not even the Grand Shaper knows about him?" Cole asked.

"No. Only one other person in the echolands knows of his existence."

"And you can give me directions?"

"I can have the Weaver's Beacon lead you to him."

"I'm being chased," Cole said.

"I am aware. And you have lost your companions. I can help you get away."

"How?" Cole asked.

"I will send you a good distance from my mountain," she said. "As I mentioned, my boundaries are irregular. My influence extends farther than you might guess along a few routes in certain directions. Far enough that those flying shapecrafters will struggle to follow. The beacon will conceal you from their weaving and their songreading."

"How do they fly?" Cole asked.

"Shapecraft. They whistle up an artificial wind with their abilities. It should not be possible. But this is what shapecraft does. It manipulates the rules."

"Can they come up here?" Cole asked.

"I control the skies near the mountain," she said. "They ambushed you just beyond one of my nearest borders."

"What about my other friends?" Cole asked. "Can you see them?"

"Mira was taken to the Fallen Temple. I can't see inside that location. Nothing blinds my vision like excess shapecraft. Honor was taken to Gamat Rue. Jace and Joe never left there. I can't see into Gamat Rue, either. I only know your friends were taken there through your memories. Desmond, Ferrin, and Drake are nearing Gamat Rue. As is Prescia. Durny was captured and brought inside the Fallen Temple."

"Can you see into Necronum?" Cole asked.

"Only the echolands," she replied.

"You can't see Destiny?" Cole wondered.

"I saw her earlier. She could have been on her way to Deepwell. Then she disappeared."

"Could she have gone to the Other?"

"I would have sensed that. She is hidden somewhere. The Warden of the Light should be able to help."

"Do you need to do something to the Weaver's Beacon?" Cole asked.

"It is done," she said. "The beacon will direct you to the Warden of the Light. The most direct route would take you across some of the central echolands. Instead, I designed a route that will keep you far from other echoes."

"Probably smart," Cole said.

"Use caution. As you approach the warden's dwelling, you will venture far into the fringe. Resist the call of the Other. The beacon will let you avoid most hazards, but you will have to cross the Pass of Visions. You will see things that frighten you. Ignore them. Do not fight them. They can only attack if you touch them. You may also see people who want your help. Again, ignore them. If you touch them, it will be taken as permission for them to engage with you."

"Sounds like a fun place," Cole said.

"Trust the beacon," she said. "It will not fail you. Are you ready to go?"

"Is there anything else I should know?"

"If the Warden of the Light chooses to help you, he will have many of the answers you seek."

"Wait," Cole said. "If?"

"Be brave. I believe he will aid you. Please give him my regards."

Cole sighed. "Fine. I guess I'm ready. What do I need to do?"

"Give me permission to send you," she said. "It makes the experience more comfortable."

"You have my permission."

"Farewell."

CHAPTER
28

VISIONS

Cole felt like he simultaneously shrank and stretched. Everything became a sideways blur. His insides lurched like he was accelerating, but it looked more like he remained still while the world streaked by.

A feeling of nausea hit, and the frantic motion stopped abruptly. He stood near a bridge over a slipstream. The gray, powdery ground seemed inhospitable to plants. Only a few small, tidy trees grew within view.

The beacon gently pulled toward the bridge. Evidently, he was supposed to cross it.

Cole turned in a circle, eyes searching the horizon. The Farthest Mountain was nowhere in view. Her domain apparently included some far-flung tentacles.

Hopefully, he had enough of a head start to baffle Sando.

His eyes swept the sky, but he spotted no gliders.

Cole started running.

He tried not to dwell on Harvan and Winston. There was nothing to do about Winston. It was horrible, but irreversible. He had to be rational about it. And he would worry about Harvan later. His list of people to rescue was getting absurd.

As he ran, Cole could not help missing his companions. Unreasonable or not, he wished there was some way to undo Winston going to the Other. He wished he could save Harvan now, partly for selfish reasons. It was no fun to run alone. The lack of company left him feeling desolate and vulnerable.

At least he possessed the beacon. He had a crucial mission and a way to reach his destination. That was big. Maybe he would finally learn where to find Destiny. And maybe he could get some information about how to get home. Was that too greedy to hope? Based on what he had learned from She Who Stands at the Summit, if anybody could help him, it would be the Warden of the Light.

Cole wondered how Jace, Joe, and Honor were faring at Gamat Rue. Hopefully, they got to see one another sometimes. Hopefully, Desmond would manage to free them.

He worried about Mira. If she was at the Fallen Temple, she was with Nazeem. Would he try to take her power again? Would he play games with her mind? Was she suffering?

He tried not to envision the possibilities too vividly.

Cole also thought about Dalton and Hunter. Were they looking for Jenna? Could they have found her by now? Everything seemed so bleak, it was encouraging to imagine something good happening.

There was plenty to wonder about and worry over.

But mostly he had to keep running.

He also kept an eye on the sky.

Just in case.

The terrain changed as he ran. Cole traversed deserts and climbed hills. He crossed plains and passed through woods. In one forest the enormous trees had thick trunks and looked as tall as skyscrapers. It made Cole feel out of scale, as if he had become tiny.

He sprinted across a landscape of smooth, black pebbles. He followed a trail through a jagged range of yellow and red mountains. He plunged blindly across an ocean of grass more than twice his height.

Occasionally, he crossed channels, but thanks to the beacon, he always arrived where a bridge was present. The beacon steered him away from intimidating music and some-times guided him away from inviting songs as well.

While crossing a wide plain made of transparent crys-tal, Cole began to discern the call of the Other more powerfully than he had yet heard it. The more detail he could apprehend, the more beautiful it sounded. The music felt familiar, as if he had somehow forgotten his favorite song along with his most cherished feelings, and they were all connected. The homesong promised wholeness and rest and joy.

He reminded himself about Winston losing his lifeforce to the Other. He concentrated on his duties and the people depending on him. He thought about Destiny and Mira and Dalton and Jenna.

And he tried not to think about how much more clearly he might hear the homesong if he shuttered the beacon. He tried to embrace his loneliness and decide he deserved the company of that inspiring melody.

He tried to concentrate on things other than the beckoning call. The crystal plain looked kind of like really clear ice. He could stare a long way beneath his feet. He wondered how far he had come. How many miles had he traveled? How many days had he run? It seemed he had gone farther than he had with Harvan and Winston, but it was hard to be sure. The duskday never changed.

At last the crystal plain ended, and Cole found himself running across a rolling prairie with occasional gigantic bushes. The call of the Other continued to beckon.

Would it be such a crime to shutter his beacon? Just for a little while?

He recalled Winston getting enthralled by the homesong before he had walked very far from the beacon. Shuttering the lantern might be the last thing he ever did. It might also let enemies pinpoint his location. He had to remember that the beacon was also concealing him. The call of the Other might sound sweet, and promise an end to his misery, but he couldn't get lured in. Too many people were relying on him.

Ominous music sounded up ahead, but the beacon kept leading him forward. A distant wall came into view. As he drew closer, Cole realized the wall was the size of a mountain, stretching as far he could see to either side.

Directly before him, right where the beacon was leading him, Cole saw a gap in the mighty barrier.

Could that be the Pass of Visions?

It was the most probable candidate so far.

As Cole approached, the barrier looked more like a huge cliff rather than a wall, though it was almost perfectly vertical, and the top was strangely level. By the time Cole reached the gap, the menacing music of the cliff drowned out the homesong. Cole felt relieved, although the new music was not welcoming.

With the beacon urging him forward, Cole entered the pass at a full sprint. Steep cliffs rose at either side, separated by about thirty yards of hard-packed dirt. The floor of the pass sloped up at a gradual incline, winding enough that Cole couldn't see how far it went.

A rumbling from up ahead caused Cole to slow down. Could it be a rockslide? He came to a stop when a large woman floated into view from farther up the pass, hovering toward him. She wore a white blouse, a long gray skirt, dark stockings, and flat black shoes. Her hair was up in a messy bun. Cole had seen this dressy schoolteacher before. She had mutilated his shaping power as she died.

It was Morgassa.

Cole's reflexive instinct was to turn and run. Instead he stared. The beacon kept tugging him forward.

"Hello, Cole Randolph," Morgassa said with a smile. "Fancy meeting you here in the realm of the dead. How about a rematch without all your little friends?"

Cole watched her glide in his direction, her feet a few inches above the ground. She was at least eight feet tall.

Could this really be her? It looked exactly like her. It sounded like her. He was in the afterlife. She could be here.

Still, if this was the Pass of Visions, it had to be a trick.

But what if it wasn't?

"I see you brought your sword," Morgassa said, her voice silky. "Are you going to leap around like a grasshopper again?" A huge sword appeared in her hands. "Or perhaps it doesn't perform so well here in the realm of echoes. Perhaps you'll have to face me in a fair fight."

What were the chances this pass had one of the beings he most feared blocking the way? It had to be a vision customized to intimidate him.

Either that, or he was about to get killed.

Morgassa was scant seconds away from him. "I challenge you to a fair fight. Defend yourself or die."

Cole reached for his sword but resisted drawing it. There was no way he could take out Morgassa singlehandedly. She was too powerful.

If she was a vision, and he attacked, she would be free to fight him. If she was real, and he attacked, he stood little chance of winning.

So his best bet was to not attack. He had to hope she was a vision.

Morgassa had almost reached him. She raised her sword to strike. She looked completely real. If he was wrong, he was about to get chopped in half.

Cole took his hand off the hilt of his sword.

Her blade remained upraised.

"Come on, coward," Morgassa urged. "Be a man. Fight me."

If she wanted, she could kill him. Instead, she was stalling.

Cole ran around her and continued along the pass.

"Don't turn your back on me!" Morgassa shrieked.

"Haven't you hurt me enough?" Cole cried out. "Go bother somebody else."

Morgassa flew in front of him, suddenly clad in a full suit of white armor, embellished with gold accents. She grew larger.

Cole wasn't worried anymore. If she was the real deal, she would have already hacked him into lunchmeat. He ran around her again.

There came more rumbling from up ahead, and Carnag stomped into view. The creature looked just how Cole remembered her, the enormous body composed of wreckage and cages.

Cole wasn't intimidated. If Morgassa was a vision, so was Carnag. He kept running, dodging around the legs.

Carnag and Morgassa dropped out of sight behind him. Cole wondered if the test was over. He ran in silence for about a minute.

Then Stafford Pemberton, High King of the Outskirts, strode into view. Cole had met the High King in Junction. He looked exactly as Cole remembered.

"Cole, you lied to me," Stafford said. "When you played errand boy in my chambers, you were working for my wife. You were hiding my daughter. You are guilty of treason."

"You're guilty of not being real," Cole said, not slowing down.

"I'm plenty real, Cole," the king said, producing a knife. His face reddened as he spoke. "Real enough to punish a traitor! Real enough to take my revenge!"

Cole knew Stafford had to be fake but disliked how

authentic he seemed. The unstable look in his eyes. The spit flying from his lips.

Stafford began to cough uncontrollably. He staggered toward Cole, swinging his dagger haphazardly.

Cole raced around him, but Stafford stayed with him, running beside him. The king kept swinging his knife, but never close enough to actually make contact.

"You imagine I'm past my prime?" Stafford gasped, still coughing. "You fancy you can outrun me? You're all going to pay. Wait until I get your friends Dalton and Jenna. Wait until I get Jace and Twitch. Hunter. Mira. They'll suffer for what they did to me. You all will!"

Cole felt tempted to argue. But it was pointless. This was some vision. It would be like talking back to a movie screen.

Stafford coughed violently but kept running. "My daughters will feel my wrath. My wife too. You'll see. I'll make them suffer."

"Enough," spoke a voice from farther up the pass.

Cole had been watching Stafford, so he hadn't seen the new person come into view. He stood in the middle of the pass, hands behind his back. They had only met briefly when Cole first touched the Founding Stone, but Cole would recognize him anywhere. Nazeem.

Standing straight, Nazeem casually waved an arm. Stafford burst into flames. Cole felt a rush of heat from the nearby fire. The High King fell to the ground screaming.

Cole ignored the spectacle.

"You can't win, you know," Nazeem said matter-of-factly.

Cole didn't answer. He just kept running. He couldn't

wait until all this was behind him. Fake or not, it was trau-matizing.

"You think I'm not real," Nazeem said as Cole neared him. "But what if I'm the one who controls the Pass of Visions? What if I have controlled this place for years, from my prison in the Fallen Temple, like how Trillian exerts influence over the Red Road."

Cole offered no reply. He kept running. Nazeem was getting close.

"What if I'm toying with you? What if this is really me?" He got down on his knees. "Torivors like sport, Cole. We enjoy contests." He pulled open his shirt, displaying his bare chest. "What if I give you a free shot with that sword? What if this is the one such offer I'm ever going to make? What if I find it amusing that you'll pass me by when you had your one chance to strike me down?"

"You're lying," Cole said. After the words left his mouth, he was mad at himself for responding.

"Torivors can't lie," Nazeem said. "I swear this is the real me. And I promise I will not defend myself. It's inexpressibly entertaining that you could end this right now, save all the people you love. I'll let you. I give my word. But you won't. You'll run right by me."

"Yep," Cole said as he ran past him. "Torivors can't lie. But you're not really a torivor. You're just another vision."

"Think what you like," Nazeem said from behind him. "You are running away from the best chance you'll ever have to win this war."

Cole didn't reply. There was no point.

The pass now sloped down instead of up. Cole hoped that meant he had crossed the halfway point.

As he came around a bend, Cole heard a voice weakly call his name.

Turning, Cole saw Winston crawling along the ground, his clothes tattered. "I can't believe I found you," Winston said with a beleaguered smile. "I was trying to catch up. It's not fair for you to face all this alone."

Cole slowed. "This is so mean," he murmured. Winston looked and sounded so real.

"I'm out of strength, Cole," Winston said. "Can you bring the beacon closer? I'm so tired. I feel like I can't go on much longer. The homesong has a hold on me. I feel like I'm slipping. I only made it this far out of devotion."

Cole stopped. He knew he shouldn't, but it was nice to see Winston, even if it was fake. "You're dead, Winston. You already went to the Other. I'm so sorry I couldn't help you."

Winston looked a little panicked. "Cole, no! I started to go. It almost had me. But I came back. The shapecrafters had left me for dead, so I followed you, and I finally found you, but I'm so tired now. Could you help me up?" He extended a hand. "I want to come with you. You shouldn't have to shoulder this burden alone. I want to help."

"The shapecrafters already took your dead echo," Cole said.

"No, it's him Cole," a voice said from behind him.

Cole turned to find Harvan standing there.

"We gave the shapecrafters the slip," Harvan said. "We

followed you. But Winston is really tired, and I don't have the strength to help him anymore. Could you lend him a hand?"

"This is sadistic," Cole muttered, and started running again.

"Come back!" Winston called.

"Let him go," Harvan said. "He abandoned us once. Of course he's leaving us again. That kid only cares about himself."

"Nazeem is back at the top of the pass," Cole called over his shoulder. "He's offering free chances to stab him. You guys should take him up on the offer."

"We'll do that!" Harvan called. "Save yourself, Cole. It's what you're best at."

Cole kept running. How much longer was this pass going to last?

Around the next bend, Cole found his dad, mom, and sister all tied to chairs and gagged. They mumbled at him urgently, but he couldn't understand them.

It was very tempting to stop and look. It had been so long since he had seen them. He knew no good would come of it, but it was hard to resist.

They groaned and grunted more urgently as Cole ran by. Was the trick to make him touch them by taking off the gags?

"I may be gullible," Cole murmured, "but even I have limits."

After he dashed by them, his dad called out in a clear voice, "Son! Please help us! We don't know how we got here!"

"How'd you get the gag off, Dad?" Cole yelled over his shoulder.

"I shook my head and it fell free," his father replied. "Please, Cole!"

"I miss you guys," Cole called, hardly able to get the words out because of the lump in his throat. Even though it was a trick. Even though they were obviously fake.

Coming around another bend, Cole could see ahead to where the pass ended. And a body lay off to the side, not far from the end of the pass. As he came closer, he saw that it was Destiny.

Of course it was. Destiny Pemberton, sprawled out in this pass full of weird visions.

She didn't move.

Cole couldn't resist. He slowed down to take a closer look.

Tessa was breathing. But her eyes stayed closed.

Cole stopped. "I'm not going to shake you awake," he told her.

She made no reply.

Cole suppressed a laugh. What if this really was her? Wouldn't it be a perfect hiding place? Everybody assuming she was a vision?

Still, no way was it really her.

He started running again.

"Help me," her voice said weakly.

"Now you wake up?" Cole called over his shoulder.

"I need a hero," she said.

"You need acting lessons," Cole replied. "You were a lot more convincing when you were unconscious."

"Please stop saying mean things," Destiny said. Desperation crept into her voice. "Come back! Help me! I'm scared!"

Cole gave no reply. Instead, he continued out of the pass.

CHAPTER
—— 29 ——

WARDEN

Short grass and sporadic bushes awaited at the far side of the cliffs. As he sprinted across the springy turf, Cole tried to shake off the memories of Morgassa's fingernails digging into his sides as she mangled his shaping power. He tried not to dwell on how much more powerful and dangerous Nazeem would be than his underlings and their creations. He did his best to push aside his guilt over leaving Winston and Harvan behind, and for leading Mira into a trap. He pretended with all his might not to miss his home and family.

Everything in the Pass of Visions had been fake. And everything had forced him to confront real fears and worries and pain.

Cole couldn't help feeling raw. He kept running. His echo body still functioned like normal. But inside he was wounded.

As Cole advanced, off to one side he noticed a wide channel. A narrow channel appeared on the other side. The two slipstreams flowed toward each other, apparently on a course to converge. The Weaver's Beacon seemed to be tugging him toward the place where the channels joined. Cole figured that must be where they had built the bridge.

The music of the cliffs receded behind him, and Cole began to hear the homesong again, along with the whistling music of the slipstreams. Directly ahead a grove came into view, graceful trees with silver bark and crimson leaves. Clover carpeted the ground instead of grass. The grove seemed to mark the place where the slipstreams converged.

When Cole entered the grove, all outside music stopped, replaced by low, peaceful strains. It surprised Cole that such a small grove with such gentle music could overpower all other sounds. As he proceeded among the trees, he still couldn't see or hear a bridge.

But he did encounter a house—a simple structure made of mud bricks with flowers growing on the roof. Two benches sat out in front. A man sat on one of the benches. He stood as Cole approached.

Cole recognized him.

"Dandalus?" Cole asked.

"Yes, my boy," Dandalus said. "Have we met?"

"I touched the Founding Stone," Cole said. "I spoke to the imprint you left there."

"Perhaps you did," Dandalus said, sitting down again. "What brings you so far into the fringe? It's much more humane to just leap into a channel."

"Sometimes that doesn't sound like a bad idea," Cole said. The beacon was pointing straight at Dandalus. "I'm looking for the Warden of the Light."

"You have quite a light of your own," Dandalus said. "Did you rob the Grand Shaper?"

"She gave it to me," Cole said. "Then She Who Stands at the Summit sent me to you."

"You think I'm the Warden of the Light?" Dandalus asked.

Cole started walking sideways. The lantern kept shifting to point right at Dandalus. "The Weaver's Beacon seems to think so."

"If we can't trust a stranger's lantern, what can we trust?" Dandalus asked, a sparkle in his eye.

"Can you read my mind?" Cole asked. "Do you know why I'm here?"

"I've gathered the basics," Dandalus said. "I'm not as quick at raiding memories as our friend on the mountaintop. It would speed this up and make it simpler if you give me permission to know what you know."

"Sure," Cole said.

Dandalus stared at him for a long moment, then gave a nod. "Thank you. I think we can keep the test straightforward. She already tested you, and the Pass of Visions was wrenching."

"Yeah," Cole said, barely keeping his voice steady.

"Without knowing the secret of the pass, it's almost impossible to make it through. I know of nobody who has done it. Even knowing how to survive it, many fail. That's part of the reason I chose this spot as my sanctuary."

"Can you only get here through the pass?" Cole asked.

"The two channels run at either side of the towering

cliffs," Dandalus explained. "They have no bridges between here and there. I'm protected by a triangle—two slipstreams and a wall of rock with a single way through."

"I'll have to go back through the pass to get out?" Cole asked.

"Unless you sprout wings, it's the only way," Dandalus said. "But you survived it once, so I expect you can do it again. Now for my test. Cole, I can send you home. Not an illusion. Not temporarily. I framed the Outskirts. I know how it all works. And I can bend the rules to send you back to your house in Mesa, Arizona. Say yes, and I'll do it. Say no, and we can discuss other matters."

"Wait," Cole said. "Can you send me anywhere?"

"I can send you back Outside," Dandalus said. "I can't send you elsewhere in the echolands or the Outskirts."

"Isn't Arizona farther?" Cole asked.

"This sanctuary effectively cuts me off from the rest of the echolands and the Outskirts," Dandalus said. "As with She Who Stands at the Summit, it was the price I had to pay to avoid the call of the Other. However, I am not separated from the ways to the Outside. That I can still do from here."

"What about my friends?" Cole asked. "Could you send Dalton and Jenna home too?"

"They would have to be here. I explained that I am separated from the rest of the echolands and the Outskirts."

Cole paused to think. Could he go home alone? Could he leave behind Dalton, Jenna, Hunter, and the other kids who were taken from his neighborhood? It would be so nice to be back in his house. The vision at the Farthest Mountain had given him a taste—his own room, his own bed.

He longed to see his parents. Even his sister. He missed living a normal life. He missed school and sports and bikes and breakfast cereal and hot showers. No running for his life. No monsters to fight. Nobody to save.

If he snuck home, who would know? Were there ways he could help there that he couldn't here? Maybe he could remind all the parents about their missing kids.

But how could he abandon his quest to find Destiny? How could he leave Mira and Honor to fend for themselves against their father and Nazeem? How could he ditch Dalton, Hunter, and Jenna?

Cole folded his arms. Did his presence here really make a difference? What were his chances of surviving the echolands? What were their chances of winning? Supposedly, there was a chance while he remained. But was that really true? How much did he matter?

In many ways, it would be such a relief to quit all this.

"Would my parents remember me?" Cole asked.

"Probably," Dandalus said. "I can't guarantee it."

"But I would be home to stay," Cole said.

"To stay," Dandalus agreed.

Cole shook his head. One day he might regret letting this opportunity pass, but he knew his answer. "I can't go. Too many people are depending on me. Can I take a rain check?"

"If you can ever find me again, sure, the offer would stand," Dandalus said. "Though finding me is seldom easy. You are a loyal friend, Cole."

"I guess," he said. "Now what?"

"You may ask me three questions," Dandalus said.

Cole figured he should get the big one out of the way. "Where can I find Destiny Pemberton?"

Dandalus smiled. "I know where you can find her. I will tell you before we finish our conversation, but I prefer to wait until the end. Is that all right?"

"Sure," Cole said, relieved that Dandalus knew the answer.

"Good. What else can I tell you?"

"How can I get home with my friends? Besides bringing all of them to you."

"Bringing all of them to me would work," Dandalus said. "I would send them. But there could be another way. Shall I explain?"

"Please," Cole said.

"Understanding the particulars involves something of a history lesson," Dandalus said. "Thank you for opening your mind to me. Among other benefits, I know that I can confide in you. Mine has become a lonely existence. I've only had one other visitor in the last two hundred years."

Cole gave a low whistle.

"I spend a lot of time in trances," Dandalus said. "Not the dangerous kind. The kind you used when running here."

"Was I in a trance a lot?" Cole asked.

"Is that your third question?"

"No."

"I'll answer regardless," Dandalus said. "You were in a trance a good portion of the way. Mostly harmless trances, until recently. When you get far enough into the fringe, the call becomes almost irresistible. Even sheltered by the beacon, your defenses were starting to break down."

"The homesong got pretty tempting," Cole admitted.

"Which is unavoidable," Dandalus said. "The whole purpose of the echolands is to prepare individuals to answer that call. Let me take you back to the beginning. Back before the Outskirts existed. Can you guess what was here?"

"I don't know," Cole said. "Outer space?"

"Wrong," Dandalus said. "There was no outer space here. There still isn't, matter of fact. This entire plane of existence was simply the echolands. Nothing more."

"So you were an echo?" Cole asked.

"That's another question," Dandalus said. "It's hard to converse without them. Keep asking and I'll tell you if you stumble onto a topic that requires you to use your third official one. I was and I am an echo. There was originally a single type of shaping here. It was most similar to Sambrian shaping, but you could accomplish all that can be done in any of the five kingdoms. And more."

"Did people shape the echolands a lot?" Cole asked.

"Quite a bit, as you might imagine," Dandalus said. "Not all the echoes were strong shapers. But everyone could at least shape a little. People carved out their own versions of paradise while waiting to heed the call of the Other."

"You came here from another world," Cole said.

"After my physical body died, yes," Dandalus said. "Everyone did. Nobody is native to the echolands. You've heard the Outskirts described as an in-between place? It really is. It's a physical realm built in the afterlife. A place between life and what comes after. A place between reality and imagination, because you can turn just about anything you can imagine into reality. A place between sleep and wakefulness, because if you can't sleep, how can you be sure you're truly awake? The echolands have a transitory, dreamlike quality. This place is intended as a permanent home to none."

"But you changed it," Cole said. "To add the Five Kingdoms."

"Some of us got greedy," Dandalus said. "We didn't mean any harm. But a handful of us were extremely powerful shapers. We learned how to cheat the call of the Other and used the time to grow in power. Eventually, we decided that we wanted to live again. So we used our abilities to create a material world here in the echolands. A mortal world."

"The Outskirts," Cole said.

"It didn't go well at first," Dandalus confessed. "We made a modest realm. We brought in mortals from some of the neighboring worlds. The easiest to access was Earth. But the mortals arrived with much more powerful shaping skills than the typical echo, and they soon destroyed the world we created. Everyone we had brought here died."

"Could you visit the world you made?" Cole asked.

"That was the point," Dandalus said. "We transformed our echoes so we could dwell there. It made us feel alive again. A detailed simulation of mortality."

"What did you do when the world was destroyed?" Cole asked.

"We escaped back to the echolands," Dandalus said. "And we tried again. We made the next world much more sturdy and complete before transplanting actual mortals. Once all was ready, we brought a new group of mortals, and within five years they destroyed the world again."

"Bummer," Cole said.

"We felt terrible," Dandalus said. "Hundreds of lives were lost. We decided that if we were going to make a third attempt, we needed to rethink everything."

"What did you do?"

"We labored to restructure the shaping power itself," Dandalus said. "Shaping had been the main problem. Mortals would come to the world we had made and destroy all we had created. So we toiled until we learned to use shaping to redesign how shaping itself functioned."

"That sounds like shapecraft," Cole said.

"Doesn't it?"

"You're hurting my brain."

"It hurt ours, too. But eventually we succeeded. Once we were finished, very few echoes besides ourselves could shape in the echolands. Those who could had limited abilities."

"And you divided the new world into five kingdoms."

"Yes!" Dandalus said. "You're catching on! We only allowed certain shaping abilities in the various kingdoms. We wanted mortals to be able to shape, but not enough to destroy what we had created. The shaping in Sambria is called shaping because it is the closest to the original shaping. Just not quite as powerful. There was also enchanting, tinkering, weaving, and minding. When we brought mortals in the next time, the experiment worked. The world held together. We had produced the five kingdoms of the Outskirts."

"And you guys were the first Grand Shapers," Cole guessed.

"There were six of us," Dandalus said. "I was the first High Shaper. The other five each supervised one of the kingdoms. Over time, a new threat developed."

"The torivors?" Cole guessed.

"They came later. The first threat was from the echoes. Too many of them wanted to migrate from the echolands to the Outskirts. There were unfair advantages to living as an echo in the mortal world, and many echoes abused their power. Though the six of us did our best to protect the mortals, other echoes commenced to exploit and enslave them. Some mortals died on purpose so they could return as echoes. It was becoming a mess."

"How did you handle it?" Cole wondered.

"Can't you guess?" Dandalus asked. "We stepped away from our creation. Together, we reshaped the world so that echoes couldn't dwell in the mortal Outskirts. The six of us withdrew and left mortal Grand Shapers in our place. There are still some places where echoes can sneak back into mortality, but not many, and not without incurring mortal weaknesses."

"What about the Shiver Moon?" Cole asked.

"We didn't want to completely sever ties between the echolands and the mortal kingdoms. The weavers of Necronum became the bridge. The Shiver Moon allowed for easier communication for all on certain nights in Necronum."

"When did the torivors come?" Cole asked.

"Right before we divided the echolands from the Out-skirts," Dandalus said. "The six of us slipped back across and captured them. Barely. It took all our ingenuity."

"So if you split up the shaping powers, how does shape-craft fit in?" Cole asked.

"Shapecraft taps into the original shaping of the echo-lands," Dandalus said. "Raw shaping. Natural shaping. The torivors have figured out ways to work around the system we established. They can sidestep many of the rules we made. If they succeed in truly unleashing raw shaping, mortal shapers will once again tear apart the world we built. Except this time, millions will perish."

"Wow," Cole said.

"And the torivors will take control of the echolands," Dandalus said. "The five kingdoms will be destroyed, and whatever remains will be ruled by an all-powerful tyrant."

"I see why you don't want Nazeem to get free," Cole said.

"Perhaps you are wondering what all this has to do with your question."

"About getting home?"

"Right. Your problem involves the fundamental nature of this world. This was originally a place for the echoes of deceased mortals to let go of their previous lives. The Out-skirts was created within the echolands. Those underlying mechanisms remain in place, but in some ways they work more powerfully on mortals who come here from Outside. When a lifeforce moves to the echolands, it is never meant to return. When a mortal comes to the Outskirts, some of the same rules take hold. Even if you manage to get home, you are drawn back."

"That makes a weird kind of sense," Cole said.

"When a lifeforce comes here as an echo, the echolands not only help the deceased individual prepare to move on—the preliminary separation helps those who mourn let go of the deceased. When a mortal comes to the Outskirts, the condition is exaggerated, and those who most love the person forget all about him."

"The echolands are about letting go and moving on," Cole said. "The Outskirts share some of those traits."

"It would require shaping at the most fundamental level to overcome these obstacles," Dandalus said. "Raw shaping of the primary aspects of this reality. It's impossible to do within the system we designed. But you have the potential of adjusting the system itself."

"Me?" Cole asked.

"It's why Morgassa attacked you so fiercely," Dandalus said. "Your power was a threat. You naturally possess what the shapecrafters have artificially tried to create inside of themselves—raw shaping power. That's why you could make the Jumping Sword work in Elloweer. Your power transcends the boundaries we established. It took you a long time to start using it because your ability was not meant to function in the system we created. But that didn't stop you."

"Doesn't that make me dangerous?" Cole asked.

"Yes. It also makes you useful. Because your style of shaping could actually challenge the torivors. I'm not sure anyone else could make them break a sweat. This must be why Trillian thought you might be able to save the Out-skirts."

"Wouldn't Trillian hate me?" Cole asked.

"Hard to say," Dandalus said. "I expect he sees you as both a hazard and an opportunity. He probably hopes you will go to him for training. Given your innate abilities, who knows how he might try to use you?"

Cole shivered. "I don't want to serve the torivors. But I'll try to stop them if I can."

"I know you mean well. I admire your courage. Cole, the answer to your question is that you have the potential to get your friends home if you can unlock your power."

"Do you know how I can do that?"

"That is a big question. Want to make it number three?"

"Yes."

"I know you wish that I could repair your power," Dandalus said. "I wish it too. But I can't. The damage is too wrapped up in who you are. It connects to your very life-spark. If I tried to heal it, I would kill you."

"Trillian thought I could get my power back," Cole said.

"Trillian was probably right," Dandalus said. "But you will have to find a way. I don't know of anyone who can do it for you."

"When I touched the Founding Stone, your imprint helped me use my power," Cole said.

"I saw that episode in your memories. My imprint didn't heal your damage. It helped you work around it. I could do the same here. I could help you work around your damage and engage some of your power. But when you left, you would remain as you were. Perhaps, given enough time, you will find methods to work around the damage on your own."

"So you can't help me fix the problem," Cole said. "I wasted my last question."

Dandalus looked beyond Cole. "I don't see a line of people awaiting their turn. The three-question rule is there to help prevent frivolous inquiries and to let me see what most matters to people. You can ask me more if you'd like."

"You seem to know a lot," Cole said.

"I am the Warden of the Light."

"Where is the light?" Cole asked. "Is it bright?"

"Brightness isn't always the best for seeing," Dandalus said. "It depends on the goal. For example, back home in Arizona, when could you see farthest?"

"What do you mean?" Cole said. "Like during the day? Or when I was on a mountain?"

"You could see your surroundings best during the day," Dandalus said. "But when could you see farthest?"

"At night," Cole realized. "The stars. Those are easily the farthest things I could see."

"But they were invisible during the day," Dandalus said. "Brightness can help, but it isn't everything."

"Is your light a lantern like this one?" Cole asked, holding up the beacon.

"It is a more important kind of light," Dandalus said. "The light of understanding. The light of discernment. The light that lets us comprehend things as they really are."

"Do you know everything?"

"I'm as close as it comes in this plane of existence. I know what the echolands once were. I know how we changed them. If all else fails, I can restore them." He considered Cole with grave eyes.

"You mean erase what you did?" Cole asked. "Hit the self-destruct button?"

"More or less," Dandalus said. "If it comes to it, I could destroy the Outskirts, flush all the echoes to the Other, and restore the echolands to their original state. I can undo what the six of us established."

"But it would kill everybody," Cole said.

"Everybody," Dandalus emphasized. "We'd all head to the Other. Including myself. I hope never to do it. But I am the final safeguard against the echolands being overthrown and corrupted. I am the Warden of the Light."

"What about my friends?" Cole tried. "Do you know where they are?"

"Like She Who Stands at the Summit, I can't see into the strongholds tainted by shapecraft. And I can't see the mortal Outskirts from here. But Prescia, Ferrin, Drake, and Desmond were captured when they tried to free Honor from Gamat Rue. Harvan was taken there as well. Mira and Durny remain at the Fallen Temple."

"It's all on me," Cole said, buckling under the impossible weight of all the people he needed to help.

"Take it one problem at a time," Dandalus said.

"I guess," Cole said. "What else should I ask you?"

"I could shed light on many issues that have made you curious. Remember, I've seen your mind. For example, I made the cloudwalls in Sambria."

"You did?"

"I felt bad for those whose wishes never came true. For the unfulfilled dreams here and elsewhere. One cloud-wall interprets broken dreams into physical realities. It was quite difficult to construct. My crowning achievement in some ways. It selects those subjects who dreamed biggest but also endured the greatest frustration. Since the cloud-wall ran the risk of eventually bringing too much material into the Outskirts, I designed the other one to dispose of the creations. I never anticipated the salvage operations that sprang up, but I'm happy they exist, so the castles provide some benefit to people beyond their aesthetics."

"I almost died in some of those castles," Cole said.

"I saw those memories. It's why I suspected you might be interested."

"What else can you tell me?" Cole asked.

"Understanding the true nature of the Outskirts resolves some of the questions you have wondered about. Originally, the echoes all communicated by telepathy. It transcended language. We left enough of that in place that everyone understands one another here, no matter what language they speak. In fact, it takes very disparate languages to create the impression of an accent."

"More," Cole said. "Read my mind."

"You've wondered about the sky. The Outskirts are not organized as a round planet like Earth. They are essentially flat, created entirely in the echolands. But the mortals we brought here all came from round worlds, so we wanted to give them days and nights. Vershaw oversaw the skies. He was the most artistic of us. He borrowed vistas from many of the different worlds that feed into the echolands, and added plenty of his own touches. Since the heavens were basically an elaborate simulation, he embraced the ruse, designing them without reliable patterns. It's enough to drive an astronomer mad."

"The sun felt real," Cole said.

"It radiates a similar spectrum as your sun back home," Dandalus said. "And the moons shed real light. But they are not actually true bodies floating in space. We faked it. The skies in the original echolands have always been as you see them here. Every now and then we allowed a duskday in the Outskirts to pay homage to the original sky."

"Cool," Cole said. "Keep going. I want to hear more."

"I could ramble on for much too long," Dandalus said. "Is there anything else specific you wish to know?"

Cole racked his brain for the best question. "What's the meaning of life?"

Dandalus smiled. "You asked Aeronomatron this one. His answer didn't satisfy you?"

"Not really."

Dandalus scrunched his face. "There are different ways to explain it. Here is one. The purpose of existence is the education of the will. And the meaning of life is to learn to love the right things."

"I like that," Cole said. "What are the right things?"

"In short? Those things that bring lasting happiness to yourself and others."

"Can you be more specific?" Cole said.

"The whole point involves discovering what those things are," Dandalus said. "Many lessons must be lived to be understood. You'll find that it doesn't so much matter what happens as you live—what gives it all purpose and meaning is who you become. You're doing a good job, Cole. An outstanding job for one so young. You're heading in the right direction."

"Thanks," Cole said.

"I have enjoyed our conversation," Dandalus said. "I miss interacting with others. Are you ready to learn where you can find Destiny?"

"Yes," Cole said.

Dandalus glanced over his shoulder. "She's in my house." He raised his voice. "Tessa! We have a visitor."

Destiny appeared in the doorway. "I was listening."

TESSA

ole could find no words. He finally went with "Hi."

"Hello," she replied. "This is the boy you told me about?" she asked Dandalus.

"Yes," Dandalus said. "He came here to help you."

Cole just stared. The most powerful people in the world were looking for Destiny. Nobody had a clue where she was hiding. People had sacrificed to find her. The task seemed impossible. Cole had only dared to hope for information that might point him in the right direction.

And here she was. A young girl.

"I met your imprint in the Cave of Memory," Cole said.

"Was I nice?" Tessa asked.

"I liked you," Cole said. "I've been helping your sister Mira."

Tessa brightened at the mention of her sister. "How is she?"

"Well, she got captured," Cole said. "Honor too. Mira gave me the mission to find you."

"Cole rode the Mare," Dandalus said. "It saved him twice. I believe your power wanted him to locate you."

"The Mare brought me here," Tessa said.

"My only other visitor in the past two hundred years," Dandalus said.

"Your own power brought you here?" Cole asked.

"I can't control her," Tessa said. "I didn't know where we were going."

"Would have been nice if the Mare had brought me here too," Cole said.

"The Mare helped you," Dandalus said. "Thanks to the Mare you met Durny and Harvan. Be grateful for that much. Destiny's power is hard to understand."

"I've started to get flashes of knowledge again," Destiny said. "At first it was a relief to lose my power. Seeing too much took away a lot of my choices. It also made people hate me. But sometimes it's nice to know what to do. To feel certain."

"Do you know what her power is doing now?" Cole asked Dandalus.

"I can't see the Mare," Dandalus said. "I don't think anybody can perceive Destiny's power from a distance. It's why nobody knows Destiny came here."

"You knew the Mare helped me," Cole said.

"Only thanks to your memories," Dandalus explained.

"Right," Cole said. He scowled. "I've searched for Tessa for a long time. But if nobody knows that she's here, shouldn't I leave her be? Where am I going to take her that's safer than this place?"

"I'm supposed to leave," Tessa said. "I've felt that much."

"The Mare put you on a path to find Tessa," Dandalus said. "Where were you planning to take her?"

"At first I wanted to reunite her with Mira," Cole said. "Now that Mira is captured, I guess I would take Tessa back to her physical body, then go after Mira."

"Sounds sensible," Dandalus said. "She'll be more vulnerable than she is here, but I can't hide her forever. Nazeem is hunting too intently. Eventually, we'll be found. And that would be unfortunate. I'm not meant to be discovered."

"But what if Stafford or Nazeem capture Destiny?" Cole asked.

"That risk persists no matter where she goes," Dandalus said. "The Mare brought Tessa here. And here she has remained until the Mare sent you to fetch her."

"I really have felt urges to go," Tessa said.

"I've had to restrain her from heading out alone," Dandalus said.

"I let him restrain me," Tessa said. "It wasn't quite time. Now it is."

Cole sighed. "Okay. I'll do my best to protect you."

"The Weaver's Beacon will help," Dandalus said. "Your enemies will struggle to find you in the echolands while you possess it."

"Is there any other place I should go?" Cole asked. "Anything else I should do?"

"Stick to your plan," Dandalus said. "Hide Tessa, then go after her sisters."

"What about Nazeem?" Cole asked. "What if he breaks free?"

"I have heard reports that Nazeem expects to win his freedom," Dandalus said. "I can't directly interact with the echolands or the Outskirts anymore, but I see and hear plenty in the echolands. We made the Fallen Temple so secure! Powerful or not, I could not imagine how he could defeat our defenses. Until I saw your memories, Cole."

"What was the clue?" Cole asked.

"Nazeem communicated with his followers in Junction using the Founding Stone," Dandalus said. "It's a brilliant loophole that I failed to anticipate. The Founding Stone is an object of considerable power. It connects to all physical material in the Outskirts. It was designed to be unbreakable, but shapecraft can thwart the most careful designs. My guess is one of Nazeem's disciples used shapecraft to break off a piece of the Founding Stone and brought it to the Fallen Temple."

"That makes sense," Cole said. "Once I shared my power with the Founding Stone, your imprint got rid of Nazeem."

Dandalus nodded. "When my imprint spoke with you, he downplayed the import of the Founding Stone. It's safer not to let people know."

"Can Nazeem use the Founding Stone to get free?" Tessa asked.

"Escape should still be virtually impossible," Dandalus said. "But given the confidence he is showing, Nazeem must have found a way."

"So we need to get the Founding Stone from him," Cole said.

"It might disrupt his chance to escape," Dandalus said.

"I'll tell my friends," Cole said. "We'll figure it out."

"It won't be easy," Dandalus said sadly. "Inside his domain, Nazeem is enormously powerful."

"Mira and Nori are in trouble because they came looking for me," Tessa said. "We have to help them. We should go."

"I need to get her back to the Temple of the Robust Sky," Cole told Dandalus.

"A long journey," Dandalus said. "I can calibrate the Weaver's Beacon to draw you there."

"Please," Cole said, holding out the lantern.

"It is done," Dandalus said, waving it away.

"Thanks," Cole said.

"Once you're gone, I will move on as well," Dandalus said.

"Where?" Cole asked.

"My next hiding place must remain a secret. I have a few other sanctuaries that I can reach without succumbing to the call. People out in the world can't know my location. Should you ever need to find me again, start with She Who Stands at the Summit."

Tessa went and hugged Dandalus. "Thank you," she said. "I'll never forget you."

Dandalus patted her head. "You have a power unlike anything I have beheld in all my days. Why Nazeem would seek to control something so untamable lies beyond my understanding. Perhaps his pride is too great to recognize the danger. But the reality remains that he wants you, Tessa. Take care."

Cole and Tessa walked away from Dandalus and his little house. They passed through trees to the short grass and occasional bushes of the field beyond. The wall of cliffs rose in the distance.

"I usually run," Cole said.

"I'd like that," Tessa said. "I've kept still for so long."

They set off across the grass.

"You really feel like you should leave?" Cole asked.

"Absolutely," Tessa said with confidence

"How can you tell?"

"It's hard to explain," Tessa said. "It's kind of like a persistent hunch. I know when I feel it."

"You're getting more of these feelings again?" Cole asked.

"Not like before," Tessa said. "It used to happen many times a day. After Papa took my power it seemed like that type of knowing had ended. But it has started up again."

They ran in silence. The wall of cliffs drew nearer.

"Do you know about the Pass of Visions?" Cole asked.

"Dandalus explained not to touch anybody," Tessa said. "I came through on Thunder last time."

"You call the horse Thunder?" Cole asked, surprised.

"That's her name," Tessa said.

"I call her Thunder too."

"You probably felt it in her music."

"The pass can be bad," Cole said. "You'll see things you really fear, and people you really love. It's all phony. I even saw you."

"Really?"

"You looked just like your imprint. You wanted my help."

"It definitely wasn't me." Her head tipped upward. "What's that?"

Cole looked up. A bunch of winged specks were soaring toward them out of the sky.

He came to a halt. A perplexing sense of unreality washed over him. This had already happened! This was how he had lost Harvan and Winston. It couldn't be happening again. Here? Now?

"No way," he murmured.

"What?"

Cole shook his head. "This is how Sando attacked us at the Farthest Mountain. There are more of them this time." He counted eleven people.

"What should we do?"

Cole looked back. The trees that sheltered Dandalus were about as far away as the cliffs. Was there any chance of making it? They had to try. "We're in serious trouble," Cole said, drawing the Jumping Sword. "Run!"

They sprinted together back toward the trees. Cole kept glancing over his shoulder, watching as the winged men swooped closer. Five glided beyond them, landing in positions that blocked retreat to Dandalus. The other six came up short, blocking access to the pass.

Sure enough, Sando stood among the six. He shrugged out of his glider and raised both hands. "A word, young sir! Do not run and we will not pursue. Allow us a moment of your time?"

Cole faced him. Destiny stood beside him. There was no place to run.

"What are you doing here?" Cole asked.

"Same as you," Sando said. "Looking for Destiny. Hello, Tessa."

She said nothing.

Cole scowled. "How did you find me?"

Sando chuckled softly. "I'm not new at this. I have my methods."

"Can you follow the beacon?" Cole asked.

"The beacon cannot be traced," Sando said. "Should I tell you, giver of silver? Why not? Consider it my offering to you. A debt repaid. I gave Desmond a message from Honor to Destiny. It was a real message that I offered to deliver for Honor after we captured her. I told Desmond that if he gave the message to you, Cole, I would keep Honor out of the Fallen Temple. She would go to Gamat Rue instead, where he might have a chance to rescue her. Desmond suspected I had ulterior motives, of course, but risked the small favor to protect his princess."

"The message let you follow me," Cole said.

"Message?" Tessa asked.

"I forgot to give it to you," Cole said. "I was excited to find you. I have it. I would have remembered."

"You have not delivered it yet?" Sando scolded, wagging a finger. "Naughty errand boy!"

"You knew we would go to Deepwell?" Cole asked.

"I believed so, yes," Sando said. "You came across at the Temple of the Robust Sky. I expected you would have the same information as Honor, and that is where she went. I am one of Nazeem's chief officers. I ordered the guards at

Deepwell to offer minimum resistance. I wanted you to free Desmond, so he would give you the message. The Mare rescued you twice, Cole. I believed you would lead me to Destiny. Congratulations, young sir. You have now delivered to me not one, but two princesses! Perhaps *you* should be a chief officer for Nazeem!"

"I'm so sorry," Cole groaned. His gut twisted with shame and frustration. Sando was right.

"I felt it was time to leave," Tessa said, sounding puzzled. "Maybe it was to protect Dandalus."

"Let's keep this simple," Sando said. "Come with us."

Cole looked and listened. Now would be a really good time for the Mare to return. The horse had bailed him out when he was cornered before. Now he was with Destiny! It was like a hundred times more important!

But he heard no whinny, no hoofbeats, no thrilling music.

Without warning, Tessa started running. Not toward Dandalus. Not toward the cliffs. She took off toward the nearer of the two channels. The narrower one.

Cole followed her. Was she hoping to get around the shapecrafters and make it back to Dandalus? The shape-crafters blocking the way ran with them. Tessa would have to sprint quite a bit faster than the shapecrafters to get around them. But the opposite was happening. The fastest shapecrafters were pulling ahead of them.

"Don't flee," Sando called, running as well. "Why waste the effort? We have you. This is over. Why draw it out?"

"You want to make it to Dandalus?" Cole asked Tessa.

"If we can," she said. "Maybe you can use that sword?"

Cole liked the idea. If he attacked violently enough, maybe he could do for Tessa what Harvan had done for him. Maybe he could buy her time to make it back to Dandalus. Once she was inside his sanctuary, he should be able to protect her. Maybe they could flee together to one of his other hiding places.

Still running toward the channel, Cole veered toward the shapecrafters who were blocking the way to Dandalus. They veered toward him as well.

"I'll slow them down," Cole told Tessa quietly. "You run through the opening."

The channel was getting closer. They were running out of room. He needed to engage the shapecrafters before he and Tessa ended up pinned against the slipstream.

Mustering all his fear and desperation, Cole pointed the Jumping Sword at the nearest shapecrafter. "Away!" he shouted. The sword failed to pull him.

Instead of jumping, Cole charged the nearest shape-crafter and whacked him on the chest. The blade didn't cut deeply, but the man stumbled, and so Cole swung at the next closest shapecrafter, who slowed to avoid the blow.

"No, no, no!" Sando shouted. "The girl! Stop the girl!"

Cole looked back at Destiny and realized what was happening. She hadn't followed Cole's lead. She wasn't trying to dash through the gap he created. She was almost to the slipstream, running hard, showing no sign of slowing or turning.

"Tessa, no!" Cole yelled. This was all wrong! This wasn't how it was supposed to happen!

Cole raced after her. The shapecrafters did too. But they had concentrated on keeping her from getting around them. They had meant to corral her. They had driven her toward the slipstream to pin her against a dead end.

Except she was going to use it as an exit.

Cole hoped she might be bluffing. Maybe Tessa would try to use the threat of jumping in to get Sando to back down.

Nobody was going to arrive in time to stop her.

Her death would also destroy her power. Thunder was about to stop existing. Perhaps violently.

"Stop her!" Sando screamed.

Two of the shapecrafters had slowed to chant and gesture. They were trying to freeze her.

Tessa never slowed.

"Tell my sisters I love them!" she shouted as she sprang into the slipstream.

POWER

No!" Cole bellowed.

This was not happening.

His job was to find Destiny. It was what Mira had most wanted. It was vital to the rebellion.

Tessa was in the slipstream. He hadn't anticipated her taking such drastic action to avoid capture. He had failed. It was over.

Her little body flowed along in the ether, arms flailing.

And Cole knew what he had to do.

He had no choice.

Impossible or not, he had to save her.

No matter the price.

Sheathing his sword, Cole ran with all his strength. He might be able to reach Tessa before the slipstream swept her out of range. Her body wasn't traveling as fast as the whistling ether.

But she was going faster than he could run.

By the time Cole reached the edge of the channel, Tessa

had swept by him. As he tried to follow, her lead kept stretching.

There was only one possible way to catch up.

Cole considered keeping the lantern, then shuttered and dropped it. Maybe Dandalus could protect it from Sando. If not, at least the Weaver's Beacon would have a better chance of survival than it would in the channel.

Cole jumped in.

The shrill whistling of the slipstream gained the overwhelming fury of a hurricane. Beneath it, behind it, the gorgeous call of the Other sang of home. The mix was exhilarating and peaceful. He felt a tremendous urge to close his eyes and zoom to the source of that beautiful music.

Not yet. Maybe later.

He had somebody to rescue first.

Swimming forward, Cole caught sight of Tessa up ahead. As he stroked downstream, she resisted the current. Their combined efforts allowed him to gain on her.

"Tessa!" he shouted, the word lost in the howling symphony of the slipstream.

Head bobbing above and below the surface, Cole struggled to keep her in view. The slipstream blurred all around him, a streaky gale of fog and tinsel. It was hard to tell if he was floating or flying—the ether had more substance than wind but less than water. He refused to inhale the substance, grateful that breathing wasn't necessary in the echolands.

Tessa drew near. Heaving himself forward, Cole wrapped his arms around her. They both sank. His feet began clipping the rocky floor of the channel. With their combined weight, he couldn't get his head back above the surface. His feet kept striking the channel floor. Gritting his teeth, Cole absorbed several impacts until he slowed enough to plant his feet against some firm rocks.

Tessa clung to him. He held her close and leaned against the wailing might of the slipstream. It took all his strength to hold steady. He could feel that if he lifted a leg to take a step, he would be washed downstream.

Squinting against the fury of the slipstream, frantic music shrilling in his ears, Cole tried to get his bearings. The near side of the channel was a sheer wall. There would be no wading out. It would require a climb.

Looking up, he found that the slipstream wasn't horribly deep where he stood. If he raised his hands over his head, his fingers would break the shimmering surface.

"Let me go!" Tessa cried, her words barely audible. "I'm not afraid!"

"I have to save you!" Cole yelled back.

"It's too late!" Tessa shouted. "Nobody returns from the slipstreams."

Cole saw a shape leaning out over the surface of the slipstream. Distorted as it was by the rushing ether, it took Cole a moment to recognize the form as Sando. His shapecrafters were holding one arm so he could lean out over the ether, his free hand outstretched toward the surface.

Cole felt a thrill of excitement. If he could lift Tessa high enough, Sando would be able to pull her out. Maybe she could still survive this!

When Cole tried to speak again, he found he had used

up all his breath on his previous shouts. He didn't need to breathe to live, but air was still necessary to push words out. Ducking his chin, Cole inhaled through his nose and discovered the ether was breathable. Inside his nostrils, it felt much more like air than water.

"You have to live!" Cole hollered, unsure whether she could hear him.

"They'll use my power!" Tessa replied, her words barely audible. "I don't want more people to get hurt!"

"Dandalus doesn't think anyone can use your power!" Cole yelled. "And I agree! I saw Thunder. I'm handing you up!"

"Let's float away!" Tessa called out. "All this will be over!"

"No!" Cole insisted.

"It felt right to jump in here!" Tessa cried.

"It felt right to save you!" Cole replied.

"That doesn't mean . . . ," Tessa started. The slipstream shrilled in his ears throughout her pause. "Well, maybe."

"Someone can still save you!" Cole called, happy to hear her wavering.

"He'll take me to Nazeem!"

"Get away! Be strong! Make their plans backfire! Get rescued!"

"All right!" Destiny relented.

"Let go of me!" Cole yelled.

She released her hold, and Cole heaved her upward. Sando leaned farther forward, Tessa's arms broke the surface of the slipstream, and suddenly, she was pulled up and away. In a blink, Sando and Tessa were no longer in view. Only the whooshing ether remained.

Without Tessa weighing him down, Cole immediately felt more buoyant. The slipstream tore at him, threatening to carry him away. He hooked one foot beneath a large rock on the floor of the channel, leaned into the current more, and struggled to think heavy, immovable thoughts.

A blizzard of ether lashed at him relentlessly, howling around him, interlaced with the heart-melting melody of the homesong. If he tried to take a step, he would be swept away. He could barely maintain his present position. If the current surged just a little stronger, he would be washed away.

Might somebody throw him a rope? Lower a branch? Extend a wing?

He kept glancing at the jittery surface, but no saviors appeared.

It was just him and the slipstream.

Maybe he should let the current take him. At this point, wasn't he resisting the inevitable? Wasn't it just a matter of time?

But somebody had to save Tessa. And so many others. He had to hold on.

There seemed to be power in his defiance. He felt a little more firmly anchored to the channel floor.

He had to think. Maybe there was a way out of this. He wasn't going to suffocate. He wasn't going to get tired. He might be able to stay put for a good while. If he lasted long enough, maybe somebody would help him.

He needed to live. He had to see his family again. He had to help Dalton and Jenna find their way home.

As Cole embraced those thoughts, once again he felt a

little more firmly planted against the turbulence. The sensation of the ether was changing. The windy fluid still mostly whooshed around him, but now it felt like some of it flowed through him. As he paid attention to the sensation, it gradually increased.

Was the slipstream really penetrating him? It made him feel intangible, like a ghost. Like his very substance was diminishing.

The call of the Other rang more clearly than earlier. In fact, as the ether passed through him, he could almost feel the homesong inside of him. When he focused on the call, a greater portion of the slipstream slid right through him. Having the ether stream through him reduced the drag, making him feel a little more stable. But it also felt like he was disappearing. Was he being washed away one particle at a time? How long before nothing was left?

"No!" he cried, his voice small against the banshee chorus. A memory stirred. When had he heard wind like this? The terminal void behind the cloudwall! He wondered if the swirling maelstrom might be composed of this same ether.

He hunkered a bit lower and leaned into the current a bit more. The slipstream hardly seemed to flow around him anymore. Yet the current still threatened to carry him away. The pull was reduced, but not as much as it should have been if he completely lacked substance.

Cole began to feel hot inside. Although the ether penetrated his body, something within him resisted the shrieking gale, causing incredible friction. The heat became uncomfortable before Cole recognized the scalding element as his power.

He was feeling his power! It had been so long! He had barely learned to recognize it before it was blocked. He had never gotten to enjoy it. And he couldn't enjoy it now as it continued to burn hotter.

What was going on? Would he burst into flames?

His entire body began to vibrate. The friction against his power was becoming more powerful than the pull against his body. Would his soul get ripped out? His lifespark? Was this how that felt?

Cole gritted his teeth. He wouldn't let the slipstream take him. Since he could feel his power, Cole reached for it. The effort caused physical pain. It was scorching, white hot, unfit to be used.

And then he could no longer hear the song of the slipstream. It was replaced by the homesong in a fullness he had never experienced. The current kept pulling but seemed remote. More important was the heavenly music washing over him. The peace coursing through him. The sublime assurances.

Somewhere deep inside he knew and loved the homesong. He adored it completely and instinctively. Was this how an orphan might feel, reunited with his mother, her beloved voice and smell reviving dormant memories? Cole had lost everything—his home, his family, his friends, his future— but this song promised restoration. Peace and joy and an endless abundance that included all he believed he had lost.

This song had been sacred to Cole since before he was

born. His life had been an illusion. This music was home.

And the music was only a promise! What would it be like to actually go there? Why was he resisting? Why wasn't he rushing toward this greatest of all destinations?

The searing heat of his power blazed inside of him. Noticing it helped the homesong recede slightly. Was his power charring him from the inside? Was he turning to ashes? Maybe that was why the slipstream gushed through him, as if he were a hologram.

The homesong resurged, more hopeful and joyous than he could absorb. Why not embrace it? Why not get lost in it?

Tessa.

Mira.

Dalton.

Jace.

Jenna.

Hunter.

People needed him.

The call of the Other decreased in volume. He could hear the slipstream again. It physically tugged at him a bit more.

Sando had taken Tessa. Mira was imprisoned at the Fallen Temple. Jace and Joe were at Gamat Rue. And it was all his fault.

The slipstream was going through him less, flowing around him more. His power was cooling, the friction decreasing.

Dalton was counting on him to return. He had promised to find Jenna. Somebody had to stop Stafford Pemberton and Nazeem. He needed to get home to his family and to help the other kids from his neighborhood do the same.

The homesong would have to wait.

The slipstream howled around him, tearing at him, but no longer sifting through him. The call of the Other remained present but not overpowering.

People needed him. They needed his help. They needed his power.

His power.

He felt it clearly. Not hot anymore. Not catching against the slipstream.

Not gone.

His power was there more clearly than he had ever felt it, even when he had used it in the fight against Morgassa, even when the Founding Stone had helped it awaken. After all this time, it was back.

And he was stuck at the bottom of a channel, on the fringe of the echolands, the fury of the slipstream threatening to peel him from his position at any moment. Cole could envision himself hurtling along the channel, a rag doll in a tornado.

But his power was back.

The glow of it gave him confidence.

And now he knew what to do.

Cole drew the Jumping Sword and pushed some of his power into it. Flames danced along the blade, bright even in the frantic blur of the ether.

He pointed the blade at the surface of the slipstream, angling it toward the near shore of the channel.

"Away!" he shouted.

And away he flew.

CHAPTER
32
THUNDER

Cole erupted from the slipstream, soaring up over the field beside the channel. The Jumping Sword always knew where he was pointing, but in his excitement, Cole had aimed too high. He rose about thirty feet over the field, then slowed at the apex of his flight before plummeting down.

Fortunately, Cole was no rookie with the Jumping Sword. As he landed, he pointed to a spot up ahead, shouted the command word, and greatly reduced the impact by taking a second smaller jump.

After coming to a stop, Cole looked around, his sword ready. He could still distinctly feel his power, and he knew that with the Jumping Sword he could give Sando a much better fight.

But Cole saw no sign of Sando, Tessa, or the other shape-crafters, not even as specks in the sky. How long had he been stuck in the slipstream?

Cole sheathed the Jumping Sword. At least he was alive.

He had never been so relieved to feel the ground beneath his feet or to see the sky overhead. He had almost left this world behind.

While Cole had chased Tessa inside the channel, the ether had carried him almost back to the wooded sanctuary where Dandalus lived. Though he felt embarrassed about losing Tessa so quickly, Cole figured he should check with Dandalus before going after her.

After his first step back toward Dandalus, Cole heard a distant whinny, accompanied by faint, thrilling music. He stopped, then turned.

In the distance, Thunder raced toward him from the direction of the cliffs. Cole gritted his teeth. Why couldn't the Mare have appeared earlier? He and Tessa might have outrun Sando.

Of course, he could still use a ride.

"Cole!" called a voice from behind.

Cole turned to find Dandalus approaching through the trees. A radiant cloud swirled inside the Warden of the Light, somehow perceivable through his clothes and skin. Cole knew from his experience at the Founding Stone that the glimmer was Dandalus's power. Cole scrunched his brow. Why hadn't he noticed it before? The luminous power was plain enough now to be distracting. Hoping Dandalus might have some advice for him, Cole trotted over and met him at the edge of the grove.

"I see you have a visitor," Dandalus said, glancing beyond Cole at the oncoming horse.

"Better late than never," Cole replied.

Dandalus raised his eyebrows. "I don't imagine Destiny's power typically arrives late."

"But I lost Tessa," Cole said. "I feel so stupid."

"Are you serious?" Dandalus asked.

"I was in charge of her for less than an hour and she got taken," Cole said.

"You were unbelievably heroic, Cole," Dandalus said. "You saved her life."

"And brought her a message that let Sando follow me," Cole said.

"A devious ploy," Dandalus said. "I noticed the message but thought nothing of it. I assumed you would give it to her later."

"You couldn't sense Sando tracking it?" Cole asked.

"He must have used shapecraft. That can be hard for me to detect. Or he might have just used the obligation of delivery to follow you, which is basically impossible to discern from outside the agreement."

The hoofbeats drew nearer. Thunder neighed.

"Come fully into my sanctuary," Dandalus said, backing up. "We don't want to risk being overheard."

Cole stepped from the turf of the field onto the clover of the grove. The outside music instantly stopped, but he could still hear the approaching hoofbeats.

"Take heart," Dandalus said. "The Mare brought you here and has now come for you. You may not have strayed far from whatever scheme Destiny's power intended."

Cole frowned. Could that be true?

"You have your power back," Dandalus pointed out. "And by very unusual means."

Cole thought about that. "I wouldn't have gone in except to rescue Tessa."

Dandalus grinned. "Who would attempt such a feat? The choice to enter a slipstream is sacred in the echolands. Once a person goes in, they do not come out."

"People don't often survive?" Cole asked.

"To my knowledge, it has never happened," Dandalus said. "If you weren't both living echoes, I doubt it could have happened. Even so, it was only made possible by your very strong will to live and your formidable power. Your will and your power helped ground you against the pull of the ether. As you held your ground, the slipstream pulled the impure shaping away. In miraculous fashion. Your power was hideously mangled. It is now completely, impossibly healed. I can no longer tell it was ever damaged."

"At least I'll have my Jumping Sword again," Cole said, patting the hilt.

Dandalus gave a soft laugh. "Yes, but Cole, your ability extends far beyond energizing objects. That is a novel side effect compared to your full potential."

"Really?" Cole asked.

"Can't you feel it?" Dandalus asked. "Of course you can, but you've never really tested it, so you're unaware of the possibilities. Cole, were it not for the threat posed by Nazeem, I might be your biggest enemy in the echolands."

"You?"

"You naturally have raw shaping ability," Dandalus said. "Since we rearranged how shaping functions, only the torivors have wielded such power here. The shapecrafters fake it in a limited way by maiming their power and the power of others. But you have it, Cole, and you have it *here*, as a bright echo. This is the original home of raw shaping. Your power will be stronger here than anywhere. Once you master it, you could undo much of what we've done."

Cole swallowed. "So why am I not your enemy?"

"Because of the threat we face," Dandalus said. "And because I can see your mind. Unlike the torivors, you don't want to ruin the Outskirts or the echolands. You don't want to rule here. You want to help. And we need help."

Thunder gave a soft whinny.

Cole turned to find the horse standing at the edge of the field. Lost in the conversation with Dandalus, he had almost forgotten about her arrival.

"Hi, Thunder," Cole said.

"Thunder?" Dandalus asked. "Ah, you felt the name, and Tessa confirmed it."

"Just a minute, okay?" Cole asked.

The horse lifted her head up and down once. Cole took it as a nod.

"What can I do?" Cole asked.

"Here you should be able to shape much as they do in Sambria," Dandalus said. "It takes time to develop that skill, especially to learn to make semblances. We designed Sambria so it is easier to shape than to unshape. We made the echolands very difficult to alter. But you will find that here, with your raw power, unshaping might be the simplest skill to learn. The stabilizing measures we took did not anticipate power like yours."

"Why do I have such a weird ability?" Cole asked.

"Your power is bound to your will," Dandalus said. "Though we built a mortal realm here, living humans were never meant to come to the echolands. Those we brought arrived with especially potent abilities. It was how they destroyed the original versions of the Outskirts, and why I chose to place restraints on shaping itself. Furthermore, almost everyone who comes to the Outskirts is brought here by others or crosses over accidentally. But you came deliberately. Since power is connected to will, those who come deliberately tend to develop extra power."

"I guess that makes sense."

"That isn't all. Under the tutelage of Nazeem, shapecrafters have blurred the limits, shaping outside the boundaries we framers established. This endangers the way we restructured the shaping power. Eventually, everything could collapse back into raw shaping. You are evidence that it is starting to happen."

"Can you fix the damage?" Cole asked.

"Not from here," Dandalus said. "If I abandon this sanctuary, I would barely have time to destroy all we made and sweep it away as the homesong claims me. Which is why I don't want to be discovered."

"Did Sando see you?"

"He at least knew there was a powerful sanctuary here. I will depart before he can return."

"If we stop Nazeem, won't I still be a threat?" Cole asked hesitantly.

"A major threat," Dandalus said. "Which is why I ask this

favor. If you can thwart Nazeem, promise me that afterward you will seek out Rinka Pryer, the Grand Shaper of Creon. With your current abilities, she should be able to teach you how to get home. You will get what you want and protect the Outskirts as well."

"I can make that deal," Cole said with a huge smile. "I've wanted to get home from the start. You really think I can do it?"

"Now that I see your power without the shapecrafted barriers in place, I am confident you can. Defeating Nazeem will be the bigger obstacle. If you trained for a hundred years, you could not face him in a fair fight. The objective must be to prevent his escape. This could be possible. Everything depends on it."

Cole nodded. "If Nazeem gets free, he takes over this whole world."

"And if it gets bad enough, I flush it all, so he doesn't trap a bunch of people, echoes, and lifeforces here with him."

Cole shook his head. "Wow. No pressure."

"Somebody believes in you," Dandalus said, nodding toward Thunder. "Let's see what you can do. Try to break the ground."

"Here?" Cole asked.

"Not under our feet," Dandalus said. "But inside my sanctuary. This domain is heavily protected, but unless I'm mistaken, the defenses won't hold against your raw talent."

Cole looked at the lush clover covering the ground about ten feet away. "How?"

"You feel your power," Dandalus said.

"Yeah."

"You remember how you pushed your power into the Jumping Sword."

"Sure," Cole said. "I get that much."

"Try to feel that patch of ground like you feel the sword before pushing your power into it."

"I'm always holding the sword," Cole said.

"And that contact is helpful when you try to share energy. But you can also reach out and feel targets at a distance."

Cole stared hard at the patch of clover. Could he sense the ground beneath? He tried to imagine the clover on fire. Or getting flattened. He tried to imagine the soil beneath splitting open.

Nothing happened.

"I don't get it," Cole said.

"Take my hand," Dandalus said.

Cole let the warden's hand close around his.

Suddenly, he didn't just see the clover. He could sense the texture and temperature, as well as the density of the earth underneath. Small rocks were buried here and there in the rich soil.

"Look harder," Dandalus said.

Cole found his perception going beyond the senses. As he focused, he understood the substance of the clover and the material of the dirt. He didn't just see it or touch it or smell it or taste it or hear it—he *knew* it.

He felt connected to it.

The clover, the dirt, and the rocks were almost part of him. It seemed he might be able to wiggle them like fingers.

"Good," Dandalus said. "Now draw on your power. Push

power into your target and tell your target what you want it to become. See it another way."

Cole could clearly sense his power. He had reached for it in vain so many times that he was still learning to trust that it was actually there. Was this how Dalton felt, able to create illusions in Elloweer whenever he wanted?

Cole focused on the largest rock within his target zone, mostly buried by soil and clover. He began to push some of his power toward the stone.

But how did he want to change it? What if he altered the substance of the rock into the same material as the soil? He could envision the necessary transformation.

He pushed harder and willed the change.

The rock dissolved into chalky brown matter.

Dandalus released Cole's hand.

Cole walked over, crouched, pushed aside some clover, scooped up some of the powdery remains of the rock, and let the fine brown dust sift through his fingers. "I did . . . something," he said.

"An outstanding effort for a first try," Dandalus said. "The echolands are designed to be unchangeable. You shaped that stone. Not into anything useful, but you transformed it."

"I was trying to make it into dirt," Cole said.

"Because you recognized and understood the dirt," Dandalus said. "A valiant effort."

"Were you letting me see things like you see them?" Cole asked.

"As best I could, yes," Dandalus said. "To get you started. Try it on your own."

Cole found that when he concentrated on another patch of ground, he could perceive the clover and the soil beneath almost as clearly as when Dandalus had held his hand. He shifted his attention to a large rock that protruded well above the clover. Should he try to make it into dirt as well?

"Don't change it," Dandalus said. "Unshape it. Destroy it. Reach out with your power."

Cole connected to the rock, pushed with his power, and tried to rip it apart. With a sound like a gunshot, the rock cracked in two.

"Not bad," Dandalus said. "Now really punish it."

Cole connected again, forcing more power at it than before. With a scowl, he tried to tear it to shreds, and the two halves shattered into fragments.

"You're getting it," Dandalus said. "Again. Same idea, but more thorough. Imagine the rock is going to kill you and your friends. It wants to conquer the Outskirts."

Cole felt his anger rise. Dandalus knew how to push his buttons. With a growl, he really released his power, and not only did the stone fragments get smashed to dust—the ground where they rested split open.

"Very good," Dandalus said. "You know how to smash now. And you know how to energize people and objects. That's a great start."

"People?" Cole asked.

"The same principle that enables you to energize the Jumping Sword should let you empower a person. You could enable a Sambrian shaper to practice her art in Elloweer, for example. Or awaken her slumbering powers here in the echolands."

"What else can I do?" Cole asked.

"Your unshaping could be useful in combat," Dandalus said. "Keep in mind that you can't directly shape or unshape a person. It just won't take. Anything with a will is very hard to shape unless the subject agrees. Even vegetation is resistant. Try that tree."

Cole focused on the trunk of a tree. He could sense it, but when he tried to push his power into it, he felt no connection.

"See?" Dandalus asked.

"Yeah," Cole said. "What about making stuff?"

"You could undoubtedly develop that skill over time," Dandalus said. "It wouldn't hurt to practice. Your power appears to be inexhaustible. But don't get frustrated. Certain disciplines take time and practice. For example, try to close the wound you made in the ground."

Cole centered his attention on the furrow he had left after pulverizing the rock fragments. He focused on the soil along both sides of the little trench, connected to it, drew on his power, and tried to force the earth together. Clumps of soil broke off, making the split bigger and messier.

"Tricky," Cole said.

Dandalus raised a hand, and the split closed up neatly, covered once again in clover.

"Wait," Cole said. "What did you do with your hand?"

"Nothing vital," Dandalus replied. "Sometimes a gesture helps my focus. My concentration and power are key, not the gesture. But mind the lesson. If closing a little ditch is difficult, imagine what it takes to shape a complex object."

"It dissolves into brown dust," Cole said.

"It can," Dandalus agreed. He crouched and scooped up some soil, then pressed it together with both hands. "Or you might produce an item like this."

He held up a golden strand just like Jace's.

"Whoa," Cole said. "Does it work?"

"Not yet," Dandalus said. "Somebody would have to charge it with Sambrian shaping energy."

Grinning, Cole held out a hand. Dandalus passed the strand to him.

Cole felt instantly connected to the little rope. He pushed, and ghostly flames flickered over the strand. Flicking his wrist, Cole willed the rope to extend and wrap around a tree trunk. It did so perfectly, as if it were an extension of his arm.

"My parting gift," Dandalus said. "I saw it in your memories and had to try."

"Will it work when I leave here?" Cole asked.

"Anywhere in the echolands, if you provide the energy," Dandalus assured him.

Cole willed the rope to release the tree and to retract into a little strand. It complied.

"Thank you," Cole said. "This could come in handy."

"Don't go looking for trouble," Dandalus reminded him. "Astride Thunder you will be hard to find. Best to remain hidden as much as possible."

"Sneak attack," Cole said. He glanced over at Thunder.

The Mare snorted and stamped one hoof. She seemed to be calling him. He looked back at Dandalus. "Think she'll take me to the Fallen Temple?"

Dandalus shrugged. "The Mare will take you where she takes you."

Cole sighed. "They have Destiny."

"And you now have your power."

Cole nodded. This was better than before. Now he had weapons—a functional Jumping Sword, a golden rope, and his power. He had already planned to challenge Nazeem to rescue Mira, basically weaponless. He now had an extra princess to save, but maybe he had more of a chance for success.

"Bye, Dandalus," Cole said.

"Be careful if you make your way to the Fallen Temple," Dandalus suggested. "If you unshape too recklessly there, you could potentially weaken the barriers that hold Nazeem captive."

"Good to know," Cole said. How dumb would he feel if he accidentally freed Nazeem?

"Don't forget the Weaver's Beacon," Dandalus said.

Cole decided not to admit that the relic had slipped his mind. "Sando didn't take it?"

"He tried," Dandalus said. "It would take stronger shapecraft than he or any of his lackeys possess to take the beacon without permission. One of his underlings got burned."

"I'll get it," Cole said.

"No need to use it while astride Thunder," Dandalus explained. "Nothing could conceal you better than the Mare."

"Thanks again," Cole said.

"Farewell, Cole," Dandalus said.

Cole ran around Thunder and followed the channel. He knew that trying to ride the horse now could lead to him galloping away without the beacon.

It was a fairly long run before finding the shuttered lantern right where he had dropped it. Thunder trotted along behind. Cole retrieved the beacon and turned to face the horse.

Thunder crouched down, and Cole climbed on. As the horse stood, Cole could feel his power flowing into the animal. Thunder brightened, light seeping through the writhing clouds of her coat.

Cole patted the horse's neck. "Are we going to save Destiny?"

Thunder took off like lightning.

CHAPTER
33

REUNIONS

Cole squeezed with his knees and clung to the silky mane as Thunder accelerated to a ludicrous speed. His previous ride seemed like a casual trot by comparison.

Thunder continued to draw power from Cole, his contribution enhancing their breathtaking velocity. Cole supposed it made sense that if the Mare was an embodiment of shaping power, then his power could boost her capacity.

The Pass of Visions quickly drew near. Just before they rushed into the pass, the terrain and sky transformed.

The sun glared down from overhead. The cliffs ahead were replaced by brown, crumbling ridges where half-dead shrubs and trees clung to life. Cole had not seen a struggling plant since coming to the echolands. Nor had he seen the actual sun! Off to one side, a meager stream trickled down a series of ledges.

The colors were less vivid. The music was gone.

Cole and Thunder had crossed to the mortal world.

But they continued at a furious pace.

The transition had been seamless. Cole had not suspected that Thunder could cross to physical Necronum so effortlessly, or that Mare could bring his echo along. Destiny had some serious power.

Beyond the broken ridges, Thunder and Cole returned to the echolands without slowing. The sky reverted to the even glow of a duskday, the music returned, and they raced across the plain of smooth, clear crystal.

Cole felt thankful for their speed. He wondered how fast they were going compared to Sando's gliders. Was there hope of beating Sando to the Fallen Temple? Maybe intercepting Destiny before they delivered her?

Thunder continued to draw on Cole's power and sporadically switched between the mortal world and the echolands. Cole thought it seemed the horse was going back and forth based on what terrain was more favorable. When riding in the mortal world, Cole found he missed the music of the echolands, but the direct sunlight was welcome. As an echo in the mortal world, Cole felt no more tired or hungry than he did in the echolands.

Thunder never reduced her breakneck pace. Landscapes came and went. Eventually, when in the mortal world, they galloped under stars and moonlight. When they returned to the echolands, the terrain became richer in vegetation until Cole once again rode across short grass between lush groves and gardens. After returning to the parklike topography of the central echolands, Thunder stopped crossing to mortal Necronum.

Trees and blossoms sped by in a colorful blur. Cole's

power showed no sign of depletion in spite of the constant usage.

Up ahead Cole heard momentous, fervent harmonies. So far Thunder had generally avoided noteworthy music, but they headed directly toward this new sound.

A large building came into view, expansive and low except for six tall, slender towers. Enclosed by a crenellated wall, the structure occupied the highest ground in the vicinity.

Cole wondered if this could be the Fallen Temple. The momentous music didn't seem threatening enough to match Nazeem's prison. But where else could they be?

Thunder slowed slightly as they approached an open gate in the wall. Startled echoes hurried out of the way as the horse zoomed inside. Cole received astonished stares as he streaked through courtyards and up stairways. Thunder galloped along covered walkways until skidding to a stop beside a large rectangular pool beneath the sapphire sky.

Cole stared in surprise. He had never seen standing water in the echolands.

Suddenly, the sky darkened and came to life with stars that reflected in the black water of the pool. The same masonry surrounded them, but he and the horse were now in mortal Necronum.

Thunder crouched down, and Cole slid off. He heard soft footsteps and waited as a figure moved along one of the covered walkways, coming toward the pool, carrying a small oil lamp and wearing a silver robe, the hood obscuring the face in shadow.

"Where are we?" Cole whispered to Thunder.

The figure stopped walking. "What?" a young, female voice said.

Thunder gave a soft whicker.

The figure threw back her hood and hurried toward the Mare. Cole gaped in astonishment, unable to breathe. It was Jenna.

She looked beautiful in the lamplight—the familiar face that he had longed to see for hopeless months. The face that had lived in his imagination long before they were brought to the Outskirts, long before he had promised to find her. His first crush. For a long time seeing her again had seemed an impossible dream. Cole had almost died more than once since their last encounter. And here she was, alive and well.

"How did you get in here?" Jenna asked the horse, not even glancing toward Cole.

"Jenna?" Cole asked, hardly able to speak. He could still barely believe this was happening. It had never crossed his mind that Thunder might bring him to her. But there she was—dark hair falling in wavy curls, soulful brown eyes reflecting the glow of her lamp.

Jenna continued to ignore him.

She began petting the horse. Thunder once again had fiery highlights in her swirling coat. It had to be the darkness. Or maybe being in the normal world?

"Animals are not allowed inside the temple," Jenna chided quietly.

"Jenna!" Cole repeated more loudly.

She turned away from Thunder toward Cole, wide eyes looking beyond where he stood. "Who said that?"

"Me. You know, Cole Randolph? From class?"

She did not appear to hear or see him. "I'm in no mood for sneaky echoes tonight," Jenna said. She waved the hand without the lamp. "Show yourself."

Cole felt a tingling, and her eyes met his.

Jenna gasped. "Cole?" she asked uncertainly.

"You see me?" Cole checked, excited and relieved.

She stared for a long, silent moment. "Yes." She reached out a tentative hand, and her fingers sank through his chest. "Are you . . . ?"

"I'm a bright echo," Cole said.

Jenna smiled widely. "Really? It's really you?" She bit her lip, and her eyes welled up. "I didn't think I'd ever see anyone from home again! Especially, well, you. But you're here! Cole Randolph. Alive! Well . . . sort of." She stopped and took a deep breath. "I'm sorry, it's been so long. I'm glad you're bright."

"My body is far away," Cole said. "This horse brought me to you."

Jenna scrunched her brow. "But I could touch it." She patted the horse again to demonstrate. "How can an echo ride an actual horse?"

"Do you know about the Mare?" Cole asked.

"What mare? This one?"

"It's a long story," Cole said. "This horse can appear in Necronum and the echolands."

"Wow," Jenna said. "I've never heard of anything like that. Although . . . I guess after everything I've seen here, nothing should really surprise me anymore."

"We're partners for now," Cole said.

"It's so good to see you," Jenna said. "Even if . . ." Her fingers passed through his shoulder.

"I've been looking for you since we got separated," Cole said. "I found Dalton."

"Really?" Jenna asked.

"If you haven't seen anyone else from home, then you haven't seen Dalton? What about a kid named Hunter?"

She shook her head. "I haven't seen any of the others since I came here, and no one named Hunter, either."

"We're at the Temple of the Still Water?"

"Right," she said. "Don't you know where you are?"

"We came here really fast across the echolands," Cole said.

"What were you doing in the echolands?"

"That's an even longer story," Cole said. "One I probably shouldn't tell for now. It could get you into trouble. Do you like it here?"

"At the temple?"

"Yeah," Cole said. "Do they treat you all right?"

"Not too bad," Jenna said. "I'm a slave, but I'm good at weaving. I have my duties. It could be far worse."

"You'd rather be home?" Cole asked.

"What do you think?" Jenna said, then noticed she had spoken too loudly and lowered her voice. "But there's no way home, Cole. We're stuck here. Even if we get home, we can't stay there. And nobody would remember us."

"There might be a way around all that," Cole said. "Have you heard of shapecraft?"

"No."

"That's probably a good thing. But it can shape the shaping power. It can mess with the rules. I'm working on finding a way to get us home for good."

A light came into Jenna's eyes. "For good? You really think you can do it?"

Cole's cheeks flushed. He'd always wanted to be her hero, even before they came to the Outskirts. After all he had experienced in the months since slavers took his friends, Cole still found the prospect exciting. "I'm not sure," he admitted. "But I believe there's a way. And I'm not going to quit until I find it."

"In the echolands?" she asked. "Are you a weaver too?"

"No, but I have some shaping power," Cole said. "Keep an eye out for Dalton. When I went to the echolands, he was planning to come find you."

"I haven't seen him since Junction," Jenna said. "Where did he end up?"

"I found him in Elloweer," Cole said.

"You get around!" Jenna said. "How do you manage it as a slave?"

"I escaped the Sky Raiders," Cole said. "Afterward I found a shaper who changed my bondmark to a freemark." He stared at her. He knew he shouldn't mention the princesses or Nazeem or anything that could turn her into a target. "I promised I'd come find you."

"I remember," she said. "You were very brave back at the wagons. Brave trying to free us and brave when they took you away. I was really worried about you. The Sky Raiders sounded like dangerous people. I worried you might be dead."

"And now I kind of am," Cole said with a grin.

"Lots of people cross over to the echolands," Jenna said. "You left your body in a safe place?"

"I think so," Cole said. "It was well guarded."

"Do you need my help?" Jenna asked.

Cole glanced at the horse. "I don't know. What can you do?"

"Normal weaving," Jenna said. "I can summon an echo, bind an echo, all that. Have you lost where you crossed over? I can point you in the right direction."

"I'm not going back to my body yet," Cole said. "Is there anything I can do for you?"

"I can always use help from a friendly echo," Jenna said. "How much time do you have?"

Cole glanced at Thunder. The Mare shook her head and stamped a hoof.

"Is the horse in charge?" Jenna asked.

"Kind of," Cole said. "It's a really smart horse. I don't think I get to hang out. I think Thunder just knew I wanted to make sure you were all right." Should he offer to have her cross over? Come with him? Wouldn't that just lead her into horrible danger?

Thunder shook her head and stamped again.

"If you find a way home . . . ," Jenna said.

"I'll be back," Cole promised. "I'm trying to get all of us

out of here. I'll come find you if I make it through this. Do you know about the Other?"

"Yes," she said. "Be careful, Cole."

"I can't make any promises about careful," Cole said. "But I'll try not to die. I mean, you know, permanently."

She looked distressed. "Can't you stay awhile? I haven't seen anybody from home for so long."

Thunder shook her head and stamped twice.

"We're kind of on a mission," Cole said. The look of desperation in Jenna's eyes caused a wave of guilt to roll through him. He didn't want to leave her here alone. It was so tempting to invite her to join him, but he knew that would only put her in more danger, and he couldn't sacrifice all his other friends for her right now. Not when they were captured in the afterlife and she was relatively safe. Life in the Outskirts seemed to mean making one impossible decision after another!

"The horse seems anxious," Jenna said, looking down at the ground.

Cole faced Thunder. "I'm almost ready. I'm just saying good-bye."

Thunder snorted.

"Dalton will come for you," Cole said. "He and Hunter can probably help you escape."

"Who is Hunter? Someone from the Outskirts?"

"My big brother. He came here before us, so none of us remember him. Think about whether you want to risk running away."

"All right," Jenna said.

Thunder crouched down.

"I better go," Cole said, climbing onto the horse. He didn't want to leave. He had waited so long, and this was so brief. But Thunder was clearly ready to go, and lots of people were counting on him. "Sorry it's such a short visit."

"Me too. But I'm so happy to see you. Good luck! I hope you're back soon. Really soon."

Thunder stood up.

"Bye, Jenna."

The stars were replaced by the uniform light of a dusk-day, and they were back in the echolands. Thunder broke into a run, once again clomping through covered walkways and across courtyards until they galloped out of the gate.

The Temple of the Still Water receded quickly. At least he knew Jenna was all right. At least he got to see her one last time.

"Thanks, Thunder," Cole said.

The Mare whinnied in reply.

If anything, Thunder seemed faster than ever. They zoomed through a rolling paradise of trees, shrubs, and flower beds. The pleasant music lulled Cole, who was growing accustomed to the thrill of the intense speed.

Distant hills came near and fell away behind them. Cole occasionally heard villages or other variations in the typical music of the landscape, but he saw no echoes. They rocketed across an abandoned universe of vibrant gardens.

At length, they entered a fairly large village. Thunder came to a halt in front of a cottage. Several echoes watched them curiously, paying special attention to the horse. Cole kept his lantern shuttered and tried to hold it inconspicuously.

Thunder crouched down, and Cole got off. "Here?" he asked, jerking a thumb at the cottage.

The Mare bobbed her head once.

"This isn't You Know Where. So where are we?"

Thunder offered no explanation.

Cole approached the cottage door and knocked. Out of the corner of his eye he noticed several echoes still paying attention to him.

A fairly tall woman opened the door. She was wrinkly and old, with bulging eyes. "Yes?" she asked.

"Hi," Cole said. "I'm not sure why I'm here."

"I know the feeling," the woman said wryly, glancing past Cole to the horse. "Is she yours?"

"Not really," Cole said. "I've just been riding her."

"Who is it?" called a female voice from out of sight.

"A boy," the woman replied. "Who are you?"

"Bryant Randolph."

The woman repeated his name loudly, then moved aside as a second woman bustled to the door. She was of medium height with a bony build and wild blue hair. Her face looked much younger than her hands. "Cole?"

"Callista!" Cole exclaimed. He hadn't seen the former Grand Shaper of Elloweer since she perished in the fight against Morgassa. "I was using my middle name."

"Cole, my boy," Callista said. "How refreshing to greet a familiar face. And a bright one at that." She glanced over her shoulder. "I'm staying with my sister, Enid. The accommodations aren't ideal to host company."

Cole looked at Thunder. The horse nodded and stamped.

"You arrived by horseback?" Callista inquired.

Cole unshuttered the Weaver's Beacon to disguise their conversation.

"Quite a light," Callista said.

"I'm trying to rescue Destiny Pemberton," Cole said. "I found her, but she was taken by servants of Nazeem."

"I've heard that name too much lately," Callista said. "I wish I could be of service, but I lost my power when I arrived here. After cultivating my gift for my entire life, I can no longer muster a simple seeming, let alone a major enchantment like a changing."

"I may be able to help," Cole said, remembering what Dandalus had told him.

"How?" Callista asked.

"I finally found my power," Cole said. "Give me your hand."

She reached out, and Cole took it. Her skin felt loose, the finger bones slender underneath.

Cole pushed his power into her.

Callista's expression brightened. She let out a giggle, followed by a cackle.

"How did you do that?" she asked. "I feel my gift as clear as day."

"It's part of what I can do," Cole said.

Callista gazed at him. "Yes, I can sense your power now. It's native to the echolands, isn't it?"

"Raw shaping," Cole said.

"Interesting," Callista said. She released his hand. "Where are we going?"

"Three of the princesses are being held here in the echo-lands," Cole said. "Tessa, Mira, and Honor. Tessa and Mira are at the Fallen Temple. I think we're going there to save them."

"You think?" Callista asked.

"I go where the horse takes me," Cole said. "This is Thunder." He lowered his voice to a whisper. "Destiny's power."

Callista hooted a laugh. "I see. So the horse found me?"

"She's in charge," Cole said.

Thunder whinnied and stamped.

"She wants to get going," Cole said.

"All right," Callista said. "Life had become wearying without my power. I felt so limited. I was hoping to find a way to be of service here. Guess I should be more careful what I wish for."

Enid reappeared in the doorway. "You're not really going?"

Callista hooted merrily. "I have my power back, my dear. You know I've wanted to help the resistance."

"I so enjoyed your company," Enid lamented.

"I'll be back this way if I can," Callista said. "If not, we'll meet again in the next realm." She turned to Cole. "Should I transform, or is there room on the horse for two?"

Thunder bobbed her head and crouched down.

"We should both ride," Cole said. "Thunder is really fast."

Callista hugged her sister, then joined Cole beside the Mare.

"Can you still feel your power?" Cole asked, wondering if she would need a constant influx of power to use her abilities.

"Oh, yes," Callista said. "I'm no novice. I just needed to find it again. My power had gone dormant. I feel good as new. I should be fine now."

Shuttering his lantern, Cole climbed onto Thunder. Callista scooted into position behind him. The Mare stood, and the village became a blur. Soon groves and gardens streaked by.

Callista cackled. "Now this is a horse!"

Cole and Callista rode in silence. Cole wondered what their next stop would be. Another old friend? A stranger who could help them? Would they visit Necronum again?

Or could they be on their way to the Fallen Temple?

Cole had no way of knowing. The geography of the echolands remained a complete mystery to him. They might have been going north, south, east, or west. Or in circles.

The terrain varied between flat and hilly, always adorned with thriving vegetation. They crossed channels, using bridges on the broad ones but simply jumping some of the narrower slipstreams.

Cole tried to calm his mind. He might be about to fight Nazeem, but at least with Callista, he had a strong ally. She had put up a serious fight against Morgassa. Hopefully, Thunder would help as well.

After a long ride sinister music began to build directly in front of them. The harsh strains tempted Cole to try to steer Thunder in a different direction. Knowing what might be coming was different from hearing the actual music. It was not a happy tune. His mouth felt dry.

A huge, blocky structure loomed up ahead, composed of

black stone and flanked by squat, square towers. A colossal iron gate appeared to be the only entrance. It was shut tight. With small windows and little decoration, the solid building looked more like a fortress than a temple.

Thunder pounded up to the gate and stopped.

"Who goes there?" called a male voice from within.

"We're lost," Cole answered. "Where are we?"

"Don't play dumb," the voice replied.

"I really don't know," Cole said honestly.

"You're at Gamat Rue," the voice replied. "And we invite you to move along. We've seen that horse before."

RESCUE

Thunder whinnied an unmistakable challenge.

"Try again, if you must," the voice replied. "We deny access. Nobody enters Gamat Rue uninvited."

"You tried to get in before?" Cole asked Thunder.

The horse bobbed her head.

"The legendary prison," Callista said. "I thought we were going to the Fallen Temple."

"Me too," Cole said. "I guess this comes first. I have friends inside. Including Honor."

Callista leaped down from Thunder.

Cole winced. It seemed like a long drop for an older woman, but by the time Callista hit the ground, she was a sleek, black jungle cat, not much smaller than the Mare.

"Open it up," Callista said.

"Me?" Cole asked.

"That gate is reinforced with a host of enchantments," Callista said. "We won't enter by force. Use your power, Cole. Let's see that raw shaping in action."

Thunder neighed.

Cole swallowed.

The iron gate looked a lot more formidable than a rock in a field of clover. The violent music of Gamat Rue belonged to something that attacked you, not something you attacked.

Cole moved to slide off Thunder, but the horse side-stepped and shook her head. Apparently he was meant to stay aboard.

"Concentrate, Cole," Callista said. It was odd to hear her voice coming from a big panther. "You can do this. They have your friends."

That got his attention.

Cole stared hard at the gate. He could feel his power inside, some of it still flowing into Thunder. Jace was in there. Harvan as well, according to Dandalus. And Joe. Desmond. Ferrin. Drake. Honor.

An echomancer named Nandavi ruled this place. She had helped Sando abduct Mira. Cole would be breaking into her territory, giving her and her guards an extra advantage. But Dandalus thought Cole had a chance against Nazeem. So he should be able to handle this.

Maybe his raw shaping would help cancel out Nandavi's home-field advantage. He had Callista and Thunder with him. And his friends needed him.

Cole focused on the gate until he felt connected to it. The sheer bulk of it was intimidating. He could feel slippery tendrils of power coursing through it.

"Send out all your prisoners, and we'll pass you by," Cole called.

The voice laughed. "Move along. If you're not careful, we might just open the gate, boy."

"Don't bother," Cole said.

It was the final motivation he needed. That sneering voice represented people who had hunted him. People who had captured his friends. People who were willing to unleash evil forces that they had no power to control. People who had driven Winston to the Other.

Cole forced his power into the gate and sensed the defensive weavings melting away. He crushed the iron monstrosity with everything he had. Metal shrieked and crumpled. Hinges burst from their moorings. The gate tore apart and crashed down amid a hail of shattered stone.

Cole connected to the base of the wall at either side of the gateway and pulverized it. A landslide of stone blocks came roaring down. Gritty clouds of dust plumed outward. Voices cried out in alarm.

Cole smiled. The dramatic results of his demolition efforts felt extremely satisfying. He wanted to do more. Tearing apart the fort would be easier than he had expected. But his friends were inside! Until he could see how things were arranged beyond the gate, Cole knew that doing more damage could harm the people he cared about.

Besides, Thunder was now charging forward, loping confidently through the rubble. Cole squinted until they passed through the dust cloud. Callista roared from off to one side.

Thunder galloped into a broad, high hall filled with scattering echoes, men and women. The echoes didn't match the formidable appearance of the building. Nobody had weapons or armor. As Cole and Thunder rumbled down the hall, they veered toward the flustered echoes, trampling whoever came within range. Callista pounced and growled, springing from victim to victim.

Cole felt his body stiffen but shook off the immobility with an effort of will. He opened the shutter of his lantern. Thunder ran so smoothly that Cole adjusted the beacon with no worries about falling. The glaring light immediately muted the music of the fortress and seemed to bother the echoes. He no longer felt the effects of anyone binding him, though he could see several echoes trying.

Thunder paused before a door. Cole forced his power into it and tore it to splinters. With the beacon shining, Cole felt energy feeding him faster than he could use it.

Echoes pressed against walls or dodged through doors to avoid the charging horse. Those who didn't were slammed to the ground or trampled.

The Mare faced another door, and Cole destroyed it, ducking as they rushed through and up a staircase. Cole blasted an iron door out of the way, and an angry echo charged from behind it. Rearing slightly, Thunder battered the attacker with her front hoofs, then stomped him when he was down.

Cole and Thunder raced down a hall lined with barred cells. They stopped where a familiar man stood clutching the bars of his enclosure, smiling at the intruders.

"Harvan!" Cole exclaimed.

"Look at you!" Harvan said with a laugh. "Riding in on the Mare!"

Cole focused on three consecutive bars of Harvan's cell and pushed with his power. Instead of bending them, he changed them to dust.

"You found your power!" Harvan admired.

"You were a weaver," Cole said.

"Once upon a time," Harvan replied.

Cole leaned down and reached toward him. "Take my hand."

Harvan complied, and Cole pushed power into him.

"Whoa," Harvan said, stepping back. "How'd you do that?"

"It's part of my ability," Cole said.

"Cole . . . it's back," Harvan said. "I feel it. Really?"

"Yep," Cole said.

"Great," a familiar voice said. "My one useful talent has been replaced."

Cole shifted his attention to a shorter, balding man in a neighboring cell. "Winston!"

"Don't get too excited," Winston said, squinting at Cole. "I'm just a dead echo. Little more than an imprint."

"But still so very optimistic," Harvan laughed.

"It was bound to happen, spending time with this guy," Winston said, jerking a thumb at Harvan. "Next time we visit the Deadlands, I can join the party."

"Is the beacon bothering you?" Cole asked as Winston continued to squint.

"It's not pleasant," Winston said. "But let it shine. You'll need it here."

Cole dissolved three more bars so Winston could get out. "Have you guys seen my friends?"

"Just the prisoners in this area," Harvan said. "Sando is here somewhere, though. Just arrived."

"Did he bring Destiny?" Cole asked.

"I don't think so. Why would he have . . . Wait, you found her?"

"And he stole her."

"He was just here trying to pry information out of me. Maybe half an hour ago."

"Halt," a shapecrafter called from down the hall, having just come around a corner.

Harvan held up a hand, and the man froze.

"The echolands just got more fun," Harvan said.

Thunder crouched down.

"Climb aboard," Cole said. "We have places to go."

"You two go on ahead," Winston said. "That lantern is a little much for me. I'll bring up the rear."

"You follow," Harvan said. "I won't leave here without you."

"I'm not going to go find a slipstream or anything," Winston said, waving them away. "Go help the others."

Harvan mounted behind Cole. Thunder rose, and they took off down the hall, slamming aside the shapecrafter Harvan had immobilized.

They dashed down more halls. Cole disintegrated doors as needed.

The echoes of Gamat Rue ran around in a state of panic. Cole met with little opposition. Thunder trampled who-ever tried to take a stand. Apparently, the people who ran this place weren't used to being attacked, especially by a rampaging horse and echoes they couldn't freeze.

After descending a level, Thunder stopped by another wall of bars. Jace stood behind them. Joe sat in the neighboring cell.

Cole felt a huge surge of relief as a giant grin spread across his face. They were okay!

"Took you long enough," Jace said, arms folded.

Cole turned some of the bars to silt. "That's all I get?"

Jace grinned. "All right. Thanks for springing me. Nice horse. Cool trick with the bars."

"Want to see a cooler one?" Cole asked, dangling his little golden rope and pushing power into it.

"No way!" Jace exclaimed, all casual pretenses disappearing. "Is that what I think it is?"

"A friend made it," Cole said, tossing it to Jace. Though it had left his grasp, Cole maintained a gentle connection to the rope, still feeding it power.

Jace caught it, then made the rope lengthen and curl around some of the remaining bars. "All right," Jace said. "Time for some payback."

"Stay near me," Cole said. "The light from the beacon will help protect you."

"Should I get down?" Harvan asked. "I'm probably faster."

"Not when I have this," Jace said, making his golden rope twirl and dance.

Joe cleared his throat.

"Hi, Joe," Cole said, turning more bars to dust.

"Good to see you, Cole," Joe said. "Unbelievable."

Thunder snorted.

"We have more to do," Cole said.

Thunder proceeded more slowly, allowing Joe to keep up. Jace stayed with them using his golden rope, sometimes grabbing distant beams or bars to sling himself forward, other times coiling the rope behind him then uncoiling it like a spring. When echoes evaded Thunder, Jace often seized them with the rope and bashed them against the ceiling, walls, floor, and any other available surfaces.

They descended many stairs. The downward angle felt precarious to Cole, but he leaned back, gripped with his knees, and held tight with his free hand. Even on stairs, Thunder remained incredibly sure-footed, keeping the ride unnaturally smooth.

Although still muted by the beacon, the music became even more threatening the lower they descended. At the bottom of a serpentine stairway, Cole crumpled an iron door, and they entered a vast cavern.

Most of the ceiling and walls looked like the natural stone of a cave, though some masonry had been added. A multitude of shapecrafters was gathered on the far side of the cavern. At the center stood a woman draped in a dark, ostentatious outfit. She faced Prescia, who knelt motionless, hands bound. Sando was among those standing nearby. Beyond the group, several cells at the far end of the cavern held prisoners, including Honor, Desmond, and Drake.

"The lady in black is Nandavi," Jace said.

"All the most important prisoners are down here," Harvan complained. "Why didn't I make the cut?"

Jace used his rope to spring toward Nandavi and the

group around Prescia. Harvan and Joe started running in that direction as well.

Thunder knelt down. Cole took it as a signal to slide off. Once his feet hit the stone floor, Thunder bolted forward with astonishing speed.

Cole drew his Jumping Sword but paused once it was out of the sheath. Jace, Harvan, and Joe stood frozen. Apparently, they had gone beyond the range of the protective lamplight from the beacon. Nandavi had her arms extended toward them, her lip curled in an angry sneer.

Cole glanced at the beacon. He had never tried to force power into it, but establishing a connection felt easy. Gritting his teeth, he flooded power into the lantern, and it brightened immensely. The brighter beacon nourished Cole faster than before. The more energy he sent out, the more he got back! Cole pushed even harder, and the glare of the beacon intensified to fill the spacious cavern. The music of Gamat Rue could no longer be heard.

Bathed in white light, Nandavi shrieked. Jace snatched her with the golden rope and began bashing her into other shapecrafters. Prescia lunged to her feet and froze a trio of shapecrafters. Thunder raced around the room trampling the shapecrafters who tried to scatter. Harvan and Joe reached the main group and attacked with their fists.

Cole's attention shifted to the far end of the cavern, where Sando and a pair of large shapecrafters had retreated to Honor's cell. Cole pointed his Jumping Sword at a spot high on one wall and shouted, "Away!" He launched into the air. When he reached the wall, he pointed his sword at the ground near Honor's cell and shouted the command again as he kicked off the stony surface.

Rushing across the upper reaches of the cavern, Cole passed over where Jace, Harvan, and Prescia were fighting. In her panther shape, Callista had joined the melee as well. Cole kept pushing extra power into the beacon as he flew.

As he approached the rocky floor, the Jumping Sword slowed him enough that he managed to stumble to a stop without falling. Sando was already inside of Honor's cell, his assistants at her sides, holding her as she squirmed.

Sando shot Cole a wink, then he, the two assistants, and Honor all disappeared.

Cole stared at the empty cell. What had just happened? Could Sando teleport?

Cole turned to his friends. Jace continued to use Nandavi like a wrecking ball. Thunder ran wild. Callista pounced and snarled, razor claws raking. Harvan threw punches. Joe had a shapecrafter in a headlock. Prescia met Cole's eyes.

He crossed over, her voice spoke to his mind.

Cole wanted to kick himself. Of course! At Gamat Rue echoes could cross to the Necronum side. Sando had done it when he captured Jace and Joe.

How would he follow them?

I can help, Prescia communicated silently.

Extending his sword, Cole jumped to her.

"Send me," he said.

"Your echo will be vulnerable there," she warned. "Easier to kill."

"Fine," Cole said.

"You'll have to leave the beacon," she said. "It won't cross."

Since Prescia had given the Weaver's Beacon to him in the first place, Cole could think of no better person to leave it with. He set the lantern down, and the light output returned to normal.

"Hurry," Cole said.

The cavern disappeared, and he was back at the ruined version of Gamat Rue in Necronum. He stood in the same bare clearing where Sando had first immobilized them, surrounded by crumbling architecture. The sun shone down from a partly cloudy sky.

Honor, Sando, and his two henchmen were just beyond the far side of the clearing, hurrying away into the maze of ruins. One of the shapecrafters carried Honor over his shoulder, while the other waved his arms, apparently weaving to keep her immobile.

When Sando saw Cole, he squealed, alarm in his eyes. His grimace showed his shiny gums. The old beggar produced a knife. "Halt!" he demanded, darting toward the henchman who held Honor.

Cole understood what he meant to do.

Echoes were much more vulnerable on this side.

Sando was going to kill Honor.

There was no time to think.

Cole aimed the Jumping Sword at a point a little ahead of where Sando was running. His power felt different here, still present, but a little less distinct, a bit harder to reach. Was it the absence of the Weaver's Beacon? Or maybe just being back in Necronum? Regardless, Cole forced extra power into the sword and shouted, "Away!"

He shot through the air low and fast like an arrow from a bowstring. Cole had never accelerated so quickly before—the influx of power had definitely boosted the jump.

The shapecrafter holding Honor had stopped. She hung over his shoulder, immobile, defenseless. Sando had his arm raised to strike with his knife when Cole cannonballed into the wiry beggar, ramming the Jumping Sword through his back. Both he and Sando collided with the shapecrafter who was weaving to keep Honor paralyzed. All three of them crashed to the ground. Cole kept his hand on the hilt of the Jumping Sword and could feel it jerking and jiggling as Sando hitched and quivered.

Suddenly, Honor could move. She thrashed, the shapecrafter carrying her lost his grip, and she flopped to the dirt. Honor sprang to her feet, brushed Cole's hand from the hilt, placed a boot against Sando, and yanked the Jumping Sword from his body. The old beggar's spasms stopped. He stared at nothing, eyes blank.

Cole's mind raced at the sight of Sando's lifeless body. It didn't get any easier—every time he had to hurt someone, even to save himself and his friends, it still sent shockwaves through his system.

Honor turned to face the other shapecrafters and found them motionless.

Cole got to his feet, perplexed by the unexplained stillness.

"I have them," Prescia called from the center of the clearing. Apparently, she had followed Cole across. The Grand

Shaper of Necronum stood with the fingers of one hand fluttering. Keeping the two shapecrafters immobilized did not seem to require much of her concentration.

"Hope you don't mind," Honor said, holding up the Jumping Sword.

"Not a bit," Cole replied. "That was quick thinking."

"Not as quick as you," Honor said. "They had me. I owe you my life. Thank you."

Cole shrugged, pleased and embarrassed. She was so tall and confident and brave and pretty. Had *he* really saved *her*? "You're welcome."

Honor returned the sword to Cole. "These two are prisoners now. Let's take them back across and lock them up."

"Can you bring all five of us across?" Cole asked Prescia.

In a blink they were back inside the cavern below the echolands version of Gamat Rue. Cole and Honor stood near the cells. The two shapecrafters huddled inside of one.

"You can adjust locations a touch when you cross if you know what you're doing," Prescia explained, picking up the Weaver's Beacon.

The cavern was quiet. Nearly two dozen echoes lay strewn about the room, apparently lifeless. A smaller group cowered on their knees, heads bowed, hands laced behind their necks. Thunder oversaw the group, with Callista, Joe, and Harvan nearby.

"Cole killed Sando," Honor announced.

"Nicely done," Harvan said. "That was quick."

"It had to be," Honor said. "Sando was about to dispatch me."

"Lucky I had the Jumping Sword," Cole said humbly, sheathing the blade. His hands shook slightly, and he hoped no one saw. He turned to the cell holding Drake and Desmond. "Where's Ferrin?" Cole asked the seedman.

Drake jerked a thumb at two trunks in a neighboring cell. "His pieces are tied up in sacks inside those two containers," Drake said. "It was all they could do to stop his escape attempts. He almost got away twice."

"Handy when you can pull yourself apart," Desmond added.

Thunder whinnied and stamped a hoof.

"Thunder's right," Cole said. "I'll open your cells, then let's get out of here. We have one last visit to make."

UNITED

M y rope stopped working when you crossed over," Jace said, holding up the small golden strand. "It shrank and wouldn't respond to any commands."

They stood outside of Gamat Rue, having exited the fortress without interference. The other shapecrafters had either fled or hidden.

"I have to keep powering it," Cole said. "When I charged up the rope, I created a connection that kept drawing a trickle of power from me. Once I crossed over to Necronum, the connection broke."

"Do you mind powering it up again?" Jace said. "I'd feel more peaceful."

"Sure," Cole said, touching the strand and nudging power into it. "Good as new."

Jace lengthened it and shrank it. "You're officially useful."

"That's a relief," Cole said.

"What about Hunter? Shouldn't his dead echo be around someplace?"

Jace lowered his gaze. "Sando knew Hunter's reputation as an Enforcer. He decided Hunter was too dangerous—even as a prisoner—and threw his dead echo into a slipstream."

"So Hunter will just skip the Echolands if he dies," Cole said.

"It isn't the funnest place I've been," Jace consoled. "Tell me how you got your power back."

Cole first explained how he met Harvan, Winston, Drake, and Ferrin. He went on to relate how they had freed Desmond and how Winston had died, allowing Cole to reach She Who Stands at the Summit. He then told about meeting Dandalus and finding Destiny. As Cole shared his tale, the others gathered to hear.

"You actually spoke with Dandalus?" Prescia asked, astonished. "His living echo?"

"His existence has been a secret," Cole said. "But he never told me not to talk about him. He was planning to change the location of his hideout. He doesn't want anybody to know how to find him. Seems like She Who Stands at the Summit controls access to him."

When Cole explained about Sando abducting Tessa, he didn't mention how exactly the beggar had traced him but couldn't help glancing at Desmond. The knight looked wretched.

Desmond cleared his throat. "I'm afraid my shortsightedness let Sando track Cole," he confessed. "I accepted a message from Honor to Destiny, and promised to pass it to Cole if he found me. The message came to me through Sando, acting as Honor's agent in the matter. It was the price for keeping Honor out of the Fallen Temple. The deal seemed so advantageous and innocent—I was getting so much for so little. I knew Sando had to be up to mischief, but was blinded to the potential harm by the chance to help Honor from my otherwise hopeless position. At the time I agreed, it didn't seem likely I would ever see Cole again. I failed to anticipate how much damage the message could do if Sando used it to track him."

"Sando fooled me in a similar way," Cole said. "He offered me a bargain that seemed too good to refuse, and it led to Jace, Joe, and Mira getting captured."

"I wanted to warn you when I gave you the message," Desmond said miserably. "I tried more than once, but the oath bound me. I couldn't deviate."

"I know the feeling," Cole said.

"You still haven't explained how you got your power back," Jace said.

"Almost there," Cole said. He related how Tessa had jumped into the slipstream and how he went after her. They listened raptly as Cole told of handing Tessa over to Sando, and then how the ether stripped away whatever was blocking his power, leading to his escape from the slipstream using the Jumping Sword. He finished by telling how he had ridden Thunder to find Callista and then arrived at Gamat Rue.

"I take it the Fallen Temple is our next stop," Harvan said. "When Sando's goons brought me here, I was worried I would miss it."

"Wouldn't want to skip the most deadly place in the echolands," Winston said. "I'll never understand how I went to the Other before you."

"At least your dead echo remains," Harvan said.

"I should go jump in a slipstream and get it over with," Winston said. "I can't form new memories. I won't recall any of our upcoming adventures."

"You can provide conversation," Harvan said. "Losing you was a blow. This is better than nothing."

Winston's expression softened. "I'm sorry, Harv. I didn't want to leave you. I'll stick around as long as I can."

Thunder snorted and stamped.

"Those who want to rescue Tessa and Mira will go where Thunder takes us," Cole said. "There could be stops along the way."

"You know I'm with you," Harvan said.

"Might be hard for all of us to fit on Thunder," Cole pointed out.

"I can help," Callista said, still in the form of an enormous black panther. "I'll change anyone who wishes to join us into forms that can run with Thunder."

"I'm in," Jace said quickly.

"Me too," Joe added.

"I go where Harvan goes," Winston said.

"It's been fun so far," Ferrin said.

Drake gave a nod.

"I have a lot to make up for," Desmond said.

"And of course I'll come too," Honor said.

Cole almost teared up, so great was his relief that he wouldn't have to fight Nazeem alone. Together they would find a way to beat him.

"I'll need to borrow your power, Cole," Callista said. "I don't have the strength to cause so many changes so close together. You should also energize Honor."

"You can restore shaping power here?" Honor asked.

"Yes," Callista said. "His ability is like none I have known."

Cole took Honor's hand and gently pushed power into her.

"I feel it again," she said, surprised. "My power went away the moment I left my body behind."

"That is typical after crossing to the echolands," Prescia said. "The power remains within, but goes dormant. Some aspect of Cole's ability wakes it up. Unlike the relics that need to constantly draw on his power, once your ability is awake, it should stay that way."

"Will you be joining us against Nazeem?" Harvan asked Prescia.

She paused. "I admire your courage and enthusiasm. But have you all considered that entering the Fallen Temple might be the same as getting captured? Have you any idea the amount of power Nazeem wields inside of his prison?"

"He has Mira and Tessa," Cole said. "We have to free them."

"I understand the intent," Prescia said. "But just because you enter the Fallen Temple voluntarily for a good cause does not mean you can prevail against the most powerful being in the echolands. You may not even stand a chance."

"Thunder is Destiny's power," Cole said. "She brought me here. If she brings us to the Fallen Temple, I think we can trust that we have a chance."

Prescia sighed. "Do we blindly trust that Destiny's power knows things we can't presently understand? Even when it contradicts experience and reason?"

"Probably," Cole said. "Thunder is the reason you're all free. At first I thought I might be going to the Fallen Temple alone."

Prescia looked at the Mare. "Nazeem has pursued Destiny more aggressively than anyone. What if her power is what he most wants? What if we're handing him victory by—"

Thunder whinnied, stamped, and shook her head.

Prescia frowned. "Maybe we should at least keep Destiny's power out of this. Cole could still lead a team—"

Thunder reared, whinnied, and bucked her rear legs.

"I think Thunder wants to come," Cole said.

The Mare gave a snort and bobbed her head.

Prescia tossed up her hands in surrender. "Who am I to resist such a power? I could name reasons this strategy seems reckless and fraught with peril, but I cannot claim to see deeper or to know more. I will join you as well."

"Sounds unanimous," Jace said. "Should we get started?"

"You just got free," Cole said. "Are you ready to charge back into danger?"

Jace shrugged. "All I've wanted since they took Mira away was to go help her."

"How was it being a prisoner here?" Cole wondered.

"Lots of waiting, mostly," Jace said. "Sometimes a bunch

of talking. They wanted information from me. I guess they couldn't read my mind."

"Persistent refusal and a strong will can block out just about anyone," Prescia said. "Well done."

"Sando spent some time trying to talk me into different deals," Jace went on. "Some sounded really good. But I'm not stupid. No offense, Desmond. Or you either, Cole."

"None taken," Cole said. "Good job."

"The worst part was the frustration of not being able to help," Jace said. "I hated all the waiting. Which is why I want to get started."

"Nazeem is a torivor," Cole warned. "I have met one before. Trillian, at the Lost Palace. He is incredibly powerful. We might not escape him."

"Did you say a torivor?" Ferrin asked.

"Yes," Cole said. "Why?"

"We had torivors in Lyrian," Ferrin replied.

"We sure did," Drake said, touching his chest.

"How many?" Cole asked.

"Dozens," Ferrin said. "But they had been enslaved by wizards long before our time. I believe they were only shadows of their former selves."

"They were still plenty tough," Drake said. "And plenty creepy."

"There are only two here," Cole said. "They were imprisoned by shapers or they would be running the place. Going up against Nazeem will be no joke."

"We know it's dangerous, Cole," Jace said. "We're ready."

Thunder bobbed her head and stamped.

"Are we agreed?" Harvan called out.

The others responded in the affirmative with varying degrees of enthusiasm. Thunder whinnied her approval.

Callista returned to her human form, approached Cole, and took his hand. "In honor of Thunder, I have a theme," she announced, then proceeded to transform the others into horses, one by one. Cole steadily pushed power into her. He felt her need increase with each changing and upped his output accordingly.

Honor held up her hands when Callista faced her. "Wait!"

"You want to be a knight again?" Callista asked.

"If it isn't too much trouble," Honor replied.

"Someone will have to carry you," Callista said.

"It would be my privilege," Desmond said, already a large white stallion.

"Done," Callista said, and Honor disappeared inside a full suit of gleaming armor.

Callista finished changing the others except for Winston, then released Cole. "Thanks, my boy. I couldn't have done so many without you."

"Happy to help," Cole said.

"What about me?" Winston asked.

"I can't change a dead echo," Callista said. "You'll have to ride."

"Climb aboard," Harvan said, now a chestnut stallion.

"Cole, I take it you would prefer to ride Thunder?" Callista asked.

The Mare crouched down.

"I think so," Cole said, mounting up.

Callista morphed into a jungle cat again.

Thunder stood and started running. The others followed.

Cole was glad to hear the music of Gamat Rue recede behind them. He wondered how long it would be until they heard the sound of the Fallen Temple. Would there be other stops along the way?

Although Prescia had withdrawn her concerns, Cole could not help thinking them over as they rode. What if they really were no match for Nazeem? What if Destiny's power simply wanted to go out in a blaze of glory? Or what if the odds of success were tiny, but Thunder had decided an infinitesimal chance was better than none?

If Sando had captured all of them, he would have probably brought them to the Fallen Temple. Now they were going there voluntarily. Might this end up being the same as if Sando had nabbed all of them at the start?

Cole thought about Jenna and Dalton. With his power back, Cole had a chance of getting them home. If they could find the Grand Shaper of Creon, their impossible dream could become a reality. But if Nazeem caught Cole or sent him to the Other, the dream was dead. If he was the best chance Dalton and Jenna had to get home, was it fair to take this risk?

Nazeem had Mira. He also had Destiny. At the moment, as far as Cole knew, those two princesses were in much greater danger than Jenna and Dalton. If Mira was in the greatest danger, didn't she deserve the most immediate attention?

Cole had long struggled with which friends most deserved

his help. He had debated the issue with Dalton. Did his old friends have a truer claim on him? Did the desperate needs of new friends like Mira trump all other problems? He was finally beginning to realize that there was simply no good answer to those questions. The old friends mattered. So did the new ones. They all mattered. He just needed to help whoever he could, as best he could, when given the chance. Right now that meant Mira and Tessa.

Besides, if Nazeem got free, he might destroy the Grand Shaper of Creon and end any hope of getting home. This threat needed to be dealt with.

Hopefully, success was possible.

They rode for a long time. Drawing only gently on Cole's power, Thunder held to a pace that let the others keep up. Paradise streamed by all around them, meadows and groves, hills and shrubs. The music soothed Cole. He realized this might be his last experience, at least on this side of the Other. He tried to absorb the beautiful sights and to enjoy the smooth speed of Thunder. Part of him wanted the ride to last forever. Another part wanted to get there and end the anticipation.

At last, menacing music began to throb up ahead. It carried a stronger warning than any of the tunes Cole had yet heard. At a deep, instinctive level, Cole wanted to flee. He had to resist trying to get Thunder to turn away.

The temple came into view, dominating a large clearing. Cole wondered if it had always been entirely black, or if that happened after Nazeem was imprisoned there. There were many towers and spires, the eight tallest equal in height.

A high wall protected the complex. A few skeletal trees stretched above the wall, bare branches contorted. A channel ran directly in front of the wall, spanned by a narrow bridge that led to an open gate. The whistling symphony of the slipstream was all but drowned out by the ominous harmonies of the Fallen Temple.

Thunder stopped just short of the drawbridge. Cole looked around at the horses with them. A knight rode on one of them. Winston rode another. And there was the panther.

"Should we return to our natural forms?" Callista asked.

Thunder nodded and stamped one hoof.

"Need help?" Cole offered.

Callista returned to her true form. "Not to restore them," she said.

One by one, the others changed back from their horse shapes.

Honor dismounted before Desmond was changed. "May I remain in this guise?" she asked.

Thunder nodded and stamped.

Callista changed all the others but left Honor as a knight.

"The gate is open," Ferrin said. "Are we expected?"

"It's always open," Prescia said. "Nazeem has always welcomed visitors. This whole area is difficult to perceive from afar. I'm sad that any echoes ever came here voluntarily."

"The music alone would keep me away," Joe said.

"Let's get this over with," Jace said.

"Cole should carry the beacon," Prescia said. "Keep it as bright as you can. Perhaps it will help shield us from his influence."

She returned the beacon to Cole, and he accepted it.

Jace twirled his rope around, making sure it functioned. Honor drew her sword. Cole met eyes with Harvan, who gave a nod.

"All right," Cole said. "Ready?"

"Lead the way," Jace said.

Cole smiled at his friend. It was nice to have him here. "Die bravely."

"Already did," Jace replied.

Cole wondered how long he had been waiting to use that line.

Thunder started forward, hoofs clomping on the bridge over the channel. Cole unshuttered the lantern as he rode through the gateway.

CHAPTER
— 36 —

RAMARRO

Much like when he had entered the Lost Palace, Cole found that the appearance of the Fallen Temple changed after passing through the gateway. For one thing, most of it was gone. Only the glossy floor remained, along with some carpets, pillars, and furnishings. A swirling sky radiated eerie light. The tempo of the music had slowed, becoming murkier and more secretive.

Thunder came to a halt, muscles twitching. Cole's friends remained with him, but otherwise the entire area appeared deserted. He could see a long distance in every direction but wondered how much of the surrounding landscape was illusory. How far would he travel before striking an invisible wall? Nothing in view matched the terrain Cole had seen moments ago outside the Fallen Temple.

"Where are we?" Ferrin asked.

"I'm afraid we're wherever Nazeem wants us to be," Prescia said.

A resonant chuckle from the sky confirmed her words.

Cole felt the hair raise up on the back of his neck.

"Not very comforting," Joe remarked.

"I'm a little glad to already be dead," Winston said.

"No need to talk like that," Harvan scolded.

"I don't see anybody," Jace said. "Where should we look for the princesses?"

"We had better find Nazeem first," Callista suggested.

"Welcome to my domain." The rich voice descended from the sky and rose from the ground, casual in tone, but powerful enough that the vibrations buzzed in Cole's chest. "You may as well relax. You are here to talk, not to fight. None of you can challenge me here. Each of you will perish if I elect to terminate you."

"Where are you?" Jace called out, rope held ready.

"I am everywhere," the voice said. "And nowhere. I may reveal myself to some of you in due time."

"Where are my sisters?" Honor demanded.

"It's a shame your mother did not name you Patience," the voice said. "Or Politeness. Do you require a demonstration? If you insist. Try to move. Any of you. Try to speak. Try to blink."

The shutter of the Weaver's Beacon snapped closed.

Cole became completely immobilized. He couldn't exhale. He couldn't twitch.

"Some of you are trying to resist me," the voice said. "You may as well attempt to lift a mountain. Go ahead and try. Keep in mind as you fail that you only remain here because I have not sent you to the Other. I would converse with Cole."

Suddenly, Cole stood in a field of thick mist that rose

to his shins. The low mist stretched to the edge of sight in all directions under a pale, hazy sky. A pair of bulky stone chairs sat facing one another. A man sat in one of them. Cole recognized him.

"Nazeem," Cole said.

"I asked some of my earlier followers to give me a name," Nazeem said. "That was what they chose. Nazeem. It suited my purposes at the time to obscure my identity. But you know my true name."

"Ramarro," Cole said.

Ramarro grinned. "That's right. Please, sit down."

Cole sat on the unoccupied stone chair. It was warmer than he had expected but not particularly comfortable.

"We met briefly," Ramarro said.

"When I was under the First Castle," Cole said.

"You're worried about your thoughts," Ramarro said. "You're concerned you may reveal something to me. Don't fret. I already know everything in your memories. You unveiled your history by trespassing here. You suspect I'm bluffing. I'm not. I know about Hunter, and Jenna, your family in Arizona, the day you lost your first tooth, your conversation with Dandalus, your hopes of keeping me trapped here—everything. Which means you can relax."

"I don't feel very relaxed," Cole said.

"I suppose not. Is there any emotion so terrible as suspense? You and your friends are completely in my power. I can do whatever I choose with you. For the moment I have not harmed any of you. But I could do so many things. Your imagination can hardly begin to envision the horrors that might await. This must produce an awful suspense."

"What are you going to do with us?" Cole asked.

"What I do depends entirely on you, Cole."

"Why?"

"It depends on what you're willing to accept," Ramarro clarified. "You possess an intriguing power. I would rather recruit you than destroy you. Same with your friends. But if you insist on resistance, my retribution will be swift."

"You're trying to take over the world," Cole said.

"I have succeeded," Ramarro clarified. "The echolands and the Outskirts are now mine to claim. You furnished the key to my prison."

"What do you mean?"

"Destiny's power," Ramarro said. "Without it, I would eventually have found another way. With it, I am free. Her power will permit me to return to the physical Outskirts. Once there, my portion of the Founding Stone will allow me to exit this prison."

"Dandalus was right," Cole said. "You have a piece of the Founding Stone."

Ramarro's grin made Cole think of a skull. "Your memories are a treasure box of information. So many delicious conversations! Dandalus trapped me here, you know. Gwendolyn as well. She Who Stands at the Summit. I had not confirmed that they remained in the echolands. Thank you."

Cole broke eye contact with Ramarro. What had he done? Would there be grave repercussions for revealing them to Ramarro? How bad would it be?

"Don't worry, Cole," Ramarro said. "Both of them expected me to see your mind. They knew I would learn about them through you. I'm sure Dandalus told you he could destroy the Outskirts and sweep the echolands bare in a desperate attempt to intimidate me."

"Did it work?" Cole asked.

"Dandalus can throw nothing at me that I cannot counter," Ramarro said. "He could probably damage or destroy the Outskirts. I'll believe that much. It's a fragile world. He might even be able to flush all life from the echolands. But not if I resist him. Not if I stop him. Even if I'm wrong, he certainly lacks the power to remove *me* from the echolands. If he had the strength for that, he would have done so long ago. If Dandalus works some unknowable form of doomsday shaping that I can't counter, if he unmakes the Outskirts and departs with all life, and if I am all that remains, so be it. I will have indirectly destroyed all who opposed me, and I will still remake the echolands as I desire and repopulate it at my leisure."

"What about Trillian?" Cole wondered.

Ramarro gave a nod. "You have traveled far and wide, Cole. You have met most of the key players in this game. Dandalus can remove Trillian no more than he can remove me. If Dandalus destroyed everything he could, the two torivors would remain. Perhaps Dandalus hopes the prospect of confronting another of my kind would intimidate me. I've never shied away from a fight, Cole. I have every reason to believe that I could either overpower or recruit Trillian. In fact, if he so desired, I might even let him go home."

"Why don't *you* go home?" Cole asked. "What's the point of taking over the echolands?"

Ramarro's eyes flashed. "At first it was simply for experience. Now revenge is in the mix. How can I explain it? Imagine you went to live in a house full of mice. And somehow, against all odds, the mice imprisoned you and took over the house. How would you feel?"

"Stupid."

Cole saw a flicker of anger in Ramarro's eyes. "Yes, I suppose so. And frustrated? And wrongfully stripped of your natural right to govern the house? You would sit and watch inferior beings control what should have been yours. If some of the mice decided to cooperate, you might be willing to share the house with them, so long as they never again forgot their place. Especially if some of the mice had qualities that made them more interesting than their more common brethren. You would need to teach the rest a lesson."

"But what if some old shaper got rid of all the furniture and all the mice?" Cole asked.

"You would have the satisfaction of knowing the mice had been exterminated," Ramarro said. "And the prospect of doing whatever you chose with the house. You could refurnish it however best suited your taste, and repopulate it with mice if you so desired."

"I'm an interesting mouse?" Cole asked.

"More than most," Ramarro said. "You killed Sando, for example."

"That makes me interesting?"

"Sando was very effective. He commanded my servants

in the echolands, just as Owandell oversees my minions in the Outskirts. If Owandell has been my right hand, Sando was my left."

"And I killed him. Doesn't that make you angry?"

"It makes me curious. Sando was cunning and powerful. You lack his experience, and yet you bested him. I prefer to work with the best. Which is why I now invite you to join the winning side."

"As your servant," Cole said.

"You're a human, not a torivor," Ramarro said. "Would you make a mouse your equal?"

"I wouldn't want to live in a house full of mice," Cole said. "I'd prefer other people."

Ramarro stared at him. "I have lived among my kind forever. I departed in the spirit of exploration. It was time for something new. And humans hold more charm than mice. I intend to control this world until I tire of the experience."

"I have a feeling you're not telling me everything," Cole said.

Ramarro laughed. "Then trust your feelings. Would you tell everything to a mouse? If a scientist had experiments in mind, would he confide fully in his lab rats? The portion I have told you is all true. Your choice is simple. You can join me, or you can watch helplessly as I do whatever I choose with you and your friends."

"If I join you, won't I be just as helpless?" Cole asked.

"You'll be helpless either way," Ramarro said. "But by siding with me you will enjoy preferential treatment. When the outcome is certain, why not join the victors? Defy me and you will wish you had stayed in the slipstream and coasted to your next phase of existence."

"What about the others?" Cole asked.

"They will have their own choices to make," Ramarro said. "But if they resist, and you join me, I may show them mercy."

"What would mercy look like?"

"I may send some to the Other," Ramarro said. "I may borrow aspects of their shaping power without torturing them. But I make no promises. I will do according to my pleasure. This is not a negotiation. Either pledge to serve me, or refuse and face my wrath."

"Don't you already know how I'm going to answer?" Cole asked.

"Not for certain," Ramarro said. "I know how you intend to answer. I also know how you should answer. Humans are so inconsistent that although I could make a very educated guess, I can't be sure about the outcome until the choice is made. You want to deny me. But it would be better for you and your friends if you change your mind. I would prefer it as well. I would rather not torment and destroy some of the most engaging mice. You could pursue a long, appealing life, Cole. I can unlock abilities in you and your friends that you could never achieve alone."

"Can you send me home?" Cole asked.

"I know of this desire," Ramarro said. "I would have to study the matter after my release. I expect that I could return you to Arizona, along with those friends who came here from your world. Would I? Perhaps one day as a reward for years of loyal service. There is also a chance you would figure out how to do it on your own while serving me. I will make no promises."

"Because you can't lie," Cole said. "And you won't send us home."

"That could be part of the reason," Ramarro said. "I find another more compelling. I don't bargain with vermin. The choice is before you. I must have an answer. The fate of many depend on your decision. Be wise."

"I'm trying," Cole said. He squirmed on the stone chair. He wanted his reply to come easily. He wanted to turn down Ramarro. Cole hated that he was hesitating. He could feel the finality of this decision. Was he ready to die? To condemn his friends to die? Was he ready to let Ramarro strip his power and shape it into a monster? Was he ready to spend eons imprisoned? Was he ready for long ages of torture? Could he condemn his friends to that fate?

Then again, would he really be condemning his friends? Wasn't it still their choice to make? And hadn't they all made this choice before, in different ways? What would Jace say to this offer? Harvan? Honor? Would they even pause? Wouldn't they have already shot him down? Just by coming here, hadn't they committed to stand against Ramarro?

In one way or another, Cole had been making this decision ever since he came to the Outskirts. Had he been content as a slave, or had he risked everything for the chance to escape? Had he stood against monsters that should have defeated him? Had he risked his life for his friends? Had he sometimes even risked fates worse than death, like when he fought Morgassa, or when he came to the echolands in the first place?

Cole had fought all along to protect his freedom and to free his friends. Would he now surrender that freedom voluntarily? Just because his enemy was calm, eloquent, and powerful, would Cole ignore that he was evil? Would he abandon his beliefs? If he served Ramarro, who would he become? He would end up like Owandell. Or worse. How many people would he harm?

The words Dandalus had shared returned to Cole. If the whole meaning and purpose of life hinged on what he chose to love and who he chose to become, the answer became clear. His heart already knew he should deny Ramarro, and now his mind was fully catching up.

"Dandalus planted those thoughts so you would choose this way," Ramarro warned.

"Who is trying to save this world, and who is trying to destroy it?" Cole replied. "Who is protecting young girls, and who is stealing their powers? I admire Dandalus! I'd much rather obey his ideas than yours."

"So be it, little fool," Ramarro said. "Lamentable but not unexpected. I suppose it is—"

Cole wasn't listening. He had focused on the stone chair where Ramarro sat. He connected to it and heaved his power into it along with an avalanche of angry thoughts.

The chair exploded into fragments.

Howling, Ramarro twisted, landing on all fours. He glared at Cole, a fathomless rage behind his eyes, furious music blaring.

Standing, Cole opened the shutter of the Weaver's Beacon and pushed with everything he had—all the defiance, all the hope, all the protectiveness, all the power. The lantern went supernova, casting a brilliant glare across the misty landscape. Some of the energy from the beacon fed back into Cole, and he increased his output. He kept one hand on the shutter, holding it open in case unseen forces tried to close it again.

The lantern was too bright. He couldn't see anything.

Had Dandalus deliberately warned him about this too? How much of this showdown had Dandalus anticipated?

The light blinded Cole, but he remained unfrozen. Nobody was attacking him. He could no longer hear the music of Ramarro's anger—or any music, for that matter.

Cole didn't want to dim the beacon too much, but he eased back on his effort enough to see.

The misty landscape was gone. The Fallen Temple looked as it had when they had first entered it. Cole stood beneath an eerie sky on a glossy tile floor surrounded by pillars. An altar sat directly ahead of him. He had moved forward from Thunder and his companions, who all remained frozen.

"You made me an offer!" Cole called. "Here is mine. Give me Mira, Tessa, and Durny. Let us depart in peace, and I won't rip this place to pieces."

"You have chosen to endure my wrath," Ramarro said, his disembodied voice falling from the sky and rising from the ground.

"Bring it on," Cole replied.

DESTINY

The ground quaked. The pillars rocked. In the distance a swarm appeared. At first Cole thought of the men with gliders who had attacked him near the Farthest Mountain and outside the sanctuary where he had found Destiny. As the swarm approached, Cole saw it was a cloud of monstrous bats.

Good, you want him angry, Prescia communicated in his mind. Glancing over his shoulder, Cole saw her standing immobile with his other companions. *It means he's not in full control.*

The freakish bats dove at him, the swarm becoming narrower and longer as it targeted him. Cole debated whether to draw his sword. It would mean taking a hand off the lantern's shutter.

The Weaver's Beacon poses a problem for Ramarro, Prescia went on. *He wanted you to serve him because it would have destroyed your protection. If you gave him your will, he would have obtained absolute power over all of us. Don't be fooled. He suggested he can destroy us at his whim. He is indeed powerful here, but he is also overconfident. Ramarro can't outright lie, but he can be wrong. Keep resisting. He can't bind you right now. He's trying to scare you. Pour on the power.*

Cole forced his full power into the beacon, and once again he could see nothing. The music of the beacon sounded like a single clear note, a ringing chime near the upper threshold of apprehension. Cole braced for the bats to collide with him, but the impact never came. The quaking ceased.

"This grows tedious," Ramarro said, his voice emanating from everywhere. "Why strive against you within my prison when I could go free?"

Thunder whinnied fiercely. Cole heard hoofbeats coming his way. He dimmed the beacon enough to see the Mare charge by him, gallop to the altar, and rear, front hoofs lashing wildly.

"Thank you for this gift, Cole," Ramarro said. "It would have cost more time to make my escape without her power. Like the other Pemberton girls, Destiny parted willingly with her ability, at the urging of Owandell, who acted on my behalf. Here in my presence, her power must obey me."

Thunder bucked and curveted around the altar, neighing angrily.

You need to see what is happening, Prescia counseled. *Ramarro is masking himself and this temple in seemings. Much of his power here comes from his ability to make us believe his illusions. He is in our minds. This place is more dream than substance. Change the nature of the light from the beacon. Demand that it reveal our surroundings as they are. Don't just make the beacon bright. Command it to let you see.*

Again Cole remembered the words of Dandalus. Could the Weaver's Beacon do more than shine brightly? Could it help him see farther, deeper, truer?

Still channeling his power into the lantern, Cole increased his output to maximum, concentrating on the nature of the light. The brilliant whiteness overpowered his vision. What if the whiteness were clear instead? What if it penetrated everything, revealed everything?

The blinding glare vanished.

Instead, Cole saw that he stood in a courtyard surrounded by the gray walls of a temple. Thunder reared near the altar, frozen now, the sparkling glory of her power flowing out of her like seeds on the wind. The power gathered and swirled around a human form, gigantic and demonic, with searing eyes. The more power flowed from Thunder, the more discernable the huge figure became, wreathed in a fiery whirlwind of shaping energy. The image made Cole recall how he first saw Ramarro—a devilish visage in the midst of emerald fire beneath the First Castle.

"We will meet again shortly," Ramarro vowed. "I look forward to continuing our disagreement in a less restrained environment."

If the slipstream was a hybrid of wind and water, the vortex around Ramarro combined wind and fire. Even though he was standing a good ten paces away, gusts of heat washed over Cole as the blazing energy whirled.

At the center of the flaming funnel, the ghostly form of Ramarro held up a small stone. Glowing white, it looked like the corner of a much larger block. It had to be the fragment of the Founding Stone! Ramarro was about to cross back to mortality. He was almost free.

Cole knew his time was running out. He had to act. Taking his hand from the shutter of the lantern for the first time since putting it there, Cole drew the Jumping Sword.

Leaping straight at Ramarro didn't feel right. The surrounding fire seemed too hot, the wind too violent. Getting blown around and barbequed wasn't going to help anyone.

Cole glanced over his shoulder to where his comrades still stood frozen. He saw the golden strand in Jace's hand, and an idea struck.

There was no time to scheme and debate. Cole could not afford to second-guess his instincts. He leveled his Jumping Sword at the ground beside Jace and shouted, "Away."

Cole streaked low and fast to the point near Jace, landing at a run and stumbling several steps past his friend before returning to his side. After sheathing the Jumping Sword, Cole yanked the golden strand from Jace's grasp and dashed back toward Ramarro.

Power no longer exited Thunder to unite with the blazing vortex around Ramarro. The Mare's coat was now a flat gray, having lost the bewitching appearance of churning clouds. Eyes ablaze, Ramarro held the white fragment of the Founding Stone above his head, the stone perhaps twenty feet above the temple floor.

"Until we meet again," Ramarro said, his voice triumphant. "It will not be long."

The fiery whirlwind around the torivor sped up. Ramarro

appeared more tangible than ever, his form solid and dark except for those incandescent eyes.

Beacon in one hand, borrowed strand in the other, Cole focused on the piece of the Founding Stone and commanded the rope toward it. The golden rope flashed forward like a striking serpent, stretching through the firestorm and curling around the white stone. Upon contact, Cole flooded his power into the rope, willing it toward the fragment.

Everything stopped.

Ramarro no longer moved. The flames no longer whirled. No music rang out.

This had happened to Cole once before.

Still forcing his power into the Founding Stone through the rope, Cole focused on the intense white glare of the little fragment. For a moment whiteness saturated his vision, and then Cole stood before an elderly man in an elegant maroon robe trimmed with gold. It had not been long since Cole had last seen his friendly face.

"Hello," Cole said. He could still feel the golden rope in his hand, although in this vision his hands were free.

Dandalus smiled. "We meet again. You have a definite knack for getting into predicaments."

"Ramarro has a piece of the Founding Stone," Cole said.

"I am aware of that much," Dandalus replied. "Would you open your mind to me? It makes it easier for me to catch up."

"Sure," Cole said.

"Oh my," Dandalus said. "This is worse than I thought. I see you met my living echo."

"You were very helpful," Cole said.

"So I gather," Dandalus replied. "And you are very brave and resourceful. Thank you for your many efforts. I feared the day would come when one of the torivors would breach our defenses. And now it has."

"Can you stop him?" Cole asked. "Can I? Can we?"

"It's too late to prevent Ramarro's escape from the Fallen Temple. He is already on his way to the physical world. Destiny's power provided the bridge he needed. Once in the Outskirts, his chunk of the Founding Stone will enable him to travel elsewhere."

"Last time I energized the Founding Stone, didn't you banish him?" Cole asked.

"When we met previously, Ramarro was using the Founding Stone to communicate," Dandalus said. "When you energized me, I was able to interrupt that communication. Ramarro could not bring his power to bear against me from his prison in the echolands. But once part of him crosses to the physical world, I will not be strong enough to stop him from using the stone to transport himself out of the Fallen Temple."

"Can I get the stone from him?" Cole asked.

"Too late," Dandalus said. "Ramarro is already more in the physical Outskirts than the echolands. When I return you to the timestream, Ramarro will be gone before you can act."

Cole slumped. "Then we lost?"

Dandalus smiled. "Not yet. Though I can't stop Ramarro from using the Founding Stone to exit the Fallen Temple, he is now in a somewhat precarious situation. Having brought that piece of the Founding Stone to the echolands, it cannot return. He must use it with one foot in the physical world, and one in the echolands. As soon as he uses the stone to exit the Fallen Temple, he will lose his hold of the fragment. If you keep the fragment energized, at that crucial instant, I should be able to alter his destination."

Cole got excited. "Could you change his destination right back to the Fallen Temple?"

"Perhaps, but it would be the Fallen Temple in physical Necronum," Dandalus said. "The connections of the Founding Stone do not extend into the afterlife. The temple was designed to hold Ramarro on the echolands side. If a disciple brought him another piece of the Founding Stone, he would be able to go anywhere. It would not take long to do so."

"Isn't trapping him for a little while better than nothing?" Cole asked.

"It would be," Dandalus said. "But I have another destination in mind."

"Oh!" Cole said. "The Lost Palace?"

"No," Dandalus said. "We worked a lot of specific holdings and bindings to keep Trillian at the Lost Palace. If I just drop Ramarro in there, he would escape in no time."

"Then where?"

"Back when we were dealing with the torivors, one of my fellow framers of the Outskirts was a man called Kendo Rattan. He was the first Grand Shaper of Creon, and he created a vault called the Void as a possible prison for one of the torivors. In the end, we went with the Lost Palace and the Fallen Temple."

"Will the Void hold him?" Cole asked, his hopes resurging.

"It will for a time," Dandalus said. "We never combined our efforts to perfect it, but it remains a unique and effective container. Ramarro will find himself floating at the center of an empty space, with no way to set himself in motion, reliving the same looping millisecond over and over again. If he gets himself moving, the space in that vacuum is designed to always return him to the center, no matter what direction he travels. And each millisecond, he would return to the center as well."

"That sounds pretty good," Cole said.

"Kendo was extremely talented," Dandalus said. "There would be no material within reach for Ramarro to shape, and all his efforts would be undone each millisecond. But he would be in the physical Outskirts, with access to the fullness of his powers. If he can learn to reshape time or space fast enough, he could theoretically work his way free. He would have as long as he needed to practice."

"How long will the Void hold him?" Cole asked.

"I can't say," Dandalus said. "Unless I'm a fool, days certainly. Weeks probably. Months possibly. Years if we're lucky. Almost anyone else would have no chance of ever escaping unless they had outside assistance."

"Will his followers break him out?" Cole asked.

"We'll have a couple of advantages," Dandalus said. "The first is his followers won't know where he is. The second is the Void is deliberately located in the farthest reaches of

Creon, in a location both secret and difficult to access. I have all the physical Outskirts at my disposal. If I could move Ramarro anywhere, I would put him in the Void."

"Sounds good to me," Cole said.

"There is a chance I will fail," Dandalus said. "But I believe I can do it. After I return you to the timestream, use the piece of the Founding Stone to converse with me again. I can tell you whether I succeeded, and we can form plans together."

"Okay," Cole said. "To make sure I have it all clear, you'll send me back to the timestream, and I'll try to keep the piece of the Founding Stone energized."

"Yes," Dandalus said. "Without your power, I will be unable to interfere. Are you ready?"

"No pressure," Cole muttered. "Yeah, we better do it."

"I'm counting on you," Dandalus said. "Keep the rope in contact with the stone and keep the power flowing."

"You got it," Cole said.

Dandalus winked. "See you soon."

Cole was back. Ramarro vanished almost instantly. Cole wasn't sure if he actually saw him for a split second, or just remembered seeing him before taking his break with Dandalus. The flames snuffed out, but the sparkling wind of Destiny's power kept twirling. The golden rope still clung to the piece of the Founding Stone. Still pushing his power into the fragment, Cole willed the rope to retract, bringing the stone to him.

"What happened?" Jace cried out. "Is he gone?"

Looking over his shoulder, Cole found that all his friends

were unfrozen. He supposed that made sense. Ramarro was no longer there to bind them.

"He escaped," Cole said. "But we may have sent him to a new prison. Let me check."

Cole focused on the stone fragment and returned to the white vision where Dandalus awaited.

"Well done," Dandalus said. "Ramarro is in the Void. He will be baffled for the first while. I wish I could see his face, but after placing him inside, I severed all contact between the Founding Stone and the interior of the Void. It should help ensure he has no foothold to the outside world."

"Great," Cole said. "What now?"

"Find the princesses and any friends you wish to rescue and then return to me," Dandalus said. "If they touch the fragment of the Founding Stone while you energize it, we should all be able to converse. I have urgent news that involves you, Honor, Desmond, and Destiny."

"You can't tell me now?" Cole asked.

"Enjoy this moment," Dandalus said. "You earned it. Release the prisoners. Then we'll talk."

The vision ended, and Cole once again stared at his companions. He realized that for them no time had passed.

"Nazeem is actually Ramarro the torivor," Cole said. "I connected to the Founding Stone using Ramarro's piece of it. Dandalus left an imprint of himself in the stone. When I energized the imprint, he was able to send Ramarro to a prison made long ago in Creon. It should hold him for a while."

"Well done, Cole," Honor said.

"Dandalus wants us to find your sisters," Cole said. "I think he has news."

"At least we can see the temple now," Honor said.

"Many of the defenses went down when Ramarro escaped," Prescia said. "I can feel Miracle and Destiny now, and should be able to lead us right to them."

Harvan approached Cole and clapped him on the back. "We weren't much of an army for you."

"Don't underestimate your contribution," Prescia said. "Every person here pitted their will against Ramarro. It was a distraction for him, and provided support for Cole."

"Especially you, Prescia," Cole said. "Thanks for your encouragement in my head."

"I helped as I could," she said with a small bow.

"We saw it all," Jace said. "Except when you were trying to burn our eyes out with that lantern."

"Whoops," Cole said. "You couldn't close your eyes!"

"A little blindness is better than losing the fight," Jace said.

"Is Thunder all right?" Ferrin asked.

Cole turned and saw the horse roaming near the altar.

"She no longer is hosting Destiny's power," Prescia said. "Otherwise, she appears unharmed."

"Is that Destiny's power in the air?" Cole asked, pointing at the sparkling whirlwind not far from the horse.

"Yes, holding to the pattern Ramarro established," Prescia said. "I expect if we bring Destiny here, she can reclaim it easily."

"What are we waiting for?" Jace asked. "Let's find the princesses."

TAKEN

They found Mira in a cell deep beneath the temple. Cole dissolved an iron door and then discovered he couldn't move or speak when he saw Mira inside. Jace ran to her and hugged her. They grinned and laughed.

Cole watched.

He felt too overwhelmed to speak. Until that moment he hadn't realized how much he had given up on rescuing Mira. His bargain with Sando had gotten her captured, and, at some level, he had believed there would be no way to set things right.

Not that things were totally right.

Ramarro was now in a temporary prison. Once he was free, Cole had a feeling that nobody on either side of the revolution would be celebrating.

But that problem would come later. For now, against all odds, here was Mira, alive and well. She approached him.

"I'm so sorry," Cole said.

"It's not your fault," Mira said. "You came all this way to help me?"

"He saved the day this time," Jace said. "Cole has his power now, and it was enough to send Ramarro into a new prison instead of letting him get away."

"Ramarro?" Mira asked.

"Nazeem's real name," Cole said. "He's a torivor like Trillian."

"Will the prison hold him?" Mira asked.

"For a bit," Cole said. "We're not sure how long."

Mira searched Cole's face. "What about Tessa?"

"Huh? You don't know?" Cole said.

"No," Mira said, looking more vulnerable than Cole had ever seen her.

"She's here," Cole said. "I found her, but Sando stole her from me. Ramarro never told you?"

Mira shook her head.

"What a jerk," Cole said.

"She's all right?" Mira asked, as if not daring to hope yet.

"Come see," Prescia said from down the hall, standing before another iron door. "She's in here."

Mira's expression lit up. "Really?"

Cole, Jace, and Mira hurried down the hall to Prescia. Cole pulverized the door. Mira glanced at him, eyebrows raised. "Not bad."

"I'm good at breaking stuff here," Cole said.

"Mira?" The hesitant voice came from the cell.

Mira turned, tears springing to her eyes, trembling hands covering her mouth. "Hi, Tessa."

Tessa walked out and stood before her sister. "I hoped I would see you here. Hi, Cole. Did you get caught too?"

Cole laughed. "We came to bust you out. But we accidentally freed Ramarro."

She gave a solemn nod. "I had a feeling he would escape."

"At least an imprint of Dandalus in the Founding Stone helped me send him to another prison."

"Was he the same as our Dandalus?" Tessa asked.

"Pretty close," Cole said.

Mira stepped forward and hugged her sister. Tessa hugged her back, but her body stayed rigid, her eyes wide.

"I missed you," Tessa said in a small voice.

"I missed you, too," Mira said. "More than I can say."

"Is this ever going to end?" Tessa whispered.

"Aren't you the one who is supposed to know stuff like that?" Mira asked.

Tessa shook her head. "The things I most want to know never come to me."

They ended the embrace.

"Dandalus wants to tell us something," Cole said.

"I should get my power first," Tessa said. "That much I can feel. And there is somebody in that cell." She pointed.

Cole unshaped the door.

An older man exited through the empty doorway.

"Durny?" Mira asked in disbelief.

"Hello, Miracle," he said, swinging his arms uncomfortably. "I came here to help but only managed to join the prisoners."

Mira went to him and they hugged. "Thank you for saving me back at the proving grounds," she said.

"It was my duty and privilege," Durny replied. He studied Cole. "Looks like you saved the day again, my young friend. I'm beginning to think you were the best purchase I ever made."

Cole grinned. "That's right. You used to own me."

"Nobody will own anybody before long," Mira said. "We'll stop my father."

"Father isn't the problem anymore," Tessa said. "If we can't stop Nazeem, he'll enslave us all."

"We'll find a way," Honor said firmly.

"Let's get Destiny's power," Jace said.

Cole walked beside Harvan as they backtracked out of the temple dungeon. The princesses walked with Prescia, Callista, and Jace. Harvan nudged Cole. "If the purpose of life is amassing stories, you have been a most profitable acquaintance."

"There may be more to all of it than stories," Winston inserted.

"And there may not be," Harvan said. "This is already one of the best. Harvan Kane and the Dauntless Outsider. Something like that."

"Now I just have to finish it," Cole said.

Harvan waved away the comment. "You're just saying that so there will be a world to tell it in."

"It's no joking matter," Winston said.

"Which lends the humor added importance," Harvan maintained. "Sadly, the story is moving on to a place I can't follow."

"Drake and I were having the same concerns," Ferrin said, falling in beside them.

"Ramarro will only return here after he has wiped the Outskirts clean," Harvan said. "We'll watch and wait."

"We could move on," Drake said. "If our chance to influence the outcome is done, the timing may be right."

"I've been having some of the same thoughts," Winston said.

"You don't count," Harvan said. "You're already dead."

"I can still end my lingering," Winston said.

"Who will be around to foil me?" Harvan asked. "Who will question my tales and call my bluffs?"

"I don't believe drawing critics will ever be a problem for you," Winston said.

"Am I that abrasive?" Harvan asked.

"You're not shy," Winston replied diplomatically.

"You'll also attract admirers," Ferrin said. "You're not afraid to be yourself, Harvan, and who you are demands attention."

"I knew I liked this one," Harvan said, putting an arm around the displacer. "If Winston rides the slipstream, I may be in the market for a partner in crime."

"I could be convinced to linger for a season," Ferrin said. "I've seen plenty of hardship and adventure, but friendship remains a novelty worth exploring."

When they exited the building, Destiny went directly to her swirling power, entering the sparkling whirlwind without hesitation. Her hair whipped around as the vortex shrank into her. She staggered when it was gone, but she was smiling.

Her eyes shone as she looked toward her sisters. "It feels like it never left. I didn't know how much I had missed it."

"I know what you mean," Honor said kindly.

Destiny looked to Cole. Her intonation became graver. "It is time we spoke to Dandalus." The words sounded like more than the whim of a young girl.

Cole got out his captured piece of the Founding Stone. "Whoever can get a hand on the stone can visit with me," Cole said. "The princesses should for sure."

Mira, Tessa, and Honor all touched the stone. Jace got his hand in there as well. Cole forced his power into the stone, and a moment later they all stood in the presence of Dandalus, surrounded by featureless whiteness.

"Greetings, Destiny, Miracle, and Honor," Dandalus said. "Congratulations on surviving your trials so far. I'm sorry for your tribulations."

"We all have our hardships," Honor said. "Cole informed us that you have news?"

"Cole allowed me access to his mind," Dandalus said. "I saw how he left the bodies of Jace, Joe, and Miracle with Hunter and Dalton. I also saw where he left his body when he came across at the Temple of the Robust Sky, in a chamber beside Honor, Destiny, and Desmond. The Founding Stone connects everywhere in the physical Outskirts, so out of curiosity I searched for your bodies. It took a little time to locate Miracle, Jace, and Joe. They are in the care of members of the Unseen. But I was disturbed when I checked on the bodies in the Temple of the Robust Sky."

"Why?" Cole asked.

"They were gone," Dandalus said.

"Did you find them?" Honor asked.

"After some searching, yes," Dandalus said. "And now that Cole has recharged me I have found them again. They remain in motion."

"What's going on with them?" Jace wondered.

"They were taken by Enforcers," Dandalus said. "Your physical bodies are rapidly moving toward Junction in a pair of prison wagons."

"Oh no," Cole said.

"I suggest you hasten back to your bodies and deal with the problem," Dandalus said.

"Don't we have to get near them to get back?" Cole asked.

"Not with the Founding Stone," Dandalus replied. "Ramarro was specifically imprisoned at the Fallen Temple. He needed to at least partly return to physical Necronum to use the Founding Stone. But you suffer from no such bindings. Your contact with the Founding Stone should let me return you to your bodies anywhere in physical Necronum."

"Then we should do it," Honor said.

"All except Cole," Dandalus said. "I take it you want Joe and Desmond restored to their bodies as well. Cole must be the last to go. Once he no longer energizes the Founding Stone, I will be rendered powerless."

"And I can't bring the piece of the Founding Stone with me," Cole said.

"It must remain in the echolands now," Dandalus said. "Like your Jumping Sword, and the golden strand crafted by my living echo, it cannot return from the afterlife. Only your echoes can make that journey."

"What about our clothes?" Mira asked uncomfortably.

"Unlike Cole's Jumping Sword, your actual clothes did not cross over with you," Dandalus said. "The clothes you have on are duplicates more akin to illusions."

"We should go," Honor said.

"I agree," Dandalus said. "The more time you have on the road in the prison wagons, the better you can plot your escape."

"I'll still have my power," Cole said.

"Yes, but it will not work as easily as it does here," Dandalus said. "You will have to learn how to control it in the physical world while inhabiting your physical body."

Cole shook his head. "The problems never end."

"Not in this lifetime," Dandalus said.

"And not when an all-powerful torivor could break loose any day," Jace added.

"Send us," Mira said. "We're ready."

"We'll be in different places," Cole reminded her.

"Which is why we better get started," Mira replied. "Don't worry, Cole. If you can't get free, we'll break you out."

"Those in the prison wagons may want to consider playing dead at first," Dandalus said. "No need to let your captors know immediately that you have returned from the echolands. It could work to your advantage."

"Sound strategy," Honor said.

"Are all of you besides Cole in agreement that I can return you to your bodies?" Dandalus asked.

They all agreed.

"Off you go, then," Dandalus said.

Cole was once again alone with Dandalus.

"I'll go get Joe and Desmond," Cole said.

"I'll be here when you want me," Dandalus said.

Cole stopped putting his power into the stone.

"Where did they go?" Desmond asked.

"Back to their bodies," Cole said. "Joe, Mira, and Jace are all right, but everybody at the Temple of the Robust Sky has been taken by Enforcers. We're in prison wagons headed for Junction."

"They're carting us to Owandell," Desmond said.

"Probably," Cole agreed.

"Don't worry, Cole," Joe said. "We'll come find you."

"We'll try to save you the trouble," Desmond said.

"The piece of the Founding Stone will remain behind," Cole said. "My sword won't come either."

"A spare sword?" Winston asked with interest,

"You're dead," Harvan said. "We'll let Ferrin have it, as long as he chooses to linger."

"I do have some experience with a blade . . . ," Ferrin said.

"Here is the Weaver's Beacon," Cole said, handing it to Prescia. "It saved us more than once."

"I'm glad," Prescia said. "But the beacon was just a tool. You did most of the saving, Cole. I'll do my best to help you on the other side as well."

"Thanks," Cole said. He exchanged farewells with Callista, Durny, Drake, Ferrin, and Winston. He looked over at Thunder. "Will she be all right?"

"She'll be extremely popular," Harvan said. "You know how difficult it is to find a horse here. I'm hoping we'll be good friends."

"Thank you, Harvan," Cole said. "I was so overwhelmed when I got here. I'll never forget you. Thanks for all your help."

"I'm glad I got to tag along," Harvan said. "You're an extraordinary young man, Cole. And your story is only just beginning. Continue as you have commenced, and I predict that nothing will be able to stop you."

"We better get going," Desmond prompted.

"Okay," Cole said, holding out the piece of the Founding Stone. Desmond and Joe laid their hands on it, and Cole pushed his power into it.

Everything went white, and Dandalus was back.

"May I have your permission to return you to your bodies?" Dandalus asked.

Desmond, Joe, and Cole all agreed.

Desmond and Joe vanished.

"Well done today, Cole," Dandalus said. "I fear some of your greatest challenges remain. But your power could save you. Learn to master it. Rescue the Outskirts. If you end up in Junction, you know where to find me."

"Thanks, Dandalus. Bye."

And then Cole could see nothing.

Rough, wooden planks rattled beneath him as the wagon jolted along an uneven road. Cole was on his side, hands bound behind his back, ankles chained together. A hood covered his head.

A flood of forgotten sensations overtook him. Hunger. Thirst. Soreness. Exhaustion.

He once again had an actual, physical body.

Though uncomfortable, the sensations were all familiar.

But one important thing was different from when he had left.

When he turned his attention inward, Cole could feel his power burning bright.

ACKNOWLEDGMENTS

Every book poses unique challenges. It was both fun and difficult to create the echolands. I had never taken my characters to the afterlife before, and I wanted to create a fantasy version of the hereafter that would feel a little different from anything we had seen. Such efforts take lots of time, and consequently require help and patience from my publisher.

Once again it has been great working with Liesa Abrams and the good people at Simon & Schuster. I also received generous understanding from my original publisher, Shadow Mountain, as they wait for me to finish *Dragonwatch*, the first book in the sequel series to Fablehaven.

Liesa helped me improve *Death Weavers*. She has the wonderful gift of being able to recognize and articulate how to make stories better. I also got useful feedback from my agent, Simon Lipskar, who also helped work out scheduling issues with my publishers. I am grateful to work with smart, talented people.

The whole team at Simon & Schuster deserves my thanks. Owen Richardson did another fantastic cover. Thanks also go to Mara Anastas, Mary Marotta, Jon Anderson, Lucille Rettino, Emma Sector, Carolyn Swerdloff, Jodie Hockensmith, Matt Pantoliano, Mandy Veloso, Jessica

Handelman, Julie Doebler, Brian Luster, Christina Pecorale, Gary Urda, and so many others.

Some additional readers like my wife, Mary; Tucker Davis; Pamela Mull; and Cherie Mull provided additional reactions and feedback. I appreciate their efforts!

This has been a turbulent year for my family. My last grandparents passed away and tight deadlines placed challenging restraints on my time. My thanks go out as always to my understanding wife and my fantastic kids.

My gratitude also extends to you, the reader. Thanks for sticking with this series and for telling people about it. One more to go. I'll talk more about that in my Note to Readers.

NOTE TO READERS

There is now just one book left in the Five Kingdoms series. Hopefully, Book 4 left you as excited to read Book 5 as I am to write it!

For the past few years I have released two books each year. With that aggressive publishing schedule, I found myself sliding a little farther behind with each book. I generally wear one of three hats—writer, promoter, or dad. I need to write the books, I need to help readers discover the books, and I need to be there for my wife and kids.

Deadlines have placed a lot of strain on my life over the past few years. I have put in the work to be proud of everything I have written, but I believe that going forward, to keep the level of quality high, and for the good of my family, I need to slow down the pace a little. I'm not retiring or anything—just hoping to get closer to one book per year than two.

As a result, it looks like Dragonwatch, my sequel series to Fablehaven, will come out a little later than initially planned. Instead of fall 2016, look for it in spring 2017. And that in turn will push my final book in the Five Kingdoms series to fall 2017. And yes, that will once again be two books in a year. Stop paying such close attention!

This postponement is being done to ensure I have time to make both of those books the best they can be. I can't wait to revisit the people and places of Fablehaven with my Dragonwatch series, and am excited to write the finale to Cole's adventures in the five kingdoms.

And of course there will be more books after that. . . .

To connect with me, look up my author page on Facebook, follow me on Twitter, and check out my Instagram account @writerbrandon. My website is brandonmull.com. If you like the stories I'm telling, share them with people. Many of us discover the books we read through recommendations from friends and family.